IN THE
SHADOW
OF THE
DRAGON

BRUCE BLAKE

ISBN 978-1-927687-47-5

In the Shadow of the Dragon

Curse of the Unnamed Book 4

Bruce Blake

Chapter 1

— · —

D ESPITE THE BANKS OF thick cloud blocking the sun, the sky remained bright, the flames flickering throughout the city reflected by the low-hanging clouds.

Baron Sylleth stood at his window, watching. The scents of charred wood flared his nostrils while shouts and screams assaulted his ears. People bustled around the courtyard below, some hurrying about, securing the compound against whatever insanity had seized the area, others fleeing somewhere else they considered safer.

His fists clenched and released, the leather gauntlets he wore creaking with the movement. A portion of him—the warrior part lying dormant under his robes of office these past decades—wanted to rush from where he stood and join whatever fray he encountered. But to what point? He'd issued directives, deployed guards where they should go. His out-of-practice sword would offer little help—better he stay put. The men needed their commander.

I may as well feed my hunger, then.

He pivoted away from the window and crossed the floor to the bell rope hanging from the ceiling, reaching out to grab it. Before pulling it, he stopped, his fingers wrapped around the purple velvet. He'd sent his guardsmen and every able-bodied servant to investigate the situation, but someone should have remained in the kitchen.

He yanked on the length of braided cord, the action triggering the chime of a distant bell, a sound unique to him to prevent doubt about who required their attention. Normally, it should be a matter of less than a minute before somebody responded; given their

1

current circumstances and the orders he'd issued, he expected a lengthier wait tonight.

When three minutes passed without response, he tugged the rope again. The bell chimed a second time.

He faced the doorway, arms crossed and toe tapping on the thick carpet as he counted the passing seconds in his head. Two minutes. Five.

He swore aloud and sighed, abandoned his place beside the bell pull.

"If I'm to satisfy my stomach, it appears I must do it myself."

He strode to the door, the armor he'd donned at the behest of his advisers clanking, the sword hanging at his waist tapping against his thigh. After yanking the portal wide, he peered along the corridor. He couldn't imagine an enemy finding their way through the city and breaching the walls. It had never happened; not in his time, or his father's, or his grandfather's before him, but better safe than sorry.

The hallway lay empty in both directions. Nobody to be seen, not even the sentry he'd ordered to guard his chamber. He frowned and cursed again as he exited, his hand falling to the hilt of his weapon out of habit as he headed toward the stairs.

On his way, he passed many closed doors and a few open. Those left ajar, he peered into, unsurprised to find them empty. He paused at some of those which were shut, leaning forward and listening for anyone hiding inside, disobeying his orders. No sounds emanated from within any until he reached the fourth.

As he leaned close, he thought he detected the rumble of a voice. The door's thickness prevented him from detecting words, so he pressed his ear against the smooth surface. At first he heard nothing, and a growl in his belly suggested him better off spending his time locating a source of sustenance. Then the muted sound came again.

Instant rage flashed in the baron. Who of his underlings dared hide when he ordered them to determine what dangers threatened his city? Why had the sky darkened, the world shaken, and his hedge maze shriveled? He stepped away, lip curled, and threw open the door.

The solid panel of wood slammed against the wall, startling the two men inside the chamber. Sylleth burst in, hand raised and lips parted, ready to spit fiery admonishment on the dalliers. When he laid eyes upon them, his ire melted to surprise.

"Rein?" he said. "You're alive."

His champion stared at him, wetness glistening on his cheeks. He made no move to greet his father, nor to hide his shameful emotions, but remained in his seat with his shoulders slumped and head hung. To the baron, he appeared a man beaten—physically, mentally, emotionally. He'd seen men appear this way before—on battlefields, at gravesides. This was neither.

"What is it?" He took another step into the room.

An unfamiliar tightness squeezed his chest, one he hadn't experienced since his son's mother died during childbirth. So many years had passed, enough he struggled to remember her face most days, but Rein's features always reminded him. They consistently prompted his memory and his resentment, but not this day.

Until his attention settled on the second man in the chamber.

Jai Aryn sat upright on the bed, any sign of illness gone from his countenance, save for the dark circles under his eyes. The knight gazed at him, the muscles in his cheeks twitching. Sylleth's gaze flickered between the two of them, his mouth opening and closing as the tightness in his chest sank lower, churning his belly.

"What's going on here?" he asked, despite not wanting to know the answer, the words tasting of bile.

"You're the baron," Jai said.

He shifted, throwing his legs over the side of the bed, and Rein reached out, offering a hand in aid. His friend ignored the invitation, concentrating instead on the fellow in the doorway.

"You remember him?" Rein asked, his voice quiet and filled with disillusionment.

The simple actions and his son's tone painted a clear picture for the baron, a man who prided himself on his ability to read subtle cues. The emotions he'd experienced in the seconds after entering the chamber—surprise, concern, disgust—coalesced into one much more familiar.

Disappointment.

Had he felt a flicker of happiness after discovering his progeny alive? Was it possible he'd tasted an instant of relief at finding out his heir had survived whatever had befallen him since disappearing on a reckless journey against the wishes of his father, the baron? The notion of it soured his mood and curled his lip. Seeing

3

Jai, reminding him of how his son lived his life, hammered the final nail into the coffin of his solace.

"He doesn't recognize you, does he?" Sylleth asked with no intention of awaiting an answer. "But he remembers me. How it must hurt you. A stake through the heart, I imagine."

Rein's face sagged further; his companion glanced between them.

"Should I know him?"

The baron did a poor job of stifling a laugh, a burst of air escaping the corner of his mouth. He shook his head, tittering despite himself.

"Better than any man should," Sylleth said, backing away.

Jai moved as though he'd rise from his bed, but Rein's father raised his hand to stop him. He didn't need the covers falling from him to reveal him naked.

"I'll leave the two of you to get reacquainted." He ensured his tone dripped with the intended flippancy of his statement.

They watched him retreat, closing the door as he exited to avoid finding out what they'd do next. Alone in the hall, he expelled the laugh bursting inside him to be free, but the sound held not a shred of mirth. Repugnance, abhorrence, disgust, but nothing resembling elation.

When his laughter ceased, he scowled and shook his head. If not for the close resemblance to his mother, he'd never have believed Rein his son.

He abandoned the doorway, determined to return to his quest to find solace for his grumbling stomach—if he retained the ability to eat and hold it down. Focused on his goal, he didn't bother with any of the other rooms he passed, cared little about whom they may contain, not after seeing his offspring.

He descended the curved staircase, this one at the rear of the castle, away from the huge, ornate steps leading to the second floor from the main foyer. His forefathers had employed the same artisans who'd built them to fashion these, and they'd paid the same exquisite attention to detail. Gargoyles leered along the railings from atop the banisters, each supported by the claws of dragons, carved of the finest timber, sanded, polished, and finished to a sheen. Potted plants sat at the edge of every step between the balusters, the green leaves adding a counterpoint to the dark wood and the red carpet under his feet.

4

Sylleth dragged his fingertips along the smooth handrail, enjoying the texture. Sometimes he pondered how many hours they'd spent creating something so perfect. No magical creature tainted this—works of art were the arena of men.

Halfway down, the glossy banister fell away beneath his touch, and he stopped, confused by what he encountered. He faced it, ran his finger over the discrepancy again as he redirected his gaze.

He stared at three dark gouges in the otherwise pristine railing.

The baron's face contorted as he wondered who'd commit such a heinous act. To him, marring the banister was akin to slashing the canvas of a priceless painting hanging in the great hall, or desecrating an idol carved in the early days of civility. No good reason existed to excuse defacing an item designed to provide delight.

His mood further soured, Sylleth rushed down the remaining stairs thinking if the damage was recently created, he may find the guilty party and see them suitably punished. He arrived at the bottom, hand gripping his sword's hilt, and encountered the same empty halls as on the second story, echoed footfalls welcoming him to the main floor.

Frowning, he crept along the side of the stairway, his spine to the curving flight. Disagreeable noises drifted to his ears, all of them sounding like they originated outside his massive abode. His eyes narrowed as he concentrated, listening, until something brushed his ear.

He jumped away, spun around to find nothing behind him but the staircase with its dragon claw balusters and green potted plants. One of the broad leaves drooped near where he'd stood, explaining the earlobe caress. He'd shifted without realizing, brushing against the foliage.

A relieved sigh shuddered into his lungs, and he returned his attention to finding out what was happening around his castle, the ache of hunger in his gut forgotten. He inched away from the staircase, glancing in each direction along the hall. A door to the outside stood ajar, sounds spilling across its threshold.

The baron pulled his sword, an action once as natural as breathing. Now, he struggled to recall when last he wore and drew a weapon for any reason but ceremony. He employed men for this, a champion, and they'd let him down. The polished steel gleamed, and he saw his face reflected in its surface, admonished himself for the fear he found inscribed on his brow.

It shouldn't be him reconnoitering, it should be Rein. But what enemy would peer upon his son's tear-stained cheeks and experience dread? More likely, he'd expect anyone seeing his so-called champion to piss themselves laughing rather than out of fright. The thought hardened his mood, transforming his own reticence into the more familiar anger and disappointment.

With a shake of his head to cleanse his thoughts, he strode toward the doorway, moving faster than before, the thick carpet muting the sound of his purposeful footsteps to a muffled thud. As he approached the exit, the acrid stink of smoke assaulted his nostrils, flaring them.

A dull gray pall lay upon the world as heavy clouds billowed into the dark sky. Smoky columns rose to join the drab pallet, some originating within the walls of the castle's grounds, the others roiling up out of the city.

Sylleth paused at the threshold, weapon pointed forward as he surveyed the courtyard laid out before him, empty of the life and activity he'd expect to find. All the servants were gone. His militiamen, too. His lips pressed together, and he swallowed a sour mouthful of saliva before stepping out into the open.

People shouted in the distance, their voices tight with panic. But what caused it? He spied no evidence of the walls being breached, no men in unfamiliar armor pillaging and lighting fires. In fact, he saw nothing but the rising smoke and the empty courtyard.

And the withered hedge maze.

The baron gaped, strode toward his treasured labyrinth, forgetting everything else. He approached not as a warrior prepared for battle, but with his sword dangling at his side, disappointment and distress evident in his demeanor.

Once broad green leaves hung from the branches, shriveled to grays and browns and thirsting for water. Desiccated vines appearing as though they'd fall to dust at the slightest touch lay on the ground like dying soldiers. Where once was an entrance, he found naught but an indentation of tangled limbs.

He stopped short of the maze, mourning its former glory. For centuries, it had presented challenge and temptation to the brave and foolhardy alike, and it remained undefeated. A dozen men a year strode to their demise along its leafy paths in search of the baron's prize. Hundreds of lost souls during his reign, and nobody knew how many in the generations before he assumed the mantle of baron. A once verdant symbol of his family's achievements now withered and ruined.

"How?" he said, taking another step closer. "What happened?"

"You did this."

Referring to the sound emanating from behind him as words felt generous, each syllable carried on the scrape of wood blocks rubbing together. Yet the meaning was clear.

Sylleth faced the speaker, his sword raised as he spun away from the ruined labyrinth. Anger burbled within him at the loss, the interruption, the accusation. He parted his lips to admonish whoever dared to speak to him thus, but stopped short when he found no one behind him.

No human.

While the courtyard remained devoid of servants and guardsmen, a squat tree stood in the path leading to the castle, though the description lacked an accurate representation of its appearance. It appeared shorter than most any he'd seen, the patchy-leafed top a scant seven feet from the ground. One branch protruded from either side, both of them thicker at their base, thinning as they went, ending in an array of smaller branches. The trunk itself wasn't of uniform thickness, but shaped more reminiscent of an hourglass.

Or the figure of a woman.

He stared, unsure of what to think. He'd never seen this unusual tree before, though it must have been there. Perhaps, like the hedge maze, some portion of its foliage lay rotting on the ground, rendering it unrecognizable, yet more than its appearance bothered him. It seemed out of place. Too near the path, too distant from other trees. He paced a tentative step forward.

Two patches of moss shifted, and amber orbs peered at him from the gnarled bark.

"You," the unsettling voice repeated. This time he noticed a crevice in the trunk open and close with the word, creaking and scraping as it moved.

The baron's eyes widened as realization dawned. Though he'd never seen it before—they kept it out of sight hidden amongst other trees—he understood this to be the Unnamed who controlled his hedge maze. A dryad. The unappealing creatures had resided within his family's estate since its construction and he recalled the guild replacing its handler at least once in his lifetime.

"Y...you," he stuttered, his feet shuffling him away from the living tree. "You maintain my labyrinth. What's happened? Where is your handler?"

The branch on the trunk's left side reached upward, stretching and creaking. The smaller protrusions at the end of it disappeared into the leaves, rustling them together in an eerie whisper. A second later, it pulled free a round object and tossed it toward Sylleth.

He didn't recognize it until the handler's head bounced to a halt a yard in front of him.

The baron gasped and stumbled backward, boots shuffling through lawn longer than it should have been. He experienced a flash of anger at the laziness of his landscapers, but it disappeared as quickly as it came as he watched the blades grow before his eyes.

Grass brushed the tops of his footwear, extended to his ankles, then his calves. His retreat slowed, the thin ribbons seeming to grasp at his feet, making the ground feel sticky. A wave of panic flowed through him, tingling along his flesh, its prickle bringing him focus. He pushed the fear aside, lifted his sword and set his stance, ready for an attack.

When he raised his eyes, he found the dryad hadn't moved.

Tendrils of grass curled around his legs, gripping him, no longer hiding their intent. He swiped his weapon at a clump, careful not to slice his own leg, and severed a clutch of them. The Unnamed cried out with a deep wail as he struggled to extricate himself. He pulled and tugged, sliced and cut until he freed his left foot, then switched his focus to the other.

The creature's lament continued with each blade he amputated, its cries lending him the knowledge he could hurt it, and the epiphany fortified him. He swung his sword in widening arcs, relishing the sight of rending grass, the sound of the Unnamed's dirge. Each swipe recalled the days of his youth, the memories invigorating his limbs.

As he worked to free his right foot, he hopped and moved with the left, attempting to keep the clutching weeds from gaining hold of him again. The movement threw him off balance, and the sharp edge of his blade nicked his leg. The baron winced, cursed, but didn't pause, and half a minute later, he was unfettered.

He stumbled backward, eyes on the creature as he noticed the wetness of his blood on his calf. Smoky air raked his throat as he heaved breaths in and out of his chest. His heart hammered his ribs. His sword arm quaked, the weight of the weapon taking its toll on his tired muscles, the illusion of his younger days dissipated. How did he let himself devolve so? Once upon a time, he'd ruled his father's tournament, much the way Rein dominated his. The most skilled and accomplished soldier in the land, surpassing even his son, in his opinion. He'd lacked the one thing responsible for impeding his champion—emotion.

And now he stood before a vile creature with his sword quaking, sweat rolling along his cheeks, and tears threatening. Too many years with his ass planted at a table, making plans, collecting taxes, and enacting laws had made him soft. Softer even than Rein.

The thought sent a surge of rage through him, tightening the muscles in his jaw and clenching his teeth. He shifted his grip on the once-familiar hilt of his blade, lowered his eyebrows, and growled in his throat.

If God meant him to die here, he'd not do it without a fight.

He moved to raise his sword arm and take a step forward, but neither limb did as directed. Confused, he glanced back, saw vines wrapped around his biceps. When he looked down, he found his thigh bound, too.

In his retreat, he'd inadvertently positioned himself at the edge of his hedge maze.

A cackle emanated from the Unnamed, its sound sending a wave of gooseflesh along his arms and drawing his attention. A crooked smile tilted what passed for its mouth.

Nothing at the bottom of the dryad moved as it made its way toward him, as though the grass beneath it gave the thing its momentum. He pulled at the creepers holding him, attempted to transfer his weapon to his off hand, but found they'd grasped that one, too, as well as his other leg. The vines held him fast, giving him no choice but to await the creature's arrival.

It halted six feet from him—close enough to strike a killing blow if he freed his sword. He focused his energy, leaning his shoulder forward and yanking at his arm. The harder he pulled, the tighter the creepers gripped him.

9

"I have been your slave for centuries," the dryad said, its rasping voice grating to his ears.

He shook his head. "Not me. My great-great-grandfather built the maze. Is it possible you've kept it all this time?"

"Yes." It drew out the word with a sibilance that provoked a shiver along his spine. "I have seen many so-called handlers live out their lives while I had none."

"It's not my fault."

The creeper gripping his arm tightened, and a tingling sensation spilled through his forearm into his hand. Without his intention, his fingers opened and his sword dropped to the ground. It didn't hit with the dull thunk of steel against dirt; the grass caught it, ferried it away. He watched it propelled across the lawn, his hope of escape carried off with it.

"I swear it's not my fault." He noticed the high pitched tone of fear entering his voice, but lacked the control to stop it. "I inherited this. None of it is of my doing."

"You could have freed me and the others," the dryad said with the same languid pace it had spoken all its grated words. "You didn't."

"No. That's not how it works." He gulped a mouthful of saliva around a painful lump in his throat, then wondered if fear caused it, or a vine threatening to crush his windpipe. "If I freed you, you'd have returned with your handler to the guild only to be put to work somewhere else. I kept you safe."

"Safe?" The dryad spat the word at him with a harsh laugh. It edged closer. "For centuries, they have imprisoned me in a cage surrounded by rocks and bars with no fresh air, no sunlight. I've had no control of my thoughts and powers. This has been no life."

Panic constricted Sylleth's chest, making the act of drawing breath a struggle. Colors flared at the edge of his vision, dried leaves rustled a death rattle behind him. His eyes darted from the Unnamed to the vines holding him, more of them wrapped around his limbs and torso than previously. His lips trembled, searching for words, for some way to talk himself out of this situation, but his years of politicking deserted him as his soldiering had.

The dryad raised a limb, drew a knotted finger across his cheek.

"Worry not. You won't be the only one who pays for your transgressions."

"No." He shook his head hard enough to set his jowls quivering. "You don't have to do this."

A smirk crossed its wooden face as the creature withdrew a few paces, creating space between them and leaving the scrape of its caress prickling on his cheek.

"I don't have to," it said. "But I will."

A leaf brushed his chin. The vines binding his arms loosened—not sufficiently to free himself, but enough for their fellows to find their way up his sleeves. The ones around his legs did the same, the interloping creepers tickling along his calves, his thighs. He struggled and pulled, his muscles knotting with effort. Leaves pushed against his mouth, attempting to insert themselves, and he clamped his jaw tight, pressing his lips firm. A vine tickled his nostril, another caressed his ear.

Terror exploded through him. He thrashed, wild eyes searching for anyone to help. The lone person he spied stood beyond the dryad—a woman holding a colorful stave, her silver hair spilling past her shoulders. She smiled and watched, giving him the impression he'd find no aid from her. But what choice did he have?

Against his better judgment—common sense being a thing which garners little attention when one's life is at stake—he parted his lips to call to the woman, to implore her to help him. Before he uttered a sound, the leafy end of a vine penetrated his mouth, stuffing it full and staying his tongue. It threatened to choke him, and he tried to cough around it, his cheeks expanding when the burst of air found no escape.

His concern increased as more of the vines' brethren entered his nose, his ears, up past the tops of his thighs. He struggled to speak, to beg for his life, but the foliage cramming his mouth turned his plea to high-pitched squeaks and muffled grunts. His eyes watered as the leaves crept closer to his throat.

Pain. In his head, his face, his bowels. The creepers took their time filling him, overtaking the space inside him with their leafy presence.

And all the while, the dryad watched, and smiled, and chuckled its wooden laugh.

CHAPTER 2

— · —

R EIN STOOD AT THE window, peering out at the courtyard, the cool air drying the tears on his cheeks, tightening his skin. A sense of duty welled inside him, bred during a life of obeying commands and doing right, as often for the wrong reasons as not.

As he watched the foliage engulf his father, it surprised him to discover how easily he disregarded his military and filial obligations. When the vines burst through his eyes, then rent his sire into pieces, he suffered less sorrow and regret than when watching the baron slaughter trapped deer for his pleasure. A sliver of guilt at the lack of remorse pressed his lips into a bloodless line, but he ignored it the same way he'd dismissed his duty as the baron's champion.

He turned from the gray sky, the blood-soaked grass, the glass pane, and faced Jai sitting on the edge of the mattress, back to him. The knight's head hung forward, his shoulders sloped. A sheen of sweat glistened on his bare spine and Rein longed to reach out, touch his smooth skin with the tips of his fingers, wipe away his perspiration. He denied himself.

How could he when the one person he was closest to and held most dear didn't recognize him?

Inside, he seethed. Anger and hatred for the witches who'd cursed Jai and the charlatan who manipulated them into the journey, threatened to boil over. He kept his rage in check, not wanting to upset his friend, but he'd remember the face of the fellow for whom he'd helped the woman search. He no longer resembled the Viden Misk he knew, but he wouldn't forget.

And he'd have his revenge.

"Do you need anything, Jai?" He pivoted from the window, abandoning the scene of carnage.

The knight raised his chin but didn't peer toward the baron's champion. "Why do you care what I require? Who am I to you?"

The question sent a spear of sadness through Rein's chest, leaving him glad his friend hadn't looked at him in case the emotion showed on his face. He paused, using the time and a chestful of breath to regain his composure, then crossed to the chair facing the bed where he'd spent days fretting, nursing the most important person in his world. As he lowered himself to the seat, he wondered what might have happened if they'd refused to search for the tome and the stave.

He'd seen some of the destruction caused by Amnayel Prisma's curse ending, but to him, it didn't compare to the chaos wrought in his life by the stave's return.

Jai glanced sideways at him, let his gaze linger for but a second before diverting it. Its brevity squeezed Rein's heart yet again.

"What did he mean?" the knight asked.

A furrow creased the brow of the baron's champion. He leaned forward, elbows resting on his knees. "Who?"

"The baron. He said I know you better than I should. What did he mean? I'd not know who you are without you telling me."

Rein sighed and stared at his feet, using the pause to choose his words. He'd already been trying to help his friend recall whatever he could, dancing around the truth for fear of his reaction. The relationship stirring between them had surprised them both at first. After their initial encounter on the tournament field, they'd both fought their attraction and urges, pretending the feelings stirred within them didn't exist because society deemed them unacceptable. But struggle as they did, circumstances always pulled them together until they stopped resisting.

Would he remember? Or would the pressure of expectations revert him to the Jai who'd existed prior to their fateful meeting?

"We have...a history," Rein said as he lifted his attention from the toes of his boots.

"History?" He continued to avoid looking at his friend. "What do you mean? Did we fight beside each other? Share pints? Attend training?"

"That, and so much more." The baron's champion paused, curled both of his hands into tight fists before releasing them again as he decided he couldn't keep the truth from the man he loved. "We—"

A shrill scream rose from the courtyard below, a panic-filled cry brimming with pain garnering their attention. Rein jumped up from his chair and rushed to the window, his eyes falling first on the spot where he'd last seen his father.

Brush grew in the place the baron had occupied, a bush with jade green leaves and flowers the color of blood. He spied no sign a man had stood there only minutes before. In his mind, he understood he should mourn the loss of his sire, but his heart refused to allow the false emotion to distract him from what was more important.

Another scream and he jerked his attention away from the peculiar shrub. Farther from the decaying hedge maze, halfway to the wall, a young woman lay on the ground. She thrashed, waving her arms and kicking her feet in the air as a horde of what appeared to be over-sized dragonflies swarmed her.

Rein let a hard breath out between clenched teeth. Opportune moment or not, the baron's champion owed a duty to his father's people. The death of his sire changed nothing about his responsibilities.

"We can't keep letting this happen without helping. We can continue this conver—"

He spun from the window to face his friend and his breath caught in his throat. Jai must have arrived at the same decision, as he'd risen from the bed and stood facing him, the swaddling coverage of sheets and blankets left behind. Naked. Rein stared for an instant at his friend's smooth skin and the muscles flexing beneath as he fought the urge to rush forward and take him in his arms. He gulped saliva and shook his head, released himself from the entrancement.

"You'll need armor. And weapons. We both will." Against his preference, he crossed the room and took a robe from where it lay, spun toward his friend, and tossed it to him. Jai plucked it from the air with a grace that set Rein's heart fluttering. "Put it on. I'll take us to get properly suited up."

The other knight nodded and threw the garment around his shoulders. Rein meant to divert his gaze but failed, leaving him to jerk his attention away when their eyes met. Neither spoke for a few seconds, producing what the baron's champion interpreted as

14

an awkward silence between them. He wondered if Jai compre-
hended it the same way.

"Come on," he said, motioning for his friend to follow as he
headed toward the door, grateful for a distraction.

Amnayel Prisma.

Viden Misk.

Alwin Pelletoot.

How many masks had he worn through the centuries? Was the
great mage the first?

Questions flitted through his mind as he scraped at the ground
around the unicorn's horn. Dirt clogged the space under his fingernails, stained his fingertips. No matter how much effort he
exerted or how fast he dug, each scoop of earth returned to its
place before he moved to shift more. Always ending where he
began.

He leaned back on his haunches, wiped sweat from his forehead, smearing it with mud as he did.

Always ending where I began.

Words, nothing more, but sometimes words carried unexpected
weight. Where had he begun? Where would he end? Everyone
asked themselves the second question; most knew the answer
to the first. Not the man who called himself Alwin Pelletoot. As
far as he recalled, he started out a full-grown adult lying on the
floor in an abandoned warehouse, an elder dead beside him. No
childhood or growing up. No good times or bad.

And what of the fellow named Waul who'd inhabited this body
before him? The one who remembered where the collected limbs,
torso, and cranium began their adventure, what occurred during
the years before he woke in a grungy warehouse. Did he exist
somewhere inside? Had the mage imprinted himself over the poor
soul, leaving a blurred image barely visible beneath? Or was he
gone, another entity's presence in this meat sheath sending him
off to some other place or snuffing his existence?

No answers came. Not from Waul, not from Viden Misk, Amnayel Prisma, or the unicorn horn stuck stubbornly in the ground,

15

its broken jagged end pointing skyward. Leaves dried and brown without an Unnamed giving them life clung to the hedges, rattling in the slight breeze, their rasp offering no more explanation than the silent ivory.

Alwin glanced over his shoulder, around the space between hedgerows. Nothing to see but dying foliage. Orania, Hum, and Shiera were gone. The injured handler had left in search of her pisky while his granddaughter likely departed with more nefarious intentions in mind. They'd left him alone with the horn and a bag full of books too small to read.

He redirected his attention toward the tip of the unicorn's mantle buried in the ground, the earth around it appearing undisturbed despite the dirt caked on his skin. He sighed, struggled to his feet, and tilted his eyes skyward.

The clouds remained, their billowy forms pregnant with rain blocking the sun and keeping him from guessing how long he'd been kneeling and digging without noticeable progress. Stopping him from estimating how much time had elapsed since Shiera broke the curse.

He presumed her chants and the resulting atmospheric disturbance portended the undoing of Prisma's magic, though Hum's disappearance and the state of the hedge maze provided his only evidence. What would it mean? Inconvenience, to be sure. Possibly so much worse. No hint of his granddaughter's demeanor suggested she thought humankind deserved a slap on the wrist for a thousand years of mistreatment.

He turned a circle, surveying the drooping hedgerows, unable to discern a clear path to find his way out and uncertain whether he should want to exit. Here, tucked away alone among the wilted leaves, he experienced a modest sense of security, or at least a lack of immediate threat.

It had been so long since last he didn't fear for his life.

Sound filtered through the withered hedges—screams and yells, the crackle of fire and the rumble of destruction. None of them encouraged him to beat a hasty exit, yet a weight pressed on him, leaving him dissatisfied with cowering in the onetime labyrinth.

"It's your fault."

The voice's appearance had ceased surprising him, even when it spoke without warning.

"I assumed you'd deserted me," he said aloud, then thought to himself, *I wished so.*

"You realize it is impossible for us to separate, no matter how badly you want to believe it possible."

"If ever I hoped you were wrong, this is it."

"You plan to hide while the world crumbles?"

He sighed, directed his gaze toward the unicorn horn protruding from the ground. "I tried."

The disembodied voice scoffed. *"That's what you call it? Tried?"*

"I don't know what to do. It won't come free, everyone is gone. I'm left with a satchel full of shrunken tomes."

"And who scratched quill on parchment to write most of them?"

"Amnayel Prisma," he responded, doing his best to make the answer sound more statement than question.

"And where is the mage now?"

Alwin's shoulders sagged. The instant he'd heard the voice speak, he'd known it would come to this. Its tone carried the weight pressing on him, discouraging him from seeking sage harbor. Its words offered naught but blame and guilt.

"He lives inside me."

"He does." A pause and he imagined the invisible speaker nodding. *"Go find your way."*

The self-proclaimed Mr. Pelletoot—the moniker of a wayward fellow possessing a body but no past—stared groundward, waiting for the voice to say more. A minute passed with no more said, so he raised his eyes, returned to the legendary artifact pointing toward the sky. He didn't fall to his knees, already knowing the result if he attempted to dig the horn from the dirt again. Instead, he wrapped his fingers around its girth.

The groove spiraling along the length of the ivory pressed against his palm and warmed his skin, as though the sun shone upon it alone while the rest of the world suffered under the cover of gray clouds. He tightened his grip, pulled up on it with hope in his heart he'd discover he'd been going about his extraction wrong.

It remained in the earth, unmoved.

"Would have been too good to be true."

Despite his lack of success, his grasp tarried, as if he expected the severed horn to offer him some assistance or counsel if he held onto it long enough. It didn't. He'd already received the lone advice he'd get.

"Find my way."

As he repeated the voice's words, he scanned the surrounding hedges again, hand remaining on the ivory. Nowhere did he spy a leafy corridor, a space for ingress or egress. He didn't know how to escape, let alone what he should do if he discovered a path.

"First things first," he said aloud, unsure why he spoke his thoughts. "No sense putting a cart before a horse."

It proved more difficult than he'd expected to release his grip on the unicorn's horn, his fist hesitant to relax, his fingers not wanting to remove their touch. After a minute, he succeeded and stepped backward from its porcelain-white length, then took another step, and a third. His heel contacted something, and he looked down to find the satchel sitting on the ground behind him, threatening to trip him. He bent and grasped the handles, noticing the difference in texture between leather worn smooth by years of handling and the mythical horn.

No warmth to these, and his skin noticed every blemish, each bump and divot in its grain. An old bag deteriorating with age, not weathered by love and use. He hefted it, heard the tiny volumes and rolls of parchment shift inside, and returned his attention to the matter of escape.

He strode to the dried and drooping hedge closest to him, examined the latticework of branches behind the brown leaves, then turned to walk the perimeter of his foliate prison. Each side appeared the same as the others, leaving him unsure when he'd completed his circuit.

"Find my way."

He repeated the three words over and over as he walked the perimeter again, as though chanting them may create a passage between the hedgerows he'd been oblivious to.

Incredibly, it did.

More likely he hadn't noticed the space in the far corner than it appeared out of nowhere, the slim opening barely noticeable on second viewing. No matter which, he reminded himself it led into a labyrinth notorious for keeping those who entered. Discovering a gap through which he might fit didn't ensure his escape. He paused.

"Find my way."

As he said the words again, he considered they may hold a different meaning than he'd presumed. Maybe the voice wasn't telling him he needed to get out. Perhaps it meant he should make a plan, formulate a course of action. The thought gave him a flash of hope, but it soon passed.

"How does that help?"

He set the satchel on the ground, slumped beside it, suddenly suspecting he'd discover for himself what happened to the centuries-worth of men who'd challenged the maze. With the magic controlling it gone, he didn't see why the murderous hedges wouldn't give up their dead.

Alwin Pelletoot tilted his head to cast his gaze skyward. The billowy gray clouds remained, hiding the sun and casting shadow across the world. How good it would be for its rays to warm his cheeks, to watch it cross the sky, and discern one direction from another.

He blinked, a frown tugging at his mouth as his desire for sunlight triggered a thought he couldn't quite define. With a sigh, he lowered his chin, concentrated on connecting the longing to something identifiable. When the two came together, his eyebrows rose.

"The sundial."

He clambered to his feet, plucked the satchel from the ground and pushed his way into the corner gap. Dried leaves rustled, their sound the hiss and chortle of an evil, petulant laugh. He ignored it, content to have a goal and intent on finding it.

Unless he died trying.

Chapter 3

L LYRIS STOOD AT THE lake's edge, staring at her feet and the liquid touching her bare toes. Mud squelched between them, the sensation both pleasant and disconcerting. She inhaled the scents of dirt and water, turned the dragon wing brooch over between her fingers. Whenever she touched it, she wished for the comfort of Flayre's smooth purple hide brushing her fingertips rather than the pin's severe edges.

She stepped forward a single stride.

Her foot splashed on the verge of the shoreline, its sole sinking into the silt. A cloud fell across her face. Had it been thus when Shiera led her out onto the lake to show her the past and tell her of her plan? She thought so. The initial steps were like any instance entering a body of water, though, after several paces, something solid and invisible had risen to support them.

She took another step, then a third, her chest tingling with anticipation, hope, worry. Her fingers gripped the dragon's wing, seeking succor from an item not designed to offer it as she sank to her ankle. One more stride, perhaps two, and she'd find the support they'd found before. She need but concentrate, imagine an imperceptible bridge solidifying under her sole.

Another pace and her foot plunged into the cool liquid, the splash frightening off a curious fingerling. She hesitated. Did she go more than four strides before? She didn't recall the water passing her ankles, but her guide and the unusual happenings had so distracted her, she couldn't trust her own recollection. It might have.

Or maybe not.

"One more," she said aloud, nodding to herself, intending the words and action to quell the concern now overshadowing everything else. "One more, two at most."

She forced herself to take a pair of confident strides forward and stopped, water lapping mid-calf, tendrils of aquatic plants brushing her skin. Silt and rocks and slender leaves pressed against her soles, nothing to support her at a lesser depth.

The handler stared down at her legs, the gray clouds above turning the lake dull, foreboding. If it sparkled and gleamed in the sunlight, she'd believe a chance existed of taking another step or two and finding that for which she searched. The grim surface suggested not, its ripples stealing her hope and washing faith away from her.

Her shoulders slumped; her fingers tightened around the brooch, its edges digging into her palm until the point of the wing broke the skin. A droplet of blood snaked along her finger, lengthened and fell, plunking into the lake.

"How long has she been there?"

Cirril Feron didn't move as Hinter asked, arms crossed in front of his chest and a frown tugging at the corners of his mouth. "Too long."

They lapsed into silence, both of them staring toward Llyris standing a yard from shore, water lapping around her knees. The handler stared downward, her shoulders slumped with defeat.

"We should get her," Hinter said without moving.

"To what end?"

"At least we'll know she's safe."

"It doesn't appear she intends to stride into the lake and drown herself."

The thief grunted her agreement but still thought they should help the distraught young woman. But she wasn't sure they could. She couldn't imagine what she'd be experiencing after losing her Unnamed, proclaiming Flayre dead.

She didn't know, but Tesfira might.

"Watch her," she told Cirril as she spun on her heel. "I'll be right back."

"What else besides watching is there to do?" he grumbled.

She hurried away up the shallow grade toward the village, not replying.

The once bustling settlement was quiet, its residents as lost about what to do in the absence of Shiera Siirist as Llyris appeared without her Unnamed. A few continued tending the fields as they'd likely done for most of their lives, but others wandered aimlessly. The ogre twins had abandoned their posts by the gate, and the man with hair growing from his ears spent his time sitting on a stump across the compound from their absent leader's hut, staring as though doing so could prompt her return.

It was here she found the acolyte's apprentice as she delivered a plate of food to the fellow who refused to leave his post.

"Tes," Hinter called on her approach.

The young woman lifted her head, smiled and waved when she spied her friend, then bent to place the platter on the ground beside the stump. She put her hand on his shoulder, leaned in to speak too quietly for Hinter's ears. The man nodded without shifting his gaze to either his benefactor or the sustenance she'd brought. Tesfira's shoulders rose and fell with a sigh before she took her leave, crossing the beaten grass to where the thief awaited her.

"Is he all right?"

The acolyte shrugged. "Like most of them here, Drobin feels lost. Trapped. They expected Shiera to rescue them from this place, give them a real life to live. But it's been days, and she hasn't returned. Their hope wanes with each passing hour."

Hinter nodded because she identified with such a feeling. Before this happened, she'd have gladly stayed here, avoiding Zeir and Carpera, leaving behind the risk of her profession. With the woman's disappearance and the handler's inability to help them, a pall had fallen over the village. An uncomfortable sense of loss and desperation permeated everything, leeching into every conversation, each movement to the point she couldn't imagine remaining.

Unless Tesfira did.

"Llyris is the same," she said, touching her friend on the shoulder and pointing toward the lake where the handler stood in knee-deep water with Cirril watching her. "We've tried talking to her, but can't get through. Losing Flayre has deeply affected her. We hoped you'd try."

"Because of what happened to Emeryn?"

Though they held no hint of accusation, her words spread tightness through Hinter's body. She considered denying the death of her mentor was the reason behind fetching her, but didn't see the point in doing so. Why should she deceive someone who meant so much to her? Wasn't when Quintan had deserted her the same?

"Yes. You are bound by loss. And grief." She sighed. "I'm sorry."

"No. You are right to find me. I should have paid closer attention to our friend, but many people need support."

The unnecessary apology in her statement set emotion tightening the thief's chest and throat, a reaction which surprised her. She pressed her lips together, preventing herself from speaking the words of admiration and love welling up in her. This wasn't the time or place.

Tesfira crouched in front of Drobin, tilted her head to peer into his face. The man with hair growing from his ears didn't refocus his attention from the abandoned hut when she spoke.

"I'm going to go with Hinter. The plate of food is on the ground beside you; please eat. I'll return soon."

She stood and glanced around the courtyard at the other residents of the settlement. Some sat like Drobin, others leaned against walls, while a few wandered without purpose. Since Shiera's departure, it was as though someone siphoned the air from the place, taking every bit of motivation with it. Villagers found themselves in the same situation as the fellow with the hirsute ears—hungry with no drive to eat, lacking intention or direction.

"Come," Tesfira said, starting toward the lake shore. "I have an idea how to help."

The former acolyte set out, leaving Hinter to follow. She paused before she did, watching her friend and noticing her bare feet. This version of Tes, the one keeping company with them since her journey with Shiera, constantly surprised her. She moved with a grace not present before, spoke with compassion and wisdom she may have previously possessed, but they'd never have known due to first her vows, then her grief. These newly discovered attributes magnified any emotion stirring in the thief.

"Are you coming?" Tesfira said over her shoulder, a smile tilting her lips.

"Of course."

She hurried to catch up, and they strode toward the lake side by side, neither of them speaking. Hinter kept quiet because she worried an admission of the passion smoldering within her may slip from her tongue. Best to remain silent and be considered a fool in love than open one's mouth and remove doubt.

Cirril stood in the same place as when she'd left, though he'd moved his hands to his hips and now resembled a parent feigning patience while awaiting their child. Except for the guardian and offspring part of it, the observation likely wasn't far from the truth.

"No change," he said as they approached. His gaze flickered away from the handler to Tesfira. "You think you can talk her to shore?"

"I don't know we need to," she replied as she strode past without pause.

Hinter started after her but stopped when the merchant's man grasped her by the shoulder. The action created a sliver of annoyance in her, and she fought to prevent herself from pulling away.

"What is she going to do?"

She shook her head. "I don't know. I suppose we'll find out together."

He didn't remove his hand as he gazed after the acolyte, now a dozen paces from where water met the shore. The muscles in Hinter's neck tightened as she waited for him to release her to follow her friend, help and support her in whatever she planned.

"We're going to die here."

With a grunt, she jerked herself away from his grip and went after Tesfira without bothering to acknowledge his comment, because she knew him most likely correct. Even as she thought it, she admonished herself in her head. She needed to have more faith in the acolyte, but faith had proved in short supply her entire life.

By the time she caught up to her, she stood at the water's edge, her bare toes sinking into the mud created where lake met land. She approached no closer to the distraught handler, so Hinter halted two paces behind her, though she longed to stand beside her, grip her hand in an offer of support. Connecting over loss couldn't be easy for her.

24

A minute passed in silence as Llyris continued staring at the lake's surface lapping around her legs, leaving the thief unable to discern if she realized their presence or if her grief hid the world, and them, from her. Hinter shifted, mud squelching under the sole of her boots despite her care.

"It's not your fault." Tesfira's gentle utterances floated out over the lake. Llyris continued without acknowledging them. "You are no more to blame for what happened to Flayre than I am for Emeryn's death."

A note of sadness squeezed the end of her statement, leaving Hinter fighting a strengthening urge to go to her, hold her. Her profession must have influenced the handler, as Llyris lifted her eyes from the water lapping around her knees, but didn't peer toward the shore. Instead, she cast her gaze across the lake, squinting against the sun's bright reflection.

"But Flayre was my responsibility. My duty to care for her, her life mine to protect, as it was the cleric's job to look after you." She faced them, lines of sorrow and concern etched across her brow. "And he did. He sacrificed and you live. I failed where he succeeded."

Hinter watched the corner of her mouth twitch and recognized her effort to subdue tears. Did they threaten because she lost her Unnamed, or because of the events on the shores of the Obsidian Fields? To her, did a jick's life outweigh the value of the cleric and his apprentice? The possibility flared anger in the thief, pressing her teeth tight together and curling her fingers into a fist, then she caught herself. She forced her hand open again, relaxed her jaw. Llyris had spent years with the purple cylinder; she'd sworn to care for her and protect her.

How can I judge her? she wondered, cheeks flushing for thinking of Flayre how she had a moment before.

Tesfira stirred, jarring the thief from her guilt-laden thoughts as the acolyte took two steps into the water, her bare feet splashing. Hinter reached out to stop her but caught herself before her fingertips found the fabric of her robe.

"In the words of God, when you find a path overgrown and impassable, a different one opens. He never leaves you stranded. And you are not alone."

The handler's expression shifted, moving from sadness to confusion, then annoyance.

"I don't require a new path. I need Flayre. She is my life." Her eyes fell again, her features slackening along with her gaze. "Was my life."

"And my vow was mine, yet you hear my voice now." She took three more strides toward her companion, water washing up past her ankles. "I mourn Emeryn Aryzath as you lament the Unnamed, and I grieved losing what I expected my existence to be. But God spoke to me. He has bigger plans for me. For us."

Hinter raised an eyebrow, pondering her friend's meaning. She'd said Shiera Siirist had taken her to God—which the thief thought a manifestation of Tesfira's grief—but she'd mentioned nothing about speaking with her deity. If she meant this ploy to tempt Llyris ashore and returned to reality, it involved the potential for emotional consequence.

The acolyte shuffled forward, her movement sending waves rippling over the surface, lapping against the handler's legs as four paces separated them now.

"You don't understand," she said, shifting her submerged feet and creating her own tiny undulations across the water, clashing with the ones made by Tesfira. "My birth didn't just happen to produce a handler. I've been meant for nothing else since before my conception."

"I get it. I may have taken my vow recently, but it came after years of effort to convince my parents and the diocese to let me. And a decade before of realizing my calling, of not fitting in."

Llyris raised her chin and peered at her friend, eyes shining with tears. "But you can start again. Your God will always be." She paused, swallowed hard, and then her voice broke on her following words. "What am I without Flayre?"

Her shoulders sagged, and she lifted both of her hands to her face, using them to cover the pain and grief straining her features, the wetness staining her cheeks. Tesfira sloshed forward, closing the distance between them. Hinter moved closer to the lake's edge until water lapped around the soles of her boots. Her heart sped when her friend rested her fingers on the handler's arm, waiting until she raised her eyes.

"You are so much more, Llyris Fildarae." The acolyte spoke quietly, forcing the thief to strain to catch her words. "It is a sad thing Flayre is gone, but you and everything you are goes on, just as I mourn Brother Aryzath's passing but God continues to have work for me."

Seconds passed as the two young women peered at each other. The gesture tugged at Hinter's heart. Part of her longed to possess the eyes into which Tesfira gazed, while another part swelled with pride at the gentleness of her voice, her careful choice of words. A lump formed in the thief's throat and she struggled to choke it down.

Finally, Llyris nodded, though anguish shone in her expression and the streaks of tears drying on her skin. Tes pulled her close, wrapped her arms around her. They embraced for what seemed to Hinter an eternity but likely lasted less than a half minute. When the acolyte released her and held her at arm's length again, the words she spoke were almost too quiet for the thief to hear.

"Let me take you to see God."

Chapter 4

—·—

THE SPACE BETWEEN HEDGES grew narrower as Alwin progressed. Branches and leaves plucked at him, each of them grasping at him with the tenacity of hands and fingers intent on impeding him, capturing him. He ducked under a thicker branch, gray bark curled along its length, and a thorn clawed at his face. With a sudden inhalation, he jerked his head away, then lifted his hand and touched his cheek, seeking to find out if the sharp tip broke the skin. His fingertips showed no blood.

"Small consolation," he mumbled aloud.

The pause in his forward progress afforded the opportunity for a peek over his shoulder, thinking he'd be well-advised to retreat rather than press on. Whatever path had led him here was gone. A shuddering breath filled his constricted lungs, and he blew air out between his pursed lips. Nowhere to go but onward, if the labyrinth allowed him to carry out such a goal.

He carried on, chastising himself for the delay, though he saw no reason why he should. What schedule had he to keep other than avoiding spending a night trapped amongst the shrubbery? Did he truly believe he'd affect what happened to the world? He'd concocted the name Alwin Pelletoot to amuse himself, but it was his identity now. So far as he knew, any remnant of the mage Amnayel Prisma living inside him died with the Unnamed his granddaughter had tossed lifeless at his feet.

Two struggling steps passed beneath the soles of his shoes before a tug on the satchel in his right hand jarred his shoulder and pulled him to a stop again. He glanced downward to find creepers snaking through its handles, gripping it and holding it tight. A frown tugged at his features as he yanked to free it. If Shiera

28

had released the Unnamed from their enslavement, as she'd said, why did the hedge maze yet live and seek to impede him?

He twisted his wrist, wrenching the bag, the tendons in his neck standing out with the effort. The creeper snapped, and he stumbled away. Dried leaves—green not so long ago—slapped him in the face. His feet tangled, and he fell, wincing at the twigs and branches scratching his hands and cheeks. He hit the ground with a whoosh of breath from his lungs and a click of teeth.

"Ooh," he moaned as he lay on the earth, the hedge pressing in around him.

The urge to stay, to give up whatever he hoped to accomplish by pushing his way through the labyrinth, overtook him. He relaxed against the dirt and decaying leaves carpeting the ground, closed his eyes. How long could he survive here lacking food and water, a blanket to protect him from the weather?

Two glowing red orbs appeared behind his eyelids.

"What are you doing?" The voice sounded weak, distant.

"Resting."

"We have no time for rest."

"No time?" Alwin chuckled, though he didn't find anything funny with either his situation or conversing with his imagination. "How is time lacking when I have naught to do?"

"Nothing but wallow in your failure."

He harrumphed.

"How can you resign when this is your fault?"

"It's not my fault." Anger snapped his eyes open, and he pushed himself to a sitting position. He didn't expect the act of opening his eyelids to vanquish the voice, but he hoped. "Prisma is to blame for this. Not me. Why can't you leave me alone? Why can't the world leave me alone?"

His unseen companion laughed, the sound mirthless and with an edge of harshness. *"You believe you are innocent? You think stealing a life and hiding in a body not belonging to you absolves you of your sins?"*

Alwin Pellctoot parted his lips to respond, intending to continue denying responsibility, but naught but a squeak of air exited his throat. He closed his mouth again, his shoulders sagging. It didn't matter how much he protested—the voice was right. This body hadn't contributed to the happenings of a thousand years ago, nor to what transpired in the present, but its usurper hiding under multiple layers of defeated souls within did. An inescapable fact, fight it or not.

"I don't know what to do."

The voice fell silent, leaving him alone. He heaved a sigh, readying himself to stand, when a flash of white on the ground in front of him caught his attention. One eyebrow rose. Something to aid him? Guide him? Give him purpose?

He crawled forward, tugging the satchel along with him lest the hedges claimed it. When he reached the spot, he secured the bag between his knees and leaned toward it, examining it before chancing a touch. Smooth and dull, it stood out against the brown backdrop of dirt and dried leaves. Nothing appeared dangerous about it.

A swipe of his hand cleared the detritus of the hedge maze, revealing more of the white item. He frowned, canted his head, dragged his fingertips across the rounded surface. Without touching it, he'd have assumed the object of his curiosity a rock, but its texture wasn't right. He laid his fingers on it, held them against it.

He sensed a vague energy radiating from it. Real? Imagined? One way to find out.

Alwin dug on either side of the item, the space under his fingernails still clogged with soil from performing the same action while attempting to free the unicorn's horn from the ground. Perhaps this thing was connected; it bore the same color and a similar texture. The thought, as nonsensical as it was, prompted him to dig faster.

This time, when he cleared the dirt away, it stayed removed, unlike before. The patch of white widened, the larger expanse now the size of the palm of his hand making the item's curvature more apparent. He increased his pace, revealing its oval shape. A fine crack ran along its surface, like a dark river cutting a path across a map's countryside. Was it a map directing him where to go?

He found a ridge, perhaps denoting a mountain range, then an impression. A crater? A lake? The edges were too uniform for either. With a shake of his head, he dismissed any attempt at guessing and increased his effort.

A minute later, he peered down at the skull, its dirt-filled eyes staring up at him—the remnant of some glory seeker who'd lost his life attempting to win the baron's prize. No map showing him a path to freedom, no clue suggesting a course of action.

A warning about his fate should he remain here.

He cursed under his breath and stood, wiped his dirty palms on the front of his filthy trousers, then picked up the satchel. He yanked hard to release it from the creepers snaking around the handles despite his attempt to protect it.

A sigh of wind rattled the hedges as he resumed his journey, as dubious about how to proceed as when he stopped. As unsure as he'd been about everything since he'd awakened with no memory.

The onetime maze continued to resist his progress, but he pushed on. He harbored no desire to end up an unidentified corpse feeding the hedgerows as his body's nutrients leeched into the ground. While he had no clue how to proceed, he realized dying wasn't the answer.

Five minutes passed like an hour as he struggled to push through the tangle of limbs and leaves, shielding the satchel in his hand from the grasping creepers. As he brushed aside another branch, he wondered what a moribund hedge or the Unnamed controlling it wanted with a bag of shrunken books, especially with the powerful Book of Shadow missing from the tiny library's inventory.

Through the tangle above his head, he spied the gray sky. No sun shone through to hint at what direction he traveled, warm his skin, or indicate the time of day. The lack of anything to suggest a larger world outside his lattice cage tightened the muscles in his jaw. He closed his eyes, hugged the satchel to his chest, the action flashing a memory in his mind of a young woman clutching a study book in the same manner.

"Tesfira," he said aloud, surprised the name came to his lips with such ease. "Do you yet live? Where are you?"

Leaves rustled as wind stirred the withered maze but, when they settled, a sound remained, one not present before. A hum. It sent a jolt through his chest, equal parts hope and worry as he forced his eyelids open again.

The pisky hovered over his head above the twisted knots of brush, a dark spot against the leaden backdrop. The creature's position hid her face from him, but what other being with a body shaped like a human's held aloft on gossamer wings might come to taunt him?

31

As soon as the Unnamed realized she'd drawn his attention, she zipped away ten feet to the right, then stopped, returned, and repeated the action. The repetition was unnecessary. He understood she wanted him to follow her, though he couldn't imagine any good coming of doing so. Hum had already tricked him...once? Twice? He wasn't sure how much she'd manipulated him to secure the Book of Shadow for his granddaughter.

Prisma's granddaughter, he corrected himself.

What did she want of him now?

He hugged the satchel tighter to his chest as he realized whatever the tiny creature wanted must be within it. He possessed nothing else and held no value himself.

Hum flitted right and left thrice more. Though her face remained hidden by the blur of her movements, he imagined impatience hardening her delicate pisky features. He glanced away toward the twist and tangle of branches, leaves, and creepers surrounding him, then whence he'd come, the narrow path all but gone. The sight of the Unnamed prompted a desire to retreat, but the now overgrown trail made it appear retirement held as much opportunity of getting lost as did pressing on.

But how did either compare to following Hum, who'd led him to Shiera the last time he dared follow her?

He shook his head, sighed. "What choice do I have?"

The next time the pisky darted southward, he followed. From the first step, the bramble of hedges eased, making going easier.

He assumed it a very bad sign.

The air ripping in and out of Ilkari's lungs burned with the intensity of a cook fire. Sweat glistened on his face, dampened his clothes, ran down the sides of his neck.

By his estimation, somewhere around two hours had passed since he and Nevan found themselves in a meadow surrounded by magical creatures hungry for revenge. Hours of fleeing without knowing where they began or where to go, barely slowing to catch their breath between then and now, because doing so possibly meant their end. They'd watched enough humans slain by the unfettered and angry Unnamed.

Their path had taken them from pasture to forest some time before, hoping for the cover of tree trunks and brush to hide them from pursuers. They'd neither seen nor heard any evidence of anyone following but, given those likely to chase them, the fact gave Ilkari no reason for relief. He knew some of them possessed wings, and didn't doubt others capable of rendering their movements silent or unnaturally swift. He'd spent his entire life around Unnamed yet understood so little about them. Despite their kind living amongst them, most of his knowledge originated in myths, legends, and rumor.

The relatively flat land they'd been traversing took on an upward angle, and the squire stopped to fill his lungs. He bent at the waist, both hands planted on his knees, as finding his air proved more difficult than he'd expected. The younger man accompanying him continued a few paces up the incline before halting to check on his companion.

"Are you all right?"

He nodded, waved a hand before returning to his struggle to draw breath. When a few seconds passed without success, a sliver of worry niggled at his thoughts. Did one of those creatures released from the cages reach him across a distance and steal his air, digging its magical claws into his lungs and squeezing them until the last of his life fled his body?

Or was he merely getting too old to run through the woods for hours?

Nevan appeared at his side, a sheen of sweat gleaming on his forehead but no other signs of distress evident in his demeanor. Recognizing this made Ilkari realize it likely his own shortfall causing his troubles. If exertion hadn't already flushed his cheeks, embarrassment would have done the job.

The young man on loan from House Carpera grasped his elbow and tugged.

"Come. We must keep moving."

The squire realized the truth in his statement, but where should they go? They had no clue about their location, let alone where their destination might be. He resisted the lad's attempt to draw him on, lifted his head, and peered at his companion from beneath his brows.

"Where?" he managed, the single-word question carried on a huff of breath.

Speaking eased his labor and the next inhalation filled his lungs near to capacity, the air fortifying him, allowing him to straighten and look Nevan in the eye.

The merchant's man shook his head. "I don't know, but we can't stay in one place for them to catch us. Did you see...?" His gaze darted away from Ilkari's, his voice quieted. "What they did to the others?"

"Aye." He nodded, expelled a hard breath through his nose as the memory of the cleric dangling from two poles with his guts hanging in the dirt flashed to mind. "And I've seen worse from some who weren't magiks."

Silence floated between them, the younger man refusing to hold the older man's gaze, and Ilkari realized this was probably the lad's first experience with death. He'd spent his life sheltered on Carpera's estate, where life's end only came for those sick or old enough to have earned it. The closest he'd likely been to evisceration was dressing a deer for a banquet. Quite a different thing.

"You're right," the squire said, disturbing the quiet. "We should carry on. Not knowing where we're going is no more risky than already being lost."

Nevan looked at him, the tenseness in his face easing now he'd found something else upon which to concentrate, taking his thoughts from the atrocities he'd seen.

"You can continue?"

The previous embarrassment returned, and the squire swallowed a mouthful of saliva along with his pride. "Perhaps slower pace this time."

The merchant's man nodded and started out, pushing aside a tangle of branches and holding them for his companion to pass. Ilkari thought to tell him he didn't need to caretake him, but stopped himself from speaking. If the lad desired to make his journey easier, even by a sliver, why stop him?

They picked a winding path up the rise at a speed more akin to a couple taking a brisk stroll, a walk with purpose. A stitch in Ilkari's right side made him wince with every second step, preventing them from traveling any faster; Nevan remained beside him, ready to help should the need arise. Having him near to offer aid deepened the squire's shame. He stayed close until they neared the apex, then rushed forward, leaving his companion to catch up.

When the merchant's man reached the top, he halted. Ilkari redirected his attention from his footing to the lad, watching him as he observed whatever lay beyond the modest summit. His expression went from carefulness to interest, then panic. He waved him up.

"What does he think I'm doing?" the squire mumbled to himself.

He put his hand against his side, exerting pressure against the stitch, hoping to stem the shock of discomfort it sent through him with each step. Had it occurred by his other hip, he'd have worried it a result of the spear someone had skewered him on, but the area remained free of both pain and scars. He gritted his teeth and pressed on. A few seconds later, he arrived beside his companion. Nevan grasped him by the shoulder as though he needed to stop him, then the two of them crouched, seeking cover behind a knot of brush.

"What is it?" Ilkari asked, the volume of his question barely the sound of a breath.

The lad responded by raising his arm to point past the veil of leaves.

A few yards beyond the foliage hiding them, the forest thinned. The trees ended in a meadow filled with thigh-high blades of grass, clumps of thorny bushes, and flowers growing in random places, their seeds deposited when dropped by birds losing the grip on their dinners. A fellow stood in the center of the field, facing away from them. Though they couldn't see his face, his posture and the sword gripped in both hands before him meant they needn't guess about his state of mind.

What caused his defensive stance eluded Ilkari.

Beyond him was a village. Smoke rose in dark curls from many of the buildings while others lay in ruin. Besides the fellow in the middle of the field, he spied not a soul against the desolate background. A ripple of wind rolled across the tops of the long blades of grass, but nothing else moved.

Frustrated, Ilkari cursed to himself, then leaned toward his companion, forcing his whispered questions between tightened lips. "What is it? Why is he on guard?"

"You don't see the beast?"

The squire frowned, squinted. Near a minute passed before a movement caught his eye, drawing his attention to what Nevan had already identified, and the thing causing the stranger's distress.

Distance made it difficult to judge the beast's height, though he stood taller than an above-average man. Dense brown hair on its head and shoulders shifted in the breeze; thick muscle rippled beneath the skin of its bare chest, the flesh the same color as its fur. Wide-set black eyes stared out from beneath a heavy brow, an iron ring dangled from broad nostrils, and two curved horns protruded beside its ears.

Ilkari's mouth dropped open. "Minotaur," he whispered, the word carried on equal parts awe and fear.

He'd never seen such a creature, though he'd heard of them. Sightings were rare, as the guild hesitated to use the beasts because their powers encompassed brutality, ferocity, and little more. The bull-men were not scalpels used with precision.

They were the hammer when all else failed.

The squire licked his lips, his suddenly dry tongue offering scant moisture. He glanced from the beast to the unfortunate fellow in its sights, then to his companion. All through his career, he'd lived by a code designed to guide his decisions: never take a life without cause; tolerate no injustice; don't question orders; leave no one behind.

As long as it cost no more lives.

"We need to go," he said, leaning toward the younger man and keeping his voice low. He didn't know what a minotaur's hearing was like. "We can't help him. We must save ourselves."

Nevan shook his head, reached for the spot where his sword should be and came up empty. When he did, he curled his hands into fists. Ilkari tensed, expecting the movement to catch the beast's attention. He parted his lips to protest his companion's action when the merchant's man spoke.

"We're not going anywhere," he said without diverting his gaze. "That's my brother."

The saliva previously missing from the squire's mouth flooded in, the shock of the lad's words practically choking him. Any thought he'd had of a judicious retreat lay dying, as they'd likely find themselves doing in short order. Nevan wouldn't leave his brother behind, and Ilkari wouldn't leave Nevan.

They'd all become victims of the beast.

He heaved a sigh and cast a glance around near his feet, found a fallen branch suitable for use as a club. The action made the younger man turn his head. The squire nodded once, a curt gesture punctuated by pursed lips and creased brow.

"Right, then," he said, straightening and taking a first step toward the field. "Let's have at it."

He didn't wait for his companion as he pushed his way through the remaining brush, but sensed him at his side as they broke cover and sprinted toward certain death.

CHAPTER 5

— · —

TWIGS SNAPPED UNDER VYLE'S broad, bare feet, his weight far too much for them to withstand. Rocks and slivers pressed against his soles, his skin too thick for them to pierce, so they did no more than leave an impression.

He purposely strayed off the trail to avoid making the acquaintance of man, beast, or any so-called Unnamed. His head spun after what he'd seen at the guildhall, and he needed time to himself to set it straight. Wandering the forest provided this, and space, too. Room to breathe.

The day dragged on with no sign of twilight since he'd left the ruined buildings which once housed him, and clouds refused to allow sunlight to break through. A creature of less significant size—a man, for instance—may have shivered, but his layers of fat and muscle helped him retain warmth except in the most frigid of temperatures. Were it so cold, he wouldn't have noticed, so distracted was he by the death and destruction he'd seen.

"Why?" he wondered aloud. "Why did they do such a thing?"

Nobody could misconstrue their time at the guildhall for living in the lap of luxury, but the Seniors did their best to keep leaky roofs patched, and fed them somewhat palatable food. Without them, here he was roaming the woods, exposed to the elements and concerned about if he should begin searching for berries or grubs before his stomach noticed the lack of nutrients he'd offered it these last few hours. Not unlike banishment to the pit, but he always knew they'd set him free, eventually. Not so now. A pile of straw and bowl of gruel sounded plenty luxurious compared to sleeping under a fallen log with rocks for pillows and worms for snacks.

His belly grumbled.

He thought of Breda. And Behrtio. And the other handlers, Seniors, and workers he'd known from his time living at the guildhall. Dead, all of them. He hadn't been able to identify every corpse, but he recognized each burned or disfigured body as having belonged to a human. Not an Unnamed expired amongst them. A tragedy. An indescribable loss of precious life.

And he'd contributed to it by not saving Breda, by walking away and abandoning her to die, breaking the Law.

Consumed by his thoughts, he didn't realize he'd emerged from the forest until his feet left prints in short grass, and then on a dirt track. He lifted his chin and halted when he saw where his wandering had brought him.

Without intending to, he'd arrived at Zalie's village, where she'd lived and died. Unsurprising, for the child had occupied his mind constantly since finding her burned and broken body in the ruined church—a punishment she didn't deserve. The result of him stepping outside the bounds of his station, not her.

A sweet girl who'd never grow up because of him.

The rest of the settlement resembled the church—many buildings lay in ruin, a few glowed with embers. Flames flickered and the stink of burned wood and charred flesh hung in the air. Vyle wondered why he hadn't noticed the stench, but the answer became obvious. Distraction, guilt, shame. Any potentially clouded his senses, but the trio combined to hide the world until he walked right into it.

He crept toward the edge of the town, his gaze darting. It appeared the citizens of the hamlet were less prepared for what befell them than the residents of the guildhall. But why should it have been different? He doubted they'd kept any Unnamed here; their reaction to him suggested none amongst them desired to keep company with a jick, no matter how useful in their endeavors. Nothing gave them reason to suspect what ended up happening, or its resultant mayhem. Their crime? Living in the settlement closest to the largest gathering of vengeful magiks.

As Vyle passed through, he recognized a handful of the dead faces, though he'd never known their names. They'd threatened him, hurled insults at him, spat on the ground by his feet, watched him perform thankless work on their behalf, but never introduced themselves. Part of him wished to experience detachment from their fate, as his brethren from the guildhall must have when they slaughtered people where they stood, but he couldn't bring himself to consider their deaths a just reward. He understood the upset experienced by magiks, but no one from this village shouldered responsibility for the desperate path of their lives. Nobody who lived today did. The blame for their servitude lay so many years in the past, it surprised him anyone remembered it.

The troll stopped when he recognized the woman who'd snatched Zalie's limp body from his arms. Her mother, he assumed as he crouched beside her, though he saw no resemblance between the two. At least, no more than he distinguished any human—they were already difficult to tell apart.

Pain twisted her face and her blank eyes stared toward the cloud-covered sky, unseeing for the rest of eternity. He extended a gnarled finger and brushed strands of hair from her blood-streaked forehead and wondered what she'd done with the little girl. Did they find the time to bury her, or did the Unnamed spilling from the guildhall into their village bent on revenge interrupt their custom? Did his tiny friend's body yet lay in repose under the rubble of one of the destroyed buildings?

He stood, took a step toward the closest hut. Two walls endured, the roof and other walls having collapsed as though crushed under significant weight. If Zalie remained above ground, he reasoned this was the most likely place to find her. He closed the space between himself and the nearest wall, then stooped, putting his hands around a chunk of dried mud. As he straightened, lifting the heavy lump, he stopped.

Why dig her dead body out from under another pile of debris? he wondered. *What good would it do?*

Other than burying her—an act he didn't understand—he saw no reason.

He let the clump slip from his fingers, shuffled backward to prevent it from falling on his toes. The time to admit the girl's death and his responsibility in it had passed. He just hadn't caught up to it yet. Until now.

The troll hung his head, fighting against the tightness in his throat, the threat of salty water in his eyes. Even with nobody near to see him, he suppressed his urge to release his grief into the world. He couldn't know for sure someone like Hispid didn't lurk in the shadows at the edge of the woods, waiting for more humans to happen along and incur his wrath. And to catch Vyle in tears.

He kicked the chunk of mud, sending it hurtling toward the ruined church, destroyed before the Unnamed broke free of their chains and brought destruction to Zalie's village, its people, and so many others.

If this is happening here, is it occurring everywhere else, too? he wondered.

He strode away from the dead woman who may have been the girl's mother, ignoring the shattered buildings and broken humans. Though he hadn't meant for them to, his feet brought him here, inadvertently giving him purpose after the surprise of the guildhall's destruction. Now he had none.

Nowhere to go. No reason to continue.

He trudged across the beaten ground, stopping beside the ruined church. The piles he'd created while removing debris remained, each heap of broken timber a reminder of finding Zalie's shattered body, each pile of stone a cenotaph to the little girl who'd harbored no fear of him.

The day he found her, the villagers had held him accountable for what happened to her, though none of the fault lay with him. He hated them for it. But he'd never have wished the fate they'd met upon them. Other Unnamed were responsible for their deaths, as the guild itself likely caused the girl's—intentional or not. It wasn't he who deserved ire and wrath, it should be those guilty of breaking the Law, and anyone—human or magik—who refused to place equal value on every life.

He hung his head, diverting his gaze from the reminders of the grim discovery. Cold, gray ash swirled around his feet, gathered from the ground and tossed about by a gust of wind. His eyelids slid closed, and he inhaled a deep breath through his nose, enjoying the breeze and pretending—wishing—to be somewhere else.

A rumble amongst the rustle of grass caught his attention, a sound akin to the far-off growl of thunder. Vyle raised his chin, opened his eyes. He waited, listening, until he heard it again.

No, a roar.

The noise galvanized him into action, and he spun around to ensure no beast tried sneaking up behind him, intent on making a meal of him. What a surprise he'd be to such a brave creature. When he found nothing stalking him, his second thought fell to

Hispid. He recalled the fellow in his bear form, imagined the sound of him voicing animalistic anger. But why should his friend have returned for him? When he left, he'd made apparent his disdain for the troll's choice to remain.

The roar reached his ears a third time, sustained long enough for him to realize it originated from a place hidden from him by the church ruins. He hurried away, taking strides capable of consuming yards as he lumbered a path through the broken building to the edge of the village. He shouldn't be concerned about the sound, but it provided a distraction from the world falling apart around him.

Left of the rubble pile once fashioned into a house of worship, his feet touched the dirt track leading out of the settlement. He followed it into the pasture beyond, where they'd first employed him to remove rocks which had appeared out of nowhere. The boulders remained cleared, but he found four unexpected figures in the field. Three men, one with his weapon drawn and held before him, all in defensive postures. The fourth had a man's body, though larger, more muscled, and covered in chestnut hair. Above the shoulders, the difference proved more distinct as a bull's head sat atop its neck.

A minotaur.

The creature balled its hands into fists as it stalked around the collected men, moving with slow purpose and showing not a sliver of fear at the sword pointed toward its body. Vyle's eyes narrowed. He'd met a similar Unnamed living at the guildhall in his youth, but many years had passed since his departure. The troll searched his memory, seeking a name, a reason for him to be taken away. It took a second, but he found the moniker.

"Runt," he shouted, hoping to find this the same fellow.

The man-beast stopped, straightened, the muscles across its shoulders tensing. When humans affixed labels to the beings called the Unnamed, they always did so in ways to taunt them. Many bore descriptive intent—like Vyle's—while others they created to demean. Who in possession of their senses named a specimen such as this Runt?

The creature stepped away from the men and pivoted toward him, its lip curled. "Do you know me, troll? If so, you'd do better not to call me by this epithet."

Vyle moved into the pasture, the tall grass sweeping across his thighs. Beyond the minotaur, the humans watched with wide eyes. He couldn't imagine what they must think—first the bull-headed fellow, then him.

"I mean no offense," he said, raising his hands, palms facing Runt. "It is a very long time ago we met. At the guildhall. I was but a whelp still learning to wipe my own ass. You left before I'd grown."

"Left?" the minotaur scoffed, expelled a firm breath through his round nostrils, the puff of air hard enough to move the brass ring dangling between them. "That's what you call banishment to a life of manual labor? Left?"

Vyle shook his head. "I knew not what happened to you."

"Of course you didn't. Look at you: you're soft. You've spent your days languishing under the thumbs of the Seniors, doing their bidding as they saw fit. Not I. Mines have been my fate. Back-breaking work, the snap and bite of whips, weeks without food or sleep. I've endured decades of pain and torture, praying for this time to come."

The troll swallowed his dislike for how the bull-headed man described him. "This time?"

"The end of the curse." Runt inhaled, flexed the muscles in his arms and chest in a display of his strength meant to intimidate. "Don't you sense it? My full power flows through me, unfettered by the mind of a handler.

"Mildr was the first I broke. My hands gave her the recompense she deserved, the same fate they'll offer these mongrels and every other human I encounter." He paused, glanced over his shoulder at the trio of men. They'd stayed put, realizing their best chance of survival was not to engage. "Three of them. Not much challenge, but I'll leave one for you, if you like."

Twenty paces remained between them, short enough distance for him to recognize the burl to Runt's lip, the flare of his nostrils. A few steps closer and he identified darker, matted patches of hair on his chest and arms, a spot of red on the left of its long, curving horns. The minotaur likely didn't kill everyone in the village, but some responsibility rested in his hands.

"I'll be hurting none of these men. Same goes for you."

As he strode forward, Vyle gathered potency in the recesses of his mind, in the place where Breda's control used to reside. He recalled little of minotaurs, but he understood their power lay in their strength. They possessed no magic to cast glamors or to enhance any of their aspects. As they were, he may be one of the few creatures strong enough to challenge a troll; Vyle lacked any intent on retaining his current state if they decided to trade blows.

"You overstep, old friend," Runt said, a sneer contorting his lips and the words they formed. "Perhaps you should return whence you came and leave the punishment to me."

The minotaur faced him, giving no concern to the unsheathed blade at his back. Every sinew in his body pulled taut, the curves and striations of his muscles visible through the dense brown hair. He snorted, pawed the ground with one foot.

"Not leaving, and nobody's doling out punishment here today." Vyle halted, let the energy gathered in his mind spill out into his torso and limbs. Its presence tingled through his veins, filling every crevice of him, waiting for him to summon it. "Best you be on your way. Go enjoy your newfound freedom and leave others to continue their lives."

"Sympathizer," the minotaur hissed. "They're undeserving of breath after the life they gave me and everyone before me. Don't you comprehend what they've done?"

"I understand their forefathers did, a thousand years ago. Why should we punish them for actions beyond their control? A mistake predating the births of their great-grandfathers."

"Because they did nothing to change it. They watched our mistreatment, at the very least, and allowed it to happen, participated in it. Magiks died at the hands of their inaction. All humans must pay."

"Not as long as I'm around."

The minotaur scowled, hesitating for less than a second before he lowered his head and plunged forward. Vyle released his hold on the power prickling beneath his skin, let it overtake him as he stepped up to greet his adversary.

Ilkari gasped as the two monsters came together.

By the time they'd closed the short distance between them, the troll had grown to at least twice its size, its hands equal to the width of the squire's head. The minotaur tilted its chin forward, aiming the wicked horns toward its adversary's midsection, intending to eviscerate the beast before it got him in its grasp.

Things didn't go according to plan.

The behemoth shifted an instant before the goring seemed assured to succeed. The tip of the minotaur's left horn appeared to graze the belly of its adversary, piercing its shirt and tearing the cloth. Ilkari winced, remembering the spearhead skewering him while trapped in what turned out to be an imaginary underground cavern. At least, it didn't exist in what he considered reality. After fleeing for their lives, the opportunity to ponder the nature of things hadn't presented itself, nor did it appear as though it would shortly.

The troll slammed its thick forearm across the shoulder blades of the bull-headed man, set him staggering. The squire tensed, expecting him to follow up with a killing attack, but he didn't. Instead, the minotaur recovered from its stumble and straightened to face its foe with a look of surprise equal to Ilkari's own.

"I don't want to hurt you," the troll said, his voice booming. "Leave these men and any others you come upon. They've done nothing to you."

The bull head shook slowly, the startled expression dispersed by a curled upper lip and bared teeth. The sight of the angry monster sent a shiver along the warrior's spine. How had he deluded himself into thinking they possessed any chance of survival against such a creature?

"They deserve what they've got coming to them," the minotaur said. "And so do you for defending them. How could you after everything humans have done to you? To all of us?"

They stalked each other, neither sparing a glance for the men watching. Taut tendons creaked and sinews bulged, boots scraped on the ground. Even from where he stood yards away from them, the musky scent of the bull and the ripe odor wafting from the troll flared the squire's nostrils. Any closer, they'd risk being overpowered before either of them laid a hand on them.

"It's the only life I've known," Vyle said, a tinge of sadness noticeable in his voice.

"Aye, and me, too. They cursed us to it. They stole any opportunity for lives of our own. Nobody should belong to another."

Ilkari's gaze flickered between them as they debated, worried the troll might see his foe's point of view. Doubtful they'd have come out on top of a fight against the minotaur; no chance they'd survive them both.

"No. None should. It was the world's way long before you and I joined it. What matters now is nobody deserves to die."

"Then we disagree," the bullish beast snarled before launching himself forward.

The troll didn't sidestep this time; he met the charge head-on, leading with a fist half the size of the bull man's skull. The meaty paw avoided the horns and connected with its jaw. Teeth clacked and bones cracked. The monster's path veered left, the strike sending him lurching away from the owner of the hand. The beast's hooves tangled, a result of his consciousness fleeing, and he sprawled to the ground, horn tips digging into the earth and spraying dirt into the air.

When a few seconds passed and the minotaur didn't climb to his feet, the troll directed his attention to the men. All of them refocused, resetting their stances to defend against his next move. Whatever threat they meant appeared lost on the creature. He took a step toward them, brushing dust from the front of his clothes with both hands. When his fingers found the hole torn in his shirt during the minotaur's attack, he paused to poke a fingertip through, then shook his head before peering at them again.

"I am called Vyle, though I suppose it's not my name anymore," he said. "Does anyone have a needle and thread?"

CHAPTER 6

—•—

H E FOLLOWED THE PISKY through the thicket, the path easier than his previous journey, but the trek still stretched on forever.

Hum hovered above him, darting forward a few yards at a time, then returning, ensuring he continued to follow. He wondered if controlling a human's doings after spending her entire existence with the opposite being the way of things gave the tiny creature a sense of relief or vindication. Giving over control to her tightened his chest with trepidation and worry sped his pulse. Was this how she'd lived her life?

The satchel he clutched grew heavier with every step forward, its bulk pulling at his shoulder, sending an ache down his arm and across his shoulders. He switched it from one hand to the other, trying his best to counter the discomfort. Inside, the tiny volumes and rolled scrolls shifted, redistributing their weight and making the task of relieving his stress more difficult. He huffed a frustrated breath and swapped hands once again.

Dark clouds and plumes of smoke roiled overhead, casting the onetime maze in deep shadow. No matter how hard he tried, it limited his vision to only a few yards in any direction, leaving him unsure where the pisky intended to lead him. The knot in his stomach suggested it somewhere he'd rather not go, and his thoughts pointed out no reason to believe the Unnamed meant him anything but harm. Unable to think what else to do, he continued following.

The brush surrounding him didn't form a trail, but neither did it seek to impede him as before. He pushed aside branches, the dried leaves rattling their death knell, and ducked under limbs too sturdy for him to move. A complicated and taxing path to follow, but easier than when he'd navigated it on his own. He wondered if Hum herself manipulated the tangle, or someone else. The possibility sent a shiver through him, jittering his teeth together. He'd just quelled it when he broke through a curtain of sickly foliage into an open space.

Alwin stopped, breath catching in his throat; at the clearing's center stood the very sundial he'd hoped to find.

He approached it with caution, unsure why he should worry but unwilling to abandon care. He didn't know whether Hum had led him here intentionally, in which case he should continue while remaining wary, or if she'd brought him to his goal without malice. The fervent beat of her wings—the sound they made the source of her name, he assumed—distracted him, but he held his gaze on the dial.

Its polished surface gleamed, a heroic feat in the dim light of the dreary day. The numbers and runes carved into it appeared to glow with a minuscule and inexplicable luminescence. He reached out, intending to brush his fingertips over the smooth face, trace the shapes they found. They seemed so familiar.

Hum interrupted.

The winged creature grabbed his sleeve in her tiny hand and pulled at him with surprising strength. He resisted, yanking the fabric from her grip and stumbling toward the sundial. He'd have fallen to the ground if he hadn't reached out and steadied himself on the very artifact he'd been reaching for when the Unnamed interrupted.

His palm settled on the strange runes he recognized as having nothing to do with marking the passage of hours. They pressed against his flesh, their forms distinct if unfamiliar, and a memory niggled at the edge of his thoughts.

He saw a craftsman carving these shapes on the polished surface of this piece of marble. It wasn't sitting here, in the midst of the baron's labyrinth, but on a bench in a workshop lit by guttering torches and flickering lanterns. Shadows danced and cavorted against the walls as the tedious scrape of chisel on rock threatened to obscure the words muttered by the man inscribing them.

Alwin gasped, though not because of the unusual scene. The air escaped him as the tiny pisky grabbed him again, this time by the collar, and jerked him away. As his hand left the cool stone, the vision disappeared. Anger rushed in, tightening his jaw and bringing a crease to his forehead. Any memory of his past, or of the men living inside him, was valuable, and Hum had stolen one from him.

He whirled around, swinging the satchel of miniature tomes and parchments at the Unnamed, but she saw his attack coming and released her grip, darting out of reach.

The clasp on the case slipped open, the two sides parting like a maw opening. His grasp on the handles failed, and the bag tumbled through the air, spilling undersized books and scrolls out, set free by the satchel's momentum. Tiny covers flapped askew and pages ruffled.

"Oh no," Alwin cried as the volumes hit the ground with a thump muffled by the layer of grass.

Dozens more similar sounds followed, like a brief storm pelting the earth with fat raindrops that stopped as quickly as it started. The case struck, bounced end-over-end to ensure the rest of its contents spilled out, then came to a stop.

He flinched at a strange, high-pitched noise, and it took a second for him to recognize it as Hum laughing. He stepped toward her, the anger that had disappeared when he dropped the bag returning full-force.

"What do you want of me?" he roared, one clenched hand raised.

As far as he knew, Waul's body had punched nobody out of rage. Even as he stood holding his fist out in threat, it felt wrong. The urge to lower it and apologize threatened to overcome him, but the others inside him kept him from doing so.

The pisky's tittering ceased. She stared at him, a firm expression hardening her visage, before she raised her arm and extended a finger. The unexpected gesture caused him to rescind his threat, and he turned his head to discover where she pointed, though hesitant to do so, glancing over his shoulder at her several times.

He saw more brush and shrugged. "I see nothing."

Hum flitted past his face, passing close enough her blurred wings tickled the end of his nose. He jumped away, startled, as she zipped to the edge of the hedges, stopped, then retreated toward him before repeating the action.

"You still want me to follow you?"

"Don't be foolish. You set out to find the sundial. You have found it," the voice in his head reminded him.

Alwin glanced from pisky to dial, then to the numerous tomes and scrolls spread across the grass. The marble monument wouldn't go anywhere, no matter how long he tarried or what he meant to accomplish. The books and bits of parchment, however, might succumb to theft, or wind and rain, especially given the age of them. A wonder they hadn't burst to dust when they struck the ground.

He spun and rushed away from the pisky, plucking the satchel from where it lay, intending to scoop its scattered contents inside where it belonged. Though the feet and legs of this body were much younger than Viden Misk's, its coordination proved lacking.

When his fingers brushed the handle but missed the grip he meant, he stretched backward to find the hold. Doing so threw his equilibrium off and he over-balanced, hitting the grass with his shoulder and coming to rest with the bag atop his chest.

"Nice work," he chided himself.

When he pushed himself up to sitting, he winced at the pain he expected. It didn't come, and it took a second for him to realize the expectation came from the last body—the one with the long white beard he'd seen dead outside the undertaker. The realization gave him pause. This was the first time he'd noticed memories and the present coming together, as though the disparate experiences inside him coalesced into a single point.

He shook his head to clear the odd sensation it caused, like someone stood close behind him peering over his shoulder, and reached for the nearest tome. It lay on the ground, out of reach, splayed open and face down. He glimpsed ancient pages between the covers, bent and creased, and leaned forward, stretching to reach it. A sound stopped him a second before his fingertips brushed the tome's edge.

With an eyebrow crooked, he raised his chin to find Hum hovering before him, arms crossed with impatience and annoyance. He waved his hand at her, attempting to dismiss the Unnamed while he collected the bag's contents, but she'd have none of it. She zipped in front of him, stomped her tiny foot in the air. He shooed her away a second time.

She fluttered farther from him, uncrossed her arms and used both hands to gesture. The movement mesmerized Alwin. He

50

stared, his eyes doing their best to follow the intricacies of her gesticulations. He kept gawking until a shudder and a rattle of paper drew his attention.

The tiny volumes and rolled-up scrolls spread around him shook as though the earth below them quaked, but he sensed no such movement himself. He frowned, reached toward the nearest volume again. Before his fingers found its leather cover this time, the book sprang to full size with a ruffle of paper.

The unexpected change startled Alwin. He inhaled a sharp breath, the air whistling between his lips as another tome grew, then a third, and a scroll after it. A second later, they all popped back to their regular sizes like dried corn held over a flame. Pages rattled and covers flapped, scrolls unfurled or rolled away to buttress against others of their kind. One gained such momentum, it didn't come to a stop until it reached the edge of the nearest hedgerow.

Alwin's mouth dropped open. "What have you done?"

He scuttled to the closest tome, a leather-bound opus with tattered corners and no markings on its cover, and plucked it from the ground. The book weighed as much as the satchel full of miniature versions. He dragged the bag over, put the volume in.

It remained its normal size and filled a third of the satchel's interior.

"No," he breathed.

His gaze fell across the others volumes—dozens of them, with more expanding to their previous dimensions. By the time they finished, there'd be hundreds. Enough to fill a library. He rounded on the pisky, anger flaring once again.

"Shrink them," he snapped.

It was his lone chance of rescuing the ancient writings, but he was unsure why the prospect of leaving all of them behind except three the satchel could hold caused him such ire.

Another memory flashed through his mind—an archaic man placing books on the shelves of a vast library. The rows of tomes reached from floor to ceiling, a ladder leaning against the bookshelf to offer access to the hard-to-reach levels. The musty scent of parchment more ancient than imaginable wafted to him, the smell carrying a weight of importance, gravity.

These weren't merely paper bound into volumes, but knowledge and stories, morals and instructions and lessons. Half-forgotten, irreplaceable, written by men long deceased, many in languages equally as dead. Wisdom not to be found anywhere else.

Alwin licked his lips, focused on the Unnamed floating in the air in front of him, her impatience etched across her entire body.

"Shrink them again," he requested, calmer than when he'd previously made the request. "Please."

Hum shook her head, beckoned for him to follow.

"Grab what you can," the disembodied voice said, its tone laced with defeat and fatigue.

Alwin's eyes flickered between the scattered tomes and scrolls, a hundred of them spread out on the ground around him, maybe more. Dark covers, light covers, some of leather, others of cloth. He even spied one with end boards fashioned of wood, another he thought might be bone.

"Which ones?"

Anxiety tightened his chest when the voice didn't respond. How should he decide which of the vast and varied collection counted as sufficiently important to rescue? No matter which he chose, he'd have to return for the others—this much collected knowledge shouldn't be abandoned to rot.

He clambered to his feet and pulled the tattered volume out of the bag, dropped the satchel on the ground as he flipped its cover open. A word scripted by an ancient hand scrolled across the first page—the book's title, he presumed—but they'd done so in a language he didn't understand. He leafed through pages of dense writings, marveling at the painstaking formation of each letter and sentence, agog at the time and effort sunk into the tome's creation. Every sheet of paper filled top to bottom and edge to spine with nary a break or pause.

He tossed the volume aside, and it hit the dirt with a disappointing thump.

Alwin inhaled a deep breath, his mouth pulled into an exaggerated frown. If he understood the swirls and loops inscribed in these tomes, he still wouldn't likely recognize which three he should save out of them. And Hum's incessant and insistent gesturing and flitting did nothing to aid his concentration.

"Please," he said. "Give me a moment."

He stared at the ground, unfocused, his vision blurring so he didn't see the books. Staring at them offered less help in choosing than did browsing their unknowable pages. When no suitable way of determining which to save came to mind, he determined to grab the three nearest—except the one filled with gibberish he'd already abandoned.

He took a step forward, intending to bend and retrieve the next closest from the ground, when Hum flew near his face. With a gasp of startled breath, he straightened, watched the Unnamed zip through the empty air and land on the edge of the sundial. She glared at him, stomped her foot to ensure she garnered his attention. When she knew she did, she waved her hands and made sounds he'd easily have confused for the peep of a baby bird new from the egg.

She radiated a bright white glow.

It reminded him of the light emanating from a round stone, and he recognized it as another memory not belonging to Alwin Pelletoot. The name Hinter sprang to mind, but he brushed it aside, intent instead on seeing what the pisky was up to.

Her luminescence fell across the gnomon, casting a shadow over its face. The dark triangle spilled over the sundial's edge and onto the ground. It stretched out like a finger, its shade falling over scrolls and tomes until the expansion stopped, its pointed end resting on a singular tome.

Alwin glanced toward Hum to see if she'd moved, manipulating the pointer. She hadn't until she saw him gazing upon her, then she waved her hand. Despite her movement, the dark and slender triangle remained stationary. Enough of a hint, even for a fellow of his ilk.

He hurried to where the shady finger ended, bent and plucked the volume from where it lay. Before he could examine it, the shadow shifted, moving away from him. Another peek at the pisky showed him she'd lingered in place, so he followed the shade.

Its shape changed as it progressed across the grass, as if the light casting it stirred, though it didn't. It shortened, narrowed, transforming from triangle to thin line. If his gaze wasn't already upon it, he wouldn't have noticed it by the time it came to rest on a second volume. He plucked it from the ground, added it to the first, and tucked both under his arm as the pointer moved again, faster.

It went widdershins around the dial's base, widening until it fell across the space behind where Hum stood upon the smooth marble face, casting a shadow with nothing blocking her light. His lips parted, a question asking how this was possible finding its way from his throat toward his tongue. He swallowed it as the short triangle of shade's point halted on a third book.

Alwin scuttled forward, careful not to kick or step on any of the other ancient texts strewn over the ground. When he reached the chosen volume and bent to retrieve it, he stopped halfway. This one he recognized out of all the books spilled from the satchel. He stretched for it, brushed his fingertips across its cover.

Traced the shape of the embossed unicorn.

The black pointer disappeared and the sound of Hum's frenetic wings stirred him to what he should be doing. He picked up the tome and stuck it under his arm with the others, returned to where he'd abandoned the satchel. As he knelt to stow the three books, his gaze flitted to the pisky now back to her normal state, then the sundial casting no shadow on this overcast day. Was this why he'd experienced the urge to locate the horometer, its role to relieve him of some of his load?

He finished stowing the tomes and clicked the clasp shut, then stood. Hum hovered where she had before this began, beckoning him to follow. With one last glance at the rest of the ancient writings lying in the clearing, he set out after her, hoping she didn't intend to lead him to his death.

If he hadn't seen his father's fate, Rein would have ignored the thing before them as a stunted tree or a large shrub in need of pruning. Anyone might have walked past with nary a second of consideration, but the baron's champion knew it hadn't been here the previous day. This was no garden ornamentation planted by one of the baron's nurserymen.

The knight leaned closer, stared at the knot in the trunk where his sire's nose had once been, two hollows for eyes, the burl reminiscent of a mouth frozen open in a pained cry. He recognized the wooden face, unsurprised by his own lack of grief. This wasn't a fate he'd have wished upon his father or anyone else, though he'd often desired to have the man out of his life.

He didn't see the creature responsible for his sire's death any-where. A shallow furrow in the earth suggested the path it had taken along the outside edge of the now-overgrown hedge maze. Rein followed the faint track with his gaze until it disappeared around the far corner.

"What happened here?" Jai asked, stepping up beside his friend. His proximity made the baron's champion tense.

"Dryad," he said, flattening his voice, revealing neither remorse at his sire's death nor excitement at the other knight's propin-quity. "The creature my father employed to shape and con-trol his labyrinth. The same one my grandfather used, and my great-grandfather before him."

Jai whistled between his teeth. "How many years has it tended the hedges?"

"As long as the maze has stood. It seems when the curse lifted, it sought revenge for centuries of servitude."

"Who expected a jick to have feelings?"

Rein pursed his lips and gazed at his companion. "Perhaps best not to slight them."

The knight shrugged. "What now?"

"The woman I told you about made me help her locate a fellow. She said he'd contributed to all this." The baron's champion waved his arm, the gesture encompassing the tattered grounds and the gray sky mottled by dark billows of smoke. "I want to find him."

He'd never lied to his friend before, but his statement held a kernel of truth. If he found him, perhaps he'd offer some expla-nation about what had happened and how to undo it, though it wasn't Rein's primary objective.

He hoped for the man to aid in returning Jai's memory.

"And where do we hope to locate him?"

"I last saw him near the maze." Rein pivoted and peered at the dried and overgrown foliage. "My best guess is he's hiding amongst the hedges."

Jai took a step toward the hedgerow. "I thought none who entered ever left."

His statement sent a pang through Rein's chest. How did he remember little things like his father's labyrinth challenge but not their relationship? It made no sense.

"Under its handler's direction and by the baron's decree, the Unnamed prevented them from finding their way out. I don't imagine it cares about such trivialities anymore."

He strode away, heading for the entry to the maze, the space now draped with sagging branches and dangling leaves. For a second, he wasn't sure his friend would follow, but the sound of his boot soles crunching against dirt relieved him of any concern.

"We best hope your assumption is correct," Jai said, joining him at the entrance. He slapped him on the shoulder and offered a smile. "After all I've survived, it'd be a shame to lose my life to a bush."

Before Rein had the chance to respond, the newly recovered knight stepped across the threshold, ducking to avoid a wayward limb. The baron's champion watched him for a second before following, worried the eventuality he'd joked about may come to fruition.

CHAPTER 7

—·—

"THIS IS RIDICULOUS."

Neither Cirril Feron's words nor his tone surprised Llyris. He wanted nothing beyond returning to Caedric Carpera's estate to resume his duties, most likely with the hope of getting back to his old life. But did that even exist anymore?

"What would you have us do?" Hinter snapped. "Languish here, waiting to see what happens?"

"Of course not, but we need a realistic plan, not something we agree with simply because your girlfriend suggests it."

The thief's cheeks reddened noticeably, no easy task given the nature of the cloak she wore. She took a step toward the merchant's man, who didn't shift to a defensive position and give her the satisfaction of thinking he saw her as a threat. His attitude only deepened her anger and Llyris thought she might have attacked him if Tesfira hadn't laid a gentle hand on her shoulder.

"It isn't up to you," she said, offering her friend a wan smile and slight nod before turning her attention to the guardsman. "Your choice is whether you accompany us or stay here."

"Is this true?" he asked, directing the question toward Llyris. "Have you made up your mind to lead us into unknown dangers? Are you willing to risk our lives on a fantasy?"

"I—" A response didn't come immediately to her lips, despite parting them and prompting a word from her tongue. "I don't know."

Cirril folded his arms and frowned. Llyris thought that, had there been the space within the hut they occupied for him to stomp away and separate himself from the others, he'd have done so. Since there wasn't he was left with naught but body language to portray his dissatisfaction, and he did his best with what he had.

"Leave her, Cirril," Mikol said. "She's lost someone she loves and yet we expect her to make decisions that affect us all."

He leaned against the door jamb, blocking the doorway but also looking as though he intended to leave at the first opportunity. This marked the first time any of them had seen him in days, other than if they went to visit him. Llyris found his dedication to the sick admirable, but worried for his health and safety at the same time. How much time could he spend with them before succumbing to one of their diseases himself?

"If anyone else has any realistic options, they best put them forth," Hinter said, still staring daggers at Cirril and leaving no doubt to him she referred.

"Realistic?" the merchant's man scoffed. "You call traipsing across an unknown land in search of an imaginary being realistic? Perhaps Mikol should have a look at you, because it seems there is something wrong with your head."

Her face pinched into a scowl, though she didn't try to advance on him this time. "And what do you suggest we do?"

"We must return whence we came. The—"

"Ha! You'd rather brave dangerous lands in search of your home without even knowing which direction to go, is that it?"

He tilted his head toward the doorway and the compound beyond. "One of them knows the way."

"They don't," Mikol said. "If they knew how to get out of here, they'd leave. They'd get medicine for the ill instead of concocting poultices and potions out of herbs and roots."

"Would they? Are we sure?"

The other guardsman shifted his position, standing straight and abandoning his spot against the jamb. "Do you forget they were banished here? Forced to live in this place with no choice?"

"Most have been here so long they don't know anything different. Why should they care?"

"Is that what happened to you, Cirril? Have you worked under Carpera's thumb for so long you don't even realize how he treats you?"

Llyris tensed, gaze darting from one merchant's man to the other. It seemed to her the tension within the hut could ignite at any moment

"Mikol. Cirril," she said, interjecting herself between them vocally if not physically in an attempt to diffuse the situation. "We —"

"You've become sympathetic to them," the elder guardsman said, ignoring her.

"You'd have to be dead inside not to," Mikol shot back. "They're not creatures or beasts. They are people with lives and emotions, fear and doubt. Their leader is gone and they are left to fend for themselves for the first time in their lives. They don't know what to do and they are scared."

Cirril's lip curled. "What's happened to you?"

"Nothing other than realizing that all lives have equal value. No matter what you decide, I will be staying here."

Before anyone could respond to his proclamation, Mikol turned and left the hut. From where Llyris stood, she saw him striding across the compound toward the front gate, undoubtedly headed for the infirmary where he spent most of his time. She worried for him spending so much time so close to the ill of the encampment, but Mikol knew the risks he undertook and he was willing to take them to repay these people for what they'd done for his mother in her last days.

"The whole world has gone crazy," the merchant's man said, waving his hands in the air near his head. "Can you believe how he's acting? Risking his life for a bunch of jicks."

"You could learn something from him," Hinter said, the sneer on her lips evident in her tone. "Tolerance. Patience. Manners."

Cirril turned his gaze on her, anger glinting in his eyes, but Tesfira stepped between them, one hand still on her friend's shoulder, the other held out toward the guardsman, flattened palm facing his chest.

"Mikol has made his choice. The decision of what the rest of us do belongs to Llyris."

The three of them directed their attention toward her and she sensed the weight of their gazes and the attached expectation pressing against her chest. It compressed her lungs, made breathing a struggle. She diverted her eyes, scanning the floor as tough she'd find the answer written in the dirt. She found naught but footprints scuffed into the dust, none of them offering the help she so desperately sought.

To their credit—mostly Cirril's as she'd suspect no other result from the others—they waited patiently as she silently weighed their options. At least, she assumed that's what they thought she was doing. Truthfully, her mind was muddled with confusion and grief. She found it impossible to sort one choice from another, one potential successful outcome from one leading them to their deaths.

"As I see it," she said, using her voice to make sense of the tumult in her head, "we have three possible paths, yes?"

She raised her eyes to find her companions nodding. For a moment, they waited for her to continue. When she didn't, they took over for her, Tesfira speaking first.

"We can seek the advice and assistance of a higher power."

"A dangerous journey to assay something which likely doesn't exist," Cirril said.

Hinter bristled but Tesfira squeezed her shoulder, stopping her from debating the guardsman's statement. Instead, she offered, "We can stay here and do nothing."

The acolyte nodded. "This might bring less risk."

"Or the jicks might get sick of us and have us for dinner like the obsidian tribe tried to do," Cirril added.

"Stop calling them that," the thief said, then moved closer to Tesfira and slid her arm around her waist. "And watch your tongue. We lost a good man to them."

The merchant's man cleared his throat and continued. "I say we should return. To Carpera's, to the baron's. Wherever we want to go, and be done with this foolishness once and for all. It's dragged on far too long."

"A journey with as much potential peril as Tesfira's," Hinter pointed out. "And, after seeing what's happened here, the changes these people have undergone, we don't know what we are returning to."

Cirril's lips parted to retort, but Tesfira shook her head and looked to Llyris again. "Do these sound like the choices you had in mind?"

Llyris nodded. Though hearing them aloud aided her in clarifying the options ahead of them, it did nothing to guide her toward a decision. She slid her hand into her pocket, seeking guidance and reassurance from Flayre's smooth hide out of habit. When her fingers touched nothing but cloth, she pulled it out again with a jolt of remembrance and sorrow, moving her touch instead to the dragon wing brooch at her throat.

Its hard surface and sharp edges were the antithesis to her Unnamed's silky skin, but the feel of it still brought the same sense of peacefulness she so often found with Flayre. She paused, closed her eyes, and inhaled a long, slow breath, using the inhalation to aid her in clearing her mind. It required she put aside visions of the small purple being, and so many other disturbing memories, until only one remained.

A robed figure standing before her in a cavern deep beneath the fields of obsidian.

Come to me.

The words floated across her thoughts. When she'd mentioned the dragon wing pin and the appearance of the robed woman to Shiera, expecting it was her, she'd been surprised and denied it. Llyris didn't doubt the woman would lie in service of whatever she needed to do to get her way, but there had been no reason for her to on this occasion. Nothing for her to gain from deception.

The woman who'd met them here—trapped them here—wasn't the cloaked figure who'd given her the brooch and saved her in her time of peril. The cowl hid somebody else's face.

But whose?

Llyris released her breath and opened her eyes. Each of her companions peered at her expectantly, hoping for her to speak the answer they wanted to hear. She didn't know what the decision was herself until her lips parted and the words spilled forth.

"Take us, Tesfira. Lead us to your God."

Hinter had doubted Cirril would accompany them, and part of her would have been happy if he didn't. Without Rein as a target for his foul moods, the rest of them were forced to endure his grumbling and his barbs. The more practical portion of her nature realized they needed his strong sword arm if they were to stand any chance of reaching their destination.

Wherever and whatever that may be.

61

As she reorganized her backpack to ensure her few treasures were stored safely away from the foodstuff with which she'd fill the rest of it, she pondered why she was so willing to follow Tes when the journey was so vague. At any other time of her life, she'd have taken the path most likely leading to self-preservation.

Except with Quint, she thought. *And look how that turned out.*

She turned the black talon over and over in her grip, running her fingertips over its serrated edge, the silver chain shifting in her palm. As always, she wondered from what creature the claw had come, a mystery she knew would remain unsolved, just as the question of whose visage was drawn on the parchment she also kept.

Instead of replacing the pendant in her pack, she let it fall from her hand to dangle at the end of its silvery strand. She unclasped the chain and strung it around her neck, careful not to catch her hair when she clasped the ends. With it secure, she let it hang against the front of her shirt as she peered down at it. The talon was all but invisible against her cloak, the unusual material usurping its color like it did everything else. After a moment, she tucked it away under her shirt, the hard surface pressing against her bare skin.

She set the tome she'd stolen from the witches' cabin on her lap, wondering as always if this small pilfering may have led to the dire consequences that followed. She suspected not—likely it was the theft of the Book of Shadow that caused the rising of the dead and the ire of the crones—but it was another mystery to which she would never have resolution.

Life was becoming more and more filled with those, these days.

The embossed dragon on the cover stared up at her, tempting her to flip it open and lose herself in the intricate illustrations contained within its pages. She thought about the colors, the details. Each drawing captured every scale on the bodies, every crook of wing and curve of tail. Teeth gleamed, nostrils flared, smoke drifted, and flaming breath flickered. If she let herself, she'd lose hours browsing.

She lifted the corner of the cover, slipped the folded yellowed parchment drawing inside to protect it, then stored the tome in her bag before it stole hours of her day. Even with it tucked away the pull to browse its beautiful pages stayed with her until she jammed her clothes into the satchel, hiding the embossed dragon.

"I should probably get rid of it," she said aloud.

She realized it made little sense for her to tote around the volume. It took up space better used for rations or first aid gear and weighed more than both of those things, unlike her other treasures that usurped little space. Despite this knowledge, she couldn't bring herself to leave it behind, though she couldn't have said why.

With its hold on her released, she sighed a heavy breath and stored the rest of her portion of their supplies—cured meats and hard bread taken from the village's stores with their permission. As she stored the last of it and stood, she noticed Tesfira approaching.

"Will he come?" the thief called out before her friend arrived.

Tes shook her head. Neither of them had expected Mikol to abandon his self-appointed position as caretaker of the ill, but they'd hoped he might. She'd have felt much safer having his sword joining Cirril's on their journey.

"He has a higher purpose, now," the acolyte said as she approached. "One different from ours."

"Right."

Hinter had never been one for higher purposes. The world she knew revolved around money and power, those who had it, those who didn't, and the ones seeking to get it. She'd started in the middle category, moved into the second at a young age, and had hoped to one day occupy the first. The dream seemed more and more doubtful with every passing day since the incident with Zeir.

"You're displeased?" Tesfira asked as she came to stand in front of her friend.

"I'd rather he came along, if that's what you mean. You can never have too many swords."

"But you can have too little faith."

Hinter pursed her lips, holding back the comments that threatened to spill forth between them. What had faith ever done for her? Or for Tesfira, for that matter? The thief had put her faith in Quintan only to be betrayed. The acolyte had placed hers in a drunk cleric and an uncaring god, believing and faithful until the moment cannibals had tied Aryzath between two trees and emptied him of his innards, and somehow her devotion continued.

Tes must have seen the struggle in her features because she stepped forward, closing the space between them. If anyone else had stood so close to her, Hinter would have backed away to avoid the discomfort of their proximity. With the acolyte, discomfort wasn't quite the right word. Her closeness made her feel awkward. Her mouth dried up and she knew she'd stumble on her words if she attempted speaking.

Her friend didn't give her the chance.

"I know this is difficult for you," she said, her expression soft, a faint smile of understanding tilting her mouth. "You weren't raised with God. If anything, religion and its practitioners betrayed you."

"You could say that," Hinter mumbled.

"I appreciate you and all you have done for me. You saved my life. You helped me through my most difficult struggle after Emeryn's death. Without you, I might have lost faith myself."

"I...I don't understand."

Tesfira's hint of a smile spread. She raised her hand and set it against Hinter's cheek, sending warmth radiating through her face, down her neck, into her chest. The thief's breath caught and she swallowed in an attempt to disguise it.

"You showed me the beauty of the human spirit. Reminded me of the good in the world in the wake of the horrible things that happened. Without you, I wouldn't have been able to return to God's path when he called me. I might not have been able to go on at all."

Hinter watched her lean forward, the movement slow and purposeful, yet it still surprised her when their lips touched. Soft, moist. The warmth spilling through her turned to heat, spread to the farthest reaches of her body and limbs. The kiss lasted for only a few seconds that somehow felt both like an eternity and not long enough.

When she eased away sooner than the thief wanted her to, Tesfira fluttered her eyelashes and said, "Thank you."

Heart racing, Hinter watched as the other young woman removed her touch from her cheek and turned to stride toward the place they'd agreed to meet for their departure. She paused for a moment, breath shortened, a sense something was missing filling her without Tes' palm against her cheek. Only once before in her life had she felt anything similar, and that hadn't ended well.

In fact, it had gotten her here.

Despite realizing this, Hinter threw the strap of her pack over her shoulder and set out after her friend, knowing she'd follow her wherever she may lead.

"I don't think so," Cirril said, the words spat as much as spoken.

"We insist." The hair on Drobin's ears fluttered when he spoke. "It's a dangerous land. You will need any assistance we can muster."

Llyris looked from the two men engaged in conversation to the pair of ogres who provided the source for their debate. The twins both wore inscrutable expressions, but she didn't know if that was how they always appeared, or if she couldn't discern one ogre emotion from another, just like she couldn't tell Hartrek from Gartrek.

"How could we know we wouldn't be in as much danger from them as anything else?"

"I've worked closely with Gartrek in the infirmary," said Mikol, who'd come to see them off. "He has been nothing but respectful and a great help."

The ogre standing to the left bowed his head in thanks and Llyris quickly searched his face for some distinguishing mark so she could tell him from his brother. She noticed a small scar above his right eye where a human had an eyebrow, and decided this the telltale sign to recognize one from the other.

"Because you are helping ease the sick to their impending deaths," Cirril snapped.

"But you are helping us with this journey, too," Drobin interjected with no trace of anger or annoyance in his tone. "If we stay here, we will die. All of us. It's only a matter of time. If you find what you are searching for, perhaps it will provide us a way to be free of this place."

The guardsman shook his head and appeared about to protest some more when Tesfira interrupted.

"As with anything else, it is up to the handler to decide." She pivoted toward Llyris and everyone else did the same. Their attention brought tightness to her limbs. "What say you?"

She glanced between those gathered near the edge of the lake—members of the village come to watch them go and the ones hoping to accompany them, her companions with whom she'd been through so much. Every set of eyes fell upon her, awaiting her decision, and it reminded her of the times Rein had asked what direction they should travel. She'd had no more idea then of how to proceed than she did now.

Before she answered, memories flashed through her thoughts. She pictured the huge python, the witches, the animated skeletons, and the cannibals clad in clothing fashioned of human skin. They'd lost two of their party for sure, with another comatose the last she knew of him, and two others missing or dead. And how many times had they all come close to death? It didn't make sense to take extra risks again, no matter how doubtful the solution may be.

"They come with us," she said finally.

The expressions on the ogres' faces remained unchanged, as far as she could tell, but Drobin appeared visibly relieved and Cirril ready to explode. To his credit, he showed the maturity of his experience and limited his dissatisfaction with her decision to a sour aspect including taut lips and a crease above his brow. Tesfira and Hinter simply nodded along with her declaration, agreeing that more muscle was better.

"A wise decision, lady handler," Drobin congratulated her.

Cirril Feron crossed the space between them and stood in front of the ogre twins, his head tilted upward to ensure their gazes met.

"I'll be keeping my eye on the two of you," he said, steel in his tone. "Don't step out of line."

Hartrek's stony visage remained, but Llyris would have sworn the corner of Gartrek's mouth twitched as though fighting back a smirk. The merchant's man turned away to stride through the middle of the crowd, those gathered parting to allow him passage.

"Let's get going then," he said over his shoulder. "Before we lose the light."

Hinter put her hand against Tesfira's lower back, ushering her friend on ahead of her. When Llyris pivoted to follow, a hand gripping her arm stopped her. She faced Mikol.

"I'm sorry I can't come," he said, guilty strain clear in his features. This was no easy decision for him, despite what they'd thought. "But they need me. I have a debt to repay."

"We know," Llyris said, nodding and offering an understanding smile that felt out of place on her lips. "We'll be fine. Back in no time."

The young guardsman returned a similar unconvinced tilt of his mouth and then the handler turned to set out after her companions, the twin ogres bringing up the rear the way Mikol would have, had he accompanied them.

They followed the lake shore, a silent, single-file line trudging the verge between firm and muddy ground. Llyris tried not to look back, worried her resolve to undertake a journey with no clear destiny might wane. But this wasn't the first time she'd set out on such a trek, was it? Journeying toward the unknown seemed to have become something of an unexpected habit.

When she gave in and glanced over her shoulder at the place they'd recently left, she found that those who had gathered to see them off had left.

All of them except Mikol.

The merchant's man raised a hand when he saw her peering in his direction. Llyris returned the gesture, wondering if she'd ever see him again.

CHAPTER 8

— · —

D ESPITE HAVING SAVED THEM, the three men seemed as fearful of Vyle as any other human he'd encountered outside the grounds of the guildhall. Besides their fear, none of them carried the tools he needed to repair his shirt, a fact which shouldn't have surprised him given the state of the oldest of them. His tunic sported more rips and tears than the troll's and appeared as though someone had dragged it through the mud and hung it to dry in the sun.

"We best be on our way before Runt wakes from his slumber." He jerked his thumb over his shoulder toward the yet unmoving minotaur. The fact he hadn't stirred worried him. He'd meant to hit him hard enough to knock him unconscious and give them time to escape, not with sufficient force to kill him.

They stared at him, motionless, as though his mouth formed words foreign to their ears. Vyle knew different Unnamed spoke other languages, but he wasn't aware of men speaking more than one. He'd only ever heard Seniors and handlers at the guild talking in the same tongue. Surely these fellows must realize the threat of an angry half-man half-bull even if they didn't speak the same language as him.

"We have to leave," he repeated, louder and slower this time, drawing the words out.

"Runt?" one of the pair of younger men with identical faces said.

"Yeah. The horned guy who'd rather gore first and ask questions later." Vyle frowned, shook his head. Anyone with a sliver of common sense must realize unimportant queries could wait, and finding safety should take priority. Instead of wasting precious time speaking, he spun away from the trio of men, heel grinding blades of grass into the dirt, and set out the way he'd come.

He preferred neither returning to the ruined village nor the destroyed guildhall, but naught but mystery lay in the other directions. Coming across one angry man-bull wasn't over-taxing, but if all the Unnamed broke free, they may encounter more trouble than a troll could handle.

As he walked away without waiting for them to follow, he slackened his hold on the part of his mind adding to his strength. His body settled into its normal state, the rush of blood in his ears subsiding. As much as he enjoyed the power coursing through his veins, he also relished it letting go.

He'd gone a few paces when he detected the footsteps of the humans following him; no sound of the one with a sword storing his weapon, so they weren't complete idiots, but they made enough noise to rival a trio of ogres.

"Where are you taking us?" one asked—the older fellow, he thought.

He shook his head and responded without glancing behind him. "Stop the stupid questions. Let's get to safety first."

They didn't pause when they passed through the ruined village, though exclamations of surprise and shock slipped from his companions. They mumbled amongst themselves, not bothering him with their concerns and comments, then fell silent again as they traversed the heart of the hamlet.

Wild animals scurried away ahead of them, frightened off at the sound of their approach. Scavenger birds and beasts had found the villagers' corpses and Vyle took care to avert his eyes when they passed the hut where he'd seen Zalie's mother lying dead out front. His breath shortened, and he again fought the urge to plunge into the abode, search for the girl's body, and give it the burial humans preferred for their deceased. But they didn't have time. Between the hungry foragers and the vengeance-seeking magiks, he barely felt confident of his own well-being, never mind the welfare of three men as meek as babes.

They reached the far edge of the settlement before any of them risked speaking.

"The entire village," the elder of the group said, his voice but a breath.

Vyle wasn't sure if he meant the words as a question or statement. "Aye. Dead or fled. Every one of them."

For the next hour, they made no sound beyond the rustle of their legs rattling through the brush. The troll led them along a similar route through the forest as he'd followed journeying to the village, avoiding the road used by humans and any sign of others passing. Each step they took, they lay their boots on soil untouched by any feet in recent times.

When they broke through into a clearing of a size for them to determine it unoccupied, they halted. Vyle faced them, readying himself to ask where they'd come from and why they decided to stand in the middle of a field attracting a minotaur, when the two men who looked alike interrupted his intent by embracing.

"I thought you dead," one of them said.

"And I you."

The troll supposed he should find the reunion heartwarming, but he found it difficult to conjure the sentiment given everything they'd seen. But how could anything warm his heart after first losing Zalie, and now discovering the destruction caused by his brethren?

"Twins, are you?" he said, seeking to distract himself from dark thoughts. "I met another set once. Ogres."

Their eyes widened and the older one tensed, swept his gaze across the surrounding area.

"Ogres?" He sounded unenthused at the prospect of encountering the behemoths.

Vyle sighed. It shouldn't bother him if people feared them more than they did trolls, but it niggled at him despite his best efforts. Big, ugly and strong, the hulking brutes were deadly but, like the minotaur, they possessed no magical abilities to speak of. The misconception both amused and bothered him; as frightened as the villagers had been when he cleared their fields of boulders, humans still didn't understand how dangerous his kind were.

"Banished," he said, pulling himself from his unpleasant ruminations. "A long time ago. You've nothing to worry about."

Not from ogres, he thought.

The fellow facing him nodded as the twins behind him chattered at each other. "I'm Ilkari. These are Nevan and Naeve."

The troll glanced at the younger soldiers, wondering how anyone discerned one from the other, then dismissed the puzzle. "I don't have a name," he said. "I am called Vyle."

Ilkari made a face. "Vyle and Runt. I sense a pattern. People with little respect for you gave you these labels."

He shrugged. "A way for handlers and Seniors to identify me from other trolls. A word chosen so I'd realize when they directed their comments toward me."

When the older one opened his mouth to continue the conversation, Vyle turned away and started across the clearing. He loathed the possibility of engaging in a discussion about his treatment under the control of humans. He'd engaged in enough of those with Hispid, who'd wanted to turn him against their keepers. Did Ilkari intend the same? If he did, it suggested his life meant little to him.

His new companions stored their sparse weapons, the hard steel whispering against worn leather scabbards, and then followed. Ilkari hurried to catch up and stride beside him, and the troll tensed, convinced he'd attempt to continue the previous conversation.

"Where are we?" he asked instead. "What's happened?"

"I don't know what the village is called." He paused. "Was called. We are a few hours' walk from the guildhall."

"The guild?" In those two short words, Vyle sensed the man's mood brighten. "Maybe we'll find safety there, somebody who can help."

"Nothing remains of it. As for what happened?" He shrugged. "My friend Hispid says the curse is done."

He glanced toward the fellow and saw any remnant of hope drain from his face.

"The curse."

Without prompting, Ilkari related a story Vyle found difficult to believe. He'd never heard of a relic called the Book of Shadow and, though he'd overheard humans uttering the name Amnayel Prisma, he didn't know why anyone should care about his stave. When he told him of the underground cavern and magiks in cages, he wondered if it was where they banished the Unnamed when they no longer considered them useful. If so, he'd not mentioned the ogre twins, a glaring omission if he did come across them.

They'd progressed well into the forest again by the time Ilkari finished his unbelievable story. When he did, he halted, as though speaking of his adventures powered his steps. He grabbed Vyle's sleeve, stopping him, too.

"Do you think we'll find horses at the guildhall?"

The troll frowned. Of course they kept horses for transportation and work—travelers weren't always available for the one, the strong backs of trolls and ogres for the other. He thought to tell him so when he realized the fellow wasn't simply asking if the guild maintained stables. He pressed his lips together and concentrated on what he'd seen when he arrived from the pit at the decimated group of structures. Like his new companions had been when they reached the destroyed village, he'd been shocked by the death and devastation. Had the barn still stood? Did he encounter horses wandering between the broken buildings? If they'd freed them, surely they'd have fled, spooked by fire and flames.

"I'm not sure."

"You need to take us."

Vyle shook his head so hard, his lips flapped with the force of it. "No. It's dangerous. If anywhere is more likely for us to happen upon Unnamed seeking vengeance, the guildhall is the place."

Ilkari nodded and scratched his chin. "Aye, they wish to see humans dead, but they have no reason to desire your death. We need horses to get to Baron Sylleth's."

"Who?"

"Baron Sylleth. If Rein survived, he'll be heading home, and we should, too."

"I think getting as far away from everyone and everything is your best plan."

"Supporting and protecting the baron's champion is my job. Doing whatever I can to prevent slaughter is my duty."

The troll's frown deepened. He figured somebody referred to as the baron's champion shouldn't need anyone else to offer him protection and support, but he knew little about the ways of humans. Like Ilkari, he'd acquired no taste for death, less so his own than others'.

"This is a poor idea."

"What about Carpera's estate?" one twin piped up.

The words the lad spoke meant nothing to Vyle, but the older fellow's reaction told him everything—he frowned and shook his head.

"Too far. After we've returned to Sylleth's to ascertain the state of the world, you can return to your home if you desire."

"But, we—"

He rounded on the speaker. "Your master sent you to the baron's, did he not? Has he recalled you?"

"No," one of them squeaked, though the troll was unsure whether Nevan or Naeve. Before long, he'd need to figure how to tell them apart.

"Then you are with me until I say otherwise. Do you understand?"

They nodded in unison, as if the same brain controlled both their heads. Apparently satisfied despite the scowl contorting his features, Ilkari faced Vyle again. He inhaled through his nose, nostrils flaring, then released the breath, using the action to compose himself before speaking. When he did, his tone sounded flat and even, but firm.

"I have been through much, master troll. Until now, I didn't expect my life to continue. Yet it has. We are delivered to you at a time when the land appears on the brink of falling apart. A time when brave men must step up or watch everything we've known descend into disarray and destruction. I cannot abide such events. As long as air fills my lungs and vitality my sword arm, I shall fight for the lives of those I love, those who depend on me. I will defend until my breath departs. Will you help me?"

The troll didn't answer. He wasn't used to humans addressing him in such a manner, unaccustomed to anyone talking to him this way at all. Seniors and handlers rarely said anything beyond giving commands and barking orders. The other Unnamed either declined to interact with him or treated him as lesser, Hispid included, whom he'd have called friend despite evidence to the contrary. This man sounded as though he truly wanted and needed his help. It seemed he recognized value in the hideous creature standing before him other than making his own life easier.

Vyle swallowed hard before the knot threatening in his throat developed enough to choke him, then nodded before his mind seized the opportunity to understand what he'd agreed to.

73

Ilkari reached up and slapped him on the arm, an expression on his lips potentially considered a smile if one held a loose definition of facial manipulations.

"No time to waste," he said, speaking over his shoulder to the twins before focusing all his attention on Vyle. "We should leave at once. Which way?"

The troll responded by grinding more grass into the dirt with his heel and setting off in the guildhall's direction. Despite his agreement, each step toward their destination enforced the possibility he'd made a mistake, and the realization this was a bad idea.

A terrible idea, indeed.

As they neared the grounds of the guildhall, Ilkari noticed a change in their guide. He'd gone silent—the exact opposite of the chattering twins trailing behind them, excitedly catching up on every second of their lives since they last parted—and his face appeared different. The skin on his cheeks looked smoother, free of the blemishes and wiry hairs normally marring it. His ears and nose were smaller by half, his teeth straighter. Other than his size hulking over everyone in their party, he might have passed for human.

"What are you doing?" the squire asked, staring up at the troll.

Vyle glanced toward him without turning his head—a bashful acknowledgment of the question. "What do you mean?"

"Your face. You look different."

"Hmph. I know not of what you speak."

The way he turned his cheek away, hiding his features from Ilkari, suggested he did.

"You've cast a glamor, haven't you? I've heard trolls possess such talents."

Vyle peeked over his shoulder at Nevan and Naeve. When he saw them too caught up in their own conversation to pay attention to theirs, he leaned closer to the squire, spoke in a hushed tone.

"I don't know what we'll find at the guild. Maybe not wise for some to discover a troll traveling with humans."

Ilkari recognized the wisdom in his words and nodded. "How much farther?"

"Over the next rise. Be prepared."

He assumed their large companion referred to the two vociferous lads trailing behind them, so turned to them as he walked. He waited for them to notice his attention upon them and cease their discussion before he spoke.

"We're close," he said. "Be ready."

Lacking swords or other weapons, he wasn't sure how they were supposed to prepare for the likes of the minotaur they'd encountered previously, or the troll with whom they traveled. If all Unnamed were like them and seeking revenge for a lifetime of slavery, prospects appeared bleak.

Or the rest of the world.

Less than a minute later, they broke through the edge of the forest into a large clearing, stopping when they did to survey the area. Buildings had stood here not so long ago, but only broken stone blocks and splintered beams remained.

Wisps of smoke rose from some piles of debris, the last vestiges of fires that had ravaged whatever flammable materials they found. To Ilkari's eye, it appeared a wonder the conflagration hadn't caught onto the nearby trees and left the entire woodland in ruins.

"These woods survived because of the dryads and wood sprites living here," Vyle said, as if hearing his thoughts. "They ensured the damage caused didn't spread to their brethren. And the forest will have passed word to the farthest reaches of the realm."

"Passed word?" Ilkari repeated, incredulous. He blew a breathy laugh through his nose. "Are you saying the trees talk?

"Buried in the earth, their roots connect," the troll said, stepping away from the verge. "Tree to tree, to brush, and mushroom, and grass. They pass messages more quickly than a horse can gallop. Faster than your words travel through the air if you yelled your tidings to the world. No system for conveying information exists more efficient than the network anchored by the forest."

Ilkari followed their guide and gestured for the twins to do the same.

"How is it possible? How do we not know about this?"

"Humans know little," Vyle said. The squire noticed a disrespectful note to his tone. "Your kind are so concerned for themselves they miss most of what goes on around them."

His words conjured a sliver of anger in Ilkari's gut. Perhaps some men acted as he suggested—Baron Sylleth popped to mind as an example—but not everyone. He parted his lips to protest, then thought better of it. This was neither the time nor place, not when they may encounter magical creatures, every one of them dangerous.

Including the one guiding us, he reminded himself.

They crept across the clearing toward the ruined buildings, ash and chunks of wood turned to charcoal crunching to dust under their soles. Ilkari gaped. He'd never visited the guild, but he recognized the layout, what structures had existed, and how severe the devastation. All of them reduced to rubble. Any hope of finding mounts to carry them to the baron's seeped out of him as they made their way into the compound.

Nothing moved. No noise found his ears other than the sound of their footsteps and the rustle of wind among the trees. The voices of the forest Vyle spoke of? Ilkari guessed not, because the troll had mentioned the connection of their roots. Still, the collapse of the hazy tunnel on him and Rein had thrown everything he'd ever known into question. He'd already seen too many unexplainable things, and suspected he'd encounter plenty more in the days ahead.

Vyle stopped, and the squire halted beside him, unsure why he'd paused. He waited for a few seconds, expecting an explanation, but the hulking Unnamed stared toward the ground, unspeaking and unblinking. Ilkari glanced down to see what had captured the brute's attention.

A corpse lay in front of him, pinned beneath a charred beam. Blistered cheeks and the bald pate where the flames had consumed the person's hair made it difficult to determine male or female, or age. The taut face could belong to a wizened apple as easily as a human.

"Someone you recognize?" Ilkari asked after what he determined a respectful time.

The troll nodded. "Her name is Breda. My handler."

A woman, the squire realized. And he presumed young, judging by the other handlers he'd met. The thought stirred concern for Llyris and the others.

"I'm sorry."

"I could have saved her, but I left her here to die."

The flatness with which Vyle spoke sent a shiver along Ilkari's spine. No matter how human-like the troll glamored himself, the heart of a beast beat inside his chest, as it did the minotaur who'd intended to end them.

"You..." The squire hesitated, unsure of his words, or if he should say anything. "You must have your reasons."

"I have friends—" He paused, swallowed. "Acquaintances in agreement with you. I'm not so sure now. It seems like any life lost in anger is a waste."

"Is this why you didn't kill the minotaur?"

"I refuse to be responsible for any more death. Runt is justifiably angry, as are so many of what you humans call Unnamed." He shook his head, blew a firm breath through his nostrils. "What does it say when you label us Unnamed and then give nicknames like Runt and Vyle and Hispid to mock us?"

"I—"

The troll raised his hand, interrupting Ilkari's protest. "His anger...our anger is misguided. You and the other humans did not enslave me and my brethren; you've benefited from happenings a thousand years before your births, most without realizing. I didn't understand the truth of our plight. Since my birth, I have been a tool for your kind to use—a strong arm to lift things, a frightening face to scare with. How can we expect you who prospered to realize the pain you caused?"

His words sent a pang of regret through the squire's chest. How many times during his life did he take advantage of a magik's abilities without the briefest consideration for their well-being? Magic hid behind so many of life's daily activities—some obvious, like the travelers, others more innocuous, such as Carpera's fountain or Sylleth's maze. Those who provided it became invisible. Sometimes because they went unnoticed, other times because they did their work hidden from sight.

"You lived here," Ilkari said, the words more statement than question.

"I did."

"Where?"

He gestured toward a heap of rubble smaller than the others. "Most of us lived there."

"Most of you? How may?"

He shrugged. "Two dozen. Sometimes more. In small rooms without windows. With too many in residence, we shared accommodations. It's how I met Hispid."

Ilkari walked away from the troll, crossing the compound toward the ruined building where they'd kept him when no humans required the tool they called Vyle. A hand poked from under the pile of stones and the squire toed the loose rocks, considered asking if he recognized who was trapped beneath. He didn't. No point making things worse.

"I'm sorry. These are unspeakable conditions. Nobody should—"

He glanced at the troll and stopped speaking when he noticed the Unnamed staring toward the forest, eyes wide and ears pricked. Ilkari faced the twins, a finger held to his lips to hush them, though neither had spoken since the last time he silenced them. Good lads, these two.

The squire crept closer to their guide, leaned in to whisper, "What is it?"

No immediate response. Vyle continued staring, gaze appearing to dart from one tree trunk to the next. The muscles in his neck and arm stood taut, and the tension seeped into Ilkari. He reached for his sword, then cursed himself for forgetting he'd left it lying at the bottom of a river rushing through an underground cavern. Never had he felt so vulnerable than at this moment.

"We're being watched."

The squire squinted, straining to identify anything beyond the tree line. Nothing—no sound, no sign of movement. Not a branch or leaf appeared misplaced. He hoped to spy a smooth brown hide rippling with muscle; steeds capable of carrying them to their destination.

"Horses?"

Vyle scoffed. "Were you a horse, would you remain here? They're all either fled, stolen, or eaten by predators, I'm sure."

"Then what?"

He shrugged. "Whoever I sensed has hidden themselves from me now."

The flesh along Ilkari's forearms prickled. "So, it's an..." He hesitated before speaking the word, not wanting to further alienate their guide, but he knew no other way to identify a magik. "It's an Unnamed?"

"Unless you are aware of any man or beast who can become invisible, I'd guess so."

Though he didn't appreciate the sarcasm, nor thought this an appropriate time, he didn't react. If pointed words were as bad as it got from the hulking fellow after all he'd been through, he'd accept them. Better than dying on the point of a minotaur's horn.

"We should go," he whispered, eyes searching and finding naught but the expected.

"Which direction to your baron's estate?"

Ilkari raised his gaze skyward out of habit, but found the sun hidden by cloud, so instead took inventory of his memories. He'd seen the guildhall on maps, but years ago. His lips pursed in concentration before he responded.

"South east," he said after a moment's deliberation. "But on foot, it will take weeks."

"Then we best get started and hope to find horses."

The squire gestured for Nevan and Naeve to follow as they set out. Vyle led them to a dirt track, opting for exposed travel rather than tempting whatever watched them from the forest.

As their feet kicked up puffs of dust, Ilkari glanced over his shoulder again. For an instant, he'd have sworn he saw a hairy beast watching them, saliva dripping from its bared fangs.

CHAPTER 9

— • —

T HE PISKY'S PACE SLOWED and Alwin decreased his speed to match, thankful for the reprieve. Going fast had prevented him from avoiding every errant branch grasping for his flesh or dangling leaf looking to slap him in the face. Not to mention the toll on his lungs.

The tiny being hovered at waist level three yards ahead of him, peeking through a screen of half-bare limbs and wilted leaves. The fragment of common sense which had proven effective in preserving the life of someone once called Waul now recommended he ignore whatever Hum was up to. His best, safest course of action was to flee, find a place to hide.

The problem with common sense—besides it not being so common—is that curiosity often gets in its way.

Alwin Pelletoot crept forward, stepping with care to keep his boot soles from crunching on leaves fallen to the ground. He shifted his shoulders, turning sideways to avoid rustling the brush. Once he'd accomplished three painstaking steps, he peered through the thicket.

Orania lay on the grass in a clearing not as large as the one containing the sundial, eyes closed and dried blood flaked on her cheek. The sight made his heart jump. He leaned closer to the curtain of branches separating their hiding spot from the open space, staring at the young woman, straining to discern any sign of life. A few seconds passed before he noticed the rise and fall of her chest.

Tension drained out of him, both because the handler lived and because her Unnamed cared enough to bring him to help her. How he'd aid the stricken girl, he didn't know, but at least he'd have the

80

opportunity. As if reading his thoughts, Hum moved aside, clearing space for him to go forth. She waved him on, her tiny hand with its minuscule fingers gesturing over and over.

An alarm bell sounded in his mind, the warning rung by his insulted common sense. Duty rather than curiosity silenced it this time, and Alwin stepped forward, passing through the veil of plant growth.

The instant his foot touched the turf within the clearing, he realized things were amiss.

He froze, eyes darting as he took stock, trying to determine if his situation warranted this panicked feeling or if fear of the unknown reared its ugly head. Nothing appeared out of sorts at first. Once-green hedgerows ringed the space, a gnarled tree stood near the center. Not until his gaze fell upon Orania again, this time taking in all of her instead of searching for a single thing, did he notice the thin vines binding her wrists. Thicker ones wound around her legs, and one about her waist.

The panic blossomed into full-blown terror and regret for not listening to his own concerns. Alwin spun, intending to dive into the onetime labyrinth. He didn't want to desert the handler, but also realized he possessed no knowledge to help her on his own. Trying certainly meant they'd both die.

Instead of plunging through dried leaves and brittle branches, leaving them quaking and shivering in his wake, a different and unexpected sight greeted him.

Jade-green foliage hung from twigs and limbs interwoven into a latticework cage. He reached out with his free hand and pushed against it. The hedge wall held. His eyes widened, and he peered through the one space remaining large enough for him to do so.

Hum hovered on the other side, a smile curving her lips.

"Help me," he cried. When she failed to respond, he gripped the lattice, shook it so the leaves rattled. "In the name of everything holy, help us."

The pisky did no such thing. Her smirk broadened, and she raised a hand, twiddling her fingers at him before she scooted away, disappearing in the tangle of brush.

Realization didn't dawn on Alwin like the rising sun; it fell across him as a wave crashing on the shore. The Unnamed hadn't brought him here to help her handler in her time of need; she'd led him

81

to an ambush. He stared at the spot occupied by Hum a second before, until a broad leaf shifted, obscuring his view.

A creak from behind him sent hard goose flesh racing over his skin.

With breath held, Alwin turned slowly, hoping to prevent whatever crept up from attacking. As he completed his pivot, everything appeared as it did before. Orania lay upon the ground, bound by leafy runners and thick ropes of vine as before; the same hedges bordered the clearing, and the tree remained at the center.

Except closer. And it wore a woman's face.

The knights walked in silence, their lack of conversation necessitated by not knowing what lay in wait around the next corner or obscured behind any obstruction. Rein wished it to be different. Given the chance to talk to Jai, to remind him of some of their shared stories and experiences, maybe he'd remember.

As they navigated the depleted labyrinth, the knight's eyes often found his friend, the sway of his shoulders, forcing him to remove himself from memories once joyful but now painful. He drew a hand across his face, hoping to brush away the heartache threatening to choke him. This wasn't the time to lament.

When the scream pierced the fraught silence, the tangle of foliage surrounding them made it near-impossible to guess from which direction it came. Jai halted, his head tilted in an effort to discern its source.

"Where?" he said, chancing the single word.

Rein frowned, gaze darting as they waited for another sound, some indication of which way they should go to locate the origin of the desperate shout. Intuition told him the very man for whom they searched created the ruckus.

No second cry followed the first, interpretable as either a good omen or a bad sign. The baron's champion bulled past his friend, taking point without any more knowledge of which way to go than Jai. He barged through a tangle of dried brush, foregoing the path. He didn't trust any route suggested by the maze, knowing his father had devised it to lead men to their doom for his amusement.

As they pushed through the hedges, brittle limbs snapping under their pressure, a gust of wind rose, moaning through the branches and leaves like a beast in pain. The sound of it sent a shiver along Rein's spine; he gritted his teeth and suppressed it the same way he'd done any time nerves threatened when a fight loomed.

Doubtless he headed for a tussle now, but with what?

Each backward step Alwin took, the soles of his boots compressing blades of grass, made him cringe. Knowing nothing about the creature advancing toward him, he understood it and the plant life around them were implicitly connected.

Every time he trod upon a creeper, or a leaf, the Unnamed before him flinched.

"Please," he said, holding both hands up in front of him, pleading, the satchel held in one, the other facing palm forward. "I mean no harm."

As he backed toward where Orania lay, the vegetation beneath his feet grew thicker. He chanced a glance down at pads of moss he hadn't noticed before, and vines extending from somewhere behind him. His mind raced, searching for a way to convince the creature to spare their lives. If the handler lived. He craned his neck to glimpse her, but she offered no resolution to his question.

The instant he faced his aggressor again, a memory flashed unbidden through his brain, provided by one of the others living inside him. In it, he saw this Unnamed in its youth, a sapling with bright green leaves and smooth bark, and a name came to him. His lips trembled, parted, and it spilled from his tongue before he could prevent it.

"Belladoris."

The tree creature stopped, its limbs shivered. Alwin clutched the satchel to his chest—an inadequate shield, but he figured it better than nothing. Thick books provided more protection than thin skin.

"No one has spoken my true name in centuries." Its jaw creaked as it spoke, the words slow and drawn out, sounding as though it exerted great effort to form them. "Not since before they sent me to tend the maze. How do you know it?"

"I...I don't know."

"Not even my handler knew what my kind call me. She named me Scrub as an insult to me and all like me."

Alwin swallowed a lump in his throat, not liking the curl to the bark forming the creature's lips, or the angered tone to its woody voice. He wished to unsay its name, but why? At least it granted him a brief respite, although he couldn't figure out how to make use of the break.

The Unnamed sidled closer, a burl resembling an eyebrow rising. "Who are you?"

"Me?" he said, the word squeaking from his tight throat. "I'm nobody."

"What's your name?"

One of the creature's roots slid through the grass toward him, like a snake creeping up on a delicious-looking rat. He took another backward step, his heels sinking into thick moss.

"Alwin. Alwin Pelletoot."

"No, it's not."

Its lack of actual human features—holes for eyes, ridges for lips, a bump for a nose—couldn't hide the suspicious expression on the face of the creature named Belladoris.

"W—Waul?"

The leaves clinging to its branches rattled as if it shook its head, though he spied no hint of movement other than its steady advance toward him. The root snaked through the grass, stalking him.

"Once, you may have been. But you contain more secrets, don't you?"

He wheezed, trying to clear his throat, using the interruption to buy himself precious seconds. His gaze flicked to both sides of the sentient tree, seeking an escape route but ultimately unable to find one. Her limbs lowered and spread, blocking his way, as the hedges behind her interlaced into what appeared an impenetrable cage.

"Viden Misk," he said, knowing it wasn't the name she wanted to hear.

"No." Her forward movement ceased and the knots above her eye holes drooped as though she squinted, peered closer at him.

Into him. "I sense many in you. Lives upon lives forced into acquiescence, like mine and all the other so-called Unnamed. But one is capable of such: the mage who cursed me to this hell. It's not possible."

A droplet of sweat rolled down Alwin's cheek, and he fought to keep himself from wiping it away. He didn't want to move his hands from in front of himself and give up any protection they provided. Not at the moment he admitted what he suspected she'd already guessed.

"Prisma," he said, his voice a guilty whisper. "Amnayel Prisma. The mage lives on in me, passed through the ages from body to body until he took mine."

The bark features changed her expression, cycling from suspicion to surprise to blatant hatred. The last halted Alwin's breath in his chest, made him clutch the satchel's handles tighter. His feet shuffled, attempting to carry him farther from the angry magik, but the moss grew up onto his boots, holding him in place and preventing escape. He glanced down, pulled hard to free one foot, and failed.

"You," Belladoris said, drawing his attention. "You did this to me. To all of us."

"No, I—"

The root stalking him wound around his ankle, squeezing tight enough for him to sense its grip through the spongy moss. It coiled up his calf, slithered toward his thigh.

Alwin screamed.

He let go of the bag, swiped at the loop of gnarled tree tightening on his leg. His hand brushed against it and it surprised him to find its surface warm, as though he'd touched a finger. He recoiled. His eyes darted from the root to its owner, the dryad closer now, the bark of its face crinkled and rippled with rage.

"You will pay for what you did to us, as the master of the estate surrendered his life for the indignities he forced upon me. For the suffering of all magiks abused by him and his family before him."

A gust of wind tore through the hedgerows. The leaves didn't rustle or move, but the branches sighed and moaned. The sound rose and the expression on the tree's face slackened. She straightened, listening to the sighs become howls. The root gripping his leg inexplicably receded, leaving a line of pain behind from where it held him. He used his free hand to rub it as he watched Belladoris creep away across the small clearing.

Despite the space between them, he suspected he wasn't close to being out of danger.

At first, Rein attempted to push through the tangle of brush, but each twig and branch plucked at him, seeking to impede his progress. He tired of pulling his arms free from the clutching plants and switched to hacking a path through the hedges with the sharp edge of his sword's blade.

The wind screamed with every swipe.

He did his best to ignore the din, straining to listen over it for any clue to indicate which direction the original scream had come from. He detected no other noises, at least none amongst the bellows of the brush.

A glimpse over his shoulder showed him Jai followed, enough room between them for him to avoid being struck by the tip of his friend's weapon. He remembered the baron, and how to soldier; why did Rein disappear from his memory? The thought tightened the knight's jaw, clamping his teeth together, and he forced the question from his mind. Without knowing what lay ahead of them, he couldn't let anything distract him.

He'd witnessed his father overtaken by the dryad.

And I did nothing.

It should have caused embarrassment, a fact to make him hang his head in shame, but it didn't. It brought no such feelings bubbling within him, no grief or sadness, no disappointment. The kingdom was a better place without his sire.

His sword slashed through a woven lattice of branches, the resistance less than he'd encountered before. The ruckus created by the blade slicing the hedge surrendered any advantage of surprise, so he jumped through into the clearing beyond.

Weapon raised, Rein stepped aside to make room for Jai as his eyes darted around this new space. Beaten grass, limp foliage, an ancient tree, and a panic-stricken man with a satchel clutched to his chest and moss growing up his legs.

The sight of the jade flora curled the knight's lip into a snarl, stirred a memory of a patch of its brethren covering a subterranean passage's ceiling. His nemesis while trapped awaiting his death.

Until she came along and offered a deal. An accord he'd upheld when she hadn't.

He stalked across the clearing toward the frightened fellow—the same one for whom the woman had searched. Although the sword he held in front of him conveyed an implied threat, the man paid no attention to Rein, his gaze steadfastly fixed on the opposite side of the grassy space. The baron's champion swallowed the anger the sight of him brewed in his belly, the curses he wanted to spit. As much as Viden Misk should shoulder the blame for what happened to his friend, this fellow may hold the key to returning Jai's memories.

"Don't worry," Rein said, sheathing his sword and drawing his dagger. "I'll get you out."

The man's gaze flickered to him and their eyes met. The tense panic hardening his features didn't relent.

"Hurry," he whispered.

The baron's champion crouched, examined the growth of moss for the best place to insert the tip of his knife and rend it to pieces. From this position, he spied the mound behind the fellow. Perhaps nothing more than an unevenness to the ground but for the human fingers protruding from it in one spot.

Rein's eyes widened—the work of the creature he'd watched kill his father. The Unnamed who'd tended the labyrinth.

"Be careful, Jai," he said over his shoulder as he inserted the dagger's tip into the thick moss. "Watch your back."

"And yours," his friend responded.

The vegetation holding the man's leg did not slice easily. It resisted the sharp edge as Rein sawed it with his knife. When he'd gotten through a few inches, the cut he'd created closed up, regrowing like the lichen on the passage's ceiling. The knight cursed, set his blade aside, and inserted his fingers into the growth.

"No," the man muttered above, but Rein didn't stop to discover if he spoke to him or if he meant to direct the word elsewhere.

His fingertips entered the moss, his flesh protected by the gauntlets he wore, and he tore at it. He ripped it away, moving frantically to stem its regrowth, chunks of green sent flying. His world narrowed to the task, as though liberating this man from the cursed lichen could aid in recovering Jai and also furnish him with knowledge about what happened to his lost squire.

After a minute, one leg came free.

"Lift it," he growled, without diverting his attention. "Take your foot off the ground."

The fellow did as he said, elevating his boot so the sole no longer contacted the earth. He wavered as though he'd teeter and fall, so Rein paused for a second.

And noticed the moss growing on his gauntlets.

"Damn it," he spat and concentrated on digging the fellow's other leg free, wondering if he'd discover his own boots engulfed by the time he finished.

Branches rustled together behind him and the baron's champion struggled to keep himself from glancing away to find out what caused the sound. Did Jai retreat into the labyrinth, deserting him? His chest tightened, the thought prompting him to claw faster at the moss. Above him, the fellow he attempted to free whimpered. A word may have hidden inside the squeak escaping his throat, but Rein missed it in his hurry to complete the task.

Then Jai cried out.

The baron's champion lifted his head from his toil and glanced over his shoulder. The knight faced away from him, his sword swinging at the creepers lashing out at him from the ground; the small, ancient tree stood closer than before. Rein realized the mistake he'd made.

He returned his attention to the moss, redoubling his efforts with the assumption his friend could hold his own for a moment.

Chicken or the egg, he thought.

If he abandoned the fellow to help Jai, he may lose his opportunity to recover his friend's memories of them. But if he stayed, the knight might not survive to remember.

He dug handfuls of moss from the man's leg, flinging them to the side in the hope they wouldn't creep in and imprison him again. Finally, he pulled the last from the fellow's boot.

"Get away," he cried, standing and throwing off his lichen-covered gauntlets.

The man stumbled—whether through following orders or from losing his balance mattered not. Rein jerked his sword out of its scabbard, turning in one fluid motion to aid Jai, but a grip stopped him, threatened to send him sprawling. Moss enveloped his boots.

He knew if he tried to free his footwear, it would take too long. Instead of wasting time, he yanked upward, twisting his right foot and pulling it out of his boot. He mimicked the move with the other and rushed to his friend's side in his stocking feet.

Side by side, their blades flashed as they fended off the roots and vines seeking to entwine them, each of the knights inching closer to the Unnamed conducting the assault. To ensure their survival, they needed to swiftly address the origin of the attack.

A thicker branch lashed out at Rein; he dodged and swung his sword, cleaving the wood. The limb fell, bounced on the ground, and a gush of brown fluid spurted from the stump it left. The jick howled in pain.

As they fought, the two knights danced back and forth on their feet, seeking to keep grass and moss from attaching itself, capturing them. Each time he shifted, the baron's champion felt the tendrils of vegetation grasping at him, his movements inhibited as though he walked upon a floor covered in syrup. The thought made him understand the fluid now oozing from the dryad.

Sap.

He spread apart from Jai, forcing their adversary to split her attention between them. Leaves and limbs lashed the air, rustling and snapping, the attacks wild and undirected. A half smile tilted Rein's lips. He'd seen many an opponent deteriorate into desperation like this.

It wouldn't be much longer now.

Around them, the hedges shook and moaned, as though agitated by an unfelt gale. Rein chanced a glimpse away; the man they'd saved cowered on a bare patch of earth, both hands clutching his satchel tight against his chest. His panicked eyes darted from the fight to the ground, to the complaining shrubbery. He appeared in little danger, so the knight refocused all his attention on their foe.

He and Jai fought on opposite sides of the tree-creature, both of them attacking as much as defending. Leaves hanging from the thing's boughs drooped as fatigue took its toll. After centuries of a sedentary life of doing nothing but control the labyrinth on the whim of its master, the Unnamed appeared unused to such activity.

Jai lopped another limb off, provoking more howls of pain. The distraction gave the baron's champion the opportunity he hoped for, and the edge of his blade bit deep into the bark of the dryad's trunk. It stumbled away, jerking his weapon from his hands.

Rein pulled his dagger from its sheath and advanced, his face contorted into a scowl he reserved for when the time came to strike the killing blow. The creature shuffled backward; the grip of the grass under his feet waned.

And the Unnamed's shape changed.

The branches shrank and sagged, the knotted wood softened. A woman stood before them, her skin a lighter shade of brown than the bark it had been a moment before, dark braids of hair spilling over her shoulders. Purple eyes blazing with pain flashed where naught but indents were seconds ago. The sword lodged in her fell from her flesh, thumping against the ground. Her one remaining hand pressed against the gash in her side, its long fingers with prominent knuckles failing in their attempt to stem the flow of thick blood.

"Finish it," she wheezed between dark lips curled in defiance to show brown teeth.

The muscles in Rein's jaw tightened as he raised his dagger and stepped forward, intending to grant the creature's wish. A hand grasping his arm stopped him and he whirled, ready to defend himself against this new threat.

The man they'd rescued released his grip and shrank away from the menace of the bare blade and the heat of Rein's anger.

"Please," he said, voice quavering, "don't kill her."

The knight stared at the fellow, confident of Jai's ability to protect him should the injured creature appear intent to re-engage. Under other circumstances, he'd have ignored the man's plea and finished his foe. Not this time. He needed his help to restore his friend's memory, or at least try.

"She..." He hesitated, corrected himself. "It meant to kill you. And what about her?"

He raised his arm and pointed at the shallow hillock. The man craned to peer over his shoulder.

"Orania." Sadness tinged his tone as he returned his attention to the baron's champion. "It is not her fault. We did this to them."

"We did nothing," he snapped. "This happened long before—"

"Rein," Jai said, interrupting.

The knight spun around, expecting his friend's speaking of his name to be a warning. It wasn't. The Unnamed continued slinking away, a trail of red-brown blood left in her wake. Four paces remained between the creature and the wall of hedges. The muscles in Rein's thighs contracted, ready to launch him in pursuit, but he stopped himself, cursing under his breath.

Allowing an adversary to survive never proved a wise decision.

The overgrown brush behind her reached out, leaves falling over her shoulders. They enveloped her until naught but her pain-taut face remained visible. Then it disappeared, too.

They stared at the space vacated by the Unnamed, none of them speaking as the hedgerow returned to its previous appearance and the inexplicable wind ceased. Foliage stopped shivering; the shaking of branches dwindled to nothing. The fellow holding the satchel broke the silence by clearing his throat. Both knights faced him.

"She didn't deserve to die," he said, voice squeaking.

Frowning, Rein ignored the man's comment and stored his dagger, then stomped across the ground to retrieve his weapon. He held it up, examining the red-brown liquid clinging to the steel, touched it with his fingertip. It came away sticky, a thread of fluid between the pad of his finger and the blade drawing out into a dangling loop. He spread them apart, breaking the strand, and fought the impulse to touch his fingers to his tongue to find out if it tasted like the syrup it resembled. Instead, he wiped it on his breeches, then did the same with his sword before sliding it into its scabbard. The task complete, he faced the man again, a withering expression cinched upon his face. He cowered, the knight's look accomplishing its goal.

"Your decision to stop me had better not have repercussions." His words squeezed out between clenched teeth. "If it does, I'll hold you responsible."

He advanced toward the fellow, who shrank away, the satchel clutched in front of him like a shield. Rein wondered what it contained, but put the question from his mind. More pressing issues concerned him.

"The stave," he said, stopping a few strides from him, his arms crossed and his face set with determination. "Where is it?"

"I...I don't know."

"Well, you're going to help us find it." When the man didn't move, Rein added, "Now."

The fellow slunk away from the low barrow where he'd stopped and headed for the closest opening in the hedgerows. The baron's champion stomped across the clearing to his boots, the grass having receded and relinquished its hold. He donned them, then gestured to his friend and the two knights followed close behind the stranger leading them. As they did, Rein took care to step over the trail of blood left by the Unnamed, a shiver quaking along his spine.

"This is a bad idea," Jai said. "We should leave this place. Now."

"She's hurt. She'll let us be," the man said over his shoulder. "For now."

"How do you know?" Rein snapped. "Who are you?"

"Alwin Pelletoot is my name these days, but it turns out I've held many others before."

The knight glanced sideways at his friend. The urge to follow up his statement and ask him about Viden Misk butted against his tight lips. Fault belonged to the old man, but if the slightest chance existed he possessed the ability to return Jai to himself, they needed to provide him the opportunity. He'd watch him closely, keep him within arm's length, but give him enough slack to either save the day or hang himself.

To his credit, the fellow who called himself Alwin Pelletoot led them with assurance through the overgrown maze. Rein had never entered the labyrinth. As a child, he'd often imagined what it must be like to challenge for his father's prize, but lacked anything to build his fantasies on other than rumors and the distant, anguished cries of those who tried. He'd pictured great jade walls shifting when one wasn't looking, thorns hungry for human blood, hidden traps. As a lad, it sounded exciting, and easy to imagine why people accepted the challenge even when nobody ever completed it to capture the baron's prize.

He reached out and dragged his fingertips across a dried brown leaf. Its brittle stem snapped, and it plummeted to the ground, landing on a patch of sagging grass at the edge of the beaten path they followed. Nothing like what he'd imagined in his youth.

They rounded a corner and emerged into another open space, but didn't pause. Alwin led them past a sundial, its base fashioned of red-veined white marble, its face carved with runes resembling no numbers known to Rein in any language. The shadow its pointer shouldn't be casting in the day's gloom crawled across its surface as they strode by, as though curious enough to follow them. The baron's champion frowned.

"Did you see?" he asked Jai, leaning closer to his friend so their guide didn't think he spoke to him.

"See what?"

He glanced over his shoulder, but they'd gone too far for him to glimpse the oddity.

"Never mind."

As they left the clearing and entered the maze proper again, he thought how good it felt having the knight walking beside him, but their circumstances leeched any satisfaction he derived from his presence. His father dead, jicks running amok, his friend remembered nothing about them, and Ilkari gone. How could he find space for peace?

Since encountering the woman and hearing her offer to restore Jai, he'd barely put a thought to the fate of the man who'd raised him like his own son. The realization sent a lancet of guilt into his heart. He sighed a long breath between his lips.

"Thinking about Ilkari, aren't you?" Jai asked.

"Yes," Rein said, one eyebrow crooked. "How did you know?"

His friend shrugged. "Intuition, I suppose. What happened to him?"

The baron's champion inhaled, using the fresh air to quell the stir of emotion knotting his gut. He remembered nothing of him and their relationship, but recalled his father, the squire, and everything else. At least he retained enough sense of him to guess what he'd been thinking.

"He climbed through a patch of moss and disappeared. It appeared unbelievable. Not so much now."

"He is resourceful and wise." Jai laid his hand on the knight's shoulder. "I'm sure he will find his way."

Rein nodded, a short, sharp motion. Saliva clicked in his tightened throat; he couldn't interpret whether the sudden rush of emotion was due to his thoughts about his squire, or the touch of his friend caused it. He suspected the latter because, when the knight withdrew, the shadow it left behind resembled heartache.

"Almost there," Alwin said.

The farther they got from their encounter with the dryad, the faster their guide led them. No crossroads or fork gave him pause. Not once did he hesitate or appear to harbor any doubt about their directions, though they'd followed enough twists and turns to leave Rein wondering. With Jai by his side and his hand on his sword, his concern waned, though he experienced more on the occasions when Alwin mumbled to himself like a madman.

They arrived at a final intersection, left or right their only options, and their guide stayed left with the same surety with which he'd led them all along. Five strides later, they passed from the hedgerow corridor into another open space.

The three clearings they'd encountered each possessed one characteristic to differentiate them from the others. In the first, they discovered the gnarled tree that revealed itself as the Unnamed who controlled the labyrinth. In the second, the unusual sundial.

A single branch protruded from the ground in this patch of grass, its bark an off-white close to the color of bone, twisting in an eerily uniform pattern. It appeared too straight and symmetrical to be what he suspected.

Rein stepped into the clearing, curiosity drawing him toward the protrusion. One of his companions followed him, but he didn't bother to find out which as he crept forward. The closer he got, the less he thought it what he'd first guessed.

He halted two strides away, staring at it, his gaze following its length to the top, then finding its way to the ground. The surrounding earth appeared churned, as though an arborist dug a hole to plant the item here.

"It didn't grow," he muttered, unsure if any stood close enough to hear him. "Someone placed it."

He reached out and brushed it with his fingertips, the surface smooth yet rough, like a fingernail, and warm in the manner of a rock lying in the sunshine. But the sun hid behind clouds, its warming rays taken from the world. He thought to take his touch away, but failed. His eyes widened.

"Is this...?" he said over his shoulder, leaving the question dangling and incomplete.

"The unicorn's horn." Alwin nodded.

Rein inhaled a sharp breath and stumbled backward, contact with the thing broken. His feet tangled, and he tripped, headed for a fall if not for Jai catching him. He righted himself, tilted his head to thank his friend, and faced their guide.

"Impossible," he said.

"No." Alwin hugged the satchel tight to his chest as though he expected someone to come along and attempt to steal it. His eyes flickered between Rein and the horn, tears rimming his bottom lids. "Nothing is impossible."

Dirt flew as the knights dug at the base of the unicorn's horn, as Alwin himself had not so long ago. Crouching halfway between where they worked and the hedges so as not to be surprised by grasping branches, he watched them, the satchel set on the grass at his feet.

Rein and Jai—he'd known their names before they told him. Every time he closed his eyes, if only to blink, new recollections of somebody else's memories flashed across his mind. Most appeared inane and unimportant, a few pleasant; some left him aghast and thinking he may prefer for his eyeballs to dry up and shrivel to raisins rather than see more like them.

The most recent hadn't been so terrible—a vision of the vast library. Shelves filled with books, racks of scrolls, a long table with candelabras set along its center, the tapers flickering and sending shadows across the collection. The memory wasn't bad, but guilt over abandoning those ancient writings when Hum tricked him niggled at him, as did the mystery of what happened to the tomes. They'd disappeared between his first visit and traversing the maze with the knights.

His anxiety and curiosity lasted until he blinked again and saw the corpse of the unicorn, its lustrous coat dulled to ashen, blood leaking from its broken horn. A gasp escaped his lips and his gorge rose. He considered closing his eyes to escape the vision, but more would come to replace it if he did, so he kept them open wide.

Air stung his orbs, forcing him to blink again, and the scene remained. This time, he stood near the slaughtered animal. Other men gathered around. These hurriedly wrapped a long, slender item in a sheet of canvas. The horn.

"I was there," he proclaimed. The knights didn't notice.

Alwin pushed himself to stand, his jaw hanging open, and the bag forgotten. He stared straight ahead, not even his companions' movements distracting him from the twisted horn pointing toward the sky.

"Of course we were," the disembodied voice said. It sounded tired. *"Do you think mere humans capable of stealing the unicorn's horn without the help of a mage?"*

"Prisma was behind it. Why?"

"Wizards require sustenance, the same things as anyone else, and more. Food, lodgings, supplies. They have to be paid for."

"Money? He helped kill an Unnamed for a few coins?"

"More than a few, I assure you."

Alwin blinked and saw them carting the horn away. His perspective switched, the eyes creating the memory lowering as Amnayel Prisma knelt beside the felled magik. His fingers came into view, stroking the creature's mane as though attempting to soothe it back to vitality.

"Didn't he realize what would happen?"

"We did not."

"Stop saying we," Alwin shrieked. "I had nothing to do with this. I'm merely a vessel, a captive."

"Are you all right?"

Rein stood, one dirt-caked hand resting on the hilt of his sword. Alwin kept quiet, anticipating the voice to elaborate further, whether with excuses absolving the so-called great mage, or fabrications about the inevitability of the situation. Though it remained silent, he could anticipate its words because they belonged to him. They formed in his head.

This time when Alwin closed his eyes to reorient himself to reality, he saw nothing. He'd never been so thankful for darkness.

"I'm fine," he said, opening his lids and bending to retrieve the satchel.

Prickles vibrated through all the muscles in his arms and legs, his fingertips tingled. Something more than discomfort and worry gathered inside him. Jai ceased digging and stood beside his friend, and Alwin peered down at the ground by their feet. Long scratches showed in the dirt where they'd dragged their fingers through it, but to no avail. The horn remained firmly planted.

"I have an idea," he said, stopping a few paces from them.

He crouched again, set the bag down and flipped its clasp. When he opened it, he remembered he'd only find the trio of full-sized tomes he'd rescued, but his heart still hoped to discover those miniature volumes tucked away inside. He sighed and pulled out the book with the unicorn embossed on the cover.

He placed it on top of the gaping satchel, using it as a pedestal as he flipped the tome open and leafed through pages with no clue what he looked for. Colorful illustrations decorated the vellum along with cursive he couldn't decipher even if he understood the languages in which they were written.

Most of the pictures depicted a single specimen. Without proper knowledge, someone could mistakenly believe a lone unicorn existed, or they existed singularly, one at a time. Alwin Pelletoot would have made the same assumption, but he carried ancient wisdom secreted away in his mind.

He paused when he came to the sole illustration the tome contained showing multiple creatures. In it, four pure white unicorns galloped across a plain, sunlight glinting on their horns, wind whipping their manes. The illustrator's expertise captured every rippling muscle, the flare of their nostrils, the sheer power and energy of their movement. Alwin extended a finger, touched the lead beast—the biggest.

The one they'd sacrificed, her horn buried in the ground a few feet away.

"What happened to the rest of you?"

He continued leafing through the pages, ignoring most of it until he reached the last sheet of parchment. The final illustration differed from the others, a sketch rather than a picture. Gray charcoal lines, thin and thick, no color and few details, and yet it caught the flight of the dragons so well, he'd have sworn he saw their wings move.

Alwin closed the book, leaving it balanced on top of the satchel as he stepped over it.

"Did you find what you were looking for?" Rein asked.

"What's your idea?" Jai added.

The knights dwarfed him, but neither did any more than step aside as he pushed between them without answering either of their questions. He stopped less than a stride from the horn—the object humans stole from the unicorn triggering first a war, then a millennium of enslavement. So much pain.

He reached out with both hands and grasped it. The twisted ridges pressed against his flesh, its surface both warm with life and cold as death.

I don't know what I'm doing, he thought.

"Do it," the voice prompted.

The muscles in his jaw flexed as he tightened his grip and yanked. To his amazement, it shifted. One knight gasped, though he didn't know which. His focus narrowed until he saw nothing but the slender bit of ivory grasped in his hands.

He twisted again. Again. The horn moved, loosening from the ground with each manipulation until it slid out.

He lifted it, clearing its tip from the dirt—heavier than he'd imagined—and his arms faltered under its weight. He'd expended a significant amount of effort trying to free it, and the muscles in his limbs were reluctant to give any more. The instant before it slipped from his grasp, Rein took it from him. The next thing he noticed was Jai's hands under his armpits, lowering him to the ground.

"How did you do that?"

The knight's face hovered over his, but he had no answer to offer beyond a lopsided smile. It wouldn't satisfy them or him, but he didn't understand how he'd known to do what he did, or how it came free.

"It doesn't matter," Rein said.

Alwin's gaze flickered to the baron's champion. "No, it doesn't," he agreed. "Now let's find the stave."

Chapter 10

— ◦ —

They'd left behind the last of the rice paddies and farms a week ago. Out on the steppes, the heat beat on them with unrelenting animosity, as though it desired nothing more than to hasten their end. The jangala, as Shiera called it, lay another day's walk ahead of them, the promise of the shade offered by its high canopy enough to keep them going.

During this time Llyris felt most thankful for the ogre twins accompanying them. They seldom spoke, and she found herself often fearful of their reasons for being there, but their size allowed them to carry more supplies than they could on their own. Even after days without encountering a stream or watering hole, they still carried plenty of water to sustain them.

The handler raised a hand and used the cloth tied around her head to wipe a droplet of sweat from her cheek. The task complete, she settled her fingers on the dragon wing brooch affixed to her shirt. At first, she'd kept it stowed in her pack with her cloak, taking it out at night after the sun set and the air grew cool, but she soon realized the bauble was the lone way to keep her mind from wandering. If she allowed it, her thoughts always ended up on Flayre and everyone they'd lost.

She wondered what aspect of the pewter jewelry brought her a sense of calm she found nowhere else. Nothing appeared out of the ordinary with its curved edges and sharp points. Any artisan could have fashioned it, a bauble for sale at any craft market in dozens of different towns. A trinket created to secure a cloak around one's shoulders, and no more to it.

Yet it was much more.

As she brushed her fingertip across its surface, tracing its details, the ridges depicting the bones hidden within it, she speculated for the hundredth time about who'd given it to her. Shiera had denied it, and what reason did she have to lie? A cloak for warmth and a pin to secure it weren't items warranting secrecy, yet the nature of its making its way into her possession was remarkable. Hinter's robe of changing colors demanded far more attention.

But the mystery of who and why haunted her, the texture of its rough surface against her fingers summoning her curiosity. If she removed her touch, it would dissipate, but then grief and sadness always took its place. Given the choice between the frustrating and somewhat concerning puzzle or anguish knotting her gut, the decision proved easy.

She licked her lips, her dry tongue tasting salt and reminding her of the thirst collecting in her throat.

"A moment," she called, her voice coming out a croak. Hours had passed since the last time she, or any of them, had spoken. "I need a drink."

She took her hand from the brooch and slid her waterskin from her shoulder. The liquid it held sloshed against the leather, the sound reminding her of Emeryn Aryzath and his wine. She resisted the urge to abandon her task and return her touch to the dragon wing pin, instead uncorking the container and bringing it to her lips.

The water flowed over her tongue, its temperature several degrees beyond warm, but it slaked her need. She filled her mouth once, twice, gulping noisily with each swallow.

"Slow your pace, handler," Cirril said. "We don't know when we may next come upon a source of water."

She lowered the skin and wiped her face on her sleeve. Her eyes met the guardsman's; she nodded and recorked the water container, though her throat begged for more. He continued watching her, as if he suspected she'd sneak another sip against his wishes.

"We shouldn't tarry," he said, breaking eye contact with her and gazing skyward. "Few hours of sunlight remain. We best travel as far as possible before nightfall."

He struck out again, expecting the others to follow, which they did. Tesfira abandoned her customary spot walking beside the thief in favor of taking up with Llyris.

"You made the right choice," the acolyte said, leaning toward her and keeping her voice quiet. "Don't let Cirril make you think otherwise."

"I won't," she replied, surprised to find her mouth returning to an arid state despite the gulps of water. "But everything else makes me wonder."

"Faith is difficult to request of someone, but I hope you trust me."

The handler's throat clicked as she swallowed. "I trust you believe we are doing the right thing."

"I can ask no more."

She put her hand on Llyris' shoulder, offered a smile, then increased her pace to return to her position beside Hinter. Left on her own, the handler set her fingertips against the pin again, searching for the sense of calm it brought before.

Hoping they'd survive.

While on the steppes, they experienced wildlife from a distance, but the jangala teemed with it. After three days trekking through the tangle of brush and vines, they'd encountered more kinds of animals than most see in their entire lives, but not the expected forest creatures. They didn't encounter rabbits or wolves, deer, bear, or skunk—at least, not like what they were used to. If those beasts existed here, they did so in distorted forms. Deer sported long, slender horns, their stature smaller than Llyris had ever seen. A rabbit-like species with stubby ears scampered away before them. Other critters chattered from tree limbs overhead, pigs with tusks protruding from their mouths crashed through the bushes to escape their advance, and fowl with plumage too colorful for words flapped amongst the high fronds of the unusual trees. Unseen mice scurried away from their steps and insects buzzed around their heads, some the size of a hand.

"Incredible, isn't it?" Tesfira asked, marveling at one of the multicolored birds.

It took flight with a raucous caw, its long red tail trailing behind it, yellow feathers on the undersides of its wings flashing.

101

Some animals employed their coloring to hide from the sight of predators, and move with stealth. The avians patrolling this place appeared without such concern.

"Beautiful," Hinter replied, though Llyris detected a note in her tone suggesting she spoke the word to feign agreement with her friend.

One thing the handler had learned about her thief companion: she preferred not to speak unless necessary, a trait the ogre twins accompanying them took to the extreme. Since they'd left the hamlet by the lake, they'd offered nothing but grunted agreements and exasperated sighs.

"Don't let their splendor distract you," Cirril said, throwing his usual wet blanket over any hint of enjoyment. "The most beautiful ones are often the most deadly."

"You sound like a man with a broken heart," Tesfira commented with a chuckle.

The guardsman halted and rounded on her, a scowl etching its lines into his face. "My personal life is none of your concern, acolyte. Keep it out of your mouth."

"And find a civil tongue in yours," Hinter said, stepping between the merchant's man and her friend.

They glared at each other and Llyris shook her head. The instances of friction between them grew daily, becoming frequent enough she worried every time they spoke to each other. As it kept up, her concern for one of them reaching their breaking point and snatching weapon from scabbard burgeoned. So far, neither had, but it did little to help her breathe easier.

Nor did the way Hartrek and Gartrek sneered and crossed their arms aid in assuaging her misgivings.

A tense second passed before Cirril scoffed and returned to leading them through the underbrush. Tesfira leaned closer to Hinter, her voice low to keep her words between them, but Llyris heard her when she spoke.

"Thank you, but you didn't need to."

"He needs to understand he can't speak to you this way."

"It's all right. Really."

The former acolyte lifted her hand and brushed her fingertips along her friend's cheek. The thief's face reddened, and a guarded smile tilted her lips. Perhaps their sentiment toward each other set the guardsman's mood against them.

Llyris hurried past the two young women, leaving them to follow as she sped her pace to catch up to the merchant's man, fingers
gripping the dragon pin affixed to her shirt. When she reached
him, she adjusted her gait to match his. Cirril glanced sideways at
her, then reverted his attention to the straightforward path ahead.

"What?"

The handler's courage wavered, and she opened her mouth,
intending to dismiss his inquiry by telling him she had nothing on
her mind. At the last instant, her resolve pushed the question she
meant to ask from her lips instead.

"Why did you join us?"

His throat made the same rumble it did whenever he'd had
enough of Hinter. "What choice did I have?"

"You could have stayed behind with Mikol."

"I'm nobody's nursemaid," he growled.

"He tends the sick because he wants to, not because they make
him. Your decision to come along."

He grunted, though not a sound of agreement like the ogres
offered when assenting to perform some task. This sounded more
dismissive, as if he thought her suggestion didn't warrant him
speaking actual words.

"You could have struck alone, searched for a path to return to
Carpera's."

"Have you looked around? I don't know about you, but I don't
recall trees or animals such as these anywhere near my home. If
you'd care to suggest which direction to head, I'd happily go."

"I can't."

"As I thought."

"So your one option is traveling with us."

"Yes," he replied, the sneer on his face obvious in his tone,
though she peered straight ahead and not at him.

"Then why make it harder for everyone?"

She squeezed the brooch, preparing herself for an angry response. He remained silent, the noise of their boots treading upon
the ground the lone sound between them. When he answered, his
admission surprised her.

"I'm scared, handler," he said, voice quiet.

She swallowed. "Because you've seen friends die?"

As the words left her tongue, she realized she'd guessed wrong.
Men who spent their lives with swords hanging from their belts

and armor strapped to their chests weren't fearful of the afterlife. She supposed most found their peace with it after ending their first life or witnessing one taken. Perhaps the initial instance they experienced their own blood leaking from a wound caused by an adversary. Certainly not decades into a career as a professional soldier.

"No. I'm not afraid of dying," he said, confirming her thoughts. "I'm used to knowing what's going on. Being in control of myself and, to a lesser degree, circumstances affecting me. This has not been the case from when I met you and your ji..." He hesitated, amended himself. "You and Flayre. Witches. Cannibals. This place. I can no longer tell heads from tails. I don't like it."

They walked in silence before he added, "I despise being frightened."

"None of us like it," Llyris said, surprised by the ease and calm in her words. "But we all are. Tesfira's joyfulness masks her fear, as does Hinter's fierce protection of her."

"And the ogres?"

She glanced toward him, saw him looking at her, the corner of his mouth upturned.

She chuckled. "Who can tell?"

He snickered. A creature in the trees above them chittered, and she looked up to find it sitting on a branch, peering at them as though holding sentry. Its long tail hung down, black in the middle with a puff of white near the end matching the whiskers framing its face. Sunlight glinted in its dark eyes as its attention followed them.

"What about you?"

Cirril's unexpected question startled her, jarring her away from the sight in the trees. She glanced at him, but he continued staring ahead, choosing his footing.

"Me?" she said with a nervous laugh. "I hardly think I'm doing anything to disguise my feelings."

"You're doing well, given the circumstances."

She considered thanking him, but chose not to; it didn't sound like a comment in need of response. Her gaze strayed up toward the top branches, but the black and white creature was gone. No trembling leaf marked its passing, and she wondered if she'd seen it at all.

"I'll try to be better," the guardsman said.

"We have a long trek ahead. It's best for all of us if we get along."

He nodded but didn't reply and she took it as a sign their conversation was complete.

The jungle buzzed with more activity after sunset than during the day. Leaves rustled with the passing of unseen bodies, branches bounced, animals called and responded. At first, Hinter glanced from one disturbance to another as she kept watch, attempting to pay attention to all of them. She soon realized the impossibility of it and concentrated on listening for larger, more predatory movements.

She'd never heard anything like the array of sounds. Tweets and cheeps and chattering. Some sounded created by a human throat imitating animals and birds. Those made her most nervous.

She crept around her companions' sleeping space, her cowl pulled up and her hand hidden within her cloak, fingers gripping the hilt of her knife. Soon, the moon would rise high enough in the sky to indicate the time to wake an ogre to relieve her— Gartrek, but she doubted her ability to recognize one from the other in the dark. She'd worry about it when she needed to.

She completed another circuit when a flicker of movement caught her eye. She whirled, yanking her dagger from its sheath in a smooth motion.

At the far side of the camp, Llyris stood, pulling her cloak from her pack. The thief watched as she threw it over her shoulders and pinned it with the brooch she often caressed. Hinter parted her lips to ask what she meant to do, but didn't. Best not to wake everyone to find out she needed to urinate.

She slid her blade into place and crept around the perimeter, following the handler as she set out away from the camp. Her feet rattled through the brush as though she gave no concern to the noise, and Hinter again stopped herself from calling out. By the time she reached the far side of their camp, Llyris was six paces deep into the jungle. The thief followed.

"Llyris," she said, the whisper forced between clenched teeth. She didn't react.

As she lifted her hand to grab the handler's shoulder, the memory of a different forest rushed to mind, where Llyris came into possession of the cloak and brooch. She'd been in some kind of trance then and Hinter wondered what would happen if she woke her from it now. Not wanting to startle her or worse, she lowered her arm and gave her some space. If she couldn't stop her, she'd at least keep her safe.

The distance between them and their companions increased and the thief glanced over her shoulder, thinking she should have roused the others after all. Too late. She didn't want to shout and risk attracting the attention of anything lurking in the jungle and, if she returned to camp, she'd be leaving Llyris unprotected. Neither choice suited her, so she kept following.

The handler's path stayed true, except to skirt the occasional tree trunk. She didn't slow as though searching for a place to void her bladder, nor did she appear unsure of her route; she walked with the confidence of a woman sure of her destination.

Hinter freed her blade again, figuring better safe than sorry. Neither the sound of the steel against the sheath nor the texture of the leather-wrapped hilt gave her the comfort she imagined someone like Cirril derived from them. Given the choice, she'd rather never have a weapon in her grip. Lock picks and files were the tools of her trade; her preference was to go without knives and swords and other pointy things. Bloody business sat poorly with her.

Ahead of her, Llyris slowed and stopped. Hinter did the same, breath held as she clung to the hope the handler needed to void her bladder. She didn't drop her breeches and squat. Instead, she tilted her head to peer up into the branches of the nearest tree. A second passed, then she raised her hand as though reaching to pluck an invisible fruit. An instant later, dark fingers appeared out of the foliage.

Hinter tensed, intending to jump forward and keep her friend from harm, but her legs refused to respond. When she opened her mouth to cry out, she found her voice wanting.

A shape emerged from the tree, dangling in front of Llyris. The thief squinted to make out the dark silhouette highlighted with hints of white and recognized it as a creature she'd spied in the high boughs during their travels. She wanted to call it a monkey, but its appearance differed from illustrations she'd seen in books.

106

It gripped the lowest branch with one hand, lowering itself to hang before the handler as its other hand touched hers.

Their fingers entwined, and Hinter's anxiety rose. The creature appeared neither large enough nor possessing sufficient strength to carry Llyris off, but looks could be deceiving. She struggled against whatever unseen force held her, again achieving no success, and instead attempted to take a step back.

She succeeded.

The thief's brow creased. She extended her hand until it met resistance. Something invisible stood between her and the handler. Magical. She jerked her touch away, shook her fingers as if she expected to free herself of any residue.

The grip between her friend and the animal continued, though Llyris showed no sign of concern or apprehension. The thief stalked to her left, reaching out in front of her to avoid walking into whatever kept her from her companion's side. Leaves rustled under her steps, but neither woman nor beast appeared to notice her presence.

She made her way to the spot beside Llyris, about five paces away from her. From this position, she saw her friend's face, her nose, chin, and mouth unhidden by the hood of her cloak. Her lips moved as if speaking, but, if she did, Hinter no more heard her words than they did her steps. She squinted, attempting to read their movements; whatever she said appeared to be gibberish.

She glanced toward where the others slept, considered waking Cirril, though doing so meant moonlight reflecting on the blade he'd surely draw. Nothing she'd seen suggested the need for weapons and violence, so she decided against involving him. One thing a thief understood: solving any problem required the proper tools. Cirril carried a toolbox as limited as any soldier.

She backed away, intending to creep farther around and get closer to the creature dangling from the tree, when the animal released its grip from Llyris' hand. As the monkey-beast disappeared into the foliage, the handler stutter-stepped backward as though stumbling. Hinter leaped forward out of concern, forgetting the unseen barrier. When she realized the mistake, she'd already passed through where it should have been, much to her surprise and relief. She caught Llyris by the arm, steadying her before she fell.

"Are you all right?" she asked, keeping her voice low and pulling her friend close.

The handler pivoted, eyes unfocused until they found Hinter's face, gave her a point of focus to concentrate on. She peered at her for a second before her trembling lips parted.

"I know what we must do," she said. "Where we have to go."

She pulled herself from the thief's grasp and lurched toward their camp. Hinter followed, memories of all her companion's oddities bubbling to the surface of her mind. She recalled Llyris using a word to freeze the witches and their undead, how she'd traveled them to unknown places and escaped from a tunnel. She hurried to catch up, caught her by the arm, stopping her.

"What are you talking about?" she said, spinning the handler toward her. "What are you?"

The fear flashing across her friend's face sent a lancet of regret through the thief. Llyris looked smaller, as though her acerbic words caused her to shrink. Hinter readied her tongue to speak an apology, but Llyris responded before she could.

"I..." she said, the single syllable quaking along with her lips. "I'm shadow-scarred."

The gazes of her companions, including the ogres, lay upon Llyris as rays of morning sun found their way through the high boughs and fronds. Waking animals and birds jabbered and cawed, prompting her to get on with what she needed to say.

The handler reached for the dragon's wing pin holding her cloak, stopped herself, lowered her hand. What should she tell them? A monkey called to her in her dreams, summoning her, then laid out a path for them to follow? Cirril wouldn't merely laugh or scoff, he'd likely call her crazy, maybe abandon their trek and return to the village. Despite the ogres' presence, the possibility of losing the guardsman's sword didn't sit well with her. Besides having gotten used to him, the vision—dream, whatever—had included him.

And what about Hinter and Tesfira? The thief already viewed her with an eye of incredulity after fetching her from her night foray. Llyris saw it in her expression as they waited for her to speak—an eyebrow raised, lips canted. Her features said 'convince me' yet gave little hope she'd meet their challenge. Behind them, the ogres appeared unaffected, as seemed the habit of their kind.

Only Tesfira acted enthused to discover what the handler had to say. She perched on the edge of a log, hands clasped, sunlight glinting in her wide eyes.

Llyris cleared her throat. "Viden Misk told me a secret."

"Misk?" The initial scoff of many assumed she'd hear from Cirril. "After everything he's done, why should anybody believe anything he utters?"

She ignored his question and pressed on. "The creation of handlers is abominable. They force human women—young women—to mate with magical creatures. They euthanize male offspring as soon as they leave the womb. Inhumane, but a better fate than what awaits female children."

She paused, dropped her gaze from the others, yet still sensed their attention weighing upon her. A slow draw of air filled her lungs, calming her and steadying her mind. She'd known about some of her heritage—residents of the guildhall often compared thoughts on the creation of handlers, though never the Seniors—but she'd long avoided putting real consideration or voice to it. The tightness it brought to her throat surprised her. When she raised her chin again, her companions continued peering at her, but their expressions shifted, softened, saddened.

"They keep the girls in captivity, treated like livestock until they are of age to conceive, then they're mated with a human male."

Hinter shook her head. "Why? I...I don't understand."

"To dilute the magic," Tesfira replied for her without taking her eyes from Llyris. "They require handlers to have the ability to restrain their Unnamed, but not enough to be magical themselves."

Llyris nodded. "Again, they slaughter the sons and place their daughters with host families who raise them until they enter training at the guild. Mothers are murdered after they've birthed a daughter or before they reach their sixteenth year if they don't."

"They kill all the males," Cirril said, his words falling somewhere between question and statement.

"Females are more powerful and have better control," Tesfira explained on her behalf again. She faced Hinter. "It's also why they make it so difficult for women to become part of the church. They fear us."

The thief offered her friend a short-lived smile and a touch on her arm before redirecting her attention to Llyris.

"How does this lesson in unfortunate history relate to Viden Misk? I hear no secret you speak of," the merchant's man said, his derisive tone returning.

She pressed her lips together, forcing any impulsive response down her throat before continuing. Without realizing it, her hand rose, and she laid her fingers on the dragon brooch. The points of the wing pushed against the pads of her fingertips, indenting her skin and drawing her attention.

"Sometimes, things take a different course."

More sunlight fell between the branches, illuminating her companions with an eerie glow, highlighting parts and hiding others—half-faces staring at her, waiting.

"My mother didn't mate with a human. She coupled with a magik. Instead of carrying a baby with the depleted power the guild desired for their handlers, she bore a shadow-scarred."

She paused again, swallowed to produce sufficient lubrication to wet her arid throat. The brief hesitation proved too much for Cirril Feron. He jumped up from his seat, impatience clear on his face.

"Can you stop speaking in riddles? We don't understand what you mean or why this matters to our situation."

"I am not an Unnamed, but I have more inherent magic than handlers. If the guild had realized, they'd have taken my life."

"But you didn't know," Hinter said, voice quiet.

Llyris shook her head. "Not until recently, when...things started happening. And then Misk explained why they did."

The merchant's man exhaled a large breath, exerting noticeable effort to control his patience. The ogres watched with identical emotionless expressions. Though she knew they understood them when they spoke, Llyris sometimes wondered if the beasts were clueless to much of what occurred around them.

Cirril pursed his lips. "So you can perform some magic. We've experienced it and are grateful. Again I ask: how does this pertain to where we are now?"

Satisfied she'd explained enough to make her companions open to what she meant to say next, she continued.

"I have been shown the way ahead for us."

"By Misk?" Feron snapped.

"No. At least, I don't think so."

When he appeared as though he'd speak again, Tesfira rose from her seat and raised her hand to stop him. Ever the protector, Hinter stood as well, positioning herself between her friend and the guardsman.

"Let her finish," the former acolyte said. When Cirril held his tongue, she prompted Llyris to continue. "Where are we to go?"

The handler's gaze slipped away from her companions and over her shoulder as sunlight filtering through the high tree boughs illuminated a path she wondered if they saw. The brooch grew warm under her fingers.

"We must travel to the heart of the mountain."

She faced the others again. Hinter looked unsurprised by her words and Tesfira beamed. True to his way, Cirril appeared doubtful.

"And what will we encounter inside this mountain? The cleric's God?"

"No, not God," Llyris said. She glanced from one face to the next. "Dragons."

CHAPTER 11

— · —

W EEKS. SIXTEEN DAYS, TO be precise, and they weren't at their destination yet.

Lacking horses, Ilkari expected it to take time to get from the guild's land to the baron's, but he hadn't estimated this long. It didn't help the troll insisted they stay off the road and took them on meandering detours whenever he sensed the tiniest hint of danger—a frequent occurrence. He'd expect a creature with the size and strength of Vyle to show more courage.

Over the last few days, their trek had become quite workman-like. They made their way through the brush, hunted and gathered when the opportunity presented itself, bivouacked when the troll decided they should stop. All without complaint, and mostly no talking. Even the twins fell into silence after endless hours of catching up on every second they'd been apart.

On this day, the seventeenth since leaving behind the ruined guildhall, they strode along a dirt track. Ilkari savored the feel of solid ground beneath his feet instead of soft moss or a patchwork of leaves and branches, appreciated the lack of twigs and thorns seeking to scratch exposed flesh as he quickened his pace to catch up to their leader, whose over-long gait set their tempo.

"How much farther?" he asked, regretting the question the second it left his tongue. It made him sound like an impatient child.

Vyle tilted his head to peer skyward, and the squire did the same. He saw nothing but thick gray cloud, the same as every day since the underground cavern had disappeared, leaving him and his companion in a field with a clutch of angry magiks. Sometimes he wondered if the sun yet existed.

"Two more days," the troll said, returning his attention to the road ahead. "We should encounter outlying farms today."

"You mentioned you've never visited the baron's."

"I haven't, but I'm not an idiot. I know how towns and cities grow."

Ilkari nodded and chastised himself. He'd do well not to let the troll's appearance sway him into thinking he didn't have a functioning brain—too easy to think of someone so brawny as simple and slow.

"We're being followed," Vyle said, his gaze holding straight ahead. "Have been since we left."

"The whole time?" Ilkari recalled the sense of being watched at the guild compound but had assumed their forays through woods and brush were to shake whatever tailed them.

"Yes. Road or forest. Whoever follows does using their nose."

"Can you do that?"

The troll glanced sideways at him. "Do I look like an animal?"

Unable to discern if he asked seriously or with a hint of humor, Ilkari chose not to respond. Answering a question meant to be rhetorical was a fine choice for upsetting people—not a result he desired to accomplish with an Unnamed.

They fell into silence, the soles of the men's boots and the troll's bare feet crunching against the dirt track. Whatever tracked them no longer needed to employ its olfactory senses to recognize their movements with the noise they created. Each clamorous step made Ilkari cringe, but he trusted the hulking Unnamed leading them out of necessity, if for no other reason. And if the creature following resembled the minotaur, they'd have no choice but to rely on him.

As they walked, the squire struggled to recall the last time he'd gone anywhere without a sword at his hip. Likely long before hair sprouted on his chest. The lack of its weight made each stride feel unusual. He missed the tap of its length against his thigh, ached for the sense of security it brought.

By mid-afternoon, they'd come upon the first of the outlying farms. A yet unharvested field of wheat moved in a slight breeze, shallow waves rolling across it like on a lake.

They saw nobody tending the crops.

A gate at the edge of the track stood half open. Its rope hinges creaked as Vyle pushed it wide and stepped over its threshold. The squire held his breath, waiting for some unseen force to strike the troll. When nothing happened, he followed, and gestured for the twins to do the same.

Somewhere out of sight, a cow lowed, and another responded. The sound gave Ilkari hope. If cattle yet survived, perhaps they'd find horses, people, supplies. Days of eating foraged berries and edible plants had left him desirous of finding more suitable food.

A few yards from the shack he considered generous to call a farmhouse, they stopped.

"What is it?" he asked. A second later, the reason for halting became clear.

A trio of red streaks stretched from the top corner of the door toward the bottom. Their angle of approach made it impossible to guess what created the mark, but caution forced the squire to assume them bloody claw marks.

"What does it mean?" one twin asked from behind him. It was more difficult to tell their voices apart than their faces.

"I'm unsure we'll be happy to know," Ilkari said.

"It's a warning," Vyle added.

With a creak of leather and a crunch of dirt underfoot, Naeve moved past him, Nevan following. They crept toward the hutch, the single sword between them drawn.

"You won't want to see what's inside," the Unnamed warned.

"Might be food," Naeve remarked over his shoulder. "Aren't you hungry? Surely leaves and shoots don't satiate a creature of your size."

They didn't wait for an answer. Ilkari looked up at the troll, half-expecting to find an annoyed expression creasing his brow for the twins not listening to him. Not only did he not, he also realized he'd expected to see Rein. Disappointed, he sighed and followed the lads.

"Don't let us die," he said to Vyle.

"You'll come across death inside, but not yours."

The troll's words sent a shiver along his spine, but he continued. He didn't know what happened to the baron's champion, or any of his companions they'd left behind, but these he meant to keep from harm.

They reached the threshold and halted, the two young men pausing to exchange looks. It struck Ilkari as odd finding the gate ajar while someone had taken the time to ensure the door latched.

Entering the house suddenly seemed like an exceedingly poor idea.

"I don't think—"

Nevan grasped the handle and threw it open before the squire finished his sentence.

The odor hit him first, the sickly sweet stench of rotting flesh assaulting his nose before his sight adjusted to discern the carnage within. It took a few seconds for his eyes to adapt to the interior's dim light, a period he wished to stretch out much longer once the hut's contents became clear.

Five corpses lay on the floor, their varied ages suggesting they'd been the family who lived on and worked the farm. Beyond the decomposition, their flesh had been ravaged, though it didn't appear the work of wild beasts. Ilkari covered his nose and mouth with his hand and stepped past the twins with their wide, frightened eyes and slack jaws. As he neared the bodies, he saw precise cuts and incisions marring their skin, not the rips and tears of teeth and claws.

He crouched a yard away from the closest victim, a boy of perhaps ten years and the youngest family member. The lad's chest lay open, the two sides of his rib cage spread like the doors of a barn, the cavity they normally protected empty. The top of his head was missing, a straight line separating the cap of his skull from the rest.

Ilkari closed his eyes and lowered his chin. "This wasn't a random attack. Someone harvested them."

He stood, swallowed the bile threatening in his throat. His focus flickered from one corpse to the next, all in similar condition. Flies buzzed around the rotting meat of the farmer's kin, landing in the open cavities for a taste of what blood remained or to lay their eggs. It surprised Ilkari the bodies weren't already crawling with maggots.

His gaze fell upon the walls. The dead family had distracted from noticing the strange symbols scrawled across their surface. Not letters or words he recognized, and not pictures, but somewhere in between. Runes, sigils, totems, things he didn't quite have the right word to describe.

"This is fae's work," Vyle said.

He stood in the doorway, displacing the merchant's men and forcing them to stand outside, a mercy for which they were likely grateful.

"Fae?" Ilkari thought the faefolk small creatures with wings, hardly capable of such atrocities. "How is that possible?"

"The fae you know from your fairy tales are but one type." He nodded at the corpses. "Some are savage and unforgiving."

The squire shuffled toward the doorway, happy to abandon the atrocities. "But why do this to these people? Surely this family couldn't have afforded to employ a handler and her Unnamed."

Vyle stepped aside for him to exit, and Ilkari inhaled a deep breath as soon as he cleared the hut's interior.

"I have done work for entire towns," the troll said. "But they may not need an excuse. Humans have kept magiks enslaved for centuries. Perhaps these people were simply guilty of being human."

Without a plausible response, the squire blinked and looked away, the statement reminding him of the peril they undertook by traveling with him. At any time, if the beast decided to exact revenge for the plight of magical creatures, they were powerless to thwart him. A sobering thought.

"We should leave," Naeve said, voice strained. "They may linger nearby."

"No," Vyle disagreed. "You saw how old those bodies are. They'd not hang around without cause."

The twins stood off to either side of the Unnamed, their faces blanched white after seeing the fates of the farmer and his family. Ilkari watched the bulge in Nevan's throat rise and fall as he swallowed hard, doing his best to keep from vomiting. If they remained close to the stink, the lads wouldn't get relief, so the squire pulled the door shut, thrusting the corpses into darkness with the flies.

"I heard cows," he said, stepping off the rickety porch. "Perhaps we'll find some horses."

The twins nodded with wan enthusiasm, thankful to escape the stench and its source. He led them around the left side of the house toward a barn appearing hastily built, and several pens. A handful of chickens lay dead in one of them, their carcasses untouched by predators, and Ilkari wondered why wild animals hadn't come to claim such an easy meal.

116

"Be careful," Vyle said as he followed them. "If you find a door, let me open it."

None of them answered, but he suspected the lads experienced the same relief at the offer as did he. If danger awaited, better for everyone if the troll assumed the lead.

As they approached the poor excuse for a barn, they heard a low, long moan. It took a second for Ilkari to recognize the sound as a cow's lowing, a moo drawn out to resemble the lament of a human in pain. It came from inside the decrepit outbuilding. The squire led them to the door, stopped, listened.

The lowing ceased, replaced by the shuffle of feet on hard ground. Perhaps naught but a beleaguered cow lay awaiting within, but they couldn't know for sure.

"Step aside," the troll said as he touched Ilkari's shoulder and nudged him. The beast likely intended a gentle pressure, but it required the squire's care to avoid losing his balance.

He shuffled to his left, instinct making him reach for a weapon absent from its normal place. When he didn't find it, he cursed under his breath, both for not having a sword and for forgetting the fact. Lacking any other option, he curled his hand into a fist and readied himself to defend or attack as necessary.

Vyle grasped the length of thick rope in his hand, his fingers wrapping around the knot tied in its end and hiding it from view. He glanced over his shoulder, first at Ilkari, then the twins, giving them each a look to ensure their readiness. Satisfied, he inhaled a breath and set his jaw.

The force with which the troll jerked the wooden slab open dislodged it from one of its rope hinges with a pop. The sound and sudden movement startled the scrawny horse standing inside the barn. It reared, front hooves pawing the air. Ilkari doubted a healthy steed capable of causing much damage to the brute who'd yanked the door wide, never mind this scrawny equid.

Despite the lack of danger from its flailing hooves, Vyle stepped aside, creating space for it to bolt. The animal took the opportunity, fleeing from the barn at an unsteady gait. It reeled toward the fence and the field beyond, must have realized its own inability to clear the wooden barrier, and amended its course. The correction made it come perilously close to falling, its feet slipping in the grass, but it remained upright. When the horse righted itself, it galloped past the house, its cadence more assured as it gave a wide berth to the place where its keepers lay dead. A few yards later, it skittered a left turn onto the dirt track and disappeared.

"So much for finding a steed," Ilkari muttered.

The troll chuckled, shook his head, and crossed the threshold into the barn, the squire following close behind.

Inside, they found the air warmer and heavy with the scent of stale hay and frightened animals—manure and urine and sweat, the odor little better than the deathly scent they'd encountered in the hut. Shadows lurked in the corners, providing spots for threats to hide. Ilkari would have crept forward with stealth and care, but their chaperon didn't appear to harbor the same concerns.

Vyle strode into the center of the barn, his bare feet kicking up dry hay and dust. He paused for a second, listening. The squire did, too, and heard nothing as the behemoth crossed the dirt floor to the farthest stall, his companions trailing.

Because the gate to the enclosure stood closed, he didn't detect the wheeze of labored breathing until their approach brought them nearly upon it, proving the troll's hearing much more attuned than his.

The cow they'd heard lamenting lay on its side, its ribs showing under its black and white hide. Its tongue lolled out of the side of its mouth as air panted between its lips, palpating the animal's chest. Its dark brown eyes rolled toward Vyle as he pulled the gate open and knelt.

"Poor thing," he said as he reached out a massive hand and stroked its neck.

If the troll's presence or actions sparked fear in the bovine, it was beyond the cow's ability to do anything about it. It panted, one leg twitched, the hoof scraping against the bare floor. A quick survey of the small space showed it devoid of any scrap of food and the trough lay empty. Ilkari pivoted toward the nearest of the twins.

"Get this creature some water," he barked at Naeve.

"No," Vyle said, not giving the lad a chance to follow orders. "It is too late."

With his one hand on the animal's neck, he inserted his other under its head, shuffled his feet to into the position he needed. Before doing anything else, he leaned closer to the suffering cow.

"Be well, sister. It's time to go home."

He jerked his hands. The cow's spine cracked with the sound of a dry twig trod upon in a night forest and the animal stopped moving. Vyle gingerly let its head rest on the ground as though he expected a lack of care to hurt it. He stroked its neck once more before standing. As he faced his companions, he drew his sleeve across his face, and Ilkari thought he spied the shimmer of a tear on the beast's cheek. He chose not to say anything.

"I fear we will encounter more of this before we arrive at your baron's," the troll said, stepping out of the stall. He crossed the barn floor, halted at the door to peer toward the field. "The Unnamed are angry, and they mean to make humans pay."

It didn't please Vyle to have his estimation proven correct.

Over the course of the next two days, they'd found red slashes marring the doors of every farmhouse they passed. Knowing what it meant and suspecting what lay within, they didn't bother stopping to investigate. How many disemboweled humans and neglected animals need they witness to paint the picture of the magiks' rise? He regretted they might have left untended creatures to suffer until death finally took them. The thought squeezed his heart.

"We should check inside," he said as they approached the next crimson-marked door. "Someone may yet live."

As with every other time he'd suggested stopping, Ilkari denied his request.

"It's too dangerous," the squire told him, like every previous time. "Our last hope is to reach the baron's."

The twins offered little input. Though Vyle suspected they'd rather not venture into another scene of carnage, he also recognized them as obedient soldiers, if inexperienced. Men who'd follow their two leaders no matter what they decided. Whether because of training or youth mattered not.

A gray pall hung over the city, fed by hundreds of chimneys and uncontrolled fires. Several columns of smoke appeared far too large to be the mere expulsion of fireplaces. The same wasn't true of the outlying buildings—no wispy tendrils rose from them.

Soon after the guardhouse came into view, Ilkari stopped in the middle of the track.

"I don't like this," he said, putting words to the most obvious sentiment. "We should find traffic on this road. Wagons, merchants, messengers. We've seen not a living soul."

"But it can't be safe off it," Nevan interjected. "You saw what they did to the farmers and his families."

"We're blessed we haven't run into them," Naeve added.

"It makes the most sense they started at the city and worked their way out," Vyle said. "Likely your Baron Sylleth employed them and their handlers."

Speaking the words curled the troll's lip. In the time since Breda's presence disappeared from his psyche, he saw more clearly the path his life had taken, and of every magik confined by Prisma's curse. He remembered when he'd scoffed at Hispid's use of the term, but now realized his mistake. They'd all been nothing but slaves, and he understood why some acted so enraged.

"I think it's best not to attempt entering by the front gate," Ilkari said. "We can find other places where we're less likely to be detected."

"Nightfall soon." Naeve tilted his gaze skyward to prove his statement. "Do we have enough daylight remaining?"

"The spot I'm thinking of is a half a day's walk." The squire raised his arm and pointed to the left of the main gatehouse. "We couldn't make it before dark."

"Then we best locate a safe place to shelter for the night," Nevan said.

It occurred to Vyle the twins weren't merely agreeing with each other, but they often seemed to share the same thoughts. He wondered if the ogre brothers he'd met in his youth experienced the same peculiarity.

"We should be able to pick a building to hide and keep safe." The troll strolled away from his companions.

He walked ten paces, separating himself to avoid having his hearing filled with their breath and the beating of their hearts. With enough space between them, he halted, leaned forward as he concentrated. For a full minute he listened to the empty buildings, the deserted streets. He heard the rattle of shutters, the creak of beams, the wind stirring dirt from the road. Nowhere amongst the noises did he detect the sound of any living thing, human or otherwise.

"Anything?" Ilkari called out upon seeing the troll's demeanor relax.

"No," Vyle responded over his shoulder without turning. "But be wary."

When he heard their steps approaching, he set out toward the nearest of the structures with no intent for them to take shelter in it—too obvious a hiding spot. A peek would at least provide a sense of the city's state.

He threw the door wide, slamming it against the inner wall to give himself an instant of surprise if needed. He'd neglected to tell the others about the faefolk's ability to remain too quiet for even his ears to detect. The quality made them sought after amongst the Unnamed, and he'd heard the guild charged more for their services. Fae made excellent spies and thieves.

And assassins.

To everyone's relief, including his own, the two rooms inside the structure lay empty of humans or other creatures, living or expired.

"These got out before it was too late, it seems," Nevan said.

"Lucky," Naeve agreed.

"Or captured," Ilkari added.

Vyle grunted. He figured the squire's assessment more likely than the twins' optimism, but he chose not to steal hope from the lads. After a search of four more nearby houses yielded the same result, they all breathed a little easier.

"They've either fled or someone's taken them inside the walls," the troll said. "If they ran, they're being hunted. If they're imprisoned, I can't guess what fate has befallen them. Either way, we should find shelter with ease."

Nobody responded to his words, but he felt the sliver of hope given them by the empty abodes wither away. He'd have let it live on if he didn't expect it to be detrimental to them. They all needed to be wary—the lengthening shadows of the approaching twilight could prove dangerous.

He led them on a winding route along the beaten paths running between the hovels. These weren't constructed streets like they'd find within the city's walls, but trails worn by many feet, grass trodden into earth to create hard-packed tracks. None of the soles who created them or walked them daily remained. Not one.

Vyle stopped occasionally, lifted a hand to signal the others to do the same. He listened. He sniffed of the smoke-tinged air. Though he detected nothing, he always paused longer than he might have. The fae confounded him, made his skin pucker with goose flesh if he pondered too much about them.

After more than half an hour, they came upon a building he deemed suitable for protecting them overnight. It was built more solidly than other abodes, set on a foundation rather than the ground. Its hardened mud walls were free of holes, its thatched roof appeared able to keep rain off their heads should the sky open and lament during the night. With twilight creeping closer, the interior lay in gloom.

After opening the door, the troll cast a glance at his companions, urging them to wait while he searched within. Relief brought smiles to the twins while Ilkari tensed as though restraining himself.

The musty air inside disguised older scents, but he sensed no unpleasantness. No dead things in here. Nothing but the scuttle of tiny feet as rodents fled from his entrance.

He allowed his vision to adjust to the dimness, which required half as long for a troll as it did for humans. Seconds later, he discerned the shape of a hulking oven at the end of the room, a narrow wooden bench against one wall, bags and barrels along the other. A thatched door beside the oven led to a second chamber. He hastened across the floor, his bare feet shuffling on its dusty surface, and rushed through the doorway into a sleeping space.

"Everything's all right," he said, emerging from the bedroom. "It's a baker's. He must have lived and worked here. There's a bed for you to fight over."

The three men filed in. Ilkari led the way, forehead creased and eyes darting; the twins followed close behind, obviously relieved to be inside where they'd feel safer, whether true or not.

"You figure we'll be safe here?" the squire asked, glancing around the interior to assess it for himself.

"As safe as anywhere," Vyle said. He slapped his palm against the wall with a loud slap, startling Naeve. "It's built better than everything else we saw, so maybe safer."

Ilkari nodded. "Surprised they left the flour and other supplies behind."

"If he fled, he'd not have taken them. If captured, a few sacks of flour, grains, and seeds mean nothing to his captors. The mice are happy for their presence, though."

The twins crossed the room to the sleeping chamber, peered through the doorway before they faced their fellows.

"Who gets the bed?" Nevan asked.

"I think likely I should," Ilkari said.

Naeve nodded. "Because you're older."

The squire's cheeks went red, and he spoke through clenched teeth when he responded. "Because a squire to the baron's champion outranks a couple of merchants' whelps. But go ahead, make yourself comfortable. Give me a sword and I'll take first watch."

Vyle stifled the chuckle bubbling into his throat and stepped between the others and the doorway.

"No, I will. Dusk and dawn are especially dangerous times. Crepuscular creatures, we Unnamed."

Ilkari faced him, a remnant of the angered glare he'd conjured for the disrespectful youths lingering on his face. He inhaled, the expression eased, and he nodded once.

"All right, but wake me next. I'll be sleeping on the mattress."

He pivoted on his heel and stomped toward the bed chamber, barging between the twins as they stumbled aside to clear a path for him. The troll couldn't contain his mirth this time, so hid it from them by exiting the bakery.

Dusk's dimness filled the trodden streets, making every shape indistinct and suspicious. He paused after closing the door, head tilted upward to stare toward the darkening sky. Night birds called to each other as they emerged from their daily sleeps. Minuscule paws padded the grass and shifted dirt, hunting for seeds and insects to feed their families. With nothing out of the ordinary to concern him, Vyle strode to the side of the building where he'd seen a bench when they approached.

He looked down at it, assessing whether it appeared sturdy enough to bear his weight. He put a foot on it, leaned forward. A joint creaked, but the wood held, so he picked it up and returned to the front of the bakery.

He didn't intend to wake Ilkari or the twins—anything they'd encounter was far too dangerous for them to conceive—so he may as well be comfortable. With the bench set in the middle of the path before the hut containing his companions, he lowered himself onto its seat. It protested, but held.

He sat for an hour or two. With moon and stars hidden by the blanket of clouds present since the night the curse lifted, naught but his internal clock provided a measure of the passage of time. As he kept watch, he pondered the happening of these last weeks and wondered why the clouds refused to leave. Could their persistence be linked to the breaking of the anathema?

The gentle wind shifted, bringing fresh scents to Vyle's nose. His nostrils flared, and he stood, hands curling into fists.

"You're stealthy, but hiding the odor of bear fur is difficult for anyone."

He waited, gaze flickering from building to building and the spaces in between, his breath held to avoid interfering with his ears. The bouquet of damp hair grew and a few seconds later, wan light glinted in a yellow eye. Then the beast stepped from the shadow.

It reared up on its hind legs, teeth bared and front paws raised. Like this, it stood taller than Vyle, and the troll tensed. He focused on the section of his mind once controlled by a woman named Breda and readied his power.

The bear made no sound and didn't advance. Instead, its dimensions decreased. Its pronounced ears flattened against its head as the long snout shrank. After ten seconds, the animal returned to the size and shape of a man.

"Hispid," Vyle said, keeping his voice quiet.

His friend stood before him, naked from the transformation but covered in enough hair to disguise the fact. The troll struggled to control the urge to rush forward and greet the guild-mate he'd shared meals with at the mess hall.

"No longer my name. Humans gave it to me and now they can have it. I have retaken my birth name, given me by my sleuth. I am Eddubu."

Vyle frowned. "Why have you been following us these last weeks, Eddubu?"

The word didn't fit his tongue well, and he knew he'd either have to concentrate to remember to use it, or dispense with the moniker altogether. The were-bear in human form stepped forward, one bushy eyebrow raised.

"It is I who should be asking you questions," he said. "Why do you risk your life to travel with three humans?"

"They have done nothing to me."

The man formerly known as Hispid shook his head. "As usual, the depth of your naivety rivals your girth. They've kept you and all magiks beholden to them our entire lives, made us slaves, offering a pittance of food and shelter in exchange for doing whatever they wanted. Our minds and bodies have been their prisoners. Nobody did anything to stop it or change it. Not the men you travel with, nor any others. Have you never imagined the life you may have led without your handler controlling you like a puppet for the amusement of the humans?"

The troll pursed his lips but said nothing. His friend moved a step closer.

"You don't realize the power dwelling within you. You've tasted it, but Breda's influence lingers, restraining you from indulging it. Let go, Vyle. No consequences exist for you, no pit to be thrown into for punishment." He paused, scratched at the thick hair on his hip. "And for your own sake, choose another name."

The troll's fist tightened with no intention of striking at Hispid—Eddubu—but a barely controllable energy flowed through him. It tingled his flesh and cinched his muscles. His heart pounded against his ribs, the sound of his pulse loud in his ears.

He inhaled a slow, controlled breath, then let it out between his lips in a long sigh, using the chestful of air to quell the feeling before speaking again.

"I will not punish humans for something they didn't do," he said, his voice quiet but firm. "And I won't stand by and allow others to do so."

"You are making a mistake, troll. Do you not perceive the storm coming to this land? You have but three choices: take cover, die, or become the tempest."

"I choose none of these. And my name is Vyle. It is the only one I have ever known, and it is mine."

"Mark me, Vyle. I can't protect you anymore." He spat his name like a piece of spoiled meat he needed to get off his tongue. "You will regret this choice. Your pets won't survive, nor you. You should have let the minotaur finish them."

"What? Protect me? What are you talking about?"

125

"Did you think me alone lurking in the shadows of the forest, watching you? Word of the troll keeping company with men has already spread, words like sympathizer and betrayer bandied about. You made it this far because I ensured you did. I wanted the chance to talk sense into you, but no more. From here, you are on your own. I can do nothing to help you."

He opened his mouth to respond—unsure if he should thank him or slap him—but the man he'd known as Hispid interrupted him by dropping to all fours. His spine arched into a humped shoulder, the thick hair grew thicker, his body expanded. Pointed teeth filled his maw and claws curved out of his widened hands, digging into the dirt. Vyle tensed again, drew power from the pocket of his mind.

Instead of advancing, the bear locked eyes with him, a hint of regret flickering in their yellowness. An instant later, the beast turned and loped away and Vyle watched him go, a chill creeping up his spine.

He stood for a minute, all his senses straining to collect any information before he squinted over his shoulder. The door to the structure where his companions slept remained closed, the rumble of snoring vibrating in his ears.

Satisfied his conversation with the newly named Eddubu hadn't disturbed them, Vyle inhaled a chestful of cool air and crept away into the night.

"Gone?"

Ilkari glanced from one twin to the other, their identical faces sporting identical expressions of concern.

"Are you sure?"

Naeve shrugged and gestured toward the door. "Have a look yourself, if you like. He's hard to miss."

His sarcasm rankled the squire, and he opened his mouth to express his displeasure, but Nevan spoke before he got his words out.

"He failed to wake any of us up to relieve him of watch and now he's gone."

"Maybe he went to fetch breakfast," his twin offered. "He'll return shortly with croissants and a nice cuppa."

Ilkari didn't appreciate Nevan's tone, but at least what he said held a vague possibility of truth, though he doubted it. He hadn't gifted them breakfast before during their journey or since they'd been in hiding. This seemed an unlikely time to start. More likely, he'd decided to watch out for himself and abandoned them to this world flipped upside down.

He didn't know why he'd expected anything different. Vyle was a troll, an Unnamed enslaved by the ancient curse like the minotaur who'd attacked them, and every other magical creature in existence. It made more sense for him to desert them in the middle of the night, leaving them unprotected, than it did he stay.

The way he'd abandoned them didn't sit well with the squire; operating without honor never did. There'd have been more honor in it if the beast killed them in their sleep. At least he'd have chosen a side, committed to a cause. Now, how could anyone guess what to expect from him?

Ilkari went to the door and pulled it open a crack, leaning close to peer out. Part of him hoped to find the troll standing beside the bakery, unnoticed by the twins—they merely belonged to a merchant's militia, after all.

The street outside the hut where they'd spent the night was neither empty nor the bustling avenue he'd have expected in the past. None of the citizens filing by appeared happy to do so. Stress and fear marked their features. Gazes darted side to side, searching every shadow and around each corner for menace.

And no troll.

He closed the door and glanced over his shoulder at the twins, who'd gone silent since he'd decided to peer at the outside world. A good thing—he didn't have the patience to listen to them defend the beast, nor did he require commiseration.

"What do we do now?" Naeve asked.

"It looks like everyone's being taken somewhere. If so, staying becomes riskier by the second."

"You want us to follow them?" Nevan stood, hands closing into fists as though he thought to fight the squire. Ilkari frowned. "What if they're leading them to the slaughter?"

"At least we'll see it coming."

127

He spun toward the door, his heel grinding against the dirt floor. He jerked the slab of wood inward without waiting for discussion or opinions from his companions. With the discoveries of the morning, his sour mood left him unwilling to hear from under-trained guardsmen young enough to be his children. They'd follow him, or they wouldn't, and he'd find peace with either.

They followed.

The squire inserted himself into the flow of pedestrians, all headed the same direction, his companions following close behind. His gaze flickered between those surrounding them and it took him a minute to realize they stood out from everyone else. He slowed his pace, spoke to the twins without turning his head to look at them.

"We need to get rid of anything marking us as fighters," he said, already unbuckling his empty sword belt. Despite its lack of weapon, he hadn't wanted to abandon it. The familiar weight around his waist connected him to a world now lost, but he'd also hoped to find a replacement to fill the scabbard. "Nobody else carries weapons or is wearing crests. Shed your belts and insignias."

He let his own slide off, leaving it on the road behind him, and awaited protest from Naeve. As the lone member of their party possessing a weapon, he expected him to be loath to part with it, as he would be were he the one with a sword. To his surprise, the twins followed his example without a word, then removed their jerkins bearing the mark of House Carpera. Someone trailing them grumbled, but he paid them no heed.

The column of captives snaked through the streets, guided to stay on track by sentries at every intersection and side street. Some of those left to guard any potential escape route resembled humans, though the squire doubted his eyes, while others clearly belonged to other races. Fae, goblin, shifters, but nary a troll in sight.

They followed in silence like everyone else, herded along the avenues of the baron's city with no idea where they were being led. Every time they reached another meeting of roads, Ilkari did his best not to make eye contact with whatever creature they encountered guarding it. After they'd traveled half a dozen blocks, their destination became clear.

The castle, or somewhere close to it.

He gestured at his companions to let them know, his intent interrupted when he caught the attention of an Unnamed nearby. The hulking man with a thick beard stiffened, his face going stony. Ilkari faced the front again as the fellow abandoned his post and trudged across the flagstones toward the line of citizens.

"You," he said in a rumbling baritone.

The squire ignored him, hoping he meant his attention for someone else. He strode a few more paces before a hand gripping his shoulder pulled him to a halt.

"I followed you from the guildhall." His stern expression turned, became harder, his bushy beard thicker. Ilkari would have sworn his teeth lengthened. "Where's the troll?"

"I'm sure I don't know what you're talking about, sir," the squire said, adding a fearful tone to his voice—easy to fake given the situation. "I've heard nothing of any such creature."

"He goes by Vyle." The man leaned close enough his breath touched Ilkari's face. It stank of decaying meat. "Though it matters not what he or anyone else calls him. You know what troll I'm speaking of."

"I swear I don't, sir. If I did, I'd tell you."

The fellow's scowl deepened. "I'll be keeping my eye on you, human."

He released his grip on the squire's shoulder and backed away, curling his lip to dispel any doubt Ilkari held about the lengthening of his teeth. Once he disappeared, Ilkari hurried to catch up to his companions.

"What happened?" Nevan asked when he did.

The squire shook his head. "Danger is everywhere around us. Be wary."

As if to punctuate his words, the walls surrounding the baron's castle came into view. Throngs of citizens herded by all manner of magiks clogged the main gate, their numbers far greater than those of their captors. Seeing the disparity, one might wonder why they didn't rise against their oppressors, overwhelm them.

The mangled bodies hanging from the parapet overhead offered ample reason why they shouldn't.

As they worked their way toward the gates with the crowd, Ilkari tilted his head to stare at the dead, as most of those gathered near him did. Ropes tied around their chests suspended headless corpses while those fortunate enough to keep their heads hung from their necks. Some lacked arms or legs, or both. Entrails dangled from a few and ravens and crows crawked and fought over the tasty offal.

"What happened to them?" Naeve asked, his words no more than an expulsion of breath.

"My guess is they attempted escape, and this is their reward. Now they're an example for the rest of us."

A sound gurgled in the lad's throat, a noise caught somewhere between a gag and a cough. Even with as much carnage and death as he'd seen in his lifetime as a soldier, the sight swirled Ilkari's gut into a state of nausea. It must be worse for young men who'd grown up living a sheltered life on a merchant's estate.

"Look away, lads. Nothing good for you to see."

He diverted his eyes, too. Naught to gain seeing a fellow's innards dangling out for the world to contemplate. After Emeryn Aryzath, he figured he'd already seen it one time too many.

Warm bodies pressed against each other, hurried on by their Unnamed herders and by a desire to escape from under the grisly warnings hanging overhead. Somewhere behind them, Ilkari heard a child crying and a woman attempting to shush him. He tried to locate them in the crowd but, with so many citizens jammed together in one place, found it impossible. Half a minute later, the cry ceased, leaving the squire to wonder if the mother covered the little one's mouth, or if someone else cut off the lament. As he redirected his focus to the path ahead, the hairy, brutish man who'd approached him before caught his attention.

The fellow leered from the crowd's edge, eyes slitted and forehead creased as though attempting to stare a hole through the squire. He gulped, worried if any of the magical creatures possessed such ability. They funneled through the gate into the courtyard beyond, leaving the angry troll-searcher behind.

Ilkari stepped into a place he'd been more times than he cared to count and yet today didn't recognize.

Once-lush gardens lay dried and shriveled, as though something greater than neglect sucked the life from them. The lawn was beaten to mud despite the lack of precipitation over these last weeks, leaving the squire to ponder what liquid combined with the dirt to create the slurry—a consideration he spent little time considering given the probable answer.

The Unnamed lining the route steered the throng toward the west side of the castle—the garden containing the baron's labyrinth. Some of those herding them did so with a simple gesture while others gnashed teeth or showed claws. As Ilkari watched, a heavy-set man in a tattered silken shirt protested. The creature to whom he directed his ire—a tall, willowy thing with stick-like limbs and a pointed nose—appeared to pay attention. At least, until one of those arms whipped out and severed the protester's arm above the elbow. He screamed and sank to his knees clutching the stump where his limb had been seconds before, eyes fixed on the missing body part lying on the ground at his feet. The magik ignored the fellow and returned to directing the crowd to their destination.

Woe be to any who didn't follow instructions.

The squire glanced toward his companions, noticed them staring slack-jawed at the events taking place around them and the adornments on the castle walls matching those on the outer barricade. Nevan's face went red, Naeve's white, as though between them they suffered every emotion such mistreatment and carnage could evoke. He felt for them, wished he knew words to pull them from their grief and anger and fear, but he didn't. He hoped that, should the opportunity to flee or the need to defend themselves arose, they'd recognize it. If not, he'd leave them behind.

Like he did Rein.

Ilkari pursed his lips and forced his own feelings down into his gut. This was neither the time nor place for him to lose his concentration. If nothing else, the twins needed him to remain focused while they weren't able.

The crowd rounded the corner toward the west garden, the sounds of their footsteps on flagstones or squelching in muddy grass beating an uneven refrain as their mouths fell silent. Most likely declined to vocalize based on what they'd seen happen to their fellows, the sight left others speechless, the same as the squire.

Like any man, he'd stood at the threshold of the baron's labyrinth countless times, dreaming of the riches awaiting him should he step across and survive to find his way out. As with most who pondered the effect of gold-filled bags on their lives, he walked away, glad to have abandoned the idea the next time the maze claimed a victim.

131

Even without its man-eating reputation, the labyrinth used to inspire awe. Its emerald leaves never appeared thirsty or in disarray, no matter the weather. Precise square corners, the bottoms of each row extended right to the ground with no hint of trunk or roots beneath. Ilkari always considered it to have at least an equal chance of withstanding an attack as did the castle's walls.

Not today.

In place of the impressive hedge maze stood a skeleton of the former behemoth. What few leaves hung from the skeletal branches were brown and withered, hanging on through force of willpower. The rest of the foliage lay on the ground at the feet of the onetime labyrinth, the piles of moldering greenery decaying to mulch.

Ilkari opened his mouth to comment, perhaps make an exclamation, but stopped himself as he remembered the screaming child silenced by some unseen hand. Instead, he turned to Nevan, who stood closest to him of his twin companions, and grasped his shoulder hoping to gird both the lad and himself. Fear glinted in the eyes of the merchant's guardsman, his youth and inexperience shining in his face. He gulped a mouthful of saliva and nodded before the squire returned his attention to the maze.

In his amazement at its condition, he hadn't noticed the figures standing in front of the labyrinth, facing the crowd. A forest of heads blocked his view, but he soon realized it wasn't the three people he expected it to be; instead, a woman stood between two squat trees he didn't recall.

Her long silver-gray hair lay flat against her white robes. In one hand she clutched a book with a plain brown cover—a tome Ilkari had seen before—in the other she held another familiar item he'd thought he'd never see again.

The stave of Amnayel Prisma.

His mouth fell open. The last time he'd seen the rune-covered wood, he'd left it behind in an unending tunnel, its wooden length gripped in his friend's fist. And now it was here.

His heart jumped. If it survived, perhaps Rein did, too.

Ilkari pushed forward, forcing himself between bodies damp with fearful sweat, moving toward the labyrinth and not caring if Nevan and Naeve followed. Without objection, the baron's subjects shifted aside, none of them desiring to be there at all, let alone close to the unfamiliar woman they'd been herded to observe.

As he got nearer to the front of the forced gathering, the squire saw the trees weren't what he'd expected. The one to the woman's right had an unusual curve to its trunk; moss hung from its branches, dangling like tresses. When he discerned facial features, arms, he realized it an Unnamed.

A dryad.

He diverted his attention to the other tree, expecting to find similar attributes. While he spotted some similarities, where the first radiated life and energy, the second stood motionless. Not dead but not alive either. Its limbs dangled at its side. Dried leaves clung to the upper branches rather than strands of moss. The trunk's features appeared carved a long time ago.

Ilkari hesitated, his focus on the decrepit tree. Unbelievably, he found some familiarity in its bark. He squinted, tilted his head before first recognizing the strange mark on one arm. After a second, it came to him.

The baron's insignia.

His heart jumped in his chest. Not a tree—a man made wooden. He pushed closer, worried if he got near enough, he'd find the attributes resembled someone he knew better than any other, a lad he'd raised as if his own child.

He stopped with but a few people between him and the stretch of muddy ground separating them from the tree standing beside the woman. His gaze swept over the woody features, his breath shallow with fearful expectation. The nose, the shape of the eyes, cheekbones and chin. They all resembled what he feared to find, but askew. The eyes too close together, the nose a hair too big.

"Sylleth," he whispered.

He tensed, ready to move forward without knowing what to do if he made his way to the edge of the crowd, when a sharp noise stopped him.

The tall, hairy man who'd accosted him before stood beside the woman, palms held pressed in front of him after having clapped his hands to gain the captive audience's attention. When all focused where he'd directed them, he nodded to her, then took his leave.

Silence reigned as her gaze swept across the gathering. When her regard touched the squire, a chill ran up his spine.

133

"I am Shiera Siirist," she said after waiting long enough to make everyone so uncomfortable they began fidgeting. "A thousand years ago, my grandfather did the unthinkable and enslaved all magic creatures. For a millennium, we did your bidding with no choice, we lived the lives forced upon us by humans. Demeaned, ridiculed, mistreated, unnamed. No more."

A nervous murmur ran through the crowd as she paused, once more taking in the faces of those gathered in the baron's courtyard. The dryad shifted, the moss hanging from its limbs swaying as though touched by a gentle breeze.

"I have returned to right my grandfather's wrongs," she continued, the volume of her voice rising. "The age of man is over."

A cheer rose, confusing Ilkari for a second until he realized the noise didn't issue from the crowd, but from the Unnamed gathered around their perimeter. He scanned them, surprised by their number, and how many of them resembled the humans they guarded.

"The time of the magiks has returned," she said, her words drawing the squire's attention. As she continued, her gaze appeared to fall on him. "You belong to me now."

CHAPTER 12

— · —

A LWIN SAT IN THE corner, knees drawn up, his right elbow
holding the satchel tight against his hip. The sound of footsteps floated through the window above him and to his left, the
mundane tromp of boots and sandals occasionally interrupted by
spoken words. The ones uttered by human tongues were short,
worried, apologetic.

Jai stood beside the closed door, a length of lumber dangling
from his hand as they awaited Rein's return, hopefully with some
morsel to provide them sustenance. As his stomach gurgled at the
thought, Alwin couldn't help but recall when he'd first woken in
the abandoned warehouse. After the confusion of his situation,
nothing had mattered but finding food. At the time, his predica-
ment felt overwhelming.

Now, after days of hiding and skulking to avoid notice, of wor-
rying about being caught and slaughtered, he wished for such
simplicity.

He'd never expected to regard his stay in the baron's jail as the
good old days.

"We have seen better times," the familiar voice in his head said.

None I recall, he thought.

He'd learned not to respond aloud to the taunts, comments, and
bits of unrequested advice offered by the disembodied speaker.
The two knights already experienced enough difficulty in trusting
him. Conversing with someone they couldn't hear and nobody
could see wouldn't increase their faith.

Yet he wanted what they wanted.

The state of the world was his fault—not Alwin Pelletoot's, or
Waul's, and partially Viden Misk's—but the responsible party lived

somewhere inside him. Often he wondered if the voice speaking to him belonged to the mage Prisma himself.

"I am Amnayel Prisma and all who came before and after," it answered, despite him not asking. *"We are legion."*

What am I supposed to do?

"The wisdom of an age dwells in you, as it did in Viden Misk before you. All you must do is concentrate. Forget your preconceptions of who and what you are. Give in to the power, dwindled as it may be. If it was gone, we'd be dead. Access it, use it. Correct a hundred decades' worth of mistakes before the toll is too great."

Not too much to ask, he thought, chuckling.

The sound drew the knight's attention, and he raised a finger to his lips. Alwin nodded, an apologetic expression lifting his brow. With nothing to do but remain quiet and do his best to ignore the hungry knot in his gut, he closed his eyes.

With the luxury of sight robbed from his mind, he became more aware of sound, smells, the feel of the satchel pressing against his side. He scented the earth under his backside, the sour odor of his sweat having dried and refreshed on his body more times than conceivable since his last washing. Awareness of the caress of his clothing against his skin grew, and the hardness of the wall pressed against his spine. He caught stray words spoken by passers-by, some in a language he understood, others in tongues he suspected one of the souls inside him capable of deciphering, but not him.

And the satchel whispered to him.

He snapped his lids open, sure his imagination must have gotten the better of him, or he'd dozed off and slipped into dream without realizing. Jai remained crouched beside the door. The light of another clouded day continued squeezing between the gaps in the ragged curtains dangling in front of the windows. Everything the same.

"Listen," the voice advised.

Alwin allowed his eyelids to slide closed again, this time ignoring the scents assaulting his nose, the feel of the world around him. He concentrated, sifting through the muffled street noise until he found the susurrus again. Difficult to separate, he focused on the tiny indistinct sound, the rustle of pages in a book, but more. The murmur of paper contained whispered words too quiet to discern, too foreign to understand.

His eyes fluttered open, and he directed his gaze toward the case leaning against his side. The fluttering continued.

He reached across his body and used both hands to snap the bag's clasps, pulled it wide. The three volumes he'd rescued from the maze after Hum grew them to full size lay wedged within, pressed together too tightly to move. Yet the sound persisted.

He shifted his position, kneeling now with the satchel in front of him instead of sitting with his spine against the wall. The scrape of his movement drew a desperate hush from Jai. He didn't respond as he pulled a tome from the case—the first time he'd taken the time to examine them since collecting the volumes indicated by the sundial.

A scrollwork pattern decorated its cover, a pebbly brown leather worn lighter at the edge by the touch of many hands. He opened it, flipped through yellowed pages of parchment. They whispered the way any book would, not in the same voice, so he laid it on the floor beside him, placing it with care to avoid attracting further ire from the knight.

The cover of the second tome was smoother, its color lighter—a pinkish white that caused a shudder at what the material might be fashioned from. He clenched his teeth and leafed through it, listened to its quiet but unfamiliar voice, then set it atop its companion.

Before removing the third grimoire, Alwin paused and drew a deep, shuddering breath, preparing himself. He knew what he'd find on the cover of this one—the unicorn. The impetus behind humanity's greed and a thousand years of suffering. His lips pressed together as his fingers dipped into the satchel, found the tome, and pulled it forth.

He held it in both hands, staring at the regal creature rearing up on its hind legs, horn pointing toward the heavens. The sight of it brought a chill along his skin. He'd been so concerned for his own safety, he'd forgotten to worry about the item they'd hidden rather than risk carrying with them. What if they found it? What would it mean to their task if Prisma's granddaughter possessed the unicorn's mantle as well as the tome and the stave?

He shuddered and forced the thought aside. The voice remained silent, but he realized if it spoke, it would tell him not to worry about it. They could do nothing but what they could do. Finding the source of the whispering pages was all he had.

The leather spine creaked when he opened the cover to reveal the illustration on the first page. The artist had used few lines to create it, each one suggesting a shape more than defining it, but leaving no doubt what he'd drawn. How anyone could draw such a delicate portrait of a creature with such conservation of ink boggled Alwin's mind, making him forget why he'd removed the book from the satchel. He blinked the hypnosis from his eyes and riffled through the pages.

The rustling sheets didn't produce the insistent tone, but, to his surprise, he found the author had drawn smaller illustrations in the bottom corner of each sheet with the same spare, fine lines as the picture on the title page. As he flipped through, a tiny unicorn galloped across a plain, its long mane fluttering in the wind its headlong rush produced.

When the last piece of vellum slipped from under his thumb, leaving him at the tome's front cover, he paused, breathless, as though he'd charged the length of the pages himself. Curious about the drawings, he opened the book to a random spot near the center. Words written in a cursive hand spilled across the parchment, framing diagrams and maps. He skipped past them and trained his eye on the bottom corner.

Blank.

A frown furrowed Alwin's brow. Did he imagine such a delight? He flipped the page and found the next sheet similarly lacking, and the next, and the next. Concerned for his sanity, he closed the volume and reopened it, this time grabbing a sheaf of parchment in his hand and fanning through them as before.

The unicorn frolicked across the open space accompanied by another pair, both smaller than it.

Startled, he snapped the book shut, eliciting a hush from Jai. He directed his attention toward the knight, offering a sheepish expression in return for his angered one, and nodded. He stared at him for a second before returning to his observation of the closed door.

Alwin passed his hand over the top of the tome's cover, letting his palm brush the animal embossed in the leather. He longed to open the book again, find out what other treasures and surprises it held, but he forced himself to put it aside with the others. Despite the entertainment rifling through its pages offered, it hadn't whispered in the voice he'd anticipated and hoped to hear.

He sighed the breath from his lungs, shoulders slumping forward. Because of their size, he'd only been able to fit three volumes in the satchel, none of them responsible for the susurration. From whence did it come? He glanced around the empty room and saw nothing capable of producing the sound. Disappointed and fighting confusion, he pulled the case toward him, intending to return the tomes.

The bag rattled.

Alwin withdrew his hand, worried he'd find some insect or vermin had crawled inside while the animated unicorns enthralled him. He leaned forward, peering into the satchel, but little of the dim light in the hovel's interior made its way past the lip of its opening. Reaching out, he grabbed the edge of the bag and dragged it closer. When nothing stirred, he tilted it toward himself. Empty.

A gulp of saliva lubricated his drying throat as he lowered his hand inside, the muscles in his arm taut and ready to withdraw at the slightest touch of anything foreign. His fingertips brushed along the side of the interior, caressing the soft leather until they touched the bottom. He searched blindly at the sides, found it empty, then moved his fingers to the corner.

They contacted a hard shape, and he jerked his hand out, fearful of being bitten or scratched. Using both hands, he pulled the bag wide, lifted and tilted it.

A small rectangle skittered into view.

"Another tome," he said aloud, forgetting himself.

Jai probably shushed him a third time, but he didn't notice as he plunged in again and came forth with a shrunken volume. It must have been hidden in the case the entire time, the satchel protecting it from the magic Hum used to restore the others. Alwin released his grip on the bag and held the tiny book up to his ear. He opened it using his thumbs, riffled the pages with the tip of one finger.

It whispered to him in the same voice as before.

His eyes widened. He didn't understand what the shrunken tome meant to tell him—a warning? Instructions?—but he figured he knew how to find out. Dirt crunched under his knees as he shuffled around to face Jai. He turned toward him, his features set with the same exasperated expression he'd worn each time he

139

insisted on quiet. Alwin spoke before he raised his finger to his mouth and forced angry air between his lips.

"The horn," he said in an exaggerated whisper. "We must get the horn."

The knight stared, unsure of what to do. His cheek twitched as the muscles in his face wrestled between humbling him for speaking aloud and asking what he meant out of curiosity. When the door opened, Jai jumped to his feet, the chunk of lumber raised in readiness to defend them from whatever or whoever entered.

Rein shut the door, using both hands to control it and keep it from making more noise than necessary. With the task accomplished, he looked first at his friend, then Alwin. One eyebrow arched.

"What's going on here?" he whispered.

Jai tilted his head toward the third man. "Best you ask him."

The gaze of the baron's champion fell upon Alwin, its weight palpable. He swallowed hard, struggled to find words to explain and came up with none, so raised his hand, the tiny tome lying on his flattened palm. Unable to recognize what he held due to the distance between them and the poor lighting inside the hutch, Rein frowned and crossed the floor to crouch before him.

"Another book?"

Alwin nodded, too fast and too many times. He made himself stop.

"What of it?"

"It speaks to me."

He regretted saying it as soon as the words passed his lips. They already thought him crazy, detestable; he didn't need to give them further proof. The knight's brow furrowed, but, to Alwin's surprise, he took his admission at face value.

"What does it say?"

This time, he controlled himself as he shook his head. "I don't know. I require help to understand what it says."

Rein reached up and scratched his stubbly cheek. "What sort of help?"

"Viden Misk's residual magic is not enough for me to decipher its whispers or to return it to its full size. I need the horn."

He watched the knight's lips press together into a thin, bloodless line as he considered his companion's words. After a few seconds, he released a hard sigh and leaned closer.

140

"What do you suppose it will tell us? The solution to our problems? Will it give us the secret to returning the world to its proper state?"

With no answers to the questions, Alwin found his mouth suddenly dry. He resisted the urge to swallow or lick his lips. His throat clicked when he responded.

"I don't know." He hesitated, then added, "I hope so."

He realized his reply wasn't enough to satisfy the baron's champion, but he couldn't offer any more. The tiny susurrations gave him no clue about their meaning, though they offered a sliver of a chance absent since the day Prisma's granddaughter plunged the horn's tip into the earth. The shard of emotion meant little.

"It's not simple sentimentality," the voice said, bubbling up in his mind. *"Ancient knowledge lives in you. Pay attention to it."*

Distracted by the disembodied words, he didn't notice Rein shuffling closer until the knight spoke close to his ear.

"Could it return Jai's memories?"

He leaned away, gaze fixed on Alwin, a desperation flickering in his eyes he'd seen on a few previous occasions. Always concerning the other knight. The baron's champion was a man who rarely gave in to frustration, lack of control, fear. Except when it came to his friend. Alwin didn't know, but saw it for the opportunity it now presented.

He spoke as quietly as possible, keeping his words between him and his nearest companion. "I think so."

Rein continued staring at him, the intensity threatening to penetrate Alwin. He wanted to look away, to escape the pressure of his attention, but he held steady. Behind the knight, Jai stirred, but he kept his focus on the baron's champion. After what felt like an eternity, he rose.

"We'll go after nightfall," he said and turned toward his friend, speaking again before he protested. "It will be dangerous, but we have no choice. Are we to spend our lives hiding in this hovel while the world burns around us?"

A long silence passed between the two men before Jai nodded. "Tonight it is."

Despite his not having moved for some time, Alwin's heart beat fast against his ribs. His gaze slid away from his companions and to the minuscule volume lying on his flattened palm.

It whispered to him.

141

The hot air inside the small hut stuck to Rein's skin and dampened his clothes. Rarely did he feel grateful for shedding his armor, but this was such an occasion.

They'd hid their protective clothing, along with the horn and their weapons, days before. Of them, he missed his sword the most. He felt exposed without his mail and plate, but naked when missing his weapon. Their situation gave them no choice. After the bloodshed in the baron's city, their trappings made them too easy to identify.

"Do you see them? Is it clear?" Alwin Pelletoot's voice shook with nerves.

"Ssh," Jai hissed to quiet him.

The knight crouched by the door he held open a crack to peer out. From where he knelt behind him, Rein saw nothing beyond his shoulder, and heard little aside from the sounds of their own breathing. Since the curse's fall, the city rested in near silence after the sun went down and the curfew began. Unless fools ventured out, then the quietness amplified their screams.

The baron's champion harbored no intention of being caught.

Another minute of stillness passed before Jai rotated to face them, his boot sole scraping the dirt floor. Even in the darkness, he recognized the sheen of sweat on his brow.

"Remember," he said, directing his whispered instructions toward Alwin. "Weapons only. We don't have time to don armor."

"And the horn," he added, louder than required.

"Yes, the horn," Rein grated between clenched teeth.

The man cringed, his face taut, then nodded his understanding. Jai glanced at the baron's champion. As their gazes met, a familiar pang tightened Rein's chest, a mixture of longing and regret. He said nothing of it, despite his hope the bumbling fool they knew as Alwin Pelletoot might cure his friend of his selective amnesia. He gestured, and the knight cracked the door again, taking one last look before pulling it wide and motioning for them to follow.

The night air cooled the sweat clinging to their skin as they left the hovel behind. Jai led the way through the streets, his memory of their layout far superior to his recollection of a relationship with a man he loved. Every time Rein saw evidence everything but he lived on in his friend's memories, it twisted his gut into a knot—one he realized may never come untangled.

They kept to the shadows, pausing at irregular intervals whenever Jai thought he detected a sound, then they'd wait, breath held, until he motioned for them to follow again. Rein herded Alwin between himself and the other knight, hoping to ensure he didn't stray or do anything to draw attention to them.

The baron's champion understood this a fool's errand, but, given the choice between living a life of oppression or dying in the fight against it, he'd choose the latter. The irony of the situation humankind found themselves in wasn't lost on him, but he couldn't spare the time to ponder it.

His head moved constantly, checking to either side and behind and above them. The creatures guarding the streets came in all shapes, sizes, and abilities. Rein knew some Unnamed were capable of flight and, if he commanded their city's watch, he'd have them involved. He and Jai had discussed this, and so the knight kept them pressed to walls and hidden in shadow unless they had no choice but to reveal themselves.

They halted at one of these—a broad intersection where three avenues came together. The deserted warehouse where they'd departed from traveling to the Obsidian Fields and chosen to hide their weapons, armor, and the unicorn horn, lay four blocks beyond. Other, more circuitous ways to arrive at their destination existed, but they'd all require more time. Time outside breaking the curfew was riskier than scurrying across an exposed crossroads, making the choice easy.

They gathered behind Jai as he crouched at the edge of the building. The night remained quiet enough to hear Alwin drawing air. The scrape of leather boot sole on flagstone sounded unnaturally loud as the knight pivoted to peer around the corner. Rein glanced over his shoulder along the route they'd taken to arrive at this spot.

The streetlamps normally illuminating the thoroughfare were dark, but the path they intended to travel wouldn't have the luxury of lighting at the best of times. Once they cleared this intersection, they'd pass into the parts of the city less cared for because they were less cared about. No streetlights, flagstones giving way to

143

packed earth, buildings in disrepair. Before he'd met the man who called himself Viden Misk, Rein had hardly set foot beyond this unofficial boundary between wealth and poverty, the haves and the have-nots. Now it happened far too frequently.

A flicker of movement at the corner of his eye caught his attention. He refocused, eyes narrowed, breath held as he searched for a shape or hint of motion along the darkened avenue. He saw neither.

"All right," Jai said from the front of their group, his words a quiet rasp. "It's clear. Let's go."

The hackles on Rein's neck rose. The streets appeared empty, but he couldn't help but feel like they weren't alone. He sensed unseen eyes watching them. He turned toward his friend, lips parted, the intent to tell him to wait teetering on the edge of his tongue, but Jai broke cover. Alwin followed. The baron's champion reached out to snag him by the sleeve and stop him, but the fellow's reckless excitement to retrieve the unicorn's horn propelled him too quickly.

"Damn it," he cursed under his breath. With no other choice, he got to his feet and hurried after them.

With his friend Jai halfway across the broad intersection, a gust of cool wind stirred the loose dirt lying on the flagstones. It picked up the sand, dust, and pebbles, whirling them around into a funnel. The trio froze, watching, waiting to discover if it was a natural occurrence or something in need of their concern. Rein already knew which as surely as he realized it too late to flee.

The detritus swirled and grew, and darkness collected within it. Jai began backing away when another gust blew through, then a third, each collecting debris and hurling it into the air. One twisted before them, the others settled at each of the other access points to the intersection, blocking their escape.

Alwin lifted his case of books, clutched it tight against his chest, and Rein wondered if he thought this some useless defense against whatever coalesced when the winds ceased whirling. He nearly laughed aloud at the futility of the gesture. Even with swords and armor, he doubted they'd survive what the whirlwind revealed.

As if hearing his thoughts, the first tornado stopped spinning. The dirt and debris borne upon the air held in place for a half second before raining to the ground, leaving a dark shape in their wake.

"What have we here?" the creature asked in a languid tone as it stepped toward them.

Long hair hung well past its shoulders while prominent cheekbones and a sharp nose marked its features. Elf, fae...Rein didn't have a name for the being, but it needed no label to coax a shiver along his spine and puckered flesh on his arms.

"They appear human, don't you think?" a second said in the timbre of a female and with considerable interest.

"Humans aren't allowed freedom at night," the third pointed out.

The baron's champion glanced from one dark shape to the next. They differed in height, but nothing else. He discerned no variance in their hair, features, or body type. And they all wore scabbards hanging at their waists. With the ability to appear out of thin air, he saw little requirement for weapons, yet they carried them.

"What say you, humans?" the first asked. "How is it we find you wandering the streets at night?"

Other than a quiet moan of panic deep in Alwin's throat, nobody responded. Jai backed away from the creature, tightening the three of them into a pack. Rein thought about warning him against this—spreading out gave at least one of them a better chance of survival—but he didn't bother. Either they all survived or none of them continued breathing. Whatever Alwin meant to do with the unicorn's horn seemed their lone hope, and recovering it needed all of them.

"You offer no reason?" the female said. "Did someone already find you and take out your tongue?"

The familiar sound of metal hissing against leather filled the air, blades filling the hands of their antagonists with such surprising speed they didn't appear to have moved at all. Their weapons glowed with an eerie green hue, casting light on their faces. Where Rein expected to find beauty, it surprised him to encounter the opposite. Mottled skin covered the high cheekbones, yellowed teeth flashed behind thin lips. He knew not what sort of creatures stood before them, but their lack of allure did little to convince him they weren't dangerous.

The baron's champion had always known he'd one day meet his end protecting his subjects, but he'd expected it to occur on a battlefield, or in a duel; somewhere people noticed his sacrifice and wrote songs about his bravery. Never had he considered he may have his life ended on the blades of monsters in the middle of a dusty intersection.

His hands curled into fists and he set his jaw, preparing to fight, ready to die an inauspicious death if fate required it of him. Beside him, Alwin began to cry.

Though many other odors tainted it, the scent held a familiarity to Vyle, a sliver he recognized. He halted, inhaled.

Ilkari.

But it wasn't the squire he'd left behind with the twins. If so, he'd distinguish it more easily. This odor belonged to someone acquainted with him, somebody who'd somewhat recently been in close quarters with the man he knew.

"Rein Shriken," he breathed.

A name everybody recognized before the world fell apart, but it meant nothing to him. Another human amongst dozens. Not until he'd saved the squire to the baron's champion did he understand more of this fellow.

He frowned. Of all the tales his companion told him—struggles and success, bravery and fighting prowess—the troll distinctly recalled Ilkari telling him his charge was lost in some unknown tunnel.

How did he get here?

When he left him, he'd done so not to desert them to their own devices, but because he realized it best for them all if he traverse the city alone. He needed to figure out what had happened and how to handle it, a task he couldn't achieve with three humans in tow.

But if Rein Shriken was the half man his squire claimed him, perhaps he knew what to do.

Vyle nodded to himself and sniffed the air again. The baron's champion had passed this spot, and not alone. He guessed he traveled with two companions, and they carried something smelling of leather and ancient paper, as if the humans' scent wasn't enough to attract the attention of any Unnamed with a nose.

The odor trail lay stronger ahead than behind—they'd come this way recently. Vyle set out, unconcerned about disguising his passing. As a magical creature in a world ruled by magiks, he didn't need to worry about consequences—a sense of freedom he enjoyed, but couldn't abide the cost.

As he advanced, his nose leading him, another scent joined the first. This one caused him concern.

Magic.

Someone else had detected the baron's champion and his companions and taken up following them, no doubt with ill intent. Vyle hurried his pace. From everything he'd seen, the Unnamed in the city held no mercy to offer their onetime oppressors. He had to warn them.

He halted when his ears picked up the sound of voices. A block ahead, no more. Three of them, none belonging to Rein Shriken or any other mortal. Magical creatures, dangerous ones, and their playful tones suggested them about to indulge their bloodthirsty desires. The song of swords being drawn confirmed his worries.

The avenue he traveled upon joined others at a crossroads and he saw shapes at the center of it—three gathered together, surrounded by another trio holding glowing blades, the light bright enough to illuminate their faces.

Daoine sith.

Fae of the sidhe. He'd met one once at the guildhall. He remembered the fellow's surliness, had asked Hispid about his nature. It turned out the barrow fairies weren't merely angry about being enslaved by mankind, but also about being unearthed from their homes; they bore the scars of this change to their lives upon their faces. Having been born with a troll's face, Vyle hadn't identified with their plight, but he understood how someone who'd begun beautiful and had it plucked from them might hold a grudge.

"Oy," he called out ahead of stepping into the intersection. The three men at the center of attention directed their gazes toward him, but none of their captors did. They'd sensed his presence as he'd known of theirs. "What's going on here?"

"Nothing for you to be concerned about, troll. We have everything in hand."

"But I am." He strode into the open space where the streets met, stopped a half dozen paces from the group. "I think you should let them go."

Not until these words did one of the Unnamed bother to spare him their attention. The fellow's mouth twisted into a sneer.

"We have no intention of releasing them. In fact, the last thing left to decide is how many more breaths we'll allow them before putting an end to their pathetic, undeserved lives."

When he'd come across the minotaur menacing Ilkari and the twins in the middle of a pasture, he'd gotten lucky. The half-man, half-bull creatures possessed a lot of muscle, but very little brains or real magic. There'd been a slim chance of the beast overpowering him, but he thought slim a generous characterization. He'd known going in he controlled the situation, so realized he'd be able to diffuse things while not hurting Runt too badly, and certainly without killing him.

He didn't want to kill magiks any more than he wanted to see humans die, but these probably wouldn't give him much choice if they engaged.

"You should reconsider," he said, accessing the part of his mind Berta used to keep from him.

Power swirled, spilled out along his spine and into his limbs. He reserved some of it, keeping it from swelling his size. The daoine sith must have sensed his release of energy because they all faced him.

"I don't know what you're up to, but each word you speak steals one more breath from these humans. My patience and humor wear thin. Away with you, troll."

The leader of the group raised his glowing sword over the cluster of men. The smallest of them—a frail fellow clutching a satchel to his chest—cowered while the other two struck defensive poses. If he didn't act, they'd slice the trio to pieces right in front of him.

He let his power free, allowing it to swell his arms and legs, increase his height. It pushed at his skin, barely contained from spilling out of him.

"My name is Vyle," he grated as he rushed them.

The eyeballs through which Alwin Pelletoot perceived the world had never spied a troll, but he felt certain one emerged from the darkness with a silence unbelievable for a creature its size.

It traded words with the three beings holding him and the knights captive. He didn't have a word for them—magical, frightening, dangerous, but those described their features, not their kind. Dark elves, or fae, perhaps. Another Unnamed with a grudge against humans.

Alwin couldn't guess why the latest addition to this unusual group wanted their release, but their captors resisted. When the brief negotiation between them broke down, the troll charged, appearing to grow larger with each step. He didn't cry out, or growl. The three creatures menacing them turned their attention and their weapons toward the attacker, the ethereal green glow of their blades brightening.

Behind him, Rein shifted. For an instant, he thought the baron's champion intended to join the impending fray—a death sentence even for a talented fighter like him, he knew. Especially lacking a weapon. To his great relief, he grabbed Alwin by the shoulder and pulled him backward instead of joining the fight, then called for Jai to retreat, too.

They managed to clear the area before the four magical beings came together. Sword blades cut streaks of emerald through the dark. The troll dodged the first two, and the third strike glanced off his shoulder with a sound like the steel struck rock. In response, the creature who'd called himself Vyle swung a massive arm. One of his adversaries ducked, the second parried, the last wasn't so lucky.

The beast's fist contacted the side of his head, crunching teeth and jawbone. The fellow stumbled but didn't fall. When he righted himself, the damage from the blow was obvious, an indentation beside his chin developing in his already-scarred face. He parted his lips and spat a slurry of blood and broken teeth onto the flagstones.

Besides the swish of blades cutting air, the clang of weapons contacting impenetrable skin, and the grunts and breaths of attack, they fought in silence. Nobody cried out for aid or in pain, not even when the troll caught one attacker by the wrist and yanked his arm from his body.

149

BRUCE BLAKE

In the darkness, the blood sprayed across the ground appeared black. Alwin wondered if—given the outward appearance of the three angry Unnamed—it looked any different in the light. He hugged the satchel tight against his chest as he peered out from behind the two knights, both of whom stood ready to defend should the need present itself.

He hoped it wouldn't.

The troll's fist crunched into the face of the female amongst his trio of attackers. Like her cohort with the broken jaw and her companion missing an arm, the blow appeared to stun her for an instant, then she returned to the fray. Despite his superior size and strength, Alwin worried the troll lacked the ability to finish his opponents. His concern deepened when the now one-armed monster took a step away from the fight.

The lips on his scarred face contorted, forming words in some foreign tongue requiring facial manipulations the likes of which he'd never seen. The air to the right of the fellow wavered, solidified until Vyle struck the man with his own amputated arm, interrupting the incantation and dispersing its results.

Alwin might have laughed at this if the sight hadn't also threatened to turn his stomach.

Angered, the dark figure leaped forward with a reckless abandon. The troll caught his head between his hands and twisted, snapping his neck with the sound of a dried twig. He released his grip and the fellow's lifeless body slumped to the ground, giving his companions a moment's pause.

The woman's upper lip curled into a sneer and the two remaining renewed their attack, coordinating their strikes, though neither spoke. Their blades struck the troll again and again, the steel clattering against his hard skin.

After a few seconds, Vyle decided he'd endured enough. He abandoned any pretense of avoiding their attacks, allowing their glowing swords to contact him unhindered. One strike grated along the top of his arm, and Alwin thought he saw the beast cringe—the first sign of anything affecting him.

It did nothing to slow him.

He pushed through, focusing on the Unnamed with the broken jaw. When opportunity arose, his hand shot through an opening and grabbed the fellow by the neck. With no more effort than hefting a chicken, Vyle lifted him off the ground, his feet kicking.

150

He dropped his sword, clutching at the troll's grip with both hands, desperate to relieve the pressure before his windpipe collapsed and he choked to death on his own blood.

He spent the final seconds of his life attempting to prise his adversary's thick fingers from around his neck, and failed.

When the fresh corpse hit the ground, the last remaining member of the group backed away. Blood ran from her shattered nose and over her torn lips, a sneer tilting her mouth, but fear flickered in her eyes. The troll took one step toward her before she turned and fled. She went three steps before the night swallowed her.

Alwin stared at the place where she'd stood a second before, wondering how she'd disappeared so quickly and thoroughly, as though she fled through an unseen door. He opened his mouth to ask his companions if they'd seen this anomaly, but stopped when he noticed the troll's attention on them.

He lingered between the two corpses he'd created, his size deflated, a trickle of blood running from his upper arm. His eyes flickered between the three men, assessing them. Rein raised his hands, palms facing the beast.

"We mean no harm," the baron's champion said. "Let us pass and we will cause no trouble."

Alwin couldn't imagine what problem they'd give the formidable creature, and he suppressed a chuckle at the idea when upsetting the current balance of the world was precisely what they'd set out to do.

"She'll tell others what happened. Bring them here," Vyle said, ignoring Rein's statement. "We have to go."

Rein lowered his hands and took a step forward. Jai did the same, offering a united front with his friend against whatever the troll may do. Alwin stood his ground and fought the urge to flee tingling through his legs. The tiny book had whispered a plan to him and he needed to execute it, even with small chance of succeeding.

"We'll be going nowhere with you. Let us pass."

"You must be the baron's champion, I presume. Your demeanor suggests it, but I can also smell Ilkari on you."

"Ilkari?" Rein repeated, a note of incredulity in his tone. "What do you know of him?"

"I parted company with him a day ago." The troll glanced along the street. "We have to go. Now."

"He's alive?" he whispered. "And here?"

"Yes, but we haven't time to speak of it." Vyle shook his head. "I have to stop making a habit of rescuing humans. You're more trouble than you're worth."

He turned away from them and began walking, expecting them to follow. If they didn't, he'd be leaving them to whatever fate befell them.

Alwin pushed between the knights, hurrying to catch up to the troll.

"We'll come with you," he said, breathless not from the effort of the creature's pace, but from coming so close to losing his life. Again. "But we have a stop to make first."

"We can't wait. They'll be after us already."

"We have to retrieve the unicorn's horn."

Vyle halted with such abruptness, Alwin walked into him.

"What did you say?"

"The unicorn's horn. We hid it in an abandoned warehouse. We're on our way to get it. It's why we're risking our lives being out at night."

The troll lifted his chin and peered over him toward the knights. "Is this true?"

Alwin craned his neck to glance over his shoulder and see both Rein and Jai nod.

"It is," the baron's champion said.

The massive Unnamed sighed an exasperated breath. "Fine. Lead me to it, then we must get off the streets." He shook his head and started out again, mumbling. "Humans always end up more headaches than help."

CHAPTER 13

— · —

T HE FARTHER THEY TRAVELED into the jangala, the harder it became for Llyris to sleep. It wasn't the way the heat stuck to her like a second skin keeping her from finding rest, though.

Everything spoke to her.

The forest was loudest at night. While larger beasts settled into their lairs, birds retreated to their nests, and flowers closed their petals with the setting of the sun, uncountable smaller creatures came to life. Bats wheeled overhead in pursuit of their insect meals. Rodents scurried through the undergrowth, spiders spun their traps. Snakes slithered and reptiles skittered. Trees, plants, animals, insects. They all had something to say, but she understood none of them.

Tesfira sat beside her as she leaned against the trunk of a tree, wishing for victory for the heaviness in her eyelids.

"It's beautiful in its own way, isn't it?" she said, her voice low, to keep from disturbing their sleeping companions. On watch on the other side of their encampment, Gartrek tilted his head, listening. "Beautiful and brutal. Nothing we've ever seen before."

"Why are you awake?'

Normally, Llyris possessed endless time for the acolyte, but her exhaustion clouded her mind as much as it weighed on her limbs. She'd abandoned her capacity for appreciating beauty a week ago, ditching it like an overburdened pack mule shedding unnecessary weight.

"I should ask you the same question."

"I'm awake because they won't let me sleep."

Tesfira raised an eyebrow. "They?"

With more effort than it should have required, the handler lifted her arm and gestured to the jangala around them. Across their camp, the ogre tensed again, ready if her movement became a cry for help.

"Everything. Can't you hear it? The jungle never stops shouting at me."

She watched the young woman shut her eyelids and raise her chin, listening to the night sounds the way Gartrek listened to them. A smile crossed her smooth face.

"Whispers," she said, opening her eyes. "Tiny feet in motion, wings beating the air, creatures chittering to each other."

Llyris sighed. "I wish that's all it was. They speak to me, every one of them. The leaves on the trees call out to me, insects buzz beside my ears, snakes hiss my name. They give me no peace and I don't understand what they are saying to me."

"Have you listened to them?"

"I..." she began, then stopped, unsure what to say.

At the beginning, when the black-and-white-furred creature told her the path they must follow, she'd tried to discern what the jangala said, thought it might be important. In frustration, she'd soon given up trying. Accepting she didn't understand was easier than attempting to decipher the clicks and whirrs God never intended human ears to comprehend. She worried if she spent too much time listening, it may drive her mad.

How could she find words to relay this to her friend? She told her companions she knew what they were supposed to do, where they needed to go. They'd put their faith in her and she didn't want to let them down.

"It is an honor to be chosen. I felt the same when God first called me." She shifted her position, staring off into the forest before returning her attention to Llyris. "But responsibility can also be a burden. Does anyone believe I or any acolyte wanted to spend years not speaking? No words, no laughter. The opposite problem to yours."

The handler shook her head. "I've never understood how you did it."

Tesfira shrugged. "Not without difficulty at first. Change is often challenging. I struggled for a while, but I kept in mind my reason for doing it. Whenever temptation threatened my vow, I closed my eyes and recalled the way I'd felt the day God summoned me."

154

"God hasn't summoned me."

"No?" she leaned closer. "What you call it is irrelevant. Think of it as purpose, if it's easier for you. Do you feel you have a purpose?"

"Like a destiny, inescapable, no matter what I do."

"The same."

"But I can't sleep nor make heads or tails of what I'm to do."

"Do you understand why acolytes take a vow of silence?"

She'd pondered the question before, but never asked. For a second, she considered venturing a guess, then decided against it and shook her head instead.

"So we can learn how to listen. Close your eyes."

Llyris hesitated. How many times in the past nights had she shut them with disappointment the result? The futility of trying to find rest brought frustration and a sense of helplessness, neither of which she desired to indulge again. When Tesfira recognized her reluctance, she tilted her head, urging her to comply until the handler gave in.

"The first step is to control your breath. Breathe with me."

The acolyte inhaled, allowing it to hiss between her lips. Llyris did the same, then expelled it when her friend exhaled.

"Good. Again."

She filled and emptied her lungs with her a second time, then a third, a fourth. The sounds of the jangala remained but, instead of a jangled cacophony of discordant noise, they coalesced into a pulse.

The heartbeat of the jungle.

It thrummed in Llyris' ears, the rhythm finding its way into her body to complement its cadence with the beat of her own heart. Tension and frustration melted from arms and legs and a sinking sensation pulled her downward into dreamless sleep.

"What's she doing?"

Despite the sneer curling his lips, Cirril Feron kept derision from his tone.

"Listening," Hinter said.

"To what?"

The thief shrugged. "Does it matter?"

"I suppose not."

They watched the handler wandering between trees, finding her way through the spaces between the brush, fingertips dragging across their leaves. Sometimes she stopped and raised her gaze toward the emerald canopy high above. If she wandered too far, they crept after her, always keeping her in sight.

"How long will this take?" the merchant's man grumbled.

"You have somewhere else to be?"

"I have a hundred other places I'd rather be."

"We all do." Hinter glanced over her shoulder at Tesfira trailing behind them. Hartrek loomed near her, watching over the acolyte as she sorted through the low shrubbery in search of leaves and flowers she recognized as useful. What use, she couldn't guess, but she'd learned to trust her friend. As a thief, she possessed many skills—they did not include botany or herbology. To her, plants were for eating, seasoning, and making tea. Tes had other things in mind.

A bird the size of Hinter's arm flew by overhead, its red, blue, and yellow feathers flashing with the flap of its wings. It landed on a high branch, tilted its head, and let out a loud crawk. As if in response, Llyris made her way toward the tree where the avian perched, stared upward at it. It expelled another raucous sound, and the handler appeared to nod before returning her attention to her companions.

"We are on the correct path," she said, wading through the brush to return to them. "But danger lies in the way ahead. Some forces don't want us to reach the mountain."

"Forces?" Cirril's hand fell to the hilt of his sword, as though the forces she spoke of might appear at any second and require him to vanquish them. Hinter thought he'd prefer it over other possibilities. "What sort of forces?"

"I know not. I suppose not all Unnamed long to risk losing their freedom."

The merchant's man's gaze flitted first to the ogres accompanying their party, then to the tangle of green vines and brown creepers surrounding them.

"There are Unnamed here?"

"Magiks live everywhere. Some who escaped the curse's effects, others never bound by it. We may find either here. Or both."

"Of course we will." He released his grip on the sword hilt. "Which way?"

"North," she said as she set out. She touched Gartrek on the arm as she passed him, indicating for him to join her as she led their party deeper into the jungle. "Be wary."

Cirril sighed. "I always am."

The birds guided them for a while, and then a furred animal Llyris didn't recognize with a straight up pointing tail and a sharp nose designed for inserting into holes in the ground. When it wandered off, no other guide came to lead them and she received fewer encouraging messages. She halted, searched the surrounding jungle for a sign. She saw none.

"Is everything all right?" Hinter asked as she stepped up beside her. Tesfira and Cirril Feron joined them a second later.

"Yes. Um." She hesitated, unsure what to tell them. "The path is unclear here."

The merchant's man scoffed. "First, we're to be wary, and now we're lost?"

Llyris ignored his barb but saw the thief out of the corner of her eye as she frowned at him.

"I...I need a minute."

She pivoted on her heel and took a step away from her friends. Their proximity interfered with her connection to the world, the hiss of blood in their veins and the whoosh of breath in their lungs too loud.

"Take your time," Tesfira said, ever patient.

"Stay close to her, Hartrek," Cirril directed.

She knew without looking he'd likely spoken the words to Gartrek. Even after the time they'd spent together, he considered the two ogres animals and hadn't bothered to note the scar over Gartrek's right eye differentiating him from his identical twin.

"No," she said, holding her hand up in a gesture to stop him. "I need space to listen."

She walked away, grateful no ogre's footsteps followed behind her. Ten paces passed under her soles, enough to separate her from her companions' whispers. She didn't need to be within earshot to guess their words. Their conversations always took on the same shape—Cirril protesting, Hinter defending, Tesfira calming. Often she wondered how to stop the cycle.

Not now, though. More pressing concerns required her focus.

She stepped through a low shrub onto an area of open earth and sat, legs crossed and palms pressed against the ground. This wasn't how she'd normally sit, and didn't know why she'd chosen the pose this time, but it seemed necessary.

Rough dirt indented her skin, making it itch, but she resisted the urge and kept her hands flat. She inhaled through her nose, scenting the trees and earth, animals who'd once passed this spot, birds overhead, more than she had any right to expect her olfactory to interpret. Her eyes slid closed and her body settled as though sunken into the lovely depths of a lush mattress.

A movement startled her—not around her, but from within. Her surprise disappeared when the nearest tree talked to her.

"You are safe, child." It spoke a language she shouldn't comprehend. *"If you stay on the path."*

"What path?" she said aloud.

Did it understand her? It appeared to have no ears, nor did it speak the languages of humans. It didn't reply, so she assumed it did not and resigned herself not to ask again.

She sank deep into the earth, felt the coolness of the dirt though the sun warmed her skin. It was loud here, filled with chittering and the scrape of digging. The rasp of her breath and the beat of her heart vanished, as if carried away from her on a watery current.

Panic flooded her, and she thought to open her eyes, but those parts of her remained a long way from where she navigated roots and dirt channels. She swept past rocks, sensed the thump of paws and hooves striking the ground above her. Did Tesfira experience this when Shiera spirited her to the mountain to meet her God?

Cold and darkness, but the sounds never ceased. They changed. The tromp of feet overhead faded and the click of mandibles and scrape of both hard carapaces and soft flesh against dirt became prevalent. She extended her mind, seeking connection with anything capable of comprehending her, to unveil the reasons for her presence and guide her in the right direction. If any of the creatures deep in the earth understood her, they pretended they didn't.

After a few minutes, the sensations threw her stomach askew. She fought the nausea, told herself her body sat in the small clearing, unmoving and safe. Her mind merely created the sense of movement. Or did it?

She broke through a thin wall into a long, gloomy chamber, equal in width and length. Her lack of physical form prevented her from determining its dimensions. It might have been huge or tiny—a massive cavern or a crack between rocks. Similarly, she couldn't assess the size of the creature staring at her with black, bulging eyes from the far end of the space.

"Who are you? Why have you invaded my home?"

Despite the absence of light under the ground, she saw its dark, rough skin marked with yellow spots the same color as its belly. The same pigmentation continued along its long tail. Sharp nails disturbed the chamber's dirt floor as it scuttled forward, closing half the distance between them. The urge to flee overwhelmed her, and she'd have done so if she possessed legs. She thought she lacked the willpower to use them if she did.

"If you're here for my eggs, you are too late. The younglings have hatched, so you can move along."

The reptile's tone suggested the words dripped of untruth, but it didn't matter. She hadn't come for eggs.

"Are you...?" She hesitated, recalling how the tree didn't respond. How all the creatures crawling through the soil had gone about their business, ignoring her. "Are you the dragon?"

Its reptilian eyes pinned her to the mud wall, the moist, warm air hanging between them growing heavier. Its head tilted. A tongue with a split end darted out of its mouth, retracted. And then it laughed.

The harsh, coughing laugh filled the dirt chamber, thumping against the walls. Llyris' face warmed, and she wondered if the creature saw color in the dark.

"Do I look like a dragon?"

She shrugged. "I've never seen a dragon in real life. Nobody has. Not in a very long while."

The reptile shuffled closer. "The king lives in the mountain and never comes down from his throne nor takes audience with anyone. If you quest to find him, I'd advise you to choose a more productive method of wasting your time. And besides," it chuckled its dry laugh again, "if you seek the epelweard, you're a bit misguided."

A frown crept across her face. Did it mean she was going the wrong way during her underground foray, or did she and her companions need to amend their course? In her physical state, it was relatively easy to see the mountain peak and ensure they kept it ahead of them. She couldn't say the same beneath the ground.

"Can you tell me about the dragon? Why won't he take audience?"

The lizard scoffed. "You think because I have scaly skin resembling his, I should guess the dragon's mind?"

"No. I'm not suggesting that, but you live closer to him than most."

"I do, don't I? He doesn't allow just anybody close to him, you know."

The creature expanded its yellow-speckled cheeks and lifted its head, its throat puffed out to match the rest. It held the pose and Llyris wondered if she should compliment it, then decided not to, thinking it too manipulative.

"What an honor to reside so near. But why doesn't he take audience with anyone?"

"If you believe the stories, the King in the Mountain had his fill of both magiks and humans alike many centuries ago. None know what happened, but he took his family and fled, swore never to return."

"The war." Llyris thought if she offered knowledge, perhaps she'd get more from the lizard. "Caused by humans. You said he left with his family? There's more than one dragon?"

"Of course. The king, his mate, and their two younglings, though none of them are young anymore."

More than a millennium had passed since the age of dragons ended. These couldn't be the beasts who'd retreated in disgust for its inhabitants. Perhaps further generations descended from those of yore? If she believed Viden Misk, the mage had transferred his essence from body to body for a thousand years, and Shiera, his granddaughter, lived on. If they continued, surely a creature like a dragon could, too.

"Does he ever come out?"

A split tongue flicked out, and the reptile moved its head side to side. "None of them do, and most close to them ensure their privacy. If it is the King in the Mountain you seek, go forth with care."

"You won't stop me?"

"I have eggs to tend and sparse time for trivialities. You've already taken up too much of my day."

"But why did I come here?"

"I don't know. Why did you?"

"I—" she began, but the sensation of motion returned and the underground chamber receded from her view.

She raced through the earth, the sounds of its residents turned to a dull hum by the rapidity of her movement. Before, she'd felt little control over her direction and progress, but now she possessed none. A force pulled her along, wending her way through a maze of roots and stone. Coolness passed above her she assumed a body of water, then she sensed a familiar area: the village they'd left behind in their quest to reach the mountain.

A sliver of panic erupted in her chest and she struggled against the power pulling her away from her task. What was she to discover about their journey by returning to where they began?

She whisked past it and traveled under the fields of bamboo. A buzzing filled the air, and she clambered with non-existent hands to find purchase in the dirt rushing by to slow her progress.

Her fear grew from an ember to a flame as she became sure this was Shiera's doing. Diverting her, undermining her plan to locate the dragon and end the events unfolding in the world. What would happen if she succeeded? What about her companions?

As the forest drew her inexorably on, she wished she'd been more careful with Flayre. If she still had the Unnamed, she wouldn't find herself in this situation.

In the jungle, seated on a dry patch of bare earth, Llyris raised a hand and grasped the dragon wing brooch at her throat.

Vyle led them through the streets toward their goal of the abandoned warehouse, his senses on high alert. Every scrape of rat toenail on dirt vibrated the hair in his ears. He whiffed each scent of owl's breath, watched the beat of innumerable insect wings.

He'd taken them as far as possible under the cover of night before he detected the daoine sith and others hunting them. Before the darkness ended, he guided them to a fresh hiding spot.

The tiny hut barely fit them all, and the roof hung too low for the troll to stand straight. Whoever lived here made do with practically nothing—a heap of dirty straw lying in one corner and stitches of threadbare clothing stacked by it suggested someone other than vermin called this place home.

The man who named himself Alwin Pelletoot stood beside the door, shifting from foot to foot like a child with a bladder full to bursting. His gaze flickered, attention lingering on nothing for more than the duration of a heartbeat. Vyle watched him, his nervous demeanor causing him concern. Whenever his eyes fell on the troll, they flashed away to someone else or to some space devoid of his companions. He observed for a minute before sidling up to the baron's champion.

"What's with your skittish friend?"

He tilted his head toward Alwin, who glanced toward the two men. Given the size of the hut in which they hid, he couldn't help but overhear the question.

"If you believe what he says, this is not a single high-strung man you gaze upon, but many. He tells me I knew him as an elder charlatan called Viden Misk, though he claims other names, too. Perhaps you've heard of one: Amnayel Prisma."

Vyle frowned, his attention fixed on the disheveled fellow as he examined the dirt floor between his feet, which he continued for some time, refusing to meet his gaze. The troll knew this name, of course. Statues and paintings and busts of the man abounded at the guildhall, and the Seniors and attendants frequently mentioned him, usually as taunts or threats.

"The mage," he said under his breath.

Were Hispid present, he'd have torn out the fellow's throat without regard for whether he had the time to shift to his bear form. Such was his hatred of the curse's perpetrator, a loathing shared by most Unnamed. Most except Vyle.

He moved to take a step toward their meek companion when a hand on his arm stopped him. His attention returned to Rein Shriken, whose eyes awaited his.

"Surely those we met last night must be searching for us," he said. His tone lacked any sliver of fear, though a hint of accusation tainted it.

The troll nodded. "Them and others."

"You sense them. Can they do the same with you? Or us?"

Vyle sighed. He knew from experience humans cared not to know when they'd been affected by magic. To some, it was akin to being burned with fire, so he didn't relish the idea of telling the knight he'd surrounded the hut with a glamor to conceal them. His mind whirled, attempting to figure out what to tell him. In the past, Breda would have handled this, leaving him to do whatever task assigned to him by the guild.

He suppressed a chuckle at the instant of missing his handler.

"We are safe for now," he said, deciding to keep his response vague as he pulled away from Rein's grip to resume his trip to speak with the nervous fellow.

When the baron's champion made a noise of protest, he faced him again, a stern expression hardening his features intended to stop him from speaking. It accomplished what he'd hoped.

"We are safe for now," he repeated before taking his leave.

As he moved toward Alwin Pelletoot, he forgot his surroundings and stood too straight. His forehead contacted a beam with a hollow thud, the impact shaking the thatched roof and quivering through the walls. He winced, rubbed his palm on the spot where a fresh welt sprang to life. No blood, so at least he wouldn't have another scar. Who'd notice if he did?

When he reached Alwin, the little man glanced up at him, then away, gripping his leather case tight against his chest like a ward capable of dispelling trolls. No such thing existed, and Vyle considered telling him, but he'd told Rein the truth—they were safe for now. Eventually, he expected a magik to detect his spell and find them.

"Is it true?" he asked, doing his best to keep his tone pleasant, always an arduous task given the voice he'd been born with. He could have used his glamor to alter it, but didn't see the point. "Does the mage Prisma live inside of you?"

The fellow's lips quivered as if he'd speak, then his shoulders rose and fell in a shrug. Vyle resisted the urge to frown and crouched before the man, getting down to his level.

"Look at me," he said as gently as possible. Alwin did, though he recognized his struggle to keep his gaze in one place. "I won't hurt you, so you can tell me the truth."

"I..." Alwin said, more a blurt than a word. "I don't know. I woke without memory of who I was. Or where. Or why. And..."

He trailed off, his sentence choked out like he fought to restrain a despairing cry. Vyle appraised him, recognized the desperation flickering in his eyes before prompting him to go on.

"And?"

"A voice speaks to me."

"Whose voice?"

"And eyes follow me. Two glowing red orbs appearing as embers pulled from a fire."

The troll wrenched himself first one way, then the other, making his observation of the hut's interior obvious. He saw Rein and Jai watching his interaction with their companion, but nothing else.

"Are they here now?"

Alwin shook his head, tilted his chin toward the case clutched to his chest.

"In the bag?"

He nodded.

Vyle reached out and laid his fingers on the satchel. "Give it to me. Let me see."

The fellow hesitated, and for a second, the troll thought he'd refuse. He prepared to curl his lip, showing his teeth in threat, but Alwin gave in and released his grasp, allowing him to take it.

Settling onto the dirt floor, he pulled the bag into his lap, lifted it, dangled it in front of his face, spun it to peer at each of its four sides, then raised it higher to examine the bottom. Nothing about it suggested that it be anything other than what it appeared. Age creased its leather at the corners, its handles worn smooth by the touch of many fingers. A few places were rubbed rough from use or discolored from exposure to water, but naught existed to suggest a pair of glowing red eyes lived within.

He set it on his legs and attempted to free the buckle, but his digits proved too large and the contraption's machinations too convoluted. Its operation eluded him, so he stopped, frowned, and tried again. The second unsuccessful attempt prompted an angry growl in his throat. He raised his eyes from the satchel to discover the man called Pelletoot cowering from the sound, so he gestured for the fellow to assist. Alwin reached forward, hesitant, placed a finger on the clasp and appeared to twist it, and the bag popped open as though it desired to do so.

Vyle harrumphed and yanked it wide, leaning over its opening to peer inside, and spied nothing but books. He pulled them out one by one, setting them on the floor beside him without bothering to browse any writing on the pages between the covers. During his time at the guildhall, nobody taught him how to read. What use was a troll with the ability to peruse ancient tomes? His kind were creatures of strength foremost, and then their glamors. People feared trolls for the power of the muscles in their arms and legs, not the one in their heads.

When the case sat empty, he held it close to his face to gaze into its depths, which proved no deeper than expected from a leather satchel of its ilk. He turned it upside down and gave it a brisk shake. A puff of dust spilled forth, but nothing else. He raised his head to peer at the fellow, but Alwin glanced away.

"What are you doing?" Rein asked.

Vyle clambered to his feet, forgetting once again about the lack of clearance and bumping his noggin on an overhead beam. He sighed, closed his eyes for a second, then bent to retrieve the books from the floor.

"Nothing," he said as he returned the tomes to their place in the satchel. "It's time we got moving again."

When he finished stowing the volumes, he offered the bag to Alwin, unconvinced the fellow was anything more than a scared man seeking refuge amongst those more capable of defending themselves in a dire situation than him.

Nevertheless, he had the unicorn's horn.

Besides the troll, they'd all been to the decrepit warehouse previously—Alwin more than any of them. He hated the place. He'd been here the first time he'd seen the crimson orbs and the voice determined to haunt and taunt him spoke to him. Whatever had wrested him from his life of drunkenness into this travesty occurred here.

Nothing positive came of visiting this godforsaken warehouse, and he expected this one to finish with no greater success than the others.

"Let's grab our things and get out of here," Rein said as he hurried down the hall toward the large, mostly empty storeroom at its end.

Alwin followed, hesitant but carried along with his companions, hurrying to join the baron's champion. As he inched down the hallway, he glanced sideways at the room where his journey as Mr. Pelletoot began. Then, he'd been a drunkard called Waul who'd imbibed too much ale and slumbered in the wrong place. He wondered if he wouldn't have been better off drinking more and dying with his throat full of his own vomit choking him.

Or perhaps that's precisely what happened and this the result.

"Don't be foolish. You may not remember everything, but you know the truth."

He diverted his gaze from the side rooms and stared ahead along the hallway, hoping to avoid seeing the glowing embers often accompanying the strange voice in his head. No matter what, he couldn't escape the sullen words spoken nobody else heard, but he'd rather not confront the red orbs.

He passed through the doorway into the storeroom, joining the others. Rein and Jai went to their hiding spots, leaving the troll to watch as they shifted aside the detritus of the warehouse's previous life to retrieve their weapons and armor. As the knights each gripped the scabbards of their swords, their expressions lightened. Relief, familiarity. They buckled their weapon belts around their waists and then turned to him.

Rein's brow rose. "Well?"

The weight of their impatience froze him, his inaction increasing their restlessness.

"The horn," the voice prompted. *"If we have any chance to correct things, it lies with the horn."*

Alwin blinked and shook his head, extracting himself from the inexplicable languor overtaking him. He crossed the dirt floor with purpose—both of retrieving the horn and keeping the impatience of his companions from overwhelming him. When he reached the far corner, he set aside the tome he clutched against his chest and searched in the darkness until he found the bundle of moldy straw he'd used to conceal his treasure. As he gripped it, readying to move it, panic blossomed in his gut at the surety of finding it gone.

He imagined one of the dark fae they'd encountered in the streets appearing out of nowhere to claim it. Or dozens of rats controlled from a distance by some Unnamed dragging it from the warehouse to bring to their master. He hesitated, fingers gripping the wilted straw. Surely if either happened, the thief wouldn't have replaced the bundle so precisely.

Would they?

He sucked a breath between his teeth, preparing himself for the disappointment he'd find beneath and the inevitable wrath of the baron's champion for not concealing such a precious item more thoroughly.

With nothing else to do but reveal his foolishness, he lifted the sheaf. A rain of hard, brown vermin droppings spilled from between the stalks and pattered against the floor. Under it lay the horn, as he'd left it, its whiteness glowing dully in the darkness.

A relieved sigh escaped his lips as he set the bundled straw aside and reached forward to wrap his fingers around the twisted ivory. The feel of its cool and smooth-but-not-smooth surface tingled against his flesh.

He lifted it and stood, holding the length of bone out in front of him parallel to the floor, as though offering a magnificent gift. The others lingered somewhere behind him, but right then, they may have not existed. For an instant, the world comprised him and the horn, everything else melting into darkness. He stared at the twist running along it from one end to the other, his eyes tracing its curve.

Until an impossible gust of wind ruffled his hair.

He raised his head, thinking to face the others and ask them if they'd felt it, too, until it happened again. This time, it flipped open the cover of the volume lying on the floor near his feet. It banged it against the dirt floor and fanned the pages.

The book whispered to him.

Alwin tilted his ear toward it, listening to the sound of the breeze flipping the sheets of paper. No more than a whisper, yet a suggestion formed in his mind. He glanced at the tome, nodded, then returned his gaze to the horn. Its restrained glow increased to his eyes, as though the item agreed with the proposition.

167

He spun around and strode to the center of the room, aware of the shapes of his companions awaiting him. The ivory pulsed in his grip, distracting him and keeping him from meeting their gazes.

"What is he doing?" one of them said.

"Pelletoot." The voice belonged to Rein Shriken. "We have to go."

He registered the words, but they meant nothing to him. Voices spoke in the dark storeroom—to him, to each other; he neither knew nor cared. His feet carried him to the middle of the room, equal distances from each wall, the troll backing away to create space for him, and he stopped. His hands worked of their own accord, spinning the horn until he'd directed the tip toward the dirt floor. He raised it, then brought it down, plunging the point into the floor.

Alwin's body tensed, his spine going rigid as his head tilted. Despite staring at the dark ceiling, a sensation overtook him. Movement. The room vanished, and the darkness rushed past; the musty odors of the storeroom disappeared, replaced by earthy scents, moist and tepid. His stomach lurched and his hands shook. He became vaguely aware of his companions gathering around him, their desperate and concerned words gibberish to his ears.

Instead, the earth spoke to him. Dirt and roots and insects whispered and chittered, directed him and carried him forward. Distance passed without his body moving, a deliberateness to it. He saw nothing as his essence rushed along but smears of brown and black, occasional unidentifiable flashes of color.

Waves of nausea clutched him and he wished for this strangeness to end. Even if it stranded him somewhere from which he'd never return, he'd be thankful for it.

As if hearing his wishes, the force carrying him slowed. The queasiness eased, panic replacing it as he realized his preference for being abandoned may be about to come true. His breath shortened, his limbs trembled.

A figure appeared before him. At first distant and indistinct but, as he drew closer, it took recognizable shape.

In the middle of a deserted storeroom surrounded by his companions, Alwin Pelletoot's eyes widened and his lips parted. A single word spilled from his tongue.

"Llyris."

She thought she remained deep beneath the earth, though where in the world, she couldn't guess.

The movement ceased and Llyris felt suspended, like floating atop a pool. She sensed creatures surrounding her, large and small, moving unseen through dirt and silt. Each tiny shift pressed against her, manipulating her skin until she saw everything around her without the benefit of her eyes.

A mass of insects drew together—beetles, termites, ants, and many-legged things for which she recalled no names. They gathered into a writhing heap, crawling over each other as they shifted dirt aside, formed a shape.

Llyris remembered the way the lake's inhabitants swirled into scenes at the behest of Shiera, and the insects' similar behavior gave her cause for alarm. If she'd possessed the ability to peek over her shoulder to check if the woman stood behind her, she'd have done it. She couldn't, so she didn't.

The tiny creatures coalesced into a shape, a single silhouette. As they continued arranging themselves, their creation took a distinct form, its facial features becoming clearer.

"Llyris."

Her name spoken by the tongue of Viden Misk, the voice she expected from the figure before her.

"What are you doing here?" she said. "Where are we?"

The insects crawled and scrambled to shake the figure's head as smoothly as if the real person stood before her. An astounding feat at any other time.

"It doesn't matter. The curse is lifted; the Unnamed are free. Everywhere."

"We've spent the last weeks at a village populated by magiks, so we suspected as much."

"Yes," he said, his expression turning grave. "I forgot you ended up there and met Shiera. I'm so sorry about Flayre."

The polite thing was to thank him, but the grief-filled knot clogging her throat prevented her, so she nodded. As she did, she

169

wondered if Misk saw the real her or if a collection of insects portrayed her, too.

"The world has fallen into disarray. Humans are being slaughtered by the dozens as Shiera and her followers wreak their revenge."

The handler gasped. The villagers knew about the fall of the curse, now they wanted to leave the place they'd spent their lives. If they desired blood, they could have taken it from her and her companions.

Or perhaps they needed them to get home first.

"I'm trying to find the dragons, to ask for their help."

The insect face went slack as the replica of Viden Misk stared at her, eyes wide and mouth dropped open. Seconds passed before he spoke again, this time in a whisper.

"The dragons?"

Llyris nodded. "Dragon, at least. He lives inside the mountain, but he likely won't see us."

"So close," he said, appearing to speak to himself, not her. "If I'd known, I'd have constructed the village elsewhere." He shook his head. "Prisma would have."

"Amnayel Prisma built the village?"

"As a prison, somewhere to keep malcontents and experiments gone wrong. A place to sequester the sick to avoid plagues decimating the humans. Her proximity to the dragon's magic must have kept her alive so long. With the book and the stave in her possession, she needs no outside assistance."

A frown tightened the handler's features, and she thought she felt an insect crawl across her face. Sitting cross-legged in a glen with her eyes closed and her companions watching, she raised a hand to brush it off. She became aware of someone far off calling her.

"You." She ignored a tug threatening to pull her away. "You are responsible for everything."

"Prisma," he said, as though expecting speaking the name to serve as a ward of defense.

"You are Prisma," Llyris snapped. "You have always been Prisma."

The visage altered, the insects forming it moving to shift the size of the nose, the set of the eyes. The first they created after Misk, she recognized. Humans had immortalized him in stone and with paint. The paintings of the so-called great mage hung in halls, his likeness in statues sat beside doors the land over. Before she said anything, it changed again and again, cycling through dozens of unrecognizable faces until Viden Misk returned, then it shifted into one more.

This one she didn't recognize, either. A fellow younger than the others, disheveled, his expression marked by surprise and fear and a sense of incongruence. His eyes darted before settling on the handler.

"I'm not." He spoke with a timbre different from the old man. "He's in here. So many in here. A thousand years' worth of souls. It's not my fault."

The anger building in Llyris eased but remained. She didn't know the disheveled fellow standing before her, but her heart ached for him. Someone stole his life, and she understood the impact; she'd never lived a life fully her own.

Like the Unnamed.

"What do I do?"

The face morphed into Viden Misk, the voice changing along with it. "Exactly what you are doing. Bring the dragon."

Her indignation rekindled at seeing him again. While he didn't contribute to the sins of Amnayel Prisma, he'd been the source of her woes, and those of her companions. Lives were scarified because of him, and he'd stolen the body of the man she'd just seen.

"And if it won't come?"

"He has to, Llyris. Without his power, all is lost."

She opened her mouth to speak again but, before any words emerged, the insects fled, dispersing into the depths of the soil, out of her sight. Her awareness stared at the vacated dirt, attempting to make sense of the impossible. What drew her here? How had she traveled? Who was responsible?

As she fretted over the questions whirling through her mind, a jerk of movement whisked her away and a journey which had taken time she couldn't estimate ended in a flash.

She opened her eyes to discover her companions standing before her, each in a pose of either annoyed impatience, in Cirril Feron's case, or concern. Except the ogres; they stood sentry behind the others, faced toward the jangala at their backs. Llyris blinked twice and inhaled a gritty breath tasting of dirt before Tesfira noticed her return.

"You're back," she exclaimed, rushing forward to fall to her knees beside her friend.

To nobody's surprise, Hinter followed her while the merchant's man remained in place, scowling.

"What happened to you?" he demanded, though his angry tone held a note of disbelief. He tilted his chin toward the two young women gathered around her. "These ones worried you wouldn't come out of your trance."

"Where did you go?" Tesfira asked, the gentleness of her words a counterbalance to Cirril Feron's.

As Llyris intended to answer, she found her mouth devoid of saliva and in desperate need of lubrication. She glanced from the acolyte to Hinter, pointed at the thief's waterskin. She needed no more prompting as she unhooked it from her belt, removed the cork, and handed it to the handler.

Cool water flowed across her tongue and down her throat, the feel of it equal parts pain and relief. She downed two mouthfuls before wiping her lips on the sleeve of her shirt and returning the skin to Hinter.

"I saw Viden Misk," she said when her voice returned.

"Misk?" The merchant's man sneered and paced three steps closer. "Hopefully you sent him to his grave."

"Viden Misk is dead. The mage has taken a new body, but it seems every soul he collects stays with him, no matter who he inhabits."

"Sacrilege," Tesfira whispered. "Those souls belong to God."

She looked away from Llyris and toward the mountain. Trees blocked her view, but the handler understood the gesture. The thief laid her hand on her friend's shoulder intending to offer the type of support and condolence nobody could supply.

"What did he say?" Hinter asked with a thief's suspicion.

Llyris glanced from her human companions to the ogre twins, her gaze lingering on their backs. Did they know the events happening in the rest of the world? They understood the end of the curse, but what if they didn't realize other Unnamed engaged in active rebellion and a search for retribution?

"Shiera has set the land alight," she said, choosing to be less specific until she had a better sense of the magiks accompanying them. "He says the dragon is needed. We're to return with him."

The laugh came an instant after she finished speaking, the sound emanating from one ogre, its deep grumble leaving no doubt about its source, though she knew not which twin.

"Bring the dragon?" one of them said over his shoulder. Without seeing their faces, discerning one from the other was impossible. "You'll be the luckiest humans in the world if you lay eyes on a loose scale."

The ogre's tone prodded Llyris. She climbed to her feet, Tesfira giving her support with a hand on her elbow, though she didn't need assistance. The handler set her jaw, her hands curled into fists.

"Then we should have little worry," she said, firm and resolute. "Because I am not human. I am shadow-scarred."

CHAPTER 14

— • —

W HEN THE SILVER-HAIRED WOMAN finished speaking—less a
speech and more a long string of threats and cruel promis-
es—the Unnamed who'd ushered the city's populace to gather encouraged them to leave. The proletariat did as instructed, exiting
the baron's compound with all the grace and organization of water
squeezing through a tiny hole in the bottom of a large pail.

Ilkari grabbed each twin by a shoulder and pulled them away
from the crowd. They looked at him, sharing the same shocked
and fearful expression as most everyone filing out of the courtyard
after her tirade.

"They mean to enslave us." Nevan's voice quaked.

Not a revelation. The squire had assumed when he discovered
the curse had been lifted humans were destined for a rough ride.

"You expected different?" he said as he surveyed the crowd.

He knew not whom he hoped to recognize amongst the sea of
faces, because he didn't know who'd survived. The baron was a
tree and Rein trapped in a magical dungeon, more likely dead; he
knew nothing of the fates of Llyris and the rest of his companions.
He held no expectation of them reversing what had happened,
anyway.

It was Viden Misk for whom he searched without realizing it
until then. But he knew less of the old man's fortunes than anyone
else. Asked to guess, he'd have said Carpera's treacherous coun-
selor caused this upheaval.

If so, why wasn't he here taking credit for it? Misk didn't strike
him as the kind of man to let others revel in his glory.

"What do we do?" Naeve yanked on his sleeve to usurp his
attention.

The squire waved a hand at him and continued his appraisal of the crowd. Perhaps he'd find the troll named Vyle who'd deserted them without explanation, though he wasn't sure finding him was the best outcome. There must be a reason for his abandonment, and he assumed it concerned him being an Unnamed among humans. Most likely he left to rejoin his kind, giving even odds, the next time Ilkari laid eyes on him, he'd be policing a mob or mounting heads on spikes rather than keeping them from harm.

The twins crowded close to him, doing their best to avoid being bumped by members of the nervous and frightened gathering as they shuffled to leave, unsure what their lives held in store. If they continued.

"Ilkari—"

He didn't bother to figure out which twin spoke his name before he waved his hand to silence him again. A disruption in the sea of citizens grabbed his attention, the head of a man taller than anyone else around him bouncing toward them, eyes locked on the squire. Ilkari squinted to get a better glimpse, his heart leaping when he first thought it the troll. He quickly realized the fellow approaching wasn't as tall, or his face as gnarled and scarred. The thick hair covering his cheeks left little of his visage visible.

"Shit," he whispered as he recognized him as the same one who'd stopped them on their way into the courtyard.

His hand fell to his hip, searching for a sword it wouldn't find. During their trip through the countryside, he'd searched farm-houses for a weapon to take as his own, but those responsible for killing the inhabitants had proved diligent at removing any for a wanderer to liberate. He cursed again.

The fellow halted five paces away, the flow of pedestrians amending its course to give him a wide berth and avoid passing through the space between them. He stared at the squire, the bits of his face not hidden beneath thick beard hard as stone, and Ilkari wondered if the man ever appeared anything but angry.

"I don't know where your troll is," he said after a minute of bearing the weight of his antagonist's attention.

"I doubt that's true," he rumbled, "but it's not why I'm here. The lady sent me to retrieve you."

A quiver of dread found its way along Ilkari's spine; he suppressed it, stretching to peer past the hairy fellow at the place recently occupied by the silver-haired woman. It stood empty,

175

the face of the tree shaped like Baron Sylleth staring out across the courtyard at his subjects, features locked in a fearful and anguished expression.

"If we say no?"

"Did I make it sound as if you have a choice?"

He bared teeth yellower and sharper than they should have been. Animal fangs in a human mouth. Nevan and Naeve pressed close behind him, whispered to each other, but he only caught a single word of what they said.

Shifter.

Though he didn't resemble the loups-garou he'd watched Rein vanquish—taller, thicker, older—the thought fell in line with the thick hair and significant incisors. If this fellow became a wolf, it would be the biggest one anyone had ever seen.

"What does she want?"

A growl escaped between the yellow teeth, deep and rumbling. He'd heard a similar sound before, once when he and Rein had accompanied the baron when he hunted bear.

"I don't care why. The only question in need of answering is whether you walk under your own power or I drag you."

The squire sighed, glanced over his shoulder at the two lads pressed behind him before returning his attention to the woman's messenger. Their eyes locked, the fellow's expression daring him to test him again. He decided not to.

"Thanks for the generous offer, but we'll walk." He took one step forward, then stopped. "Where will we find her?"

The hairy fellow jerked a thumb over his shoulder toward the wooden baron.

"In the maze."

Ilkari didn't wait for him to say more before striking out. The twins followed without protest, though he felt their reticence. As soon as they'd passed the messenger, he fell in behind them.

"And don't try anything," he said, the deep growl underlying his words. "Or I'll tear your heads from your necks."

When Alwin Pelletoot released his grip on the ivory horn, his body slumped to the ground. Vyle got his fingers under the fellow's head to keep it from bouncing against the dirt floor—he understood how much it hurt to bump your noggin more than most.

"What's happened?" Rein asked, hand on the hilt of his newly donned sword to steady it. "Is he all right?"

"To answer your second query first, yes, he'll be fine. The horn borrowed some of his energy, but it will return." The troll rested Pelletoot's head on the floor and raised his gaze to peer at the ivory. "Regarding your initial question, the unicorn's mantle yet holds magic. It used him."

"For what?" Jai asked, stepping up beside his forgotten friend.

"To find out, we'll have to wait until he recovers."

Vyle shuffled forward, moving closer to the bone shaft protruding from the dirt. He didn't think he'd ever seen anything quite so beautiful and extraordinary in all his life, except for maybe Zalie. The thought gave him pause—how odd to compare a human child to a stolen piece of the most magical of beings. But he'd sensed magic about the little girl, at least to him. If he'd not met her—if she hadn't recognized the real him despite his hooked nose and scars—and if the guild wasn't responsible for her death, would he still be here aiding the humans?

He shook the thought from his mind and reached out toward the length of ivory protruding from the ground, its white swirl tempting him. Before his sausage fingers touched it, he hesitated. A man lay unconscious on the floor after touching it. How much magic survived inside this piece of bone after so many centuries? It didn't seem possible.

After a deep inhalation, he gripped it, expecting to feel some shock of power or hear the clop of a unicorn's hooves, but he experienced neither. His skin touched cold, hard ivory, its surface ridged and pitted despite its smooth appearance. He grunted, braced it, and wrenched it upward to jerk it from the ground.

It didn't move.

Vyle raised an eyebrow and gathered a sliver of his power, sending it to his arm. The second attempt achieved no further success than the first. A frown crossed his face, and he concentrated more of his magic. His muscles swelled, veins wound twisting paths beneath his skin, the blood racing through them making them pulse with the beat of his heart. He gritted his teeth, reset his grip, and yanked upward a third time.

The horn remained.

"Blast." He released his hold and stepped away. He wiped unfamiliar beads of sweat caused by effort from his forehead.

"What is it?" Jai looked up from tending their fallen companion, who hadn't rejoined the land of the conscious.

"It won't come out."

"It has a habit of this," Rein said.

"But we'll have to leave it behind."

The baron's champion shook his head. "Don't worry. It will sort itself out."

His strange choice of words deepened the troll's frown but, unable to see any point in continuing, he abandoned the conversation. If the horn of the powerful magical creature needed to stay put, why should he argue?

He turned away from the mythical object and strode across the chamber, amending his course to arrive at an uncluttered spot. His heel ground in the dirt as he spun around, leaned his spine against the wooden wall, and let himself ease down until his rump touched the floor. From this vantage point, he watched Jai and Rein tend to the unconscious Alwin Pelletoot and wondered why he felt such a connection to them.

But it wasn't just these men. It began with Ilkari and the twins. Leaving them to die on the minotaur's horns would have proved the easier choice, but for the sense of being drawn to them. When he'd happened upon the man-beast threatening their lives, the possibility of not aiding them hadn't occurred to him. He'd dismissed it as a guilty response to deserting Breda but, the more time he spent with them, the more he experienced the drive to help—and protect—them.

The last thought made him chew his bottom lip. While Rein, Jai, and Alwin were safe here with him—if not conscious, in Pelletoot's case—he'd abandoned Ilkari, Nevan, and Naeve to fend for themselves. He regretted doing so but the late-night visit from the man once known as Hispid had convinced him others likely to come and figure out his secret. So he left.

Vyle filled his lungs and huffed a sigh, the air fluttering his lips, a sensation he normally enjoyed. He closed his mouth and finished exhaling through his nose.

Jai moved from where he stood, choosing to kneel beside their fallen comrade across from Rein. Their eyes met and held, then the knight redirected his attention to Alwin; the baron's champion continued gazing at his friend.

Another unexpected trait about trolls people found surprising? Intuitiveness. Vyle's heart squeezed at the wave of anguish emanating from Rein, though he didn't understand what caused it. Surely not Pelletoot's lack of consciousness; the sensation hadn't presented until he looked at Jai, therefore it must involve his friend. He didn't ask—the instinct of curiosity belonged to more feline-leaning creatures than himself.

A minute passed. The knight busied himself with ensuring their unconscious companion rested in a state of comfort while Rein watched. Vyle glanced from the trio to the horn poking stubbornly from the floor, its slight angle chiding him, daring him to attempt its removal a second time. He shifted but remained in his place—he need prove nothing.

Alwin Pelletoot stirred. The troll stood, careful not to bump his head on any low-hanging ceiling beams, and joined the men as his eyelids fluttered and opened. A quiet moan escaped the prone man's lips.

"Are you all right?" Rein asked, leaning forward and taking the lead in the manner of someone used to doing so. "Do you remember where you are?"

Alwin blinked three times and glanced between the concerned faces peering at him from above. When his attention came to rest on the troll and he didn't react with surprise or disgust, Vyle realized his memory of them to be intact.

"Warehouse," he said, voice ragged. His eyes darted toward the unicorn's horn he'd jammed into the floor and he lowered his head. "But I wasn't here."

"Where?" The baron's champion leaned in, rested his hand on the fellow's upper arm. "Your body remained here. Where did you go?"

Alwin swallowed, the lump in his throat rising and falling as the saliva clicked along his parched gullet. His eyes closed long enough for Vyle to sidle closer to see if he'd lost consciousness again. They popped open with the suddenness of a person who'd recalled things forgotten.

"I don't know, but I saw Llyris. Talked to her."

179

"You spoke to the handler?" Rein squeezed his biceps; when Alwin flinched, he released the pressure. "How is it possible? Where is she?"

"She is alive, and the others, too."

"Good news," Jai said with a nod.

The baron's champion glanced at his friend and another wave of wistfulness wafted from him to the troll. Vyle shifted from foot to foot, uncomfortable with being privy to the pain he felt. He focused on Alwin instead, hoping to keep himself from shedding tears.

"You spoke to this handler," he said. "She is definitely alive, not slain by her Unnamed?"

Three sets of eyes fell upon him. Jai raised an eyebrow; Rein repositioned the hand resting on Alwin's arm to the hilt of his sword. This last action made him realize what he'd suggested.

"When the curse lifted, many magiks took revenge on those who'd oppressed and controlled them their entire lives. Not me. I wasn't with Breda when it happened. I didn't kill her."

Despite the truth to his statement, a flash of guilt jilted the troll. The memory of his handler lying on the ground, incapacitated and surrounded by fire, filled his mind. He hadn't killed her, but neither had he saved her. After unpinning her, he'd left her to fend for herself. Perhaps she'd survived, but he couldn't imagine how.

"But you would have?" Jai asked.

Vyle shook his head. "They raised me with the law forbidding us from harming humans."

They continued staring at him in silence, but he guessed their thoughts: with the curse lifted, the laws no longer held sway over him or any other magik. If he wanted to, he could tear them all limb from limb and eat their hearts without repercussion. He harbored no desire to, but they didn't know his mind. They'd always look upon him with suspicion and fear.

Some things never change.

"Her Unnamed is gone," Alwin said, breaking the tension. "Stolen from her, then used beyond its capacity."

"I saw it," Rein whispered. "The woman employed Flayre to travel us here. The Unnamed appeared a withered shadow of herself. It surprised me to find out Llyris let her go."

"I saw it, too," Alwin added. "I didn't know what it was. Looked like naught but a burnt chunk of wood."

Vyle sighed. Losing any life warranted grief. Though he'd known none of the travelers, he'd heard about them—creatures of exceptional intellect and emotional capacity despite their inability to interact with those around them. Others said they created a far greater bond with their handlers than any other magiks did with theirs. His heart squeezed again, this time for the woman they called Llyris.

"What did she say?" he asked, putting effort to keep his voice from cracking. "Why did she visit you?"

Alwin scuffled himself up to his elbows, then struggled to sit. Jai caught him under the armpit to assist him and he found his feet, swaying enough the knight didn't let go. Once he'd steadied himself, he pushed Jai's hand away and tottered across the floor toward the unicorn's horn. Upon reaching it, he grasped it, using it to support himself. His knuckles whitened with the forcefulness of his grip.

Seconds passed, and they all watched, waited, every one of them expecting something to occur, including Alwin Pelletoot. Vyle saw the anticipation in his expression dissipate as time ticked by. When he gave in to the realization nothing would happen, he twisted his wrist, rotating the horn a half-turn as he wrenched it from the floor. Easy. The troll frowned, raised an eyebrow.

Alwin Pelletoot kept many more secrets than they realized.

The scruffy fellow pivoted, the length of ivory in hand like a stick meant to aid him in walking. He propped himself against it, stared at his companions with a grim and stony expression.

"They are questing to find the dragons," he said. "She means to undo what has been done."

"Impossible." Rein stood. "A thousand years have passed. They don't exist anymore."

"They do." Vyle knew little about the history of humans and Un-named, but these details every magik had learned. "Dragons have always been and will always be. They don't require the attention or belief of men."

They fell into silence again, and the troll sensed the two knights struggling with whether to believe them or not. Given their circumstances and the state of the world, they had no choice.

"How long?" Rein asked.

181

Alwin shrugged and shook his head. "She doesn't know, or if they'll permit an audience. Your handler is worried she won't accomplish her task."

Hand resting on the pommel of his sword, Rein's fingers drummed against the hilt. Vyle took it as a gesture of thought, or perhaps his own concern.

"Regardless, we need to be prepared. Do you agree, Jai?"

For an instant, the knight appeared surprised at the baron's champion asking his opinion, but he recovered quickly.

"Aye. We must spread the word, ensure every hand capable of gripping a weapon is ready when needed."

Rein nodded. "First, we find Ilkari."

The two knights agreed, and what their companions thought of their plan meant nothing. Vyle and Alwin followed them as they strode out of the room with purposeful steps. The man using the unicorn's horn did so with apparent trepidation. Any semblance of confidence he'd shown in the wake of his experience with the magical creature's power was gone, its last remnants disappeared like dust borne upon a stiff wind.

The troll pressed his lips together and his brow creased as he brought up the rear. He realized Alwin's dread grew from his fear for his own life, a concern Vyle didn't share. Trolls were extremely difficult to kill to begin with, but his kind also believed their lives were but one step in a much longer journey. He didn't know what came next for him, but it didn't end.

His vexation sprouted not from worry about himself, but the knowledge more would suffer and die.

Many more.

CHAPTER 15

— · —

F OR DAYS, EVERYTHING FOLLOWED them.

Birds flocked overhead, passing them by, then wheeling en masse to fly by again. Animals kept pace, most of them hidden by green foliage, their presence undetectable except for the occasional stirring of leaves or snap of a branch. Other creatures didn't bother attempting to hide as they swung from branch to branch above them, some high in the forest canopy, others much closer. Amongst them, Hinter spied the strange black and white creature with which Llyris had appeared to communicate, with its long tail and wispy coat.

And the insects.

Armies of ants marched along with them, hurrying to keep pace but inevitably falling behind, their place taken by what the thief assumed another colony. Flies and stinging bugs swarmed around them, never coming close enough they needed to shoo them away, though the sound of them provoked the response more than once. All those creatures, tiny to large, seemed meant to not only accompany them, but guide them. They steered them, kept them on a route toward the mountain jutting skyward ahead of them.

Over three days, they closed the distance with the help of gnats and birds, monkeys and cats, until they stood at the base staring up its craggy face, the top concealed in a swirl of mist.

They spent more than an hour searching, hoping to find a path wending its way around jagged boulders and between trees bent by the wind, but to no avail. If they were to progress any farther, it meant climbing.

Hinter surveyed the sharp slope before them, her practiced eyes locating hand- and footholds. She deemed it a moderate climb, one possible for her and Cirril with little difficulty, and perhaps the ogre twins, too. She doubted Llyris and Tesfira capable of navigating their way to whatever lay above, though she didn't want to speak her misgiving aloud. Thankfully, the merchant's man relieved her of the burden, as he so often did.

"Well, this is it then." He slouched onto the nearest rock of a size to permit sitting. His tone held equal measures of anger, disappointment, and relief. "This is where the foolishness ends."

"No," Tesfira said as she stared up the mountainside, her mouth open in awe. "He's up there."

"Doesn't matter if we can't find a path."

"We don't need one." The former cleric's student withdrew from her worship of the peak and redirected her attention to another member of their party. "Llyris?"

The handler flinched as though startled by the sound of her name, glanced sideways at her companion but refused to meet her gaze.

"I..." she said, then paused like she needed to collect her thoughts, figure out what to say. A few seconds went by, a gust of wind stirred her hair. "I can't go any farther."

Tesfira moved closer, raised her hand as though she'd touch the handler's arm, but stopped herself. She glanced toward Hinter, offered her a smile, and the thief's own concern over their situation lifted a bit.

"What did they tell you?" the acolyte asked, her words quiet. "The creatures, Misk...what did they say?"

Llyris shook her head. "They showed me the way here, nothing more. None of them knew how to get beyond the epelweard's defenses."

"If anything resides within besides rock and dust," Cirril mumbled.

Neither woman commented, so Hinter took it upon herself. She strode past the ogres standing with their arms crossed, waiting to see what the silly humans wanted them to do next, and crouched beside the merchant's man.

"We've come this far," she said, keeping her words between the two of them as much as their proximity allowed. "Give them some time. If they can't figure anything out, we'll return to the village."

184

Cirril Feron shifted on his rocky stool to glance over his shoulder along the path they'd followed to arrive at the foot of the mountain, as if in doing so he saw the distant dwellings and all the trials and tribulations they'd encountered. He stared for a moment, then sighed and nodded.

"A bit more time won't hurt anything, I suppose. Dinner can't get any colder."

He turned his gaze to her and they both tilted their mouths in humorless smiles. She slapped him on his knee and stood, refocusing her attention on Llyris and Tesfira but remaining at his side. With the interruption complete, they returned to their conversation.

"Shiera took me inside the mountain," the acolyte said, her voice filled with the same wonder as her expression when she'd stared toward the misty mountaintop. "She did it the same way you did when you spoke with Misk."

"I don't know how it happened." Stress tightened Llyris' features and Hinter suspected her on the edge of tears. "The ground took me."

The acolyte nodded, and this time she rested her hand on the handler's arm. "Then let it take you again."

"I can't do it alone."

"We'll go with you."

"But how?"

Tesfira thought for a second before responding. "It can't be too different from traveling."

At the mention of her former function, grief became evident in the creases in her forehead, the tremble in her lips.

"I directed Flayre. She controlled the magic. If I could travel us myself, we wouldn't have walked so far."

"Would have been nice," Cirril said. Hinter slapped him on the shoulder.

"You sell yourself short, Llyris. You reversed course in the tunnel Shiera created. Isn't that impossible?"

"Apparently not."

"Do you know anyone else who has ever done it?"

The handler found a sudden interest in her boots, the toe of one which she used to kick a pebble. It skittered across the dusty ground and came to rest at the spot where the mountain slope began.

"No one," she said, the words barely audible.

"Then it can't hurt to try, can it? As Cirril mentioned, nobody is keeping a meal warm, anticipating our arrival."

Llyris raised her eyes toward the acolyte, who proffered a lopsided smile the handler didn't return. Instead, she nodded.

"All right."

She peered up the slope and Feron jumped to his feet beside Hinter, his unexpected action startling her into jumping away and reaching for her dagger. It required but an instant for her to realize he meant no harm to anyone.

"Wait," he said, voice raised. "What have we decided?"

"Llyris will take us inside the mountain the way she visited Viden Misk. How Shiera brought me here."

"You mean the way she hallucinated conversing with the old bastard? Doesn't sound like any way to get where we're going."

"Cirril," Hinter said, attempting to interrupt him. He'd have none of it.

"Besides, while in your trance, I could have strolled up beside you and pushed you over, or slit your throat. You couldn't have protected yourself. If what you propose is real, we'll all be sitting ducks to a stiff gust of wind, falling rocks, hungry animals. Anything."

"We will stay and guard you," Gartrek said, stepping forward. Hinter had learned to identify him from his twin by the faint scar over his right eye mostly hidden beneath his scraggly hair. "We can't pass any farther, anyway."

The merchant's man reacted in the manner she'd have expected.

"We're to trust you with our safety? Two Unnamed? Perhaps you've been awaiting this opportunity to dispose of three more humans and a handler?"

Gartrek's stony face hardened. "If we meant to kill you, we wouldn't have walked so far."

Cirril opened his mouth to offer further protest, but Hartrek stepped up beside his brother. Individually, the ogres were intimidating; together, they may as well have been a stone wall.

"We gain nothing by killing you," the second twin offered. "But if you live and you succeed, maybe we can return to the world, our lives."

"I don't trust them," Feron said, addressing his companions while staring at the Unnamed.

Hartrek made a sound either clearing his throat or a growl starting. His brother put his hand on his arm, stopping the noise before it revealed its true intent.

"Your choice is easy: figure out how to believe in us or hike to the village and live out your life tending a rice paddy." He paused, glaring at the merchant's man with such intensity Hinter wondered whether the ogre remembered the rest of them existed. "Which will it be, human?"

The thief didn't think the magical creature intended his words as a threat. Perhaps more like a warning. Either way, his statements made Cirril Feron stand a little straighter, puff his chest out, and curl his fingers around the hilt of his sword. He glared at the ogre as though his gaze were a weapon capable of boring holes in the beast. Half a minute crawled by before Hinter realized she held her breath; she released it, curious if the others were doing the same.

"Fine," Cirril grunted, released tension from his body, the action giving his companions permission to do the same. He turned his attention to the handler, who watched them with a fearful expression as she gripped the brooch securing her cloak in one hand. "Can you do it?"

Hinter suspected her shrug in response wasn't the answer he wanted, but she offered no more.

Llyris made them sit in a circle and join hands, a suggestion the merchant's man scoffed at. The thief thought it meant she didn't have any idea how to make this happen. The ogre twins stood at either side of them, backs to the mountainside as they surveyed the surrounding area for any sign of trouble.

"Close your eyes," the handler said.

"Really?" Cirril's doubt surprised none of them.

Before doing as Llyris asked, Hinter inhaled a deep breath, steeling herself for what may come next, whether it was some supernatural journey to meet a dragon, or finding themselves

187

seated in the dirt, watched over by a pair of ogres. To her right, Tesfira must have noticed her reticence and squeezed her hand. She faced her, saw her friend's comforting smile.

"It will be fine," she said and, though she looked at her, the thief suspected she meant the words for all of them, including Llyris. "You'll see."

Hinter did her best to return the expression; she thought her face failed her. Tesfira closed her eyes, and she continued watching her, marveling at both her beauty and her faith. How she'd been through so much and retained her belief in God and others was beyond her. Someone had betrayed the thief once and she'd lost trust in the world.

Until Tes.

She released her grip on both her friends' hands.

"Hinter," Llyris said.

"A moment."

She opened the pack sitting in her lap and dug to the bottom, unaware why she needed the pendant hidden away in the secret compartment, but it suddenly seemed of great importance. She fished it out and pulled the cord over her head, letting the talon dangle inside her shirt, its smooth surface pressing against her chest. With her goal accomplished, she grasped Tesfira's hand, then Llyris', surprised to find an item in the handler's palm not present before.

She looked at her, saw her eyes close, then glanced across the circle at Cirril Feron. He'd already followed instructions, so she snapped her eyelids shut, worried if she didn't and the handler did transport them, they'd leave her behind.

Seconds passed, a minute. Hinter counted them off in her head the way she'd marked the interval between sentries guarding a treasure she intended to steal. Two minutes. Three.

How long should they wait before they realized their plan was a failure?

Across from her, she heard Cirril stir, shifting his position. As if triggered by his movement, she noticed her own buttocks knotting with the pressure of the rough ground pressing against it. In her life, she'd spent innumerable hours hidden, unmoving, blending into her surroundings while she awaited one thing or another to happen. How much time did she spend waiting for the perfect opportunity, the exact timing to accomplish her goal? So much, she shouldn't require a shift of her seating to relieve a discomfort in her ass cheek after a few minutes, yet she did.

Hinter fought the urge, counting the passing seconds in her head to distract herself. Shy of four minutes, the need overwhelmed her.

She kept her eyes closed and her hands clasped with Tesfira's to her right and Llyris' on her left as she shifted, leaning toward the handler to relieve her discomfort. It disappeared as soon as she lifted her cheek. Satisfied, she settled into her original position, only to find the ground gone from beneath her.

And Hinter fell.

Though no wind rushed past her, she sensed the movement. Her brain commanded her eyelids to open; when they did, she saw nothing different from when closed. Darkness. Her mouth moved, and no sound emerged.

Panic flared in her chest, spreading through her body, tingling along her limbs. Her disquiet focused her, and she noticed her hands were empty. Her heart jumped.

Tesfira?

The name crystallized in her mind but lived nowhere else.

The falling sensation slowed and stopped. Hinter glanced around, perceiving nothing other than the darkness at first. An impenetrable night surrounded her, filling both her eyes and her ears, the complete silence broken by her own pulse whooshing in her head. The panic set a sour taste upon her tongue and she recognized if she didn't control it, fear threatened to overcome her.

She returned to counting seconds as they passed, though she felt they held no value wherever she was. She reached twenty when things shifted.

The sense of movement restored itself, this time pulling her forward, and with it came a presence. She wasn't sure how she knew it, but she understood Llyris to be with her. Darkness lifted, everything around her lightening to differing shades of gray, striations and layers marking one from another.

We are inside the mountain.

"Yes, we are," the handler's voice responded to her thought. "And do not worry. Tesfira and Cirril are with us."

At her words, Hinter sensed the others. She attempted to touch the acolyte, first with her hand, then her mind, but located her with neither. She could only trust her present, and safe.

They followed veins and cracks in the stone as though water seeping through. Their path twisted and turned, often doubling back on itself before finding an alternate way forward. If they'd been on foot, their journey would have sent even Hinter's finely tuned sense of direction spinning, but here, it didn't matter. Movement mattered. Progress.

The gurgle and rush of a river reached the thief's ears, though she knew not from where it came. Maybe from below, beside, or above, and she mused about whether the water flowed through the mountain itself, overtop, or around it. She considered turning her head, finding Tesfira to ask if she heard it, but it wasn't possible. She wasn't a body built of bones and muscle to house a brain filled with thoughts. That container sat at the base of a slope, holding her friends' hands as two ogres watched over them. Might as well have been a thousand miles distant.

The rush of water grew, then faded again, as though they passed it by. A rumble replaced it, low and ominous, emanating from deep in the earth. Small at first, but as it grew, Hinter sensed it shaking her consciousness. It started out a shiver, then expanded until she imagined it rattling her teeth and quivering her bones.

It's the mountain fighting us.

She concentrated her thoughts, forcing herself to feel Llyris' grip pulling her forward as her other hand held Tesfira's. Their pace slowed, the rock fighting their progress. The rumble became a roar, deafening if she'd had ears to hear it. The urge to cry out filled her, and she wondered if her mouth did what her mind desired. Did two ogre twins stare at her, curious what caused her to shout?

The moment she worried it would become unbearable, the sound ceased. Silence overtook them before they tumbled out of the stone into a vast cavern.

Despite her body sitting cross-legged some distance away, Hinter hit the ground hard. The impact jarred her shoulder, clicking her teeth and making her release her grip on both the hand leading her and the one following. The sudden pain she could handle, but losing track of Tes sent a flare of panic through her chest. She adjusted herself, rolled with the momentum, and came to her feet, right hand darting beneath her cloak to retrieve the dagger hidden within.

Except it wasn't there.

Her mind developed by years of quick thinking and adjusting on the fly ignored this oddity as it paid no attention to the pain in her shoulder. Her gaze flickered over the cavern, taking in her surroundings in broad strokes before finding her three companions.

Cirril Feron was already climbing to his feet, a frown tilting his mouth, as much pained grimace as dissatisfaction. Llyris and Tesfira sprawled on the stone floor nearby, the handler stirring while the fourth member of their group lay unmoving. Hinter rushed to her, falling to her knees at her side.

"Tes," she said, grabbing the young woman's shoulder.

She gave her a gentle shake, cautious not to disturb her too much lest she'd broken a bone in their fall. Cirril stepped up beside her, staring down at the proceedings, then Llyris joined them.

"Is she all right?" the handler asked.

"I..." Hinter began, then swallowed around the strange tightening in her throat. "I don't know."

She gave Tesfira's shoulder a firmer tug, using her other hand to cushion her as she rolled her onto her back. The onetime acolyte let out a sigh, her wide eyes staring at the cavern's ceiling somewhere overhead. The thief's heart jumped—she'd seen dead men stare in the same manner.

"Tesfira!"

A smile crept across the young woman's lips and her gaze shifted to meet her friend's.

"We're here." Her words carried on a breath filled with wonder. "Have you found him yet?"

"No." Worry clipped the word shorter than she intended. "Are you hurt? Can you move?"

Tes blinked, glanced at the others gathered around her. "It's wondrous, isn't it?"

"It appears to be a cave," Cirril said. "I've encountered a few of them before."

The young woman giggled and returned her attention to Hinter. "Help me up." She held out her hand.

Hinter stood, grabbed it but didn't pull. She worried her friend may have injured herself without realizing, so she gave her a solid base. With a deep breath to ready herself, she first sat, then drew her knees up and levered herself to her feet. As she did, she tilted her head, directing her eyes upward. The thief followed her gaze, peering up into darkness.

"It's beautiful," Tesfira said.

Where she found beauty in the inky black, Hinter didn't know, nor did she bother asking. Now they'd determined they were safe and unharmed, they needed to direct their attentions to remaining so.

"Where are we?" she asked, directing the question toward the handler. "Are we inside the mountain?"

"I think so," she replied.

"How did our bodies get here?" Cirril added. "And my sword?"

"They're not our bodies," Llyris said as she glanced around the chamber, responding despite her distraction. "They are manifestations so we can interact with our surroundings."

Hinter frowned. "Did you create them?"

The handler abandoned her survey of the cave to observe her, then her other companions, before shaking her head. "No. I didn't."

"Then who?" Cirril demanded.

A swirl of hot wind strong enough to lift dust from the cavern floor responded to his question. The thief covered her face with her forearm to prevent particles from battering her eyes. When the shifting air subsided, she lowered it, her attention drawn in the direction whence it came.

Guttering torchlight illuminated the walls, throwing light across a vast expanse appearing as though it may go on forever.

Despite the assurances of the troll, Rein's companions appeared no different to him than usual. He didn't know how the creature's glamor worked, but to him, he saw it accomplishing nothing.

"You're sure about this?" he asked for the third time.

"Of course," Vyle replied with no sign of annoyance at his doubt. "To others, you appear as Unnamed who should travel with someone like me. Trust me."

Rein sighed, faced Jai. When their eyes met, the knight shrugged in a gesture suggesting he saw no other choice. The baron's champion didn't, either. In the days since they'd left the warehouse, every hour the streets had become more dangerous. Patrols of magiks enforced the curfew with an iron hand, forcing them to spend too much time in hiding to hope to accomplish their goal. If they wanted to succeed, they had no alternative but to believe the troll.

And so Rein gave control over to the beast, despite every fiber of his being warning him against doing so. Never trust the enemy.

"What do I look like?" Alwin said, an excited note in his voice at being someone else concealing the fear it normally held.

Vyle pivoted toward the fellow and lifted an eyebrow. "A dwarf."

"A dwarf?" he repeated, disappointment replacing his previous enthusiasm.

"Oh, don't sound so unimpressed. Though short in stature and prettier only than trolls, dwarfs are strong, and experts in manipulating the earth. Formidable adversaries and faithful allies."

Pelletoot's expression shifted, a smile creeping onto his lips. "Will I have—?"

"No," Vyle replied before he finished his query. "My glamor changes your appearance but gives you none of their power."

Alwin nodded and Rein watched the man's cheeks go pink with embarrassment for asking a question with such an obvious answer. Their exchange made the baron's champion wonder what visage the Unnamed gave him, but he pushed the childish curiosity aside. Frustration replaced it, and concern at their inability to locate his squire.

"Enough," he snapped. "We have no time for games. Take us to where you left Ilkari."

The troll stared at him and Rein tensed, concerned this might be when the magik showed his true colors; he made no threatening move. Instead, he tilted his head forward in deference. "As you wish. Follow me."

Vyle led them out of the abandoned mercantile where they'd spent the last night, foraging what little foodstuff others hadn't already pilfered. Alwin exited after the beast, then Rein gestured for Jai to go before he brought up the rear.

They filed through the doorway, the door it was meant to frame missing, ripped from its hinges after the lifting of the curse. As

193

they made their way down the boulevard cluttered with garbage and excrement, the baron's champion noticed all the jambs empty. They'd removed the doors, leaving few places for humans to hide.

Anyone they saw as they followed Vyle cowered from them, hiding from the troll, the dwarf, and whatever their companion made himself and Jai resemble. Some peered at them from their open doorways, their bodies hidden behind walls, most of them disappearing when the baron's champion came close enough to making eye contact. Did they appear so unappealing? Or were the residents of his father's city so accustomed to abuse from the Unnamed, they expected it from any they spied?

He suspected the latter.

By the time they reached the one-room building where the troll had abandoned Ilkari, they'd scared multitudes of citizens into hiding while seeing no magiks. Rein knew the varied magical beasts patrolled the streets after dark, streetlights fed by their magic igniting as required, but perhaps they left humans to enjoy a modicum of freedom during the day.

"Empty," Jai said as they peered in.

Did they really expect to find them here? Rein had known his squire his entire life. He'd grown up with him, trained with him, learned from him. One person in the world meant more to the baron's champion than Ilkari. His gaze flickered to the knight, then away to the vacant space.

Of course he wasn't sitting here waiting for them. Inaction was no more in his nature than in Rein's.

"What now?" Pelletoot asked.

He gripped the unicorn's horn, leaning on it for support as if their journey had proved too arduous to endure. Seeing him in this pose—as though his own comfort outweighed the missing squire, or Jai's memory, or the mistreatment of humans—curled the lip of the baron's champion.

"We find him," he snapped. "Our plan has not changed."

"They could be anywhere, Rein," Jai interjected, the sound of his voice leeching some of his friend's anger away. "Where should we start?"

Hearing his friend speak his name and feeling his attention upon him dissipated the last of his disappointment in the man who called himself Alwin. Despite his desire to maintain it, he abandoned his precious eye contact with the knight and faced their troll companion, who remained outside the hut, peering in.

"Any idea where they went?"

Vyle held his gaze without speaking before leaning away from the doorway. He straightened, his face disappearing from the view of the baron's champion, so Rein moved to the door to watch the Unnamed.

The troll's nostrils flared, each of them as big as a man's nose when he expanded them. He tilted his head, turned it first one way, then the other. After a few seconds, he shuffled his feet, turning his body to his right.

"Faint, but I have them," he said. "I'd judge a couple of days have gone by, but they went in this direction."

He raised his arm to point and Rein stepped out into the street, Jai and Alwin Pelletoot following close behind him. A few citizens milled about in the distance but, compared to the normal hustle and bustle of the city's avenues at midday, it may as well have been empty. The flagstone road lined by doorless homes and shops led toward the towers of the baron's castle visible above the roof lines.

"Do you think...?" Jai said, leaving the end of the question dangling. They all knew what he meant.

"It is likely," Vyle replied. "But I cannot say whether they went themselves, or if someone took them."

Rein stared at the distant ramparts, his lips pressed into a thin line, his throat tight. Even if the woman and her Unnamed hadn't usurped his father's stronghold, he harbored little desire to return to the place where he'd been raised. As an adult, he'd moved his residence out of the castle and into the city, returning only when required. He hated it and everything it represented.

"No point wasting time."

The baron's champion set out down the avenue without waiting for his companions, his gait long and determined, his expression hard.

Today he'd burn the place to the ground.

The hirsute brute led them through the courtyard, shouldering aside humans who weren't smart enough to clear a path. Ilkari's gaze darted, searching for an escape, though he realized running was likely a fruitless plan. Not only did he doubt their ability to outrun their captor, but other Unnamed of all sizes and shapes filled the place. Despite this, his decades of training kept him alert to any possibility.

No matter how remote.

The twins pressed close behind him, whispering to each other in tones too quiet for him to hear, the fear in their voices unmistakable. He felt for them. So young, so inexperienced. Carpera had sent them on a simple mission and they ended up in the middle of a magical insurrection. With all his experience with battle, he struggled to maintain a brave face; he couldn't imagine how they must feel.

Every few paces, the hairy fellow peered over his shoulder at them to ensure they weren't lagging. One more reason not to attempt fleeing. The squire hoped for some opportunity to present itself once they reached their destination.

When the baron's labyrinth came into view, Ilkari was struck again by the change. How many times in his life had he walked past the hedge maze? Sufficient to no longer pause to appreciate the emerald green foliage or marvel at the precise shapes of the hedgerows.

No more.

Once verdant, dried brown leaves now drooped on brittle branches. Holes in the hedges allowed one to peer through between paths, an oversight Sylleth wouldn't have tolerated when challenging the foolhardy to solve his labyrinth. No colorful butterflies flitted amongst the foliage, no birds chirped from hidden nests.

A skeleton of a maze stood before them, its flesh shriveled, its bones showing.

"What happened to it?" Nevan asked.

"She did," Ilkari replied.

"No talking," their escort barked over his shoulder.

He led them toward the labyrinth's entrance, the space now guarded by a lonely hedge made of twisted brown vines. The squire stared at it, entranced by its shape. He'd never seen it before. As they neared, the coiled and twined branches took on a distinguishable aspect—legs, arms, a torso. A face.

Baron Sylleth's face. Frozen in a tortured expression, mouth open, eyes wide. Ants crawled over the peeling bark lips.

"By God," Naeve whispered.

The brutish Unnamed halted before crossing the maze's threshold and, distracted by the arborous nobleman, the squire walked into him. Nevan and Naeve did the same to him.

The hulking man jerked around and the three of them jumped backward. He didn't lash out or gnash his formidable teeth, instead fixing them with a glare suitable for giving a heart attack to lesser beasts.

"You first," he said, glowering at Ilkari.

The squire hesitated at the verge where lawn ended and labyrinth began. Over his decades serving the baron and his son, how many challengers had stepped over the brink in search of their fortune? Dozens, to be sure. No one ever returned.

The Unnamed laughed. "Oh, you'll likely never leave the maze, but not for the reasons you're thinking. Now move."

He gave him a push, and Ilkari stumbled into the labyrinth, heart hammering in his chest as his boot came to rest on the beaten path between the hedgerows. He'd often wondered what happened to the men who'd challenged the baron's puzzle. Did they get lost and wander the paths until succumbing to thirst and hunger? Did ravenous beasts live hidden behind veils of broad leaves, waiting for their quarry to take the wrong turn and walk into their clutches?

He'd hoped never to find out.

The brute ushered Nevan and Naeve in after him and then followed.

"Move."

"Which direction?"

"Don't matter. Just go. You'll get there."

Three choices lay before him: right, left, or straight ahead. Four, if you counted returning the way they'd come, but the Unnamed blocking the exit removed the fourth possibility from the list.

The twins stood beside him and he glanced from one to the other.

"What do you think, lads?" he said, attempting to keep his voice calm. With fear obvious on their faces, he wanted to do anything in his power to lend an air of normalcy to their dire situation.

Before either of them answered, the shifter shoved him, sending him stumbling down the path ahead of them.

"Get going," he urged again. "No more talking."

Ilkari caught his balance, wishing all the while for his sword to be hanging at his side instead of lying at the bottom of an underground river. He doubted he'd best the Unnamed in a fight, but he'd damn sure draw blood and leave the bastard with a souvenir to remember him by.

It should have been a relief when the hirsute fellow followed them into the maze, confirmation it no longer held the power it once possessed. Small consolation when it meant being accompanied by a brute capable of transforming into a murderous beast.

They walked for fifteen yards before coming to the next intersection. Ilkari paused, looked along each path before choosing the right. No particular reason for it—every direction appeared identical, as difficult to tell apart as the twins accompanying him. Delicate, brittle remnants of the once-vibrant maze clung to peeling branches, the papery leaves russet and intricately etched, ready to fall to dust at a touch or under a stiff breeze.

They walked in silence, even Nevan and Naeve thinking it the best choice to follow the Unnamed's growled command, unusual as it was for them to keep quiet. Ilkari had no siblings or offspring, so he didn't understand the depth of their connection. Never the chatty type himself.

A left. Two rights.

He attempted to track their direction of travel, but cloud cover obscured the sky, leaving him disoriented. Did it matter? Somewhere like this, all paths led to the same destination.

Death.

The space between the hedgerows curved, which they hadn't done to this point. Each path usually ran parallel or perpendicular to the others, sometimes coming to a dead end, other times a sharp corner or switchback, mostly arriving at an intersection offering two or three choices, but always straight.

Until now.

The road ahead bent at an angle, keeping Ilkari from seeing what lay beyond the curve. it remained thus until it opened into a wide space carpeted with vibrant grass, its color out of place after passing the dull earth tones leading them here.

The silver-haired woman awaited at the center of the clearing beside a tree little taller than her. At least, the squire thought it a tree. He recalled the baron, frozen in a wooden pose by the entrance to the labyrinth. This might be anything, or anyone.

She cradled a tome in one arm, held against her chest like a babe waiting to suckle. The fingers of her other hand gripped the shaft of a walking stick. Ilkari's heart jumped when he saw it.

The squire's jaw tightened, his teeth pressing together hard enough to cause him pain. He didn't stop. His hands curled into fists.

"Squire," she said. "Thank you for coming."

"You greet us as though we had a choice," he growled.

"There is always a choice. Yours was attend me or die, if I know Eddubu. Perhaps not the best either or, but a choice, nonetheless."

"What do you want, woman?"

The hairy Unnamed shoved Ilkari, sending him stumbling forward. "Keep a civil tongue in your head."

He recovered and glanced over his shoulder at the fellow. He'd retreated and placed a hand on each of the twins' necks, holding them to prevent them from following, the implicit threat of his touch easily recognizable.

"You smell of a man I took the stave from. Rein, I believe his name."

Ilkari's lips pressed into a thin line. He glared at the woman, wishing for the ability to injure her with his stare. The tree beside her shifted, not as though stirred by a breeze, but a limb moved to a different position.

"What have you done to him?"

"Done? Nothing. I made the mistake of allowing him to live, an error you are going to help me correct."

"I'll do no such thing."

"Hmm," she said, the sound denoting amusement. "Loyal to the end. How appropriate. I'm sure the same quality in him will be both your undoing."

"I won't do anything to aid you. If Rein Shriken lives, I hope he does so to a ripe old age."

"Doubtful. I need precious little of you but to stay where you are. Your champion will take care of the rest."

Ilkari raised an eyebrow. The tree rustled, drawing his attention, and he'd have sworn the pattern of bark on its trunk differed from before. It resembled a face, though not one he recognized, with hard eyes and a severe nose. He refocused on the silver-haired woman, thinking he must be mistaken.

"Why would I do such a thing?"

"I suppose you have little choice this time."

The creepers Ilkari hadn't noticed snaking their way around his calves tightened to the point of pain, causing him to cry out. When he recovered from the surprise, he reached down to insert his fingers between the vines and his legs, attempt to prise the things away from him and free himself. They cinched tighter, soliciting a grunt from him and ensuring no chance to work his fingertips beneath them.

Worse, they continued growing, winding up past his knees, binding his thighs. If they kept going, they'd encircle his rib cage and squeeze the life out of him the way the witch's python attempted to do.

"You may as well kill me now. Rein won't fall into your trap."

As he spoke, he wondered if he was alive and here, or if this was her ghoulish method of torturing him before letting the tree's pets crush him. If he lived, the baron's champion wouldn't waste time saving one man when so many required help.

"As much as I'd enjoy ending your life, you mean nothing to me." She moved closer to the tree, caressed its trunk. The bark shifted, like a face changing its expression. A slash mid-way along crinkled into a smile. "And, if you must know the truth, it's not even your baron's son who concerns me, but the street urchin accompanying him. I didn't expect him to be a problem. Another example of my mistake in extending mercy. No more."

"Yet you let me live."

"For now. You have a use to me." She raised a hand and gestured past Ilkari. "They do not."

Sudden concern flared in his chest and he pivoted, the coiled creepers holding him tight. The hairy Unnamed still held the twins by the scruffs of their necks, like a mother cat chastising her kittens. Their faces were blanched white, their wide eyes fixed on a spot the squire couldn't see. He twisted, his gaze passing over the woman and the tree adorned with smiles.

When he discovered what distracted Nevan and Naeve, he gasped.

The minotaur stood blocking the far path, its nostrils flared, eyelids narrowed, lips parted to reveal broad, flat teeth. It huffed a breath and pawed the ground with a hoof. One twin let out a squeak, and the beast launched itself forward as though waiting for this sign.

"No," Ilkari cried. He twisted the other direction, doing his best to face his companions. "Run!"

To his surprise, the hulking Unnamed released them, but they remained where he'd held them. It took but a second for him to realize creepers similar to the ones holding him also bound the twins.

"No," he shouted again, the word nearly drowned by the pounding of the beast's hooves on the ground.

An instant later, it came into his line of sight, chin lowered, each forceful step throwing up clods of turf. Naeve's voice returned, and he screamed as the brute slammed into his silent brother. The thing cocked its head before it made contact, ensuring both of its formidable horns found their target.

The impact lifted the unfortunate lad off the ground, snapping the vines holding him and sending a mixture of breath and blood spewing from his mouth. For a second, he folded around the minotaur, his top half bent over the thing, legs wrapped around it. The beast skidded to a halt, and Naeve's limbs flopped like those of a child's doll.

He hung limp on the creature's horns as it laughed.

"Make him stop," Ilkari yelled, twisting to face the woman.

She and the tree were gone.

Ragged breaths burned his lungs as he faced his companions in time to see the minotaur pull Naeve free and toss his slack body to the ground. Blood glistened in his brown fur, shone on the flesh of his wide nostrils. A pink tongue snaked out and licked it from his lips. It strode toward Nevan, savoring his fear as it approached. The lad screamed again.

"Please. Don't." Ilkari considered dropping to his knees to beg for the lad's life, but the creepers held him fast. Any attempt to kneel would leave him lying on the ground, his face in the grass. "Let him live. Take me instead."

The hairy Unnamed who'd brought them here laughed. "You heard the lady. You have use; they do not. You'll get your due once your champion shows up." He rubbed his palms together like a starving man preparing for a feast. "Everyone will get their due."

The minotaur stood in front of the shrieking guardsman. It set its hands on Nevan's ears, holding him as it lowered its head and placed the tip of one horn under his chin. With an upward jerk, the lad's screams turned to gurgles, and then he fell silent.

The horned beast yanked its weapon out of the lad without grace or care, the movement splitting his face in two. He released his grip on the poor fellow and he sank to the grass beside his brother, their blood pooling together in their final grotesque connection.

"You bastards," he spat, hoping if he pissed them off, they'd end his life and, in doing so, maybe he'd save Rein. "They didn't deserve that. You're nothing but monsters."

The minotaur ignored him as it cleaned the twins' lifeblood from his horns and face. It wiped it away with its hands, then licked its palms clean. While it did, the hairy Unnamed approached the squire, his expression stony and eyes blazing. Ilkari steeled himself for whatever blow, bite, or attack the brute used to end his life. He didn't halt until he stood nose to nose with him, stooping to lower himself to the human's level.

"You all deserve it after what you've done," he said, forcing the words between his clenched teeth. The next ones he punctuated with stiff jabs of his sausage-sized finger to the squire's chest. "Every. Last. One. Of. You."

He spun and walked away, the minotaur having already finished its version of bathing itself and taken its leave. The Unnamed stepped over the dead and bleeding twins, his boot squelching in the mud their deaths created. When he reached the nearest path out, he stopped and spoke to Ilkari over his shoulder without turning.

"Keep quiet, now," he said. "Wouldn't want you to spoil the surprise."

He left the clearing, disappearing between the hedgerows, and the squire's gaze fell to the gaping holes in Neave's chest, Nevan's face ripped in two.

He wondered how long before he and Rein and the rest of the world joined them.

202

CHAPTER 16

— • —

IT DIFFERED FROM WHEN the woman brought Tesfira here.

She'd seen no cavern, nothing but a bright light, pulsing and warm, she thought of as representing God's love. No shapes, merely a sense of happiness and care perceived through faith and benevolence.

The illumination was gone except for the shifting glow of huge torches held by sconces too high on the stone walls to reach. By the acolyte's estimation, Hartrek and Gartrek couldn't have stretched enough to set them alight. The fire dancing and crackling at their ends illuminated a vast cavern, its ceiling lost in shadow, the floor uneven and littered with varied items. From where she stood, Tesfira spied three different desks—one plain and more aptly described as a table, the others huge and ornate and out of place. Many urns of varying sizes and shapes occupied the space, as well as stacks of books and chaotic piles of scrolls. As she surveyed them, Hinter stepped forward, separating herself from their small group.

"No," the acolyte said in a whisper as she reached out to grasp her friend's sleeve and missed. "Please wait."

The thief waved her hand and continued. Eight paces brought her to the first pile of tomes where she stopped and knelt.

She ran her fingertips along the cover of the top volume, the scabrous ancient leather familiar after exploring the witches' library. It was the largest of the unruly stack of nine books, each set at odd angles as though someone made a game of seeing how high they could pile them without the tower toppling but lost interest.

The binding creaked as she opened the cover; archaic paper crinkled and the scent of age wafted to her nostrils. Her memory flashed to the cellar where she'd found the Book of Shadow beneath a now-destroyed house. She reached behind her, grasping for her backpack as she remembered the dragon tome stored within. Her pack hadn't come with her on their unusual trip through the mountain.

Of course it didn't, she thought, chastising herself.

Despite the self-admonishment, her hand crept under her cloak, searching for the hilt of her knife. Missing, too, but she felt the outline of the talon pendant resting against her chest below her throat.

She flipped the tome's cover closed with a puff of air and stood, moved to the nearest of the desks. Experience assessing items of value suggested it of some exotic wood she didn't recognize, its color dark, the veins running through its surface wide. A metal box too small to be called a chest sat in the center on four short, curved legs, torchlight glinting on its silver lid. Hinter raised her hand, her innate sense of curiosity making her reach out to open it, but a word from Llyris halted her.

"Wait," the handler said.

She lowered her arm and pivoted to face her companion, who'd already parted from the others, headed for the desk.

"It looks like the box Misk kept Flayre in."

She stopped beside her friend without taking her attention from the curiosity, though she registered the other woman withdrawing.

"Impossible," she muttered, not intending the observation for anyone but herself. "It couldn't be here."

She lifted her hand as the thief had, extended it toward the item, but paused when she noticed the quivering of her fingers. She curled them into a fist, opened it and flexed them; the shake dissipated but remained, so she continued despite it.

She touched cold metal, ran her fingertips along the beveled edge. As much as she desired to grasp the corner and flip the lid open, she hesitated. What if she found Flayre secreted within? Worse, the Unnamed dead inside? She couldn't bear the thought of discovering her blackened corpse. If the box contained her shriveled body, finding it might be the final ingredient toward loosening her tenuous hold on reality.

She pressed the tip of her index finger under the corner, watched it form an indentation in her skin as she lifted.

To her relief and disappointment, green velvet lined the empty chest—not the one Viden Misk used to heal Flayre, but she suspected it for similar usage. Nothing to be seen, but she reached inside anyway, feeling around the soft fabric lest some unnoticed spell hid things from her eyes.

Her touch revealed it was as vacant as it appeared, with no evidence of hidden compartments or anything nefarious. She allowed the lid to drop closed with a muffled thunk, then lifted the box, turning it in her hands to view it from all sides. Fine scrollwork crawled along its sides, but the way it looped on itself with no break in its lines led her to believe it decoration rather than runic lettering.

The top and bottom were smooth and free of markings, polished to a high sheen. As she turned the item to peer at the bottom, she glimpsed Cirril Feron reflected on its surface, his visage cast in writhing shadow by the guttering torches. His unexpected appearance startled her, and she thumped the box down on the desk, spun to face him.

"Where is it?" he demanded. "Where is this dragon we've come to meet?"

Llyris shook her head and shrugged, her features drawn into a fearful expression. He hated the idea of stirring the young woman's concern, but life had taught him directness was the most efficient path to any goal. Of course, this knowledge was also why he'd lived most of his time alone—a lesson he'd never learned.

The handler crept out from between him and the desk as though she suspected he wanted access to the box she'd held, but he had no use for the bauble. He cared about nothing but locating the damned dragon they'd come for—if it existed. Then they'd be on their way home.

He stepped past the piece of furniture with no right to be in the middle of an immense cavern—who'd decide to sit themselves here to write a letter or conduct their business? As he advanced, his gaze flickered, never resting for more than a second in one place, though he perceived each item it touched. He saw the books and scrolls, urns and goblets, glass phials filled with colored liquids, sculptures of mythical beasts. All of it lay in shadow and dimness, the torches doing a poor job of illuminating them.

"Damn it," he grumbled under his breath. If he meant to survey their surroundings, he'd need more light.

He abandoned his visual search of the cavern and glanced at the left wall, assessing the height of the sconces. Too high. He glimpsed a short ladder leaning against the cavern's right side and set out toward it.

"Cirril. Be careful," Tesfira called out.

He didn't let her words deter him nor acknowledged her concern with anything more than a wave of his hand.

A motley assortment of clutter forced him into a zigzag path to his goal. He paused when he came upon a lantern, picked it up and shook it; when no oil sloshed inside its reservoir, he returned it to its place. Possessing nothing with which to ignite it, he'd have needed a torch to use it, anyway.

He stepped over a crate of scrolls, ran his hand over the top of a sealed barrel as he passed, stared at a jar containing what he suspected a pig's foot floating in a yellow fluid; closer inspection suggested it something other than porcine. Jars, urns, a looking glass, mirrors, rolled-up rugs; the cavern appeared more a depository for unwanted items than the lair of some magical beast.

When he reached his goal, he found the ladder in good repair—no makeshift ladder of dubious quality formed by lashing chunks of wood between two side rails. A tool built by someone with a solid knowledge of woodworking. He pushed it against the wall where it leaned, testing its strength. It didn't flex at all, so he gave it a shake. No rattles or squeaks. Satisfied, he lifted it, intending to carry it to the closest sconce and retrieve a torch.

It proved lighter than he'd expected, and he picked it up with ease. He wended his way through the ragtag collection of forgotten junk until he stood beneath the nearest torch holder. The ends of the ladder clunked as he leaned it against the wall. Without hesitating, he set his foot on the lowest rung and climbed.

"It's not tall enough," he heard the thief call out. "You won't be able to reach."

He didn't bother to acknowledge her assessment. What irked him so about the girl, he wasn't sure, but she'd gotten under his skin from their first meeting. He'd done his best to tolerate her, but the times he'd desired to knock the attitude from her with the flat of his hand numbered too many to estimate.

He put his disgruntlement with Hinter aside and ascended the ladder, eyes on his feet to ensure he didn't misstep. When he reached the top, he tilted his head and looked up at the torch above him, hand outstretched.

As the thief had suggested, it lay outside his reach.

"Blast," he grumbled to himself.

He advanced one more rung, the flats of his hands against the wall because he'd progressed beyond the tops of the side rails. He stretched and fell short again. The torch's flame crackled and popped, as though laughing at his failure. If he climbed higher, he didn't think he'd be able to maintain his footing, so he extended to his fullest.

To his amazement, the torch grew closer. Dumbfounded, he relaxed his reach, and the distance between him and his prize increased again.

"Keep reaching." Llyris calling out this time. "When you do, the ladder grows."

Cirril frowned and fought the urge to pivot toward his companions and offer them an incredulous expression. Surely the handler must be incorrect in her estimation—ladders don't grow.

And yet he'd noticed the torch nearly within his grasp.

Since no other, taller ladders lay about the cavern, he figured he had no other choice but to keep trying.

Cirril reset his feet, jamming the outsides of his boots against the side rails. He tested his new footing, then leaned toward the wall, pressing himself against it. His right hand stretched upward. He pushed himself up on his toes.

A sense of movement startled him, jostled his positioning, the surprise of it setting his heart racing. The stone of the cavern grated against his chest as the rung of the ladder pressed against his boot soles, pushing him higher. He wanted to peer upward, to allow his eyes the opportunity to dispel the notion his other senses portrayed, but worried about such a movement sending him tumbling from his perch. The floor wasn't far below, but he couldn't know what he may land upon, or how pointy it might be.

The sensation continued, and he concentrated on keeping his cheek from scraping along the rock. A moment later, his fingertips brushed the metal sconce. He felt about until his fingers closed around the torch's support and gave it a tug to test its sturdiness. It proved solid, so he gripped it and tilted his head.

The torch hung above him, its heat touching his cheeks as he squinted against its brightness. It appeared to be as big as him, its wide, lit end tapering down to a point too large for him to wrap his fingers around.

Cirril cursed to himself. Why did he think he could handle it on his own? Had he forgotten the effects of distance and perspective the way a child might? How could he grasp the huge torch and descend the ladder without falling? His choice was to tempt fate or to retire empty-handed. Choosing the former likely meant a fall, but the latter would give the thief fodder, and he'd already stomached enough of the young woman's barbs despite their ceasefire.

With a heavy sigh, he clenched his teeth and stretched higher, using the sconce as an anchor with one hand while he reached upward with the other. The ladder extended along with him and his fingers wrapped around the torch's girth. He steeled himself, ready for its weight to unbalance him, and lifted to free it from its holder.

To his surprise, it weighed the same as any other torch he'd ever carried. Despite its length and width, he held it in one hand.

"Now to get down," he grunted to himself.

He released his grip on the sconce and shifted to grasp the ladder's side rail. The move accomplished, he lifted a foot, intending to step down to the next rung, but a rush of air startled him. His hold on the ladder failed and he went backward, arm pinwheeling as he expected to topple to the floor to land on his ass.

His boot touched hard ground.

The shock of it sent him off balance, but he maintained his footing, the torch flame wavering over him as he flailed his arms to keep his balance. Heart hammering against his ribs, he settled himself and glanced toward his companions, eyes meeting the thief's as he expected her to toss him some snide comment about his gracefulness. She refrained.

Hinter gaped at Cirril. How he held the massive torch aloft with one hand was wonder enough; she didn't want to ponder the ladder extending and contracting as though it possessed its own brain and a goal of aiding the guardsman. His spare glance toward them lasted a fleeting second before he turned his attention to the vast cavern.

"Wait here," she said to Tesfira and Llyris without taking her eyes from Feron. She didn't so much as pause when the acolyte protested and reached to grasp her sleeve.

"Hinter. No."

Her fingertips brushed the sleeve of her cloak, but the thief moved quickly enough to avoid her getting a hold. Though she wanted to stay with her friend to ensure her safety, years of instinct forced her onward. The cavern full of antiquities laid out before her sufficed to prompt her innate curiosity. What may lie beyond their sight tempted her more.

She wended her way through the labyrinth of curiosities, avoiding the urge to examine them as she passed. Considering how she and her companions arrived here, she suspected she possessed no capacity to return with anything, so why tantalize herself? Instead, she concentrated on catching up to the merchant's man, staring at him to avoid temptation.

She held no love for the fellow; offered a choice, he wasn't someone with whom she'd have associated—not difficult to ascertain given how few people she'd chosen to associate with over the course of her life. Sometimes she wondered if the problem lay with her, but she always dismissed the possibility realizing it the safest decision.

"Do you see anything?" she called.

More than ten paces ahead of her, Cirril shook his head in response without diverting his attention from the darkness receding before his torch. Hinter increased her pace, intent on making sure she stayed close enough to help him if the need arose. Though she didn't like the man, she'd never abandon him.

She directed her own gaze to the cavern being revealed by the advance of the guttering flame. Shadows writhed and danced, their shapes resembling creatures fleeing the light, any of them potentially that. As she closed the space between herself and Feron, she slowed to match his pace. Best to be careful.

But was it necessary? Her body sat on the rocky ground grasping hands with her companions at the base of a cliff, their group overseen by a pair of identical twin ogres. With their corporeal selves some distance away, could anything hurt them here?

She didn't want to be the one to find out.

Ahead of the merchant's man, the clutter of mismatched sundries ended and torchlight spilled out over a flat, empty expanse of cavern floor. He stepped over the last item in his path—an urn as tall as Hinter's shoulder, with a chunk broken from its neck and a crack running down its side. His boot touched clear ground. As soon as it did, a spark of panic ignited in the thief's chest.

"Cirril, wait."

Hinter increased her pace, and to her surprise, her companion heeded her plea. He halted, waiting for her to catch up. When she did, she stopped beside him, tilted her head to gaze up at him as he glanced at her sideways.

No matter what she said or how she acted, he couldn't help but suspect the thief's motives and intent. By choosing a life of stealth and deception, hadn't she brought it on herself? Shouldn't anyone with a brain realize to never trust someone of her profession?

Either way, he appreciated the support.

The now-empty cavern stretched away from them into inky darkness. Nothing moved, and no clutter marred the floor but for the occasional ridge of dirt.

"You want to do this?" the thief asked.

Cirril stared straight ahead, straining to make out anything in the blackness. He didn't answer for a second, then diverted his eyes to peer down into Hinter's face.

"We have no choice," the merchant's man murmured. "Have the others advance here, no farther."

He stepped out into the flat, open space, and a shiver ran up her spine. She swallowed hard and faced the companions they'd left behind. Her gaze met Llyris' first, then Tesfira's before she waved them on.

"Come wait for us here," she said, then pivoted to follow Cirril.

The handler took Tesfira by the arm and drew her forward. The acolyte allowed herself to be led, and she trailed along in silence. Llyris understood the struggle happening within her—the battle between faith she'd nurtured her entire life and the evidence laid out before her—because she'd experienced a similar conflict. Since her earliest memory, she'd believed in the power of the Unnamed, thought her job a noble one when others spurned her and treated her like an outcast. Now, a haze of grief and confusion hid the truth. Tesfira had lost her mentor, and Llyris her constant magical companion. The acolyte pondered whether her faith had been misguided; the handler knew she'd been misled. There was nothing noble about a thousand years of mistreatment at the hands of humans.

Nothing honorable about oppression and genocide.

She led the young woman through the peculiar assortment of nonsensical trinkets, diverting her eyes from her companions only when necessary to avoid some impediment threatening their footing. As they neared the cusp where the collection ended and the flat dirt floor began, the torch Cirril carried pressed on, Hinter keeping pace a few steps behind, her shape rendered all but invisible by her unusual cloak.

Llyris halted when her toes touched the dusty ground, and Tesfira stopped beside her. The light borne by their companion illuminated a circle twenty feet around, then a swath lay in darkness before the torches held in the wall sconces brightened the cavern again. Not far ahead of their companions, they ended, and a blackness capable of hiding anything began.

"Be careful," Tesfira called out, her voice quaking.

The thief slowed her pace and peered over her shoulder at them.

The acolyte's tone gave Hinter pause. Her heart urged her to stop, go to her friend and comfort her, but the self-preservation bred into her through a life spent ever in some level of peril denied her. With a sigh, she abandoned any thoughts of retreat and refocused her attention on the darkness ahead of them.

With her diminished pace, Cirril increased the gap between them, leaving her on the edge of the torch's light as they passed beyond the illumination cast by the sconces. Blackness pressed against her from two sides and she scurried forward to catch up to the merchant's man.

"Do you see anything?" she whispered, the hushed question sounding vociferous in the dark.

"Nothing yet," he growled.

Now striding side by side, they slowed their pace, both choosing a path of caution without speaking of its necessity. Each had experienced similar situations in their pasts and knew how best to proceed. She may not like the merchant's man as a person, but she respected his abilities and knowledge. Rarely did his actions precede thought, despite his propensity for anger.

The line of illumination leading them crept forward with each step they took, its glow revealing the dusty cavern floor inch by inch. She counted three paces before Cirril halted without warning. He said nothing as he raised his hand and pointed to a spot on the ground ahead of them.

Hinter squinted as the flickering flame threw juddering shadows. At first she believed her companion fooled by a trick of the light, then she recognized the shape in the small hills and valleys of dust.

"Is it...?"

"A footprint," he confirmed. "A big one."

They crept forward, the torch casting its glow across the outline in the dirt, illuminating it, defining it. By the time they reached its edge, the leading line of light barely extended beyond its far side.

"What the—" Cirril began before Hinter interrupted.

"Shh. Listen."

They both halted, frozen as if turned to stone. The torch hissed and the thief's pulse whooshed in her ears—nothing else. She'd detected a noise an instant before, though she wasn't sure what. An ominous sound disguised beneath Cirril's exclamation, felt as much as heard.

Seconds passed, and she laid her hand on her companion's arm to ask for his continued silence. He tilted his head, glanced sideways at her, their gazes meeting before they both returned to staring into the darkness.

The merchant's man detected no sound—not before Hinter hushed him, and not since. Anyone else insisting on inaction, he'd have scoffed and carried on, but he knew the thief had spent her life honing her skills. Best to listen to her.

A soft release of breath, long and steady, with a low grumble concealed within. A scraping on the ground. Cirril reached for his sword out of habit, despite knowing he'd find no scabbard dangling from his belt. The torch tottered in his grip and he replaced his hand, using both to steady it.

The red glow began with a single point a distance off the floor thrice his own height. It spread in thin lightning bolts that didn't fade, like scarlet light shining through cracks in a stone wall. It kept expanding, outlining shapes, puzzle pieces of something larger. Much larger.

Green eyes winked open.

"Why have you come here?"

The words met his ears an instant before the heat carrying them touched his face. All the cavern's torches flared and brightened, as though prompted to greater life by the speaker to reveal it.

Before them loomed a beast unseen by humans for more than a millennium.

At first impression, he thought the dragon's bulk filled the cavern, but quickly realized this wasn't true. It stood on its thick rear legs, membranous wings spread behind it, a faint luminescence radiating from its translucent ruby skin as veins of black ash pulsed beneath the surface. Its wide mouth revealed rows of spiked teeth. Droplets of fire spilled over its lips, illuminating the air as they fell to the floor, splashing in bright impacts like deadly rain.

The merchant's man swallowed hard. Anyone with battle experience knew fear. Those claiming fearlessness had either never put themselves in a position to feel it, or they were damn liars. What marked a person as brave wasn't their lack of fear, but how they reacted.

Never more in his life had Cirril Feron wanted to flee, but he held his ground, eyes fixed on the lambent emerald orbs.

"I asked a question," the dragon said.

Its tone didn't change—no added threat or note of impatience in its words. None were necessary. Its throaty growl, the timbre of rocks rubbing together, needed nothing further to raise the hair on Cirril's arms.

"Why have you come?" Droplets of molten saliva dripped from its lips as it spoke. "Why are you here disturbing me?"

"The curse has been lifted."

The patter and scrape of footsteps followed the handler's response, and both Hinter and Cirril looked back.

"Llyris," the thief said. "I told you to stay put."

She wasn't sure why she'd rushed forward. How could she protect her friends against a creature like this they couldn't do themselves? She'd inadvertently used a word to halt two witches and a collection of bones, but she doubted the ability of such party tricks to affect the most magical of beings.

"We are here to beg for your help," the handler said, ignoring Hinter's chastisement. "The curse is ended. A war is at hand."

"The curse?" Genuine surprise shaded the dragon's tone. "Magiks are free? Then why should there be war?"

"It's not their fault. It's—"

213

"Shiera," the beast finished for her. "I did my best to keep her away so she wouldn't steal any of my magic. I should have realized my power wasn't the only left for the taking." It leaned forward, green eyes flickering with emerald fire. "It was you, wasn't it?"

"I—"

The dragon straightened again before she answered. Its long, broad head tilted to one side, the pose held for a few seconds before relinquishing it.

"Nothing can be done."

"You can't let it happen," Tesfira said, appearing beside Llyris. Their eyes met, and the handler saw desperation in her expression.

"Tes," Hinter cried, making no move toward her friends. Perhaps she thought them safer with herself in between.

The acolyte swallowed hard—she knew what they'd come to request, and the winged creature had already refused before they asked. Out of the corner of her eye, she saw Llyris fill her lungs with a shaking breath.

"She leads them in a war against the humans," she said, louder than the first time she spoke. "She seeks vengeance against people who had nothing to do with casting the curse."

"No, but they did nothing to change it." The dragon tucked its wings away, leaned forward to stand on all four of its legs. "Perhaps they are not responsible, but they are complicit."

"People are dying. Shiera will not stop until she has had her fill of vengeance and bloodshed."

"Are humans so arrogant they believed consequences would never arise? Did you believe yourselves capable of subduing all magical creatures for the rest of eternity? One amongst you must have realized the potential repercussions should the magiks gain their freedom."

"Viden Misk," Hinter said, and Tesfira glanced at her, but the thief stared at the dragon. "He knew. He sent us to find the items he needed to lift the curse, but the woman stole them. As though she guessed his plan."

"I know not of this man." The creature's nostrils flared. It blew out a hard breath and sparks danced from its nose. "Are you suggesting I had anything to do with this? What here in my self-imposed exile do you see that implies this?"

214

"Only the exile itself," Cirril said, his words compressed between tight lips.

"But you know Viden Misk." Llyris ignored the conversation and took another step forward. "By a different name. Amnayel Prisma."

The dragon's head jerked as though the handler slapped its face. Flames flickered in its jade green eyes.

"Prisma?" The name sounded more snort than word. "The mage can't possibly live after so long. He may be a wizard, but he is human."

"He lives of a fashion," Hinter said. Every time the thief spoke up, a sliver of worry for her friend's safety insinuated itself in Tesfira's chest. Part of her wished she'd let the rest of them handle this and reduce the possibility of her getting hurt. "He's passed himself down through generations, transferring from one body to another to keep his essence alive. Viden Misk is but the latest."

"And you are all foolish enough to think he held the best interests of the magiks at heart when he sent you to collect his baubles? Prisma made them the Unnamed."

The constriction in the acolyte's chest expanded to the point she realized it wasn't simply concern for her friend. Other emotions wound themselves in with the worry, and it took her a minute to unwind them. When she did, she recognized the one chief amongst them: disappointment.

When Shiera brought her to the mountain, she thought she'd found the God Emeryn Aryzath had taught her about. Instead, they stood now before an uncaring, argumentative beast who spent its time hoarding treasure rather than mending souls and spreading love. The tightness in her spread, expanding through her torso, down her legs, along her arms until it reached her hands and they curled into fists.

"You should have stopped it," she said, the words mired in disillusionment and anger. "You are the most powerful magik alive. You have your name. If you'd taken action to prevent a war instead of fleeing, none of this would have happened. People wouldn't have died. You are as responsible as Prisma."

The dragon stared at her, its lip curling to reveal teeth like short swords. Hinter slipped a hand onto her forearm.

"What are you doing?" she whispered.

Tesfira shrugged.

215

"I did not flee," it responded, nostrils flaring. "Nor could I have deterred the fallout from the unicorn's death. But I need not explain myself to a mortal. Your kind killed the unicorn to steal her power, and one of yours cast the spell of enslavement. How dare you blame me?"

"Yes, humans are responsible," the acolyte said, stepping forward and away from Hinter's touch. "But you alone could have stopped it. Or lifted the curse once he placed it. Centuries of suffering and misery are equally your fault as ours, and now the deaths of innocents, too."

The dragon stared at her, and Tesfira struggled to hide the fear threatening to quake her limbs. Overtaken by angry disappointment, she really didn't know what she was doing. Had Emeryn Aryzath both lived his life and died for nothing?

"Shiera brought me to you before she stole Flayre and disappeared. Don't you remember?"

The dragon laughed, dual plumes of steam escaping its nostrils. "Foolish human, none have visited me in a thousand years. I know not how you got here but, as soon as you're gone, I'll be having a word with my defenses."

Tesfira pressed on. "But I saw you."

"No. You did not."

"Then what...?"

"Whatever she wanted you to see."

"No. It's not true." In her mind, the radiant light burned, and she sensed the warmth and love emanating from it. Until this moment, she'd been convinced of what it represented. Could she have been so wrong? "Brother Emeryn gave his life."

She didn't know why she said it; the words spilled forth without giving her the chance to consider them. What use did knowledge of his death have to a creature capable of killing them with a single breath?

The acolyte hesitated, unsure what to say. She'd expected their journey through the mountain to end the same as when she came with Shiera. Now it didn't, confusion left her uncertain of her experience.

She opened her mouth to repeat her previous statement, because maybe this was God in another form, and he hadn't heard her request for help. If some magiks possessed the ability to alter their forms, the almighty must, too. He'd created this image,

216

this space filled with treasure, to appease the expectations of his friends. Always with faith came explanation.

Or maybe Shiera had deceived her, as the dragon suggested.

"His death can't have been for nothing," she said. "Despite his flaws, he was a good man. You know this, don't you?"

The creature grumbled. Its eyes flickered away from Tesfira to somewhere in the darkness before returning. "I know not of whom you speak."

A jolt of grief climbed up from the acolyte's chest, clogged her throat. She opened her mouth again, unsure if the knotted despair threatening to choke her would allow her to form words. Llyris touched her shoulder, stopping her, the expression she wore offering solace where it couldn't exist.

With a nod of reassurance to the young woman, the handler stepped forward, hand sliding into her pocket. Out of habit, she expected to brush Flayre's smooth flesh, though she knew they'd never do so again. Instead, they found the hard edges and curves of the brooch.

She didn't remember putting it there.

Her fingers closed around it, the familiar shape pressing against her flesh calming her mind. She took three paces forward, moving closer to the formidable beast standing before her.

"Llyris!"

Cirril's voice this time; she ignored his distraction. She needed to convince the dragon to help, or many would lose their lives. Or everyone.

"You are the greatest of the magiks. The others will listen to you. If you do nothing, thousands will die."

The creature appeared to hesitate, shifted its head to the side and cast its gaze into the darkness. Llyris squinted, attempting to identify what it distracted it. When the dragon caught her doing so, it took a half step to its right, hiding something from her view.

"It cannot be helped," it said, an edge to its tone, as though the words it spoke tasted bad. "We left the human world centuries ago and vowed never to return. It's better for all if we keep this vow."

"We?" Hinter asked the question already finding its way to the handler's tongue.

The dragon glared at her. "I'm not the last of my kind."

"Maybe another will help," the handler ventured.

"I speak for all." Its eyes flickered away. "Nobody leaves here."

217

The air within the cavern warmed as the beast became more unhappy and agitated with them. Llyris wondered about their fate if it decided to fill the space with its searing dragon breath. Would they be safe because their corporeal bodies sat at the foot of the mountain? Or would the scorching heat incinerate their essences and send them to the afterlife as if it ravaged their flesh? She swallowed hard, attempting to dispel the thought.

Llyris took two more steps forward, closing some space between her and the mythical creature. As she stopped, she pulled her hand from her pocket, thrust it out before her and uncurled her fingers, revealing the pewter dragon wing resting on her palm.

The beast's head jerked. "Where did you get this?"

"At first I thought it from Shiera, but she claimed it wasn't her who gave it to me. From your reaction, I presume you didn't present me with it, either."

"I have not left this cavern in a thousand years, yet this bauble you yield should be among my treasures, as should the talon your friend wears around her neck." The dragon shot an angered glance toward the thief. "I can only imagine where you got them."

Again the creature pivoted, as though peering at someone hidden in shadows. The repeated action proved too much for the merchant's man and Cirril erupted forward, rushing the beast.

"What are you hiding?" he barked.

Llyris' heart jumped, and she opened her mouth to plead with him to stop, faced Tesfira and saw her doing the same. The dragon cut them off as it reared up on its hind legs and spread its wings so wide their tips scraped the cavern's walls.

"I have entertained enough of your delusions," it said in a puff of smoke. Llyris glimpsed a fire in its throat. "Do not presume to approach me."

Hinter jumped forward and snagged Cirril by the sleeve. The merchant's man tried to pull away, but she maintained her grip, stopping him from doing anything foolish. The dragon turned its hard expression on the handler.

"You and your friends are misguided, shadow-scarred. Your mage is the only one capable of changing fate's path, and he left it too long, and then failed. I'm no god, and you can blame none but yourselves. You should return your party whence you came before it's too late." The dragon pivoted from them in a motion quicker and more graceful than a beast its size should have moved. "Now leave my home."

Faced away from them, the creature flapped its wings once. A gust of air buffeted their cheeks and stirred their hair. Tesfira lifted her arm, bringing it in front of her face to avoid debris stirred by the breeze from finding her eyes. Her mouth opened, her lips pulled into a sneer, more words of accusation perched on her tongue. This wasn't how the God Brother Emeryn taught her about would act. The Creator in his stories was kind and just, caring, thoughtful, and wise. Aryzath's God would never leave his people to die under the vendetta of a madwoman. He'd never let the world suffer. He'd—

A realization struck her, hitting her with the force of an open-handed slap she hadn't seen coming. It sucked the breath from her, leaving her gasping and wondering why she'd never realized it before.

The Unnamed were God's creatures, too, and he'd abandoned them.

And then the room disappeared.

They traveled out of the mountain at a far greater pace than they'd come, colors of stone, veins of minerals, pockets of insect colonies flying past until they emerged into their bodies.

Llyris gasped, closed her eyelids against the light, and fell over from her seated position. Her cheek hit the dirt, scraping it, and she winced at the pain but didn't right herself. She waited as sensation returned to the rest of her body; she felt the ground pressing against her side, smelled the earth's scent, heard the scrape of footsteps. A second later, a hand gripped her under her arm, tugging at her to help her rise.

She opened her eyes to find Gartrek looming over her. Though a heavy fatigue weighed her limbs, she allowed the ogre to pull her to her feet. Across from where she stood, she watched Hartrek attempt to offer the same aid to Cirril, but the merchant's man refused. He shook off his attempt and got up shakily on his own with a grunt as the twins shifted their assistance to Hinter and the acolyte.

"A waste of time," the guardsman said with no pretense of hiding his ire. His angered gaze found Llyris first, then Tesfira. "Days upon days lost because of you, girl. You said the dragon—your God in the mountain—could solve all our problems. If we'd decided instead to go home, we'd be halfway there by now."

"Leave her alone." Hinter stepped in front of the merchant's man. "She didn't know. It was a better idea than yours. If we'd attempted to return to the village, we'd likely be dead."

Cirril scowled, refusing to stand down. "Now we must find our way to the accursed settlement before thinking about our journey home. More opportunity for us to die."

"I..." Tesfira started, then swallowed. "I don't understand."

"What's not to understand?" he snapped, and lifted his arm to point up the mountainside. "The beast living in this mountain doesn't care about humans, or jicks, or anything but itself judging by its hoard. Your so-called God is a fake."

Before any of them realized what was happening, Hinter slapped him across the face, her palm contacting his cheek with a loud crack. The surprise of it froze him, giving the thief the time to jump away, her hand darting inside her cloak to retrieve her dagger.

"I've endured about enough of you," she said through tight lips.

The merchant's man pulled his sword from its scabbard, the song of steel on leather loud in Llyris' ears. Her heart jumped; they'd come so far and failed, now they intended to kill each other. And it was her fault.

"Stop it," she screeched, the words exploding from her mouth before she put so much as a thought to speaking them.

Her companions froze. Not just Hinter and Cirril, but Tesfira and the ogres—none stationary by choice. Only their eyes followed her as she stepped forward, her fatigued legs protesting as she made them carry her.

"This is nobody's fault but mine," she said, and lowered her gaze to her feet. "If I hadn't allowed her to seize Flayre, none of this would have happened."

Nobody responded—they couldn't. Despite the silence, she felt their eyes upon her as she stared down at the earth beneath her boots. How did she let this happen? Life had seemed so simple during her time at the guildhall. They'd laid out her meals, gave her a place to sleep, sent her and Flayre out to work when required. Rarely pleasing work, and she was seldom treated well, but at least no one died. Not until they assigned her to Caedric Carpera or, more accurately, Viden Misk. Now a path of corpses lay behind her—friends, enemies. How many innocents may lose their lives before Shiera sated her thirst for revenge? It seemed to Llyris the portrait of her recent days was painted with blood.

She couldn't let it happen anymore.

Her hands clenched into fists and she raised her chin. Her companions stared at her, frozen by her words. The wan light filtering through the clouds glinted on the steel of Hinter and Cirril's weapons like beacons to guide her.

She went to the thief first, taking the blade between a finger and thumb. "You may release it," she said, and she did, her hand relaxing enough for the handler to pluck it from her grasp. No other part of her friend moved, other than her eyes following as she stepped toward the merchant's man.

"And you." When she tried to take the weapon, he refused to loosen his grip. Half a step brought her within inches of him. She tilted her head and stared up into his face, her teeth clenched as she spoke again. "Let. Go."

This time, her words compelled him, and he released his sword. Llyris took it from him, surprised by the weight of it, and stepped away from her five companions, separating herself from them the length of six paces. A minute passed as she studied them, all of them watching her with no other choice but to wait. She wondered for how long her command might hold them. Enough time for her to escape? She dismissed the thought quickly.

"Too many ways already exist for us to die without killing each other." She tossed the sword and dagger onto the ground, the thump of their weight hitting the earth punctuating her words. "What's wrong with you? Can't you put your petty grievances aside long enough to create a strategy?"

She stared at them, gaze moving from one to the next. With none of their muscles under their own control—including those in their faces—their eyes became their lone way to communicate, to express their thoughts and emotions. Grief and disappointment flickered in Tesfira's; Llyris recognized it from when the cleric met his end and before she thought she'd found her God. In Hinter's she saw anger and concern for her friend. Unsurprisingly, Cirril's betrayed his irritation, annoyance, impatience.

The ogres, she couldn't read. Their black and yellow eyes continued to appear foreign to her, even after spending every minute of their trek to the mountain with them. It reminded her of how she'd always identified as an outsider, no matter whether accompanied by humans or Unnamed. With Flayre alone had she ever felt comfortable.

Now what? she thought. *What do we do?*

She knew she needed to start by releasing her companions, but the merchant's man would be irate, the acolyte grief-stricken, and the thief intent on caring for the young woman for whom she'd fallen, all leaving her no better off than when her words froze them. If she released them, could she stop them again if she wanted to? This was all new to her, unknown.

"We have to act," she said. "We can't give up and attempt to blunder our way home. Can we agree on that?"

She directed her attention toward Cirril, knowing his desire to return to Carpera's. His frozen features gave away nothing, but angry sparks flickered in his eyes; the handler proceeded with her pondering.

"And this is no time to debate or seek to prove God's existence. Too many lives are at stake." She looked to Tesfira, stepped closer to lay a hand on the young woman's arm. "You have been through so much. I know how desperately you desire to make sense of Emeryn's sacrifice, but don't you think he'd want us to save as many people as we can?"

She couldn't imagine how the words spilling from her lips must sound to her companions, because they rang empty to her. With the failure of their plan to involve the dragon in rescuing humans, what choices did they have? Four of them against an uncountable throng of magiks. No chance, yet she kept speaking.

"Hinter," she said, taking her hand from the acolyte's arm and moving closer to the thief. She leaned in, bringing her lips nearer her companion's ear to whisper. "Tesfira isn't the only soul in need of help and protection."

As she paced a few steps away to view the entire group, she fought to keep a quake from her hands. Why did she say these things? She felt as lost and disappointed as she assumed her friends must. Wasn't it what caused the tiff between Cirril and

222

Hinter—the disappointment of traveling so far to find they'd done so for nothing? Lacking plan or purpose, some of their companions dead, and humans at the mercy of a woman bent of vengeance. What could they do?

Llyris realized the muscles in her neck and jaw had tightened to the point of pain, her teeth clenched so tightly together they threatened to break. She relaxed the knotted tendons, drew a hard breath through her nose. When she'd regained her composure, she surveyed her companions again, noticed the red hue to the merchant's man's cheeks as he struggled against her hold on him. She gulped, unable to believe she held such sway over him and the others, but her nerves and disbelief disappeared as she raised a finger, pointed at him, and uttered a single word:

"Speak."

He sputtered like a man breaking the surface of a lake, his lips and the muscles in his face moving while the rest of him remained frozen.

"Travel us." His words surprised Llyris. "The dragon said you should."

"I..." She hesitated, thought about Flayre. "I can't."

"Did you think you could transport us through a mountain?"

She gazed at him, the anger evident in his expression despite his control of it as he spoke. Her throat dried up, and she shook her head, then waved her hand.

"Be free." The charm gripping her friends lifted.

Tesfira sighed her relief, and the ogres grumbled.

"He's right," Hinter said, her agreement with the merchant's man as surprising as his decision to show his support instead of hostility.

"No. Flayre opened the portal. I merely...guided her power." She almost used the word controlled but stopped herself. It felt wrong when she described her relationship with the magik as one of restraint, though it was the truth. She'd kept the Unnamed from being herself, from doing what she'd normally do, relinquishing control when it suited her needs. "No human can travel on their own."

"But you're not human, are you?" Cirril said.

"No handler is—"

"Nor are you merely a handler," Hinter interrupted.

"The dragon called you shadow-scarred. You told us the same," Tesfira said, her voice quiet. "What does that mean?"

"It's not real," Llyris snapped, regretting having released them. "A ridiculous myth."

"It is real," Hartrek rumbled. "Shiera told stories about the shadow-scarred—the offspring of handler and magik. A hybrid. Humans think they're myths because so few have existed. They find and execute those born before they discover their power."

"Why should anyone believe anything she said?" Llyris turned away from her companions, hiding the tears threatening at the corners of her eyes.

"You took us through the mountain," Cirril reiterated.

"And froze us with your words," Hinter added. "You did the same thing to save our lives."

The handler wiped wetness from her cheeks, realized she held the severe dragon wing brooch in her fist. She dabbed her tears on her wrist and slid her hand into her pocket, replacing the pin where it should be. A second later, she felt a touch on her shoulder. She knew it belonged to the acolyte.

"You escaped the tunnel," Tesfira said, voice quiet as though she intended the words for the two of them alone. "That's not supposed to be possible."

The truth, but she didn't know how she'd done any of it. It just happened, like an infant learning to swim when thrown in water because not doing so meant losing their life. If she hadn't paralyzed the witches, or guided them through the mountain, or reversed course in the tunnel, one or all of them would be dead.

"But I gave up Flayre," she said, her head sagged forward. "She died because of me. All of this is because of me."

The last few words squeezing through her tightened throat threatened to choke her.

Perhaps the world would be better if they did, she thought before facing her friends. When she did, she found all but the ogres had gathered close behind her, their proximity explaining the quietness of Tesfira's voice.

"If it's your fault, then you should find a remedy for it," Cirril said, the familiar edge returning to his tone.

"What's to lose?" Hinter added.

"Our lives," Llyris said, her tone flat.

The thief shrugged. "What's our choice? Get lost finding our way home and starve to death? Eaten by wild animals?"

"Not much choice." Tesfira stepped closer to Llyris, put her arms around her and pulled her close in a hug. "We believe in you."

The handler couldn't help but bury her face in her friend's shoulder and release the sorrow and anxiety built up inside her. She cried and snuffled, embarrassed by her own display. The acolyte held her tight, and none of the others said anything while she wept for Flayre and Emeryn, Aryzath and everyone else who'd suffered because of their journey.

Because of her.

When the tears stopped and she extracted herself from Tesfira's embrace, they all watched her and waited.

Hinter stood beside Cirril, their earlier disagreement she'd worried about ending in bloodshed forgotten as their weapons lay on the ground where she'd dropped them. The ogre brothers observed from farther away, arms crossed in identical poses, awaiting her decision. Tesfira remained before her, her own cheeks damp.

"Try," she said.

Llyris surveyed them all again, expecting someone to protest, to disagree, or call her out as a fraud. They didn't. They waited in silence. Waited for her.

"You all agree?" she asked when she'd regained enough control of her voice to form words. They cracked, anyway. She directed her attention to Cirril. "All of you?"

Stony faced, the merchant's man nodded. "I haven't the energy or inclination to hack our way through the damned jangala again."

She didn't bother asking Hinter—if Tesfira agreed, she would, too—so she looked to the twins.

"And you two?"

They shrugged in unison, as though one mind controlled four shoulders.

"They sent us to ensure your safety," Hartrek said.

"Wherever you *go*," Gartrek added.

She inhaled a deep sigh through her nose as her gaze flickered across the faces of her companions once more. They'd endured so much together: witches and dead men and cannibals and more. Recalling it made her wonder about the fate of the others. Were Rein and Ilkari alive? Jai? And what of Viden Misk?

225

The last set her teeth grinding. She accepted responsibility because she'd given up Flayre but, but if the old man hadn't sent them on his quests, none of this would have happened.

"All right," she said.

Her companions stepped away in silence without her needing to ask them to give her space, though she didn't know if she'd need it. Nobody cheered or clapped for giving it a go, not did anybody jeer or laugh at her attempting the impossible. They gave her room and kept to themselves.

Llyris didn't know what to do.

She filled her lungs again, let the air out in a long, shuddering sigh. Somewhere in the forest leading away from the mountain, a bird cried out, its raucous song harsh yet beautiful.

Life is beautiful, she thought. *That's why I have to try. Even though it might kill them.*

She closed her eyes, cast her mind backward in time to her days at the guildhall where she'd learned the craft of handling Flayre. She remembered the first day she held the smooth purple cylinder, her appearance like nothing more than a colored candle, an improbable form for a creature with such power.

Her heart swelled with the memory of her magical friend, the feel of her energy against her palm. She recalled the way it tickled her skin when Flayre began spinning, the scent of cloves and jasmine accompanying the wisps reminiscent of smoke she emitted. Most of all she remembered the sense of connection, of belonging, of oneness they'd shared.

"It's working," Cirril said, disbelief clear in his voice.

Llyris opened her eyes, more surprised than the merchant's man to find the swirl of white forming in front of her. No bigger than her fingertip, but there.

She let out a nervous laugh and closed her eyelids again, finding the sense of togetherness, nursing it, growing it. Out of habit, she extended her hand and swore she felt the Unnamed spinning upon it, whirling about her stretched-tight palm like the first day they bonded, and so many times since.

Like she never would again.

A minute passed. The sound of rushing air filled her ears, though no wind touched her cheeks or stirred her hair, and she knew it was time.

She opened her eyes.

The tunnel's mouth gaped before her, more than large enough to accommodate beings taller than ogres. It glowed with a purple light at its edges she'd never seen before.

"I'll go first," she said. "Let me get a ways in before anyone follows. If this fails, I want to be the only life lost."

She swallowed hard and stepped forward, concentrating to avoid making eye contact with her companions. The passageway made it easy as the unusual color mesmerized her, drew her forth. It calmed her, as though Flayre's way of prompting her on, of telling her everything would be all right.

Llyris held her breath as she stepped across the threshold without knowing if she'd survive to come out the other side.

CHAPTER 17

— • —

"**I**T WAS YOU, WASN'T it?" the dragon said.

"Whatever do you mean?"

"You know what I mean. The talon and the wing brooch. They belong to me and yet they ended up in the hands of humans. I presume you know something about that."

"Perhaps I do."

The dragon sighed, a plume of steam billowing from his nostrils as he settled onto the ground. He hadn't expected the visit; his defenses, normally so vigilant, had let him down. Over a thousand years, it had never happened, but he understood why it did this time.

"Shadow-scarred," he said aloud.

"I told you there was one. You should have expected her."

The dragon shook its head. "I didn't think it possible. Or necessary."

"You should have believed me, Aeryz."

"Those items didn't belong to you. Worse, you should never have left here."

"Why did you send them away? They need your help."

He frowned in the best way a dragon can frown. "It's my job to ensure your safety. I can't do so if I go to aid mortals, nor can I do it if you sneak away to hand out baubles."

"But this is serious. Lives will be lost."

"The humans will only get what they deserve."

"They deserve death no more than our kindred deserved enslavement. A fresh evil does not reverse a previous one."

228

"I don't understand you," the dragon said. "How can you show such compassion to them after they killed your mother?"

"A heinous act perpetrated by a few greedy humans. I can't hold an entire population responsible for their actions. Neither should you. Centuries have passed."

The dragon stretched its neck out to lay its chin flat on the cavern floor, closed its eyes. As so often happened when he shut out the torchlight, Aeryz pictured rolling hills, lush green grass. He imagined daisies, the taste of fresh air, the warmth of the sun heating his scales. How he missed the feel of the wind flowing over his wings.

The clop of hooves on hard stone echoed into the heights of the cavern and Aeryz opened his eyes.

"What do you want me to do?"

The unicorn strode into his line of view and he'd have sworn he saw her smile.

CHAPTER 18

—.—

L LYRIS COULDN'T HAVE GUESSED how many times she'd traversed a portal going from one location to another. Proud of her new life and intrigued, she'd counted at the beginning, but the number grew quickly, first through training at the guild, then when they assigned her tasks. In the hundreds, to be sure. And her enthusiasm had waned, both with familiarity and as she realized the contempt with which others viewed her and her fellow handlers.

Two things had remained consistent during those trips: the nature of the path itself, and Flayre.

Neither were the same this time.

Her magik was gone. Dead. She'd sensed it happen. A piece of her soul ripped out, a strip of skin flayed from her. The pain and grief continued living in her, filling the void left when her connection with the Unnamed had been torn away. That would never change.

She hadn't expected the tunnel to be so different.

Where every other path she'd traversed was white and opaque, this was misty and translucent. She viewed the world outside through its walls and experienced no struggle to her steps. As she walked at her usual pace, she watched the ground whisk by beneath her, saw the insides of trees and hills through which the tunnel passed. They hadn't taught her at the guild it worked this way, nor had she put much thought to it. At her regular gait, she moved faster than any living thing.

Despite herself, she giggled and heard the sound produced by her amusement. Another difference.

She slowed her pace and pivoted, intending to signal for her companions to enter the portal, and found she'd traveled far enough to no longer see the end. It turned out she needn't have worried, for her friends already followed her. They appeared as dots, two larger than the others, but they trailed her. She stopped and awaited them and it surprised her to find her forward progress continued even when her feet weren't moving, though at a slower speed.

Three minutes later, her companions joined her.

"This is so different," Hinter said, her gaze scouring their surroundings as the handler walked again to keep up.

"We knew you could do it," Tesfira added.

"We haven't arrived yet," devil's advocate Cirril Feron interjected. "Let's not get too excited. Be wary."

Llyris experienced a familiar pang at the merchant man's words. So often during her life, others had feared and diminished her—this felt no different. She chose not to respond, instead concentrating on pressing forward and reaching their destination as quickly as possible. Old hurts or not, lives were at stake.

The acolyte must have sensed her distress as she hurried to walk beside her, leaned close.

"I'm proud of you," she whispered.

The handler nodded her thanks and allowed herself a smile when Tesfira slowed to rejoin Hinter, then pressed on.

They'd cleared the jangala, and the plains sped beneath their feet. A minute later, they traveled over the water of the lake, then stepped out of the exit portal onto solid ground.

Llyris managed three steps before she dropped to her knees, turned her head and retched. This explained why the tunnel existed the way it did—the sense of speed halting so abruptly threw off one's equilibrium. She glanced over her shoulder at her companions experiencing the same reaction as she did, except for the ogre twins, who apparently had much more robust constitutions than humans.

As she wiped sputum from her mouth on her sleeve, she wondered if Mikol had become so nauseated because he experienced traveling differently from others.

"Mikol," she said aloud as she scrambled to her feet.

Her cheeks burned as she realized she'd put little thought to the fellow who'd stayed behind. They'd been gone for weeks, leaving him alone with a collection of Unnamed when they all understood what had happened in the outside world.

She clambered away from the lakeside, stumbled, righted herself, then found her footing and balance. She straightened, broke into a run despite the hammer and anvil pounding in her head. Behind her, she detected the scrape and thump of the others following her.

As she crested the rise and passed from the lake onto the path to the rickety village, she noticed the lack of sentries at the front gate, the position normally occupied by Hartrek and Gartrek. With the ogres gone, they'd not bothered to post anyone else in those positions. It didn't seem right. Mikol was a militia man in the employ of Caedric Carpera, and she'd seen first-hand the security at the merchant's estate. Surely one of his guards would have the sense to protect their perimeter.

A second curiosity caught her attention: the lack of smoke rising skyward from cook fires—a constant in any hamlet. Not a single wisp marred the blue sky.

Llyris pushed herself to go faster, her gut reeling, mind imaging the worst, though she didn't know what the worst entailed. An attack by humans who'd found their dwellings? Shiera returned to spirit them all away to fight her fight? The dragon seeking retribution for their intrusion? Not the last. They'd left the mythical beast, but not irate. And if he had attacked, they'd find more smoke, not less.

She burst through the open gate, her feet pounding the hard, flat ground. What she saw slowed her instantly, and she skidded to a stop.

Bodies lay scattered across the central courtyard—at least eight. Her chest tightened, and she put her hand to her mouth as her gut churned again, threatening to expel whatever it hadn't already discharged. A second later, the others appeared beside her.

"Oh no," Tesfira exclaimed. "What happened?'

Llyris shook her head. She saw no blood, no twisted and broken bodies. But for the faint scent of death carried on the breeze, she might have guessed them sleeping.

Before any of them thought to move, the ogres rushed forward. Gartrek dropped to his knees beside the first of the fallen, grasping the body by a shoulder and rolling it over. Hartrek did the same at the next. The space of three heartbeats later, he let out a howl.

The sound prompted the humans of their company forward again. Gartrek moved, too, going to his brother, kneeling beside him. He put his arm around Hartrek's shoulders, and they both hung their heads.

Llyris arrived beside them and didn't immediately attempt to identify the dead. Part of her refused to look. The wail the ogre made upon discovering the fellow reminded her they'd grown up with these people, spent their lives with them day after day. Who it was didn't matter. These were the twins' friends. Friends they'd lost.

When she overcame her reticence and stepped up, she recognized Drobin, though it took a second. Pustules oozing thick yellow fluid marred his features; a line of dried blood ran from his nose, along his cheek to his ear.

"Get back," Cirril barked as he shuffled backward. "A pox has claimed him."

"And the others. All of them," Gartrek said, head hung.

"Mikol," Hinter whispered.

She and the merchant's man rushed away, leaving Llyris and Tesfira staring at the sickly corpse. A moment later, the thief returned to collect them.

"We have to find him, then leave this place of death."

They searched from hut to hut, finding the dead everywhere they looked. A few had passed a while ago, their stench so putrid after baking in the sun, they couldn't enter. Llyris recognized them all from the time they'd spent in the village and she fought tears for every one of them.

"He's not here," Cirril said as they finished searching the last hut, blissfully empty. In the center courtyard, Hartrek and Gartrek had begun dragging the dead together, lining them up in a row.

"I know where he is."

Llyris walked away without explanation or waiting for the others to follow, heading for the front gate. Once she passed through it, she went right, following the hard-beaten path running along the outer edge of the palisade bordering the village. Her heart beat fast, her breath came in short gulps.

How many people have to die? she thought.

Mikol lay on the trail outside the compound where they kept the sick. She approached with care, her arm drawn across her nose and mouth against the odor emanating from behind the stout wooden fence. When she arrived beside her fallen companion, she stopped and stared down at his slack features, the welts and blisters marking his face.

"Mikol," she said, her voice a breath expelled to create space for more grief.

The guardsman opened his eyes.

"Llyris."

A croak more than a word, but she recognized her name in it and dropped to her knees beside him. Seconds later, Cirril, Hinter, and Tesfira joined her.

"Stay back," the merchant's man barked. "Breathe his air and it will be the death of all of us."

The handler ignored him, taking the poor fellow's head in her lap. She pivoted toward the thief.

"Your waterskin," she said. "Give it to me."

Hinter reached into her cloak and produced it, handing it to Llyris. She popped the cork out with her thumb and tilted it, letting a few drops fall on Mikol's cracked and peeling lips. He lapped at it with a swollen tongue the color of over-boiled peas. When he attempted to swallow, his throat clicked and any liquid he'd taken into his mouth spilled out.

"What happened?" Cirril demanded from his spot four paces behind the others.

"Let him get a breath," Hinter snapped.

Llyris clenched her teeth. She'd tolerated enough of the petty bickering between the thief and the merchant's guardsman, and this wasn't the time for them to renew the annoying habit. As she tensed, readying to chastise them, Tesfira placed her hand on her shoulder and the young woman relaxed. The handler returned to tending their ill friend.

She tilted the waterskin again, allowing a thin dribble of water to cascade into Mikol's mouth. He lapped at it, smacked his lips, then raised a finger half-an-inch. He took the gesture as a request to stop.

"Shiera," he grated, the word like sandpaper scraping across an unfinished board.

"She did this?" Cirril asked, taking a step forward.

Mikol shook his head once and closed his eyes, as though the action loosened his brain and he needed a second to return it to its proper place.

"No. She protected them."

"What? What do you mean?"

"Stop it!" Llyris rounded on the merchant's man, unable to abide him anymore. "Give him a chance."

He frowned at her, but relented.

"She...kept..."

Mikol's halting words ceased, and he licked his lips with a sticky sound. The handler took it as a request and poured more water on his tongue. He swallowed, coughed, the spittle flying from his mouth red with blood.

"She kept them...safe from disease. A spell. To pro...to pro..."

"To protect them," she finished for him. "Of course. I should have seen."

"Everyone?" Tesfira asked, her voice quiet. "Everyone is dead?"

He nodded once and his eyelids slipped shut in a long blink again. "I tried...to save them. I'm the last."

"What can we do for you?"

His rheumy gaze fell on a spot over Llyris' shoulder. "Kill me."

She craned her neck to peer at Mikol's compatriot standing behind her. His eyes widened at his friend's request; he made no move for his sword.

"Mikol...I...I can't."

"It hurts...Cirril. P...Please."

"Too many have died. First Linian, then Kove." He shook his head, diverted his gaze from his friend. "I can't."

The younger man groaned, his muscles tensed, the cords in his neck stood out as he bit down hard, eyelids squeezed tight shut. The spasm lasted a few seconds. When he opened his eyes again, tears spilled out of the corners, running along a path toward his ear. Llyris' throat clogged, stopping her from adding her voice to his to plead Cirril to end his misery. One way or another, he'd die. Why did he have to suffer first?

It turned out she didn't need to beg.

Tesfira moved fast. Her hand darted into Hinter's cloak and came out with the knife secreted within. The blade pierced his chest before any of them knew what was happening. Mikol jerked once and lay still.

"What did you do?" Cirril said, his voice filled with disbelief.

The acolyte fixed them all with a grim expression belied by watery eyes.

235

"I did what I wish I could have done for Emeryn as he watched his stomach cut open and his entrails yanked out. A courtesy I pray someone offers me, if there is no hope and only pain."

Hinter put her arm around her friend and pulled her close. Tesfira melted against her chest, tears streaming down her cheeks, and Llyris cried right along with her.

They stood on the hill at the edge of the bamboo forest over-looking the village in silence. Nearby, the river flowing into the lake gurgled. Birds hidden from sight chirped and sang. Insects buzzed. The world carried on despite the death and decay filling the commons.

The buildings and palisade themselves appeared not different from when they'd arrived, but nobody worked the fields, no smoke rose from chimneys. A pall lay over them, a weight caused by what they'd seen.

Every fiber of Cirril's upbringing rebelled against them having left the bodies—Mikol's especially—without burying them, but they couldn't spare the time. He presumed the ogres would do so, though he knew nothing of their customs. For all his knowledge, they might eat the dead.

The thought roiled his stomach, a feeling with which he'd become familiar since they'd returned from the mountain. First, the unusual travel through the handler's tunnel set it churning, then the sight of the diseased corpses. Finally, Mikol. Not because of his friend's request, nor the acolyte fulfilling his wish.

His own inability to provide Mikol's relief tightened his gut and sickened him.

Wouldn't he have requested the same were it him succumbing to a pox without hope of recovery? Wouldn't he have expected Mikol to relieve him of his suffering?

He reached across his body and wrapped his fingers around his sword's hilt, looking to it for comfort, but it offered none. He doubted he'd ever find it again after failing his friend.

"What now?" Hinter said, breaking the silence.

The thief's arm still draped over Tesfira's shoulders and, though the acolyte's cheeks showed red, she'd stemmed her. When she raised her eyes and met Cirril's, he found somewhere else to place his attention.

"We go back." Llyris' tone held an edge unusual for her.

"Go where?" Tesfira asked.

"She went to the baron's. We must end this."

Cirril swallowed hard and readied himself to speak, intent on keeping his emotions from his voice.

"And how will we do that?" To his ears, he failed.

"I don't know," the handler said. "But we have to try. We can't leave the world to die."

Did she look at him as she spoke? Her way of acknowledging his failure in Mikol's ultimate time of need? He didn't think such things were in the handler's nature. Of course, he'd never expected to see the acolyte kill a man, either. If he'd discovered anything during their cursed excursions done at the behest of Viden Misk, it was the unbelievable was possible.

"You're right," he said, then used a mouthful of saliva to swallow the reticence and self-loathing trying to clog his throat. "We have to try."

He glanced between his companions, each of them staring at him, and he wondered what they saw. Did he appear different to them now, his air of authority and courage replaced by timidity and fear? Did they sense his heart and grow concerned he'd fail them in a time of need, as he did Mikol?

Saying it aloud wouldn't convince anybody, but he swore to himself never to let it happen again.

"We can't hide," Tesfira said. "Hinter?"

"You know I'm with you, Tes." She squeezed her friend tight against her. "Wish Hartrek and Gartrek were coming with us, though."

"They have their own paths," the acolyte said. "We shouldn't force ours on them."

Hinter nodded, and they all turned to Llyris. The handler studied them, eyes hard, her mouth pulled into a shape somewhere between frown and grimace—anger and in pain. Cirril understood and wished he could find a path out of his shame to where she was.

She remained silent. Her eyelids slid closed and the firmness of her face increased until she resembled a bust carved from stone, hardness and edges and hatred. She appeared so much older now than when the merchant's man first met her.

How long ago was it? Not so long for her or the world to have changed so much.

Energy spilled out of her, filling the air around her and touching her companions. The hair on Cirril's forearms rose as it prickled across his flesh. His mouth dried up and his hands clenched into fists.

The space in front of the handler shimmered and wavered, like heat rising in the summer. It coalesced into a dot, expanded. As it grew, a sheen of sweat formed on the guardsman's brow. His breath shortened to pants.

What's happening to me? he wondered. *What have I become?*

The swirling air took on a familiar, misty aspect. The merchant's man squeezed his fists tight enough to dig his fingernails into his palms, hoping for the pain to pull him from this uncomfortable, fearful place he'd slipped into. He looked away from the forming portal to the handler instead. A line of blood ran from one nostril, across her lips, unnoticed.

"Llyris, you're bleeding."

She didn't respond, and Cirril hated the quiver in his voice. He sucked his bottom lip into his mouth and bit it hard, punishing himself for revealing such an unwanted emotion.

When the entrance grew large enough to accommodate a full-sized human, Llyris opened her eyes. She stared straight ahead at the tunnel's misty translucence, strode forward without a word to her companions. As her foot crossed the threshold, Cirril's heartbeat increased, and perspiration formed on his brow.

Arm in arm, Tesfira and Hinter followed the handler with no hesitation, and without checking to ensure the merchant's man brought up the rear. They didn't think they needed to. Despite his shortfalls, they expected to count on him and his sword to support them.

Cirril didn't move.

Somewhere high above, a bird cried out, its call raucous, distant. He tilted his head, lifted his hand to shield his eyes. It took a few seconds before he glimpsed the creature—red and orange feathers, its long tail streaming out behind it like a kite. They'd seen it a few times before.

What if I stayed? he thought. *Would they miss me? Would they care?*

The bird's call rang out a second time as it wheeled and darted away toward the plains, the jangala, the mountain. He watched it for a handful of seconds before lowering his hand, pivoting to face the misty path.

It had grown to ten times his height—bigger than any passage he'd ever seen. It gave him pause, both in awe of its size and out of reticence.

"Coward," he said aloud, then darted into the tunnel, leaving the opportunity for safety behind and following his friends toward certain death.

CHAPTER 19

— • —

I T SURPRISED JAI WHEN they strolled through the gates of the baron's estate unchallenged. In fact, they'd seen no one at all.

"I don't like this," he said as he scanned the grounds.

He recognized them—every shrub and statue, the marble columns guarding the doors, the pennants waving in the breeze. He'd been here thousands of times and recalled them all.

And yet he'd forgotten everything about Rein.

It struck him as so unlikely, he wondered if this so-called baron's champion told the truth of them.

Truthfully, it wasn't so much he didn't remember the man. Blank spots riddled his recollections, like a shadow moved through his mind, a dark and unrecognizable placeholder for someone. Did the phantom represented Rein Shriken? Why? And why did neither memories nor emotions attach to it?

The baron's champion's presence made him feel a bit as though he was losing his hold on reality.

"Anything?" Rein's question pulled Jai from his thoughts.

"Aye, he's near," the troll said, head tilted and nose raised. "And blood fouls the air."

The knight tightened his grip on the hilt of his sword. The familiarity of the weapon did much to allay worries about his sanity. Armor, bared steel, a challenge ahead—these were the places he lived. He determined to concentrate on these and forget the holes in his memory.

"Which way?"

Vyle nodded toward the left of the expansive castle, and Rein set out without waiting for the others.

With the baron's champion now leading, Jai walked beside the horn-bearing Alwin Pelletoot, and the troll brought up the rear. Under other circumstances, he'd have been reticent to allow a magik behind him; given their situation, he deemed it the best choice.

Despite its size, the Unnamed moved in near silence, so quiet he peered over his shoulder to ensure he followed. Without fail, he did.

Alwin Pelletoot pressed on, regardless of the fear etched on his face. He gripped the horn so tightly his knuckles gleamed the same white as the item he held. Rein strode with purpose, as though he knew their destination.

They rounded the corner to discover a dozen corpses dangling from ropes against the side of the castle. Their presence startled three crows from their grim repast, sending them into the air flapping and cawing their discontent. Jai covered his nose from the stench emanating from the dead and wondered how the birds tolerated it.

Rein led them through the empty gardens, past overgrown shrubs and lawns far beyond due for a trim. The baron wouldn't have accepted such unkemptness. At the edges of the flowerbeds and amongst the plants stood familiar statues of former dukes and kings, nobles of note, some missing bits and chunks. One lacked an arm, someone had chipped another's nose off. One statue lay in rubble, and it took the knight a second to recall whose likeness was now a pile of jagged fragments of marble.

Amnayel Prisma.

Alwin's eyes found the ruined tribute and his gait faltered. Jai grabbed him by the elbow, drew him on.

"No time," he told the man.

"What are we doing?" Alwin whispered as he used the unicorn's horn as the rarest of walking sticks. "Shouldn't we be finding the woman? Or better yet, fleeing?"

"Is this what you want? Retreat?"

The fellow sighed and shook his head. "I'm to blame. I must do anything possible to restore balance."

The case he carried banged against his leg when he walked, and Jai wondered what good a man with no combat training carrying nothing but a satchel and an ivory walking stick would be in a fight.

Not much.

"They're in the labyrinth, aren't they?" Rein said without facing them.

"Yes." The troll laughed. "You humans think you have no scent but, once I meet one, I can't get the stink out of my nose."

None of the rest of them shared his humor.

They reached the maze's entrance and stood on the verge. Like every person who'd visited the fabled labyrinth, Jai had lingered here a dozen times before, curious about what hid within and what drew men to challenge it. Whenever he'd tarried here in the past, what he gazed upon appeared different. Sometimes, paths lead left and right, or three options lay ahead. Occasionally, the path extended straight for yards before branching, turning, or offering another option. A unique puzzle each time.

Today, the entrance ran direct and uninterrupted by breaks in the decrepit hedges. He'd never seen it like this.

"Rein?" he began, intending to find out if the baron's champion had experienced this version.

He glanced toward the knight, the usual sadness glittering at the edges of his eyes, but his determination set his face with an immovable expression. Without answering, he stepped forward into the maze known for claiming lives.

Jai pushed Alwin to follow, then he and the troll went after.

Vyle didn't like any of this. Not at all.

They'd seen no Unnamed outside himself for far too long. He smelled them, and the air held the bite of magic, but no matter how hard he sniffed, or how much energy he expended, he couldn't locate its source.

It worried him not for himself, but for the others. He'd grown to like the quirks of these humans, especially the little one called Pelletoot—such a funny name. If they came upon a group of magiks, he wasn't sure if he could protect them. He'd do his best, but even a troll has his limits.

They stalked along the unusual path with its dried leaf walls and yellowed grass floor. Both fighters brandished their swords as though they thought steel posed a threat to whatever they may encounter. More likely the stolen horn offered more menace to an Unnamed if wielded by someone who understood its power.

He doubted Alwin Pelletoot was the man.

The scent left by Rein's squire grew, as did the tangy odor of blood. Fresh, wet. Its stink flared his nostrils. How could the humans not detect it? Better they didn't—it would probably send at least one of them running for cover.

Other smells hid beneath those—skin and fur and fangs. Difficult to tell if they were days old, or purposely hidden. He wanted to warn them but realized doing so would alert anyone listening to their presence, as well as having the potential to drive Pelletoot into a panic. Best to trust the knights and keep from adding more fear to their timorous companion.

Rein slowed his pace, raised his hand in indication for the others to do the same. Jai and Alwin strained to see past the baron's champion; Vyle experienced no such issue. Since he stood three heads taller than the tallest of them, he'd already spied the bend in their path ahead. No way of knowing what lay beyond it.

They halted and Rein faced them.

"Be ready," he said unnecessarily. This aspect of humans Vyle didn't understand—they often spoke things aloud they meant for themselves, not others. "Are we close, troll?"

He nodded, debated whether to mention the cloying scent of blood thickening the air, and decided against it. Ready was ready, no matter the cause.

The baron's champion set out again, both hands gripping his weapon, knees bent and prepared to dart any way dictated by whatever came at him. Vyle admired him for his efficiency, though he too often allowed emotion to taint his decision making, a trait the troll wouldn't have identified with if not for meeting Zalie.

The thought of the little girl set an ache in his chest, a sensation he held onto in case he required motivation for whatever came next.

Closer and closer. The intensity of the stink in the air meant death. He worried they'd find Rein's squire staring skyward, his life drained from his veins and arteries. His olfactory senses weren't so attuned as to discern such things.

They reached the start of the smooth bend, the path curving right, hiding what lay before them, revealing it a few feet at a time. Vyle resisted the urge to quicken his pace, to take point and protect the others. An attack may come from the rear.

At the front of their entourage, Rein stopped without warning. His sword wavered for an instant before he spoke a single word.

"Ilkari!"

He rushed out of sight, Jai hurrying along behind him, Alwin reluctantly following. The troll maintained his pace, glancing over his shoulder, expecting the surprise attack. None came.

He rounded the final bend and encountered an opening into a clear space. At the center of it stood the squire, his legs wrapped in vines, two men lying in pools of their blood near his feet—the rank odor explained. Vyle recognized them as the twins who'd accompanied them—Naeve and Nevan. Good news one of his former travel-mates lived, but the sight made his eyes watery.

Rein and Jai rushed to their friend's side, stepping around his dead companions without knowing their names or how they got there. The baron's champion spoke to Ilkari, but he didn't answer. Instead, he stared past them, toward the troll, eyes wide and eyebrows raised as though he'd lost his voice and used his features to communicate.

Vyle straightened, wiped his face on his sleeve. The distinct scent of bear reached his nostrils an instant before the creature's bulk slammed into him.

At first, Ilkari felt relief when Rein appeared.

Alive, he thought. *He's really alive.*

Next, he worried it an illusion. Some new torture perpetrated upon him by the silver-haired woman or one of her Unnamed. He didn't know why she'd torment him in this way when she could as easily kill him or have him slain. Both the minotaur and the hairy brute appeared the types to enjoy killing.

Finally, he panicked. She'd laid a trap for the baron's champion, and left him as bait.

"Rein! Watch out!"

His tongue moved, lips making the shapes required of them to form words. His throat tightened and struggled. No sound emerged.

"Ilkari," the knight said and rushed across the brief expanse separating them.

To the squire's surprise, Sir Jai followed him, his appearance as healthy and vibrant as when he'd last seen him. Behind him came an unfamiliar fellow carrying a leather satchel and a long, white walking stick tapered to a point at one end. At the rear, the troll appeared in the space between the hedges, stopping to watch.

"I didn't think I'd ever see you again. What happened to you?"

Ilkari's head spun. Rein alive. Jai recovered. The curse lifted and Unnamed slaughtering humans. Was this why Vyle accompanied them? Was he the trap to be sprung?

The baron's champion went to his knees, laid his sword on the ground and drew his dagger, inserted the tip between two lengths of vine and began releasing his friend. Ilkari ignored him, peering instead across the clearing at the troll, wondering if he'd reveal his true colors.

If not for his concern, he wouldn't have seen the danger creep up behind him. He tried to call out, and his mouth again produced no sound. He widened his eyes, raised his brow. Nothing happened for an instant, then the beast appeared to understand his warning.

Too late.

The mass of black hair barreled into him, throwing Vyle forward and bearing him to the ground, the creature's maw reaching for his throat. The sudden movement and the troll's grunt startled the other men, pulling their attention away from the bound squire.

Then the minotaur came into view.

He rolled with the impact, cursing himself for not being more aware.

Smooth teeth grazed the skin at the back of his neck as he pivoted, turning toward his attacker looming over him.

An unfamiliar face with recognizable eyes.

"Hispid," he grunted. "You don't have to do this."

Vyle didn't know whether he could speak in this form. If so, he didn't respond other than with gnashing teeth and groping claws. One of the sharp nails sank into the troll's shoulder. He clenched his jaw and his power gathered without needing him to think about it. He grabbed handfuls of fur, jerked to the side, and threw the beast clear. With it off him, he leaped to his feet, fists clenched as he ignored the blood trickling down his arm.

"You betrayed us," the bear he'd known as Hispid said, proving his ability to speak in any form, though a throaty growl disguised his words.

"Nobody deserves to die."

Vyle reached inside himself, took hold of the power swelling within, guided it the way Breda did when she controlled him. He directed it into his arms and legs, felt them swell as he increased in both size and strength. The display didn't deter the were-bear.

"Put on whatever show you like. It won't stop me from tearing your throat out." A pink tongue darted out, dragging across dangerous white teeth. "I've often wondered how trolls taste."

"I don't think you're going to enjoy it."

They came together in a grunted exhalation of breath. Vyle grasped the bear by the fur under its chin, avoiding its formidable incisors and holding it away from their intended target of his throat. It left him with one hand free, but his foe with two claw-filled paws available for attack. It raked at his face, scratching his cheek and drawing more blood while he avoided its swipe at his midsection.

"Don't make...me hurt you...Hispid."

A sound reminiscent of a laugh issued from between the shifter's teeth, the hideous noise cut short by its attempt to clamp its mouth onto his head. As it lunged forward, the troll shifted, using the beast's momentum in his favor.

Holding the fur under its chin, he grasped another handful on its lower stomach and hoisted the creature into the air. It made a surprised yelp more reminiscent of a dog as its feet left the ground. Vyle spun around, slamming its spine hard against the dirt.

His onetime friend stared skyward, gaze unfocused, chest heaving as he struggled to recover the breath knocked from him. The troll loomed over him, fists clenched.

"Yield, Hispid."

For the space of three heartbeats, he thought the shifter might comply. His eyes ceased spinning, his breathing eased. For an instant, he recognized the fellow he'd sat beside in the guildhall mess, the man with whom he'd worked so hard at being friends.

"Hispid is what humans called me to berate me, Vyle." He pushed himself up, coiled. "My name is Eddubu."

His onetime lunch-mate sprang, but he was ready. He pivoted and caught the shifter in a headlock. Surprised, the beast thrashed, deadly claws slicing the air dangerously close to his face and chest, intent on killing him.

Vyle concentrated all his power into the arm holding the bear. Squeezed. Twisted.

A long crunching sound came from the beast's thick neck, followed by a pop, and the thrashing ceased. The troll held him for a few seconds before lowering him with the same care as settling a babe into its crib. By the time he'd released him, Hispid had already transformed into the state Vyle recognized.

"I'm sorry, friend," he said, brushing hair from his face.

He hadn't killed Zalie, but felt responsible. At night, when he lay awake, he told himself walking away from Breda when she needed help hadn't killed her, but he knew it a lie.

This time, he couldn't fool himself. He'd ended Hispid's life. Him and no one else to blame.

He hung his head, wishing for a different outcome, and may have stayed put but for the sound of pounding hooves and a pained cry.

The creature came out of nowhere, its two cloven feet thumping on the hard ground the lone clue to its presence. By the time they detected it over the tumult of the ogre and bear wrestling, it was already too late.

Jai shifted at the last second, turning sideways to accept the impact on his side. One horn tore through his shirt at the back, the other grazed the flesh of his stomach.

The force threw him, catapulting him away from the ferocious creature, knocking the air and sense out of him.

The instant he fell, Rein leaped forward without hesitation. He swung his sword at the bull-headed monster, hoping for the sharpened steel to create enough space for him to insert himself between the beast and his fallen friend.

The swipe produced the intended result, and the minotaur jumped away to avoid the flashing blade. When it saw the baron's champion standing before him, the creature laughed with a sound no man's throat had ever produced. It reverberated through the air, brought a chill to the knight's skin. He clenched his teeth, the muscles in his jaw bunching. No matter what, he wouldn't let this beast end Jai's life, not after everything they'd been through.

"Puny human," the minotaur said, its nostrils flaring as though it found Rein's odor too rank to bear. "You all think—"

He didn't wait to find out what insult the creature intended. Waiting on it prolonged the inevitable. If any chance for survival existed, he needed to use surprise as a weapon as important as his sword.

Without a sound of warning, Rein jumped forward, his wrist loose as he swung his blade horizontally, arm extended to his fullest reach. The tip struck the minotaur on the left side, digging into its muscled flesh and cutting a path along its belly. The beast threw back its head, cried out in pain and anger as blood spilled down its torso from the fresh wound. For an instant, the knight thought he held the advantage. He pivoted, shifting his grip on the sword's pommel to reverse its course into a backhand swipe, but the creature proved too agile. The length of steel cut empty air and the minotaur's brawny forearm came down across Rein's shoulder blades, the mighty blow sending him sprawling.

He hit the ground hard, the impact knocking the air from him and filling his chest instead with distress. During so many years competing in his father's tournaments, he'd learned not to struggle to fill his lungs—he'd find his breath eventually, and taking the time to force it allowed his opponent to continue his attack. During a tournament duel, he may have survived such an onslaught, but not against this monster. Any advantage he granted would be the last.

Before his body came to a halt, Rein tucked and rolled away, shifting his grip on the hilt of his sword. The minotaur's cloven foot slammed down on the spot he'd vacated, the collision of hoof to ground shaking the earth and sending a spray of dried dirt into the air. The baron's champion scrambled to put some space between himself and the beast, raised his weapon in defense as his lungs burned and his ribs ached to draw air. He continued to resist the urge.

The Unnamed laughed again, its hand pressed to the gash across its midsection as it gave him time to climb to his feet.

He's playing with me, Rein thought. *I cannot best him in one-on-one combat.*

He glanced past the creature at where Jai lay, arm pinned awkwardly beneath him. Broken, no doubt, but he lived. Nothing else mattered. He didn't need to beat the beast fair and square, he merely needed to ensure his friend's life continued.

"You waste both our time," the minotaur said and blew a stiff gust of breath from its nostrils. "You know your days will end at my hand. Why not set your sword aside and make it easier for both of us?"

The knight allowed his gaze to stray from the creature, sure it wouldn't attack him with his attention elsewhere. It wanted him to see his death coming.

Nobody else was close—the troll engaged in defending his own life, vines binding Ilkari, and Alwin...the fellow couldn't contribute anything more than watching in fear. He didn't blame him; some people weren't made for battle.

There'd be no help from them, nor the injured knight. If the threat of the minotaur was to end, it was his task and his alone. He refocused on the beast threatening him, allowed his lungs to draw air, and they complied. He filled his chest, then expelled a long breath between his lips. Seconds passed as he stared into the beast's eyes. Neither of them diverted their gazes and memories flooded Rein's mind, most of them remembrances of the good and loving times he'd shared with Jai. When his thoughts strayed to the life stolen from them when the witch ensorcelled him, the one dangled in front of them until neither the woman nor Viden Misk returned his friend to himself, he brushed them aside. A fight is no time for ill feelings.

Holding the minotaur's gaze, he nodded once and set down his blade. The creature's eyes widened as he hadn't expected Rein to take him up on his offer. To its credit, the Unnamed stopped itself from commenting on his choice or belittling him for it. A smile canted its lips, then it lowered its head to point the wicked tips of its curved horns toward him.

The beast exploded forward, the thick muscles in its legs launching it with a speed and force no man could ever hope to achieve and few could avoid. In the instant it took the creature to cross the space, Rein released his grip on his sword and drew the dagger at his belt with his other hand. He timed the movement so, as the horns penetrated his torso, the blade's sharp edge opened the minotaur's throat.

The force of his foe's charge threw them both to the ground. With every trace of focus and control remaining in him, the baron's champion sank the blade into the beast's side as its hot blood fountained from its slashed arteries, soaking him with its coppery stench.

The beast twisted its head, horns churning his insides. Rein choked down the pained cry finding its way from his chest to his tongue, concentrating instead on burying his dagger in the creature's flesh as many times and with as much force as possible before strength left him.

The minotaur gasped and gagged. It reached upward, grasping for his face while supporting itself with a hand planted against the ground. The baron's champion grimaced and swiped away its groping fingers, the movement sending a fresh wave of pain through his body. He stabbed again and again, wondering if he'd have enough strength to kill the monster.

He got his answer when its elbow buckled and the muscular beast's bulk came down on him, pushing its horns harder into him. This time, he couldn't stop himself from crying out and a pained bellow tore from his throat. As he expelled his breath and agony into the world, his energy went along with it. Rein sagged backward until his head rested against the ground. Each inhalation became a labor, the weight of the minotaur and its tines in his gut too much for him to overcome to fill his lungs. Blood bubbled to his lips whenever he exhaled.

He closed his eyes and did his best to calm himself. If any chance of survival existed, he must extricate himself from beneath the man-bull. He needed to be bandaged to stop the bleeding before he lost consciousness.

With another breath sending a shock of pain through his belly, he gathered his energy, pushed his hands against the dirt, and raised his head. His muscles bulged and knotted, the tendons in his neck tightened as he gritted his teeth.

He didn't budge. His strength failed.

He sagged to the ground, sweat beading on his brow. A cough shook him, warm spittle expelled from his mouth falling on his lips and cheeks, and he knew it was blood without seeing its color. A man coughing blood was someone with precious little time remaining in his life.

The sound of armor scraping against dirt caught his attention and he let his head sag in that direction. His heart swelled when he saw Jai dragging himself toward him.

"Jai," he said. "Worry not. It's not as bad as it looks."

He attempted a laugh, but it devolved into a cough shaking his body. He winced with the pain, closing his eyes and holding his breath as he waited for the worst of it to pass. When he opened them again, the man he loved lay beside him.

"Naught but a flesh wound, champion. You'll waltz at the ball in no time."

Rein managed a pained smile. "If anyone knows I shouldn't be dancing, it's you."

He glanced away from his friend's face, saw the way he cradled his arm against himself and the pain etching his features.

"You're hurt."

"As are you. These things sometimes happen during fights."

Rein attempted to nod his agreement, but his neck didn't have the strength to do so anymore. First coughing blood, now his fortitude waning. How often had he seen other soldiers experience this? He knew one day his expiration was due, but he'd always hoped to die surrounded by those who loved him. He'd long expected it to include two people: Jai and Ilkari. And here he was, his wish fulfilled in such a cruel way, with one bound and the other having forgotten his love for the baron's champion.

A slow exhalation escaped his chest, and he noticed a swirl of gray impinging at the edge of his vision. One more sign.

"It's getting cold."

"It's all right," Jai said, grunting as he shifted his position. He touched Rein's face, wiped blood from his cheek and brushed hair from his forehead. "I remember, Rein. Seeing you here like this, I remember everything."

The baron's champion inhaled a sharp breath. "You do?"

251

He nodded. "I do. And I can't tell you how much your love has meant to me, how often it's gotten me through tough going."

Rein struggled to laugh again, the action conjuring another painful cough. The rusty taste of blood tainted his tongue and threatened to choke him. Through it, he maintained his gaze on his friend, hoping doing so would stop the gray haze's encroachment on his vision.

"We had quite the times, didn't we?"

Jai nodded. "We did. Good ones and bad. And even during the worst time, you stayed with me. You had faith and believed in me, and now I have returned to myself."

A tear rolled from Rein's eye and onto Jai's hand pressed against his cheek. The other knight wiped it away with his thumb. When did they last touch this way? Before the cabin in the woods. It felt like so long ago. So much had changed. A lifetime had passed.

The baron's champion suppressed a shiver, his teeth chattering. The gray at the edge of his vision expanded until he saw nothing but Jai's face. Given the choice, this was how he'd want it at the end. He opened his mouth to speak, lips quivering.

"I love you, Jai."

No sound came out, or his hearing ceased. Whichever the truth, his friend understood his intention. His features tilted with a sad smile, then his lips formed the same words. Rein focused on Jai's palm on his cheek, anchoring himself to it as the haze stole the last of his vision.

Then night overtook all.

Alwin Pelletoot snuffled and wiped his face with his sleeve, smearing tears and snot across his cheeks. For the first time since he'd been watching, Jai raised his eyes to peer upon him.

"He's gone."

He took his hand from the cheek of the baron's champion and struggled to reposition himself, wincing at the pain caused by the broken arm he held against his chest.

"You remembered," Alwin said, his voice breathy with awe.

The knight continued holding his gaze without responding. Finally, he shook his head. He lowered his chin as he spoke, refusing to meet the man's eyes.

"No. I didn't."

The words struck Alwin like a punch to the heart. "But you said..."

"He gave his life to save mine. Offering him a final moment of happiness before he died was the least I could do."

"He loved you so much."

Jai raised his head.

"I know. I wish I remembered. I wish I knew how it was to be loved that way, but I don't."

"Most of us will never know."

The knight grimaced as he pushed himself to sitting, then struggled to his feet. Beyond him, the troll sat upon the body of a man recently a bear. Alwin gaped—so much death.

Jai shambled across to where vines bound Ilkari, his face slack. His eyes didn't move from Rein until he approached within an arm's length.

"Ilkari—" he began.

The squire shook his head, mouthed soundless words Alwin suspected were 'release me.' Jai interpreted them thus and knelt before him, pulling his knife from his belt and sawing at the bindings. A faint howl like the wind gusting through a small space shuddered through the desiccated maze. The knight ignored it and continued working at the vines until sweat ran from his forehead and his face contorted with pain.

The troll laid his hand on the knight's shoulder, stopping him, and Jai crawled aside. Vyle hesitated, regarding the squire with drooping eyes.

"I'm so sorry," he said, before reaching down to rip the bindings away.

The force of it sent Ilkari to the ground, but he bounced up and rushed to the fallen champion, knees skidding in the grass as he fell beside him. Tears already wetting his cheek, he took Rein's head in his lap, bent over the man he regarded as his son, and sobbed soundlessly.

The former Viden Misk watched along with the others. He thought about going to the squire, setting his hand upon his shoulder to offer consolation, but abandoned the idea. Was it the right thing to do?

A minute passed before Jai spoke.

"Our adversaries will assume us dead. We need to take advantage."

"Give the man some time," Alwin protested.

"Time is not in abundance."

He opened his mouth to protest again and was interrupted when Ilkari raised his eyes, Rein's blood smeared on his cheek and across the front of his jerkin. He nodded, leaned forward and kissed his friend on the forehead, then lowered his head to the ground with the care and gentleness reserved for the dead.

"But we can't leave him here," Alwin pleaded.

"We have no choice," Vyle said. "Soon, we may all be joining him. Then what will it matter?"

Pelletoot scowled. Leaving him to rot, to become food for the carrion eaters made the loss of the baron's champion seem so trivial. All of this because of the lifting of Prisma's curse.

"Our curse," the voice reminded him.

Even now, its unexpected appearance startled him and he cast about seeking the speaker before returning his attention to Jai, who stood nearest him, to see if he'd heard. The knight had sheathed his dagger and shifted his focus to his injured left arm, peering down at it as he touched it gingerly with his good hand.

"Broken?" Alwin asked before silently chastising himself for posing such an obvious query.

"Most certainly. I'll need a splint and sling, but it can wait. We have more pressing concerns." He straightened, paused to collect himself, then surveyed what remained of his companions. "Ready?"

He swallowed hard. Was there really an answer to that question?

Vyle let Jai lead as they crossed the clearing toward the path which had led them to this place of death.

He understood the need to move on, but it pained him to leave them this way. They were all friends except for Runt, who'd always been bull-headed, literally and otherwise. He even considered Hispid his friend, despite his attempts to kill him.

Now his blood stained Vyle's hands.

As they left, the troll craned to peer over his shoulder at the twins he could no more tell apart in death than in life, at the minotaur lying atop Rein Shriken, the surrounding ground soaked with their blood, and at the fallen shifter, his head canted at an impossible angle thanks to him. He recalled Breda, and Behrtio, and the others who'd lived at the guildhall. Dead, all of them. Finally, he remembered Zalie, and his heart ached.

Someone needs to pay, he thought, and from what everyone told him, they were likely to bump into the woman responsible soon.

Chapter 20

— · —

O NCE THEY ROUNDED THE bend to the straightaway—it hadn't changed from when they'd entered the maze—they saw out into the courtyard beyond. At the end was the tree they'd seen accompanying the silver-haired woman.

Alwin gripped the horn tighter, hefted the satchel. Why did he bring the bulky bag, lugging it around the city without knowing if anything within would help them, or how to use it if it could? The thought set a sour taste in his mouth as he realized he didn't know what to do with the length of unicorn ivory, either.

They pressed on, their field of view widening as they got closer to the exit, though he wished for it to remain narrow. Nothing pleasant filled the new slivers of space.

An insect buzzed near Alwin's ear. He waved the end of the horn at it, bonked himself in the head and cursed under his breath. The bug dive-bombed him a second time, the noise louder than it should have been. He ducked, caught a glimmer of light at the corner of his eye before a shape came into view.

"Hum."

The pisky danced and weaved, taunting him. She zipped away and in, daring him to continue forward. He swung at it again, missed. She circled his head, flying too fast for him to follow before hovering in front of his face, wings humming a monotonous tune until Vyle plucked the tiny creature from the air.

He brought her close to his mouth and Hum's eyes widened, obviously concerned the beast meant to eat her. She struggled against his grasp, tight enough to hold her but not so firm as to crush her. His lips parted. The pisky flinched.

256

"Tell your master we're coming," Vyle growled. "Tell her she has much to answer for. Tell her I said so."

The troll less released the flying Unnamed and more threw her toward the exit. Hum tumbled through the air before she got her wings going, righted herself, and zipped away.

"Friend of yours?"

Alwin let out a nervous, mirthless giggle. "Not exactly."

The tiny winged being didn't return, much to his short-lived delight.

As they approached the egress from the maze, the field of view widened. More than a tree awaited them.

Jai pushed forward, sword raised as he surged past the troll. He may not have remembered Rein, but he retained clear memories of witches, animated dead men, an enormous python, and the comforting feel of his weapon in his hand. It calmed him, focused him, readied him for whatever lay ahead.

Nothing could have prepared him for what they discovered beyond the end of the hedgerow.

The tree with the likeness of a woman. The silver-haired temptress who'd visited him in his dreams and woken him from his sleep. Dozens of others of all shapes and sizes—tall and slight figures with dark complexions and pointed ears; winged creatures; a hairy fellow with a pronounced snout, and so many more. His eyes passed over them, but his brain refused to comprehend.

How they appeared mattered not to the knight. They were killing people, a threat to humanity, and he must stop them. He gritted his teeth, tightened his grip on his sword and prepared to rush forward, ready to give his life until the woman spoke, stopping him in his tracks.

"Welcome, Sir Jai," she said with a wave of her hand. His legs became like stone. "I suppose your appearance suggests you and your friends dispatched the shifter and the man-bull. Impressive, but a disappointment and a tragedy. I enjoyed the company of the hairy brute."

The knight's companions emerged from the labyrinth, garnering her attention. She nodded toward them and they froze.

"Wait your turn," she said, then returned her formidable scrutiny to the knight.

He struggled against her hold, jaw closed tight, the tendons in his neck taut bands on the verge of snapping. She tittered at his attempt and sauntered to him, tilted her head as she gazed up into his face.

"I woke you from the witch's curse to punish the baron's champion." She walked around him like a tailor appraising their client, intending to create them a new suit. He followed her with his eyes, watching her until she disappeared behind him, picking her up again when she reappeared. "The trouble with you humans is you never do what's expected of you. We merely wanted peace and freedom, and look what you did to us."

A murmur spread through the gathering, grumblings of agreement and hatred.

"I suppose with you I've learned a lesson about mercy thrice over." She halted in front of him, a smile lacking any sense of mirth or comfort slashed across her pale face. She raised her hand and set it against his cheek. "I think it's time you remember."

Where he and Rein had met wasn't far from the labyrinth's entrance. For years, he'd admired him from afar, sneaking into more than one contest to watch him fight, the champion's prowess pushing him to work harder and inspiring him to enter the baron's tournament. He convinced himself it was a decision made in search of glory, a raise in station, not simply to get closer to Rein Shriken.

He got it all and much more.

Visions winked through his mind, sounds and emotions attached to them. Laughter, sweat on bare skin, satisfaction, clanging swords, desire.

Love.

His belly knotted. His chest ached.

He'd told the truth of them. How could he not see? Not remember?

The woman's smile widened. She removed her palm from his cheek and stepped away, and her touch took all the knight's energy with it.

His sword became an unbearable weight, his armor too heavy, his legs incapable of holding it all. His hand opened, the weapon clunking to the ground. His arm dropped, his knees buckled. Sir Jai Aryn folded to the grass, resting on his haunches with his head hanging forward. He raised his hands to his face to hide the tears streaming down his cheeks.

"Rein," he said, his voice weak and distant. "Oh, Rein."

The woman turned her attention toward Alwin Pelletoot.

He watched as she approached, his eyes darting between her, the distraught knight sobbing on his knees, and the magiks gathered, watching. The odds appeared stacked against them.

What do I do? he thought.

"Nothing left to do," the voice responded.

His gaze flickered about, searching for the red orbs so often accompanying it. Could an Unnamed have assisted him all this time?

"Don't be a fool," it chided. *"You know I am you and you are me."*

"What did you expect to do with these?" The woman gestured at the items he clutched. "A worn satchel and a piece of bone? Disparate things. Useless to most men. But you aren't most men, are you?"

She leaned in close, glaring into his eyes. If he possessed the ability to withdraw, he'd have done so, posthaste. Lacking the option, no choice remained but to sweat.

The woman reached down and plucked the bag from his hand, his fingers opening without his consent to allow her to take it. She hefted it but didn't open it before tossing it backwards with the casualness of someone disposing of a piece of trash. It thumped on the lawn halfway between her and the other magiks. They watched it land, but none came forward to claim it.

"And this," she said, dragging the tip of her index finger along the length of the unicorn's horn until it rested on his hand. He shivered. "I can allow you to keep this for now. Perhaps it will help me call out the man hidden inside you. What is it you named yourself? Alwin?"

259

He swallowed because he possessed no other method to respond. She nodded, as if receiving the answer she'd hoped for.

"I've no more issue with you than any other human. Which is to say, I'd prefer you dead." She wrapped her fingers around the horn, stared into his eyes. "Are you in there, Amnayel Prisma? Are you, grandfather?"

She tapped him on the forehead with the tip of one finger, a woodpecker's beak knocking on a tree. Colors and images flashed through his head, swirling together in an incoherent mess. She gave him enough time to hope they stayed before he saw himself—a drunkard without name or memory who'd become Alwin Pelletoot—waking in a dark room. Confused, disoriented, and shocked to find someone dead beside him.

A flash of light and he became the old man, Viden Misk. A series of images unfurled: trapping a guardsman in a traveler's tunnel; lying to a merchant to take advantage of his power, influence, and money; sneaking into a child's sleeping chambers in the darkness and casting a spell to make him ill. A row of slack and staring faces, the color drained from their cheeks, the life stolen from their eyes. A dozen of them, more. Hundreds.

He gurgled, but no other sound arose. He thought he heard the woman laugh, but the horrible memories demanded he watch the truth of his existence, of the men behind the voice guiding him and taunting him since he awoke in the storeroom.

Now he became someone else whose name he knew not. Alwin Pelletoot didn't recognize him, but others hidden inside him did. He watched the man enlist two women to aid in his quest, then banish them to a forest-bound cabin when they stole a sliver of his power for themselves.

Deaths and suffering, all at his bidding. Destruction wrought by his numerous guises over the course of a thousand years.

The final face, he recognized. Amnayel Prisma. The great mage, immortalized in story and song, the savior of mankind. The one who'd plucked humanity from the brink of extinction at the hands of the magiks, saving it from certain death in a war it couldn't win.

This version of Prisma bore small resemblance to the proud and powerful fellow portrayed in paintings and statues in every noble's halls and gardens. This man appeared haggard and broken at first, on his knees, weeping.

"What have I done?"

The words floated through his head, though not spoken in the same tones he normally heard when a voice nobody else registered filled his ears.

The vision rolled farther backward into the past, and the same man stood on a bluff overlooking a series of wood and stone cages. Each contained magical creatures awaiting their time to be bred, but not to create more Unnamed. They were to be mated with humans—the first step in creating handlers. Forced breeding.

Faint in the vision's background, he heard anguished wails.

"No." Alwin Pelletoot attempted to say the word, but his lips failed him.

Another flash of light and a younger Prisma sat on a chair in a claustrophobic chamber. The flame of a single taper cast eerie shadows across the cheeks of those gathered with him—hard men with scarred faces and steely eyes. Mercenaries who'd seen death and dealt it with no compunction or regret.

The mage's mouth moved without producing sound, but Alwin recognized the shape of the words without hearing them.

"The horn," Amnayel Prisma said. *"Bring it to me."*

Alwin's gorge rose. His fingers went limp, and she relieved him of the unicorn's mantle stolen a thousand years before, and he watched her do it, glad to have it gone as his body revolted from what he'd seen.

"He did it," he whispered, the woman relaxing her hold on him to allow his lips to move and his confession to be heard by all those gathered. "He stole the horn. It's his fault." He hesitated, swallowed. "My fault."

A tumult of sound spilled through the crowd of magiks, every indistinct word carrying the tones of anger and revenge. And he couldn't blame them. Amnayel Prisma was neither savior nor hero to humans or the Unnamed. Nobody took advantage of him or subverted his power. The mage was the villain to everyone.

And he lived inside a man who'd named himself Alwin.

Vyle didn't exactly understand what was going on.

First the knight broke down sobbing, then Pelletoot blanched as if he'd seen a ghost before blurting out nonsense about the horn. If he put his mind to it, he'd decipher these happenings—contrary to popular belief, his kind weren't unintelligent because they were large and strong. Ogres, maybe, but not trolls.

He didn't bother putting his thoughts to it, though, because of distractions.

During Alwin's convulsions and mutterings, a shimmer appeared in the air near the castle wall. Having lived his life at the guildhall, he was familiar with such a sight and what it meant.

An arrival, he thought.

He couldn't be sure who'd travel here, but he harbored suspicions based on things he'd heard from his new friends. If it was the return they hoped for, he'd best distract everyone until they arrived.

The silver-haired woman's magic held his body in check, not his will. Not how Breda did when she controlled him. Powerful though she was, she didn't possess a handler's skills, hadn't been trained in the ways to suppress the abilities of magiks.

Vyle concentrated, focusing on building the power secreted away in the recesses of his mind. He drew more than ever before. More than he'd needed to clear the remains of the church or used in his fight against Runt. More than he thought resided within him.

It coursed through him, sending ripples of gooseflesh along his arms, standing the patchy hair on his head on end. He curled his hands into fists, clenched his jaw tight.

The troll broke free of the woman's hold.

Deep down, Vyle didn't want to hurt anyone, no matter the cause, but he was also pragmatic. Left to do as they wished, this gathering of magiks meant to kill him and his companions, an eventuality he couldn't abide.

A ferocious roar tore from his throat, a sound deeper and more frightening than any he'd created. He leaped toward the nearest of the woman's Unnamed—one of the dark fae who'd accosted them on the streets. His sausage fingers wrapped around the man's head before he ever realized Vyle's movement, and he squeezed without malice.

Everyone gathered gawked at him, frozen with surprise. Behind them, a misty circle formed and expanded and a woman stepped through.

Tesfira watched Llyris step out of the passage onto a swath of grass leeched of color. She didn't falter to her knees like the last time she'd traveled them thus. Instead, she straightened, her body tensed. It worried the acolyte, but also gave her hope of avoiding nausea.

No such luck. It hit her the instant she and Hinter passed from the tunnel into the real world, knotting her gut and doubling her over. Her chest and throat convulsed in an attempt to rid her of unnecessary cargo, but found nothing, the meager contents of her stomach left on the ground beside the lake.

The thief knelt, heaving as well. An instant later, Cirril joined them.

"Never thought I'd miss an Unnamed," he wheezed between spasms.

None of them laughed, not even the merchant's man himself. They took another minute to catch their breath and Tesfira realized the handler hadn't moved.

"Llyris?"

She struggled to unfold herself, the muscles in her abdomen protesting every inch of the way. With her body close to upright, she raised her eyes to find out what gave their friend pause.

A crowd awaited them.

She noticed the magical creatures first, the most cursory of appraisals enough to reveal their nature. At the front stood Shiera, near her Jai and Ilkari and another man the acolyte didn't know. The knight was doubled over on his knees, and the new fellow appeared distraught, haunted. The squire was frozen, his gaze fixed on the same fight raging beyond them as everyone else.

A troll tussling with several of what she guessed were elves.

A second passed until Shiera Siirist faced them.

"I'd wondered if you survived our last encounter," she said, her tone equal parts annoyance and amusement—a tired parent agreeing to play one more game before bedtime. "But if you've come for your traveler, I'm sorry to say it's too late."

The handler's hands curled into fists and she stiffened.

263

"I felt it when she died," Llyris grated. "A part of me went with her."

"Oh, isn't that darling?" Shiera laughed.

Several of the Unnamed close to where they'd arrived had noticed the newcomers and abandoned the game of watching a troll fighting a match it must surely lose. The nearest took a step toward them and the handler raised her arm, palm extended outward.

"Stop!" she said.

The word cut through all noise like a heated blade sliding through a block of lard.

And everything stopped. The troll froze with an elfin creature dangling from one hand, its other fist planted in a second's gut. The thing moving toward them—a goblin-faced beast with spindly arms and long fingers—halted mid-step. Lacking the balance to remain upright, it toppled over, hit the ground and bounced like a felled tree.

Only Shiera remained unaffected.

"You already know your tricks mean nothing to me."

Tesfira climbed to her feet, wishing for a weapon, or at least her prayer book for comfort, but she'd let her friend stow it away in her pack. The thief liked to take care of her, and she appreciated it when she did.

As if reading her thoughts, Hinter came to her side, knife in hand, and grasped her arm.

"Stay close," she said.

Then Shiera waved her fingers, relieving them of a choice.

It felt similar to when Llyris made them stop, but not identical. She couldn't put her finger on the difference but, forced to try, she'd have called it intent. There was a malevolence to it absent from the handler's, a malignancy. Power born of vindictiveness and malice.

Either way, she lost the ability to move, as did Hinter and Cirril. The merchant's man stood nearby, sword half out of its scabbard, features drawn into a grimace with equal chance of being caused by the nausea of traveling as ire for the silver-haired woman. Llyris was frozen, as well.

All of them beholden to Shiera's whims.

She crossed the lawn as though somnambulant, her face tilted skyward, her path meandering.

"It feels so good to have the damned horn out of my spine," she said as she tipped her gaze toward Llyris. "Do you realize how difficult life was with it? Horrible!"

She ambled a full circle around the handler, sparing brief, contemptuous glances for the rest of them. When she completed her circuit, she began it again, speaking all the while.

"I'm sure you've had your difficulties too, my dear. It can't have been easy growing up in the guildhall, not knowing the identity of your mother. And shadow-scarred, too. Does it hurt finding out the man you thought your sire wasn't? Maybe not, considering the way he treated you." She continued her pacing, beginning a third. "Of course, your real father hasn't done much better, has he?"

She laughed. Tesfira stared, confused. She'd known little of handlers before meeting Llyris—they were all female and possessed enough magic to control their assigned magiks. When the handler learned more details about herself from Misk, she'd mentioned they were produced through a union between humans and half-breeds—women purpose-bred from the coupling of a human and an Unnamed. The entire concept made Tesfira's head spin and her stomach roil.

Shiera's diatribe continued. "The good news, for your mother, at least, was it happened before he stole the body before this one. What did you call him? Viden Misk? No, he possessed a much younger and more attractive fellow when he took her." She stopped in front of Llyris and shook her head. "I hadn't thought of it, but I guess this means you're my auntie. It's no wonder you turned out the way you did. Understandable that you couldn't keep your Unnamed alive."

The handler's hand flashed out, the flat of her palm contacting Shiera's cheek with a bright crack. The silver-haired woman stumbled backward, eyes wide with shock. A sense of pride bubbled in Tesfira's chest and she'd have laughed if she could. She suppressed the satisfaction, for her prayer book warned her pridefulness was a sin.

The granddaughter of Amnayel Prisma straightened, lowered her hand from her face to reveal a clear, red imprint where Llyris struck her. Her features affected no hint of her previous good humor. Her eyes blazed with anger.

"How did you...?"

"Your little tricks mean nothing to me."

265

Shiera took three steps away, her expression shifting from surprise to disdain, a look Tesfira imagined a bishop offering her mentor when at his lowest.

She didn't strike back. Instead, she hefted the white walking stick, peered up and down its length, then appeared satisfied about whatever measure she'd taken of it.

"I will not punish you, Llyris Fildarae," she said. "Not yet."

The silver-haired woman raised her other hand, wiggled her fingers.

Cirril moaned and came to life.

Energy raced into the guardsman's limbs and he nearly stumbled. When Shiera paralyzed them, she'd caught him about to take a step and, though he lacked the momentum of the movement, his muscles remained primed for it.

He steadied himself, grasped his sword's hilt with both hands, waiting to find out happened next, what Llyris wanted to do. Hard to believe he thought to follow her lead rather than the other way around, but the crackle of magic in the air convinced him he'd chosen the best course.

Behind him, the misty tunnel swirled. He glanced at it, the opening a few feet away. How easy for him to perform an about face and dart into it, leave this war.

The possibility stirred a sour taste to his mouth.

How can you consider it? he thought. *Coward.*

The word brought steel to his limbs. Never in his life had Cirril Feron backed down from a fight. A different opponent than he'd ever tussled with, but today wouldn't be the day he fled.

The woman stepped forward, brandishing the white length of...wood? Its surface shone like no walking stick should, polished to the high sheen of a piece of marble. Could it be made of stone?

No, not stone, he realized. *Bone. The unicorn's horn.*

The merchant's man wasn't a superstitious fellow, nor did he believe every story he'd heard; he remembered them, though. He knew tales of Amnayel Prisma and how the curse started—always thought them flights of fancy.

Yet she held the catalyst for a war, and now a rebellion.

Cirril surged forward, not understanding why she'd let him go while everyone else remained bound by her words. He didn't appreciate the threatening way she brandished the horn as she approached the handler and saw an opportunity to make recompense for the cowardice in his heart.

He stepped between them as she swung her weapon. Cirril raised his sword to catch the blow.

A sound rang out like a hammer striking an anvil, the force of her attack greater than any he'd endured. It drove him to his knees, forced a grunt from his chest.

And broke his blade in two.

Somewhere inside his warrior's brain, he knew better than to kneel there, staring at the broken piece lying on the dead grass in front of him. He realized doing so gave his adversary the opportunity to attack with a killing blow, but he couldn't take his eyes off the way it shone in the dim daylight, or the jagged line where she'd snapped it halfway down.

The strike still reverberated through him as he raised his gaze, expecting to see the ivory horn arcing through the air toward his head. Given the weight of the impact on his blade, it should crush his skull and kill him instantly.

Hopefully.

No more pain from losing his friends, his love. No more cowardice. Nothing but the darkness after the light.

The blow didn't come.

The woman loomed over him, the horn raised, but the handler stood beside her, a hand gripping the weapon, their eyes locked.

Cirril launched himself forward to skewer her on what remained of his sword.

Llyris surprised herself. To say she'd moved with surprising speed was an understatement. More she existed in a place one second, and a different spot the next.

She'd watched the merchant's man defend her and the unexpected outcome, seen him go to his knees and Shiera raise the staff to strike again. An instant later, her fingers were clutching it.

It wasn't wood.

She felt the swirling ridge wrapping along its length. Its opalescent sheen reminded her of the inside of a seashell she once found in the forest. She'd never known how the shell made its way amongst the trees.

Cirril lunged forward, driving the remainder of his weapon toward the woman's side.

It bounced off her as if he'd attempted to skewer a statue.

Shiera flicked her foot, caught the merchant's man in the shoulder, and sent him tumbling. He rolled away, the broken half of his sword flying from his hand, and came to rest at the feet of Hinter and Tesfira.

The silver-haired woman jerked the horn, attempting to tear it from Llyris' grasp, but she held firm. Their eyes met. Fire seethed in Shiera's and a sinister smile tilted her lips.

"What now, handler?"

She drawled the final word in the manner she'd heard it spoken before—dripping with derision and disgust. A term so many mouths despised speaking. A label painted with loathing. An epithet more than a title.

"Let my friends go," she said between clenched teeth. "They are no threat to you."

"I tried that before, and they've been nothing but thorns in my side. Being careful where one offers mercy is a lesson well learned." She tilted her head, eyes fixed on Llyris. "Don't worry. I'll set them free. Free to discover the afterlife."

Anger swelled through the handler. She released her grip on the horn, shoved with both hands, intending to send her adversary flying backward away from her.

It produced the opposite effect.

Her palms met a stone wall, jamming her wrists. The energy of them contacting sent her backwards, past her friends. She struggled to keep her balance and failed. Her feet caught on one another and she tumbled, hit the ground and rolled.

Into the tunnel's entrance.

Llyris took a second to gather herself, appraise her condition. Bruised, not broken. She gathered herself and stood at the end of the path, facing the silver-haired woman. Shiera laughed.

"My, how unfortunate." She strolled past the handler's companions, giving a sideways look to Cirril as she did to ensure he attempted nothing foolish. When she reached the mouth of the passage, she stopped, inches separating the two women. "If you hurry, perhaps you can reach the other end and return before the last of the blood drains from your friends."

A knowing smile crept onto the handler's face. "Oh, I won't need to rush."

Her hand shot out, breaking the plan between the tunnel and the world. Shiera inhaled a shocked gasp as Llyris grabbed the front of her shift and yanked her forward.

The silver-haired woman stumbled across the threshold, and Llyris stepped out.

The skull clutched between Vyle's fingers cracked, the sudden, unexpected sound startling him. He opened his hand and let the daoine sith drop to the ground as the other one wrapped on his fist fell. He glanced around, wide-eyed, and found his companions free of their bindings while the rest of the Unnamed remained held. The troll rushed to the squire, who stood closest to him.

"What's happening?" he asked, forgetting they'd left the squire's voice-box behind in the labyrinth.

"I don't know," the fellow croaked, surprising them both.

"She's trapped her." Pelletoot spoke with a voice not his. Older.

"Misk?" Ilkari said.

He shook his head, like a man attempting to loose himself from a spider's web he'd walked through. "She can't exit the tunnel without traveling to the far end first."

"The other one did," Vyle pointed out.

"Shadow-scarred," Alwin whispered, again in the elderly tone.

The troll frowned. The words his companion spoke made no sense to him. How could a shadow be scarred? Or leave a scar? A shadow couldn't touch or be touched. It offered respite from the sun on a scorching afternoon, but little more.

He faced the squire, the more intelligent of the pair, in the troll's opinion.

"What's he talking about?"

Ilkari shrugged. "Not sure, but the woman can't reverse within the tunnel. Llyris has the upper hand. She could close it and vanquish her to somewhere else, or let her go to whatever's at the other end and trap her."

Vyle's frown deepened, and he glanced toward the crowd of Unnamed held in the young woman's thrall. In his opinion, no matter what happened to the silver-haired one, they'd have their hands full.

Llyris stared at Shiera, enjoying her shocked expression. This wasn't an appropriate time for gloating or self-congratulations, but after a lifetime frowned upon as less-than, she considered a second of appreciation acceptable.

"Close it!" Cirril's voice. "Close it now."

The woman's eyes flickered away from Llyris to some-where over her shoulder—presumably toward the merchant's man—then returned to the handler.

The shadow-scarred, she reminded herself.

When their gazes met again, memories flashed in her mind. She recalled the witch lopped in half by the closing of the tunnel, the wild-eyed cannibals panicking at their situation before they disappeared. Her chest cinched around her heart. All this time, she'd despised the deaths caused by the tasks Misk sent them to complete, yet she was responsible for as many. She alone.

Her expression must have changed, because Shiera's shifted along with it. A wry grin crept across her features, a knowing glint twinkled in her eye.

"You can't do it," she said, the words muffled by the couple of inches of passageway between them.

Her head rocked, and she laughed before turning and rushing away through the tunnel. An instant later, Cirril appeared by her side.

"Close it," he implored. "This is your chance to end it."

She glanced over her shoulder at the Unnamed her words held in place. "Is it?"

She felt him seethe beside her, his anger and hatred radiating from him like heat from an ember.

"If you won't, I will."

He moved to take a step; Llyris caught him by the arm.

"She'll kill you." Their eyes met. "I can't close the passage, but it is up to me to stop her."

She used her grip on the merchant's man to launch herself forward, sending him stumbling away from the tunnel's ingress. The world went misty and indistinct.

And then she ran.

Tesfira watched Llyris disappear into the passageway and Cirril stagger backward. In the brief time since Shiera's hold on them disappeared, she hadn't moved because Hinter gripped her. She struggled and shook off the thief's grasp, ignoring the hurt expression it brought to her friend's features.

"We have to do something," she said.

"You heard her, Tes. If we face Shiera, it will cost us our lives."

"Not that." The acolyte pointed toward the crowd of magiks, a few of them beginning to flex their hands or stretch their necks like waking from a deep sleep. "That!"

Jai was vaguely aware of goings-on around him. Shadows moved. He detected incomprehensible noises he recognized as words—a world out there, but not for him.

271

Not now Rein was gone. Dead. And in his last moments, he'd lied to the love of his life about his feelings because he'd forgotten he had them. How could he ever forgive himself?

The noise outside his self-imposed prison grew. More activity flickered at the edges of his vision. He supposed he should be concerned, couldn't bring himself to so much as raise his head. If not for the huge and powerful hands grabbing him by his shoulder and dragging him to his feet, he guessed he'd have died on his knees.

A goodly part of him wished he did.

When Vyle saw the slightest movement from the nearest magik—a kobold, he believed they labeled themselves, but they were difficult to identify because you rarely encountered them in their natural state—he sprang into action. Powerful as a troll may be, he was no match for dozens of what the humans called Unnamed.

His fist mashed the creature's nose, flattening it into its face, and the tricky thing folded to the ground. Ilkari realized what was happening and took charge.

"The passage!" he shouted, already moving. "We have to get to the passageway."

A good plan. Vyle knew one fact about the tunnels created by those capable of initiating travel—no other magic worked while inside it.

The squire ushered the two young women the troll didn't know ahead of him, the fellow called Cirril followed, and Pelletoot, but the weeping knight remained. Vyle summoned his power again, concentrating it in his arms, and grabbed Jai by the shoulders as he passed, dragging him along with him.

Four steps lay between him and the passageway when he caught more movement from the corner of his eye. With the array of magical ability gathered, he couldn't guess what to expect, and didn't intend to stay to discover the answer. With a burst of power, he launched himself and the knight forward, diving through the mouth of the tunnel as a blast of energy struck behind them. It dug a hole in the earth where he'd been an instant before.

He hit the misty ground and rolled, doing his best to protect the man he held. He popped to his feet and pushed Jai ahead of him into the waiting grasp of Cirril Feron.

"Go," Vyle roared at the others. "We have to make it to the other end before they catch us."

They set out at their fastest pace, the troll bringing up the rear. Within the passage, he lost his magical abilities, but he was still bigger and stronger than any of the humans and most Unnamed.

As he lumbered along the misty passageway, its influence inserted itself in his mind, a weight suppressing him. It reminded him of how it felt with Breda's fingers in his head, controlling him. So much time had passed he'd forgotten the dampening effects of the handler. He'd gotten used to the sweet taste of freedom.

Hinter adjusted her pace to match Tesfira's, keeping the acolyte a half-step ahead of her during their flight through the passage.

She glanced at Ilkari and Cirril, the fellow she didn't know who'd held the white stick before Shiera took it, and a troll guiding Jai. This last confused her, but the sight of the magiks boiling into the tunnel's opening behind them dispelled any concern about the beast.

Despite having darted into the passageway mere seconds after the handler, Llyris was some way ahead of them, the distance increasing. Hinter sought to quicken their own pace, her pack thumping against her spine as she ran.

"Hurry," she said to Tesfira.

The acolyte didn't respond with words, instead answering by hastening her speed. The gesture swelled Hinter's heart while increasing her concern equally. After Quintan and how he'd betrayed her, she'd never expected to fall for anyone again.

With a pack of angered magiks chasing them and Shiera ahead, how long could it last?

Alwin himself had never entered a traveler's tunnel or even considered what it was like. The Waul part of him hadn't thought it a possibility so hadn't bothered wasting what little sober brain space he had on fantasizing about it.

Other parts of him knew.

As distinct memories bubbled and percolated inside his head, released by the silver-haired woman, he longed for the freedom of his previous amnesia. When he couldn't recall anything, he'd desired to remember, if simply a fragment. He hadn't realized how bad such a sliver of the past might be.

He loped along beside Ilkari, the satchel he didn't know why he bothered to carry banging against his leg. His breath came in ragged gasps as he pushed himself to keep up with the older man, visions of other lives assaulting him all the while. The others living inside him tried to convince him they'd performed the heinous acts playing through his brain without malicious intent.

It didn't change the outcome.

A thousand years of slavery and mistreatment. Forced breeding. Murder, deception, oppression. Not enough excuses existed in the world to justify such monstrous actions.

And we consider them the monsters, he thought. *But I am the monster.*

His gait faltered. The man called Ilkari grabbed him by the sleeve, tugged him along.

The passageway ran straight and Alwin let the novelty of passing through trees and thick brush as though ghosts distract him from the death and genocide rattling around his brain.

Llyris knew the woman she chased couldn't reverse and meet her head on, but nothing stopped her from halting and making a stand. It meant they'd clash without benefit of magic, two women wrestling to save the world.

The thought didn't appeal to her, so she hoped Shiera was doubtful about how her powers worked in this unusual passage. She'd seen Llyris reverse course; maybe she wondered whether it acted as a suppressant to her abilities or not. Concerned about the possibility, the handler considered calling out, telling her to stop, but she'd had no effect on Prisma's granddaughter before.

She needed to catch her before she reached the far end of the tunnel with sufficient time to prepare for Llyris' exit, or to reenter.

To push herself harder, she brought poor Flayre to mind, remembered her shrunken frame. Yes, she'd pushed the Unnamed hard out of necessity, but Shiera had consumed her power, snuffing the life of a tender and caring creature.

She gritted her teeth, willed her aching legs to move her faster.

To her surprise, they did.

The space between them decreased. She stared straight ahead at the woman, her silver hair flowing out behind her as she ran, the unicorn's horn bobbing in her hand with each stride.

Closer. Closer.

They neared the tunnel's end, daylight streaming in though the opening, so close to her quarry now. A few strides between them. She lifted her arm, reached out toward her, the tips of her fingers feeling the silky touch of the ends of her hair.

Shiera exploded from the passage, Llyris right behind her but not near enough to grab her. The handler stumbled, her feet caught, and she hit the ground with a whoosh of breath. Her shoulder dug a furrow in the dirt as she skidded to a halt, stars dancing before her eyes.

She lay on her belly, struggling to find air, and blinked hard to clear her vision. Once Twice. Three times. She rolled over, gasped to fill her lungs, and found herself lying in the shadow of the dragon.

CHAPTER 21

— · —

T HE WINGED CREATURE LOOMED over her, its bright emerald eyes staring down at the fallen handler until a clamor rose behind her.

She resisted the urge to turn, but the dragon raised its head and she thought she should also find out what followed her.

Her companions spilled out of the passageway, lurching across the open ground toward her. The ones who'd previously accompanied her at the village carried on, but the others—Ilkari, Jai, the fellow she didn't know, and the troll aiding them—skidded to a stop at the sight of the mythical beast. Cirril backtracked to gather them closer to himself, Llyris, Hinter and Tesfira.

And a good thing he did.

Close behind them came Shiera's gathering of Unnamed. Kobolds, fae, goblins, shifters, and more. The dragon's presence halted the first ones out, stopping them with mouths gaped and eyes wide. They left no space for their compatriots to clear the passage, forcing them to push their way out or end up trapped, and the crowd of magiks became a tangled pile.

Nowhere amongst them did Llyris spy Shiera.

She raised her hand and Hinter came to her, offered support in climbing to her feet.

The handler didn't expect the silver-haired woman to be awestruck by the dragon—she suspected she'd known about its lair all this time. It explained her talking of the god in the mountain, the epelweard.

Had those who'd banished her and the others here been aware? Unlikely.

"Where's Shiera?" she said, breath burning in her lungs.

"I don't know," the thief replied, head swiveling to scan the area. "But we better act fast before they get organized."

She gestured toward the crowd of Unnamed. Most had found their feet, but they all stared at the dragon, trapped by the swirling passageway at their backs.

"I'm not worried about them. I think our friend will keep them in place."

"Our friend?"

The tone in Cirril's words caught Llyris' attention. She spun to face the creature as it reared up on its hind legs, tilted its head skyward, and roared a column of flame toward the heavens. The orange and crimson bird they'd seen when they first arrived burst through it, its feathers trailing fire and leaving a bright path scalded on their eyes.

Screams, yells. Some of the Unnamed dropped to their knees, pledging their allegiance to the king of all magiks.

Llyris grabbed Hinter by the sleeve and tugged.

"This is our chance to find her. Grab the others."

She set out without waiting for a response from the thief, glancing over her shoulder as she went. As she suspected, the dragon enthralled the magical beings too much for them to notice her.

She hurried past the beast, heading for the village's front gate. No part of her desired to return to the house of suffering and death, but she could imagine nowhere else for the silver-haired woman to flee. She assumed when she'd exited the passage and come face to face with the dragon, Shiera must have headed somewhere seeking refuge.

Llyris crossed through the entrance, half-surprised not to find Hartrek and Gartrek having taken up their old positions. She didn't see them anywhere. Odd; they were awfully big to miss.

Footsteps behind her—Hinter and the others catching up. She glanced at them and took a quick inventory: one sword sheathed on the hip of a distraught knight, a pair of daggers wielded by a thief and a guardsman, a sad man carrying a satchel, a weaponless squire and acolyte, and a troll she didn't know if she should trust. She'd been too busy to notice another detail before—no Rein Shriken. The combination of his absence and Jai's demeanor left her concerned.

Llyris sighed and considered crossing her fingers. A little luck never hurt.

They crept into the village, expecting to encounter rotting corpses, their faces covered in burst pustules, skin hanging in sheets. They found none. The ogre twins must have been busy during their brief absence, and she wondered what they'd done with them. Her memory flashed to the tribe of cannibals living on the shores of the Obsidian Fields and their habit of harvesting the dead for tools and clothing. An angered gurgle in her gut prompted her to change her focus.

Ahead and to the left lay the hut providing Shiera shelter for centuries. As good a spot as any to search.

She padded across the beaten ground, passing the gathering circle, the stumps and stools arrayed around the fire pit crowded with long-dead ash and chunks of blackened logs. A breeze shaded with the tang of brimstone found her nose, making her curious about what the dragon was doing. After their encounter with the creature, she didn't know what to expect.

Llyris stopped short of the doorway into Shiera's hut, attempting to peer inside from a distance. Shadows. Any of them either her or nothing. She waited for the others to catch up.

"I'm going in," she said, tilting her head toward Cirril Feron.

The merchant's man nodded. Though he gripped his dagger, ready for whatever may come next, his slack features told a different story. Gone were his intense stare and set jaw, the mien of a soldier prepared for battle. Llyris understood—they'd seen things capable of breaking a person—but she needed him.

"Cirril," she said, touching his forearm.

His eyes flickered toward her; she didn't have to say more. He nodded, his expression hardened. When the need arose, he'd be ready.

She crept forward without looking at the others. Seeing the worry on their faces wouldn't help with her own bravery. She slipped her hand into her pocket, pulled out the dragon's wing brooch. It lacked the quiet energy of Flayre she'd used to calm herself, but its hard edges provided a measure of comfort, a familiarity to concentrate on.

Her progress halted one stride away from the hut's entrance and she leaned forward, peering into the dimness, eyes straining. Packed dirt floor, a simple bed of straw. Nothing else. Breath held and muscles tensed, she went the last step and poked her head through to ensure the woman wasn't hiding beside the doorway.

Empty.

"She's not here," she said, relaxing.

She paced away from the structure where Shiera had lived for centuries, overseeing the village and its inhabitants. In the end, she'd forsaken them when she saw the opportunity to strive for her bigger goal. Did she know what would happen to them without her protection? How could she not?

Not abandoned—sacrificed.

The thought brought a sour taste to the handler's mouth. Dozens of living beings dead in service of her wish to free the Unnamed from the curse.

But she wasn't the only one who'd sacrificed others.

Llyris' gaze fell on the man she didn't recognize. He stood near the troll, the worn leather satchel clutched to his chest like a shield to protect him from whatever he may encounter. She frowned and stomped across the commons. He flinched as she pulled up in front of him.

"Misk," she said, the name an accusation. "I know you're in there."

The fellow cowered, lifted the bag higher as though he sought to hide behind it. To his credit, he nodded once.

"Where is she?"

His gaze flickered away from her, darting between the huts spread throughout the village. He shrugged. Llyris glowered at him, considered pressing him further until the troll stepped between them. The handler tensed, expecting him to get physical. Why didn't her companions come to her aid?

"Leave him be. He doesn't know where she is," the beast said, sounding more articulate than she'd expected. "He's a victim like everyone else."

She stared up at him, a million things rushing through her brain—dragons and death, Flayre, her life before. Never in her wildest dreams did she expect to yearn for a return to those times. Fraught as they were, at least she understood her place.

Nobody asked her to save the world.

Her grip on the brooch tightened, its edges digging into her palm, and her mind flashed to her time at the guild.

Unlike herself, the Seniors separated most handlers from their Unnamed, the magiks living on a different part of the grounds from their counterparts. As with all travelers, they tasked her with caring for Flayre, not merely coaxing the magic from her. During those years, she'd seen many magical beings come and go.

"I know you," she said. "They call you Vyle."

Surprise flashed through his eyes, disappearing as he nodded.

"Why are you helping us?"

"Nobody needs to die."

Despite his hideous appearance, she recognized the pain and regret in him. Beneath the gruff exterior lived a sensitive, caring creature, one forced all his life to lean into the expectations of a population who considered him a monster. Not so different from her experience as a handler.

They deserved their freedom, but nobody needed to die.

"She's not here," she said, spinning away from the troll to face the others.

"How do you know?" Ilkari asked, his voice gruff.

"She's not someone who hides. She'll be looking for ways to twist the situation to her advantage."

Her companions watched her, waiting for her to say more, wanting her to provide guidance. How had they come to this place? How did a simple handler, destined for nothing greater than following the instructions laid out for her by the guild Seniors, end up here?

A hand on her shoulder startled her. She spun around to find the nervous man, an apologetic expression on his face, knuckles white as he clutched the satchel tight against himself. Despite his appearance, the words he spoke came out steady and confident.

And spoken in Viden Misk's voice.

"You are shadow-scarred."

The phrase wrapped around her, sank into her, permeating her muscles and penetrating her until it found her bones, her guts, her heart.

Llyris inhaled a deep breath and closed her eyes.

The immediate sense of sinking made her stomach lurch, but she didn't let it distract her. She concentrated, feeling herself slide down her body, along her legs, into her feet. She jumped through the space taken up by the soles of her boots and entered the earth.

This time, it felt comfortable, familiar. The chatter of burrowing insects and the grind of worms sliding through dirt carried on as always, as though nothing unusual happened around them.

She went deeper, listened more closely.

The roots spoke of the dragon coming down from the mountain, a sense of concern and excitement in their whisperings. She allowed them to draw her away, guide her. They showed her things she already knew—the misty passage swirling outside the village's walls, the group of magiks held at bay by the dragon's threat.

And Shiera standing on the shore, horn in hand, arms raised.

Llyris' eyes popped open. "The lake."

The nervous man stumbled as she pushed past him. Out of the corner of her eye, she saw the troll gather him, and then the others rushed to follow her.

Through the village gates, she went right instead of left, intending to take a tight path following close to the palisade and avoiding the throng of magical creatures. She assumed the dragon wouldn't let them pursue her, but she didn't know the beast's intent. The other concern was this route took them past the spot where Tesfira relieved Mikol of his suffering. She set her jaw, gripped the brooch tight enough to feel it bite into her flesh, determined to keep her attention from wandering to the gate.

She needn't have worried because Shiera left something else to distract her.

Vyle needed no introduction to these humans, especially the woman who'd first appeared from the misty passageway. Ilkari and Jai knew them—good enough for him. Plus, it became clear pretty quickly they wanted to help, not to harm.

So, when the one they called Llyris whisked past him, hurrying toward the gate with no word of explanation, he scooped up Alwin Pelletoot and followed without hesitation.

As he loped along behind her, it surprised him to notice a warmth creeping in his chest, and he took a moment to observe it, wonder what caused it. With everything going on, why should he experience this unusual sensation? What was it?

Purpose. Belonging.

All those years confined at the guildhall, trying to connect with Hispid and others, and he'd failed. Even the so-called Unnamed ostracized him, left him out, made him an outsider.

But here, in the most desperate of times, these humans accepted him. A corner of his mouth crept upward, tilting his lips into what some might consider a smile.

They rounded a bend and Llyris halted with a suddenness that forced him to amend his course to avoid running her down. When he saw what gave her pause, his smile disappeared like a drop of water on a red-hot stone.

Two ogres blocked the path ahead, one lying on the ground, the other kneeling beside the first.

"No." The handler rushed forward.

Vyle followed her, abandoning Alwin Pelletoot to fend for himself. The warmth in his chest fled as quickly as his smile when he saw the blood.

"Hartrek," the shadow-scarred said. "What happened?"

The troll's eyes widened. He'd briefly encountered the ogre twins in his youth, but they'd left an impression. Of all the Unnamed he'd met throughout his life, they matched closest with his kind—big, brawny, and misunderstood because of their appearance. And what idiot forgot a matching set of behemoths weighing more than a thousand pounds between them?

Hartrek and Gartrek, he recalled. This is what happened to them.

Some places worse than the pit existed.

The burly fellow raised his eyes to Llyris, tears glistening on his cheeks, and shook his head. Vyle came to stand with her, the others soon joining them.

The ogre held his brother's head on his lap, blood at the corners of Gartrek's mouth—nothing compared to the amount soaking his shirt from the wound in his chest. Llyris knelt beside him, put her hand on his arm. Hartrek winced, her touch causing him pain.

"She did this," the handler said. A statement, not a question.

The ogre nodded, lowered his chin.

"Where is she?"

He pointed toward the lake. Llyris glanced the direction he indicated, then took a moment to ensure their eyes met. What passed between them, Vyle couldn't say. Grief, perhaps. Sadness. An insurance to exact revenge.

She stood again and set off, continuing to follow the palisade. The others followed, but the troll hesitated, lingering at the side of the ogre. A second ticked by before Hartrek realized his presence and tilted his head to peer up at him. He stared at Vyle for a moment before his expression changed.

"I know you," he said, his voice choked with tears. "We met many years ago. At the guildhall. Kurth, isn't it?"

The troll's eyes widened. He had no memory of being called this name, but a sense of familiarity accompanied it. A surety it belonged to him.

Kurth, he thought. *I have a name.*

Ilkari tugged Jai along with him, the tip of the knight's sword dragging behind, the sound of it grating in the dirt, setting the squire's teeth on edge.

He didn't know where they'd ended up or what was happening—familiar feelings since the day they set out from Caedric Carpera's on missions they didn't truly understand. Knowing the outcome, he felt certain every one of them would have risked their own deaths and refused.

Now Rein and so many others were dead.

His gut wound itself into a tangled ball at the thought. He'd spent most of his adult life looking out for him, first as a teacher and mentor in his childhood, then serving as his squire when he grew to manhood.

Every fiber of him wanted to release, to fall to the ground in a heap, curl into a ball, and mourn the man he'd considered his son, but he couldn't. He needed to stay strong. For Jai. For Rein's memory.

And until somebody paid the price.

Llyris led them around the outside of the strange compound in this ramshackle village he'd never been in and didn't know existed—like so many places they'd visited of late. Hinter and Tesfira followed close behind her, then Cirril Feron. The merchant's man gripped his weapon, but he noticed a difference in his demeanor, a quality Ilkari didn't recall seeing from him before.

Hesitation.

Recognizing it worried the squire almost as much as Vyle's absence.

The troll had stayed with the ogres. Llyris and the others appeared to know them, their familiarity all he had to trust the remaining one wouldn't sneak up behind him and crush his skull like an overripe melon. Faith in their judgment and his hope Vyle wouldn't let it happen.

He'd grown to appreciate their guide over the weeks they'd spent together. Like and trust him, though he'd abandoned them. As they approached the unknown ahead of them, he wished the brute strode beside them, hoped for his return.

The lake's scent found Tesfira before they reached the top of the rise. All lakes possessed a particular odor—mud and decaying plants, the redolence of the sun heating the water. At other times, such odors stirred happiness in one's heart.

Not today.

Besides the danger lurking ahead of them, this lake represented a place of disappointment for her. She'd stood beside it, placing her trust and belief in a woman she didn't realize intended to wipe out humanity. Shiera had taken her to the mountain, pretended to show her God, and now Tesfira wondered what trickery she'd performed, because God didn't exist. Not in the mountain, at least.

And if her days continued beyond this one, she'd likely spend the rest of it doubting He'd ever existed anywhere else.

Understanding this hurt her heart. What would Brother Emeryn think of her? He'd given his life doing God's work, and she'd lost her faith because a devil woman tricked her.

She squeezed Hinter's arm more tightly and, awkward as it made it as they followed Llyris, the thief glanced over at her friend. She wore a question on her features: *are you all right?* They both knew the answer, leaving no reason to speak it. Instead, the acolyte's eyes darted toward the fence surrounding the compound where they'd kept the sick. The place responsible for wiping out the village's residents.

Where she'd slain a man.

"I killed him," she said, her words jarred by their hurried pace. "I killed Mikol."

"You did what needed doing."

She shook her head. "God won't let me into his kingdom." *If there is a God*, she added to herself.

"Any god who wouldn't allow you in isn't worthy of wasting breath on prayers, Tes."

Hinter offered a strained version of a smile, the expression meant to give support, to suggest understanding. How out of place it appeared given their circumstances.

I shouldn't have said anything, she thought. *Not now*.

She knew her friend cared for her, as she did in return. This wasn't the appropriate time to distract her from the looming threat, but she couldn't prevent it from slipping out. After a lifetime of leaning on her faith, believing in a higher power to whom she owed all, she felt like she'd been left floating in the very lake they rushed toward—water over her head, under her, all around her.

How could she find her way?

They crested the rise and stopped at the end of the path winding down the incline to the shore.

Sunlight glinted on the churning water, and Cirril wondered what so agitated it when no wind disturbed the air. Ripples and waves wrinkled the lake's surface, the undulations heading all directions, clashing against each other, appearing like liquid boiling in a vast pot, but no steam rose toward the sky.

"What's happening?" he asked, leaning closer to the handler.

He didn't expect her to have an answer, but he needed to expel the question from his head. If he left it to rattle around by itself, unanswerable, it would have distracted him. He required all his focus to overcome the overpowering urge to flee.

"The creatures of the lake are unhappy," she said.

As if hearing her words, a fish broke the surface, arching through the air before splashing into the water again. In the second of its exposure, Cirril glimpsed a row of quills along its spine, a long snout filled with needle-pointed teeth. Then it disappeared.

"What the devil?" he muttered and adjusted his grip on his dagger. "Why do they behave this way?"

Llyris raised a finger in response, pointing at the edge of the lake.

Distracted by the churning waters, Cirril hadn't noticed the silver-haired woman. She stood two paces from the shore, waves lapping around her ankles as she held her arms in the air, the twisted horn extended toward the sky.

The guardsman gulped down a mouthful of sour spit. It tasted of fear.

Over the course of his career in Carpera's militia, he'd crossed swords with uncountable men. Brigands and thieves, men of a rival merchant's militia, the occasional duel. Whenever the time came to exchange blows, his muscles quivered with anticipation. His mind focused to a fine point, everything in the world disappearing except the opponent before him. Not once did one of them lay a blade on him.

But this...

Witches. The animated dead. Cannibals. Troll and ogres and other magical creatures for which he didn't have names. A dragon, for God's sake. A dragon. How should a soldier fight these menaces with naught but a short length of sharpened steel? An impossible task.

One likely to end in death—his.

Llyris sensed the doubt and despair radiating from Cirril beside her and the rest of her companions as they arrived to join them at the crest of the hill. How could she blame them? They were but a rag-tag collection of humans set to face the granddaughter of the greatest mage who'd ever lived. A woman born a thousand years ago.

What possibility for survival, let alone success, did they have against her?

The handler turned from the lake, her gaze falling across each of her friends. A thief sentenced to a life of servitude after failing in her chosen career. An acolyte losing her faith, doubting God's existence. A knight overcome by despair, another by doubt, and a third struggling against unfamiliar fear. A troll who'd abandoned them, and a fellow clutching a satchel to his chest as if it contained the most precious items in the world, but with nothing else to offer.

She smelled the reticence on them. It filled the air like the smoke from a poorly made fire, wrapping around them and permeating everything. What happened to her companions she'd met at the merchant's estate? The thief who'd crept into the witches' cellar to steal the Book of Shadow? Or the fighters she'd seen stand with nary a glimmer of fear against undead foes and enemies bent on harvesting their bones and eating their flesh? Who was this young woman masquerading as the acolyte who'd dedicated her life to the service of God, forsaking everything else?

They watched her like sheep awaiting directions from their shepherd, and she saw in their eyes they hoped she'd release them, let them flee, or hide, or break down and cry.

Because who was she to guide them? A waif given to the guild without a fight. An outcast, derided by the citizens she sought to serve. A handler responsible for the death of her Unnamed. A freak. A loser. A...

A shadow-scarred.

The words floated to her as if on a breath of air. She glanced between her companions, wondering if any of them heard it as well. None gave any sign they had.

The daughter of the mage.

She faced the lake, positive Shiera attempted to manipulate her, but she remained the same as when they arrived—arms raised, droplets of Gartrek's blood tainting the horn she held aloft.

Llyris lifted her hand, uncurled her fingers. The dragon's wing brooch lay on her palm, its shape outlined in her flesh. The silver-haired woman hadn't given it to her. It surprised the dragon to discover she possessed it. If neither of them, who had appeared in the forest and presented it to her?

You know the answer, Llyris Fildarae. You are the answer.

She closed her hand on the totem again, sensed the warmth radiating from its edges. It flowed into her, following a path up her arm, through her veins, into her chest. It spread through her body, filled her, forced the worry and hatred out of her.

She turned to her friends.

"It's her," she said. "She's doing this to us. The doubt. The fear. The lack of faith in ourselves. In each other. In God. Everything is her doing."

The group glanced at each other, surprised to find their companions experiencing something similar to themselves. Hope glimmered in their eyes.

Llyris turned her attention toward the man she didn't know. She held out her hand, expectant.

"Give me the bag."

Alwin's mouth fell open. He couldn't guess why the dial had chosen him, or why this trio of volumes, but he suspected it meant for him to protect them. Or perhaps they him. But to what ends? How would he know what to do with them? Was this it?

"Pelletoot. Give her the satchel."

The sound of the troll's voice startled him. He'd crept up behind without Alwin noticing. A being of his size shouldn't possess such an ability to creep, but he managed it.

He diverted his gaze to his arms wrapped around the leather bag, its edges pressed into the crooks of his elbows. Not holding it, hugging it. Though he held it close to his nose now as before, he just then noticed the worn cowhide's scent, the metallic tang of the clasp in his nostrils. He drew a sigh, his expanding chest pressing against it.

"Give it to her," the long-absent voice in his head told him. *"This is why you have it, you fool."*

Alwin swallowed hard, raised his eyes to the handler awaiting him to do as she'd said, though she didn't ask a second time.

He shifted, moving his hands to the sides of the satchel, and extended it. The weight of the tomes inside it threatened to drag his arms groundward. When she took it from him, he exhaled in relief.

Llyris knelt and put the bag on the ground, her fingers finding the clasp and working to open it. When it didn't cooperate, Alwin parted his lips, intending to offer direction. The finicky contraption gave up before he spoke.

The young woman reached in and extracted a book, leafed through its yellowed pages before setting it aside. Alwin strained to see which one, then stood on his toes to peer over her shoulder and into the satchel's dark depths.

She took out the next tome, followed the same procedure as the first, then pulled forth the third. His heart sped as she passed her hand over its cover. He imagined the feel of its grainy leather, the scent of the ancient vellum, the magnificent illustrations hidden away inside.

"This one," she said, and stood.

She shifted her position, facing the lake again and the woman standing ankle-deep in its waters. Llyris cradled the book with her left arm and flipped it open, riffling the parchment as though she knew exactly where to find what she wanted. Alwin wished to be holding the tome and gazing on the intricate pages of text, the swooping lines brought together to form likenesses of the fantastical beast.

The handler traced a path along the scrawled words, the pad of her finger whispering across the page. She closed her eyes. Her lips moved.

Llyris didn't know what she was doing.

The instant she'd laid fingers on the tome, she knew it was what she sought, but not why. Everything after happened the way anything born of habit did.

But whose habit? Not hers.

Her fingertip followed the tangled web of letters across the rough parchment, and pictures appeared in her head. An interpretation of what her finger traced on the page. Meadows and flowers, the scent of honeysuckle carried on a warm breeze. Peaceful. Tranquil. A place anyone would yearn to be.

In her mind, she stood in the middle of the meadow, fresh air tickling her nose and filling her lungs, sunlight warming her skin. But it wasn't her nose, or her skin.

It tempted her to wonder who and where she was, but she resisted. She realized she needed to focus, a difficult task in the face of such an idyllic scene. The urge to sniff flowers and chase butterflies, to roll in the grass and lap at pools of cool water bubbled inside her.

"Llyris."

Hinter's voice pulled her from her reverie. She opened her eyes, vision momentarily blurred, and peered toward the lake.

Its surface was in upheaval. It splashed around Shiera's legs; fish jumped and twisted in the air, which itself spun, coaxing waves upward to join it.

The handler snapped her eyelids shut again, flipped the pages in the tome resting on her arm. She scanned the sheets of parchment, browsing each without pausing to enjoy whatever they showed her. The rustle of the ancient paper sounded as loud in her ears as the tumult of the lake. It whispered to her, encouraged her to continue, told her what she searched for was close.

Am I going crazy?

Her hand passed a dozen pages of dense text followed by an illustration. She stopped, laid her palm flat on the picture, and filled her lungs to capacity, drawing energy in with the air. A vision coalesced—the hooded figure she'd met in the forest, and then in the cavern under the Obsidian Fields. She heard it speak and repeated what it said.

"Come to me."

A whisper. A simple movement of breath between her lips.

The energy she'd drawn left her. It rushed out of her body, spreading out in all directions. When she faltered, hands grasped her, held her from crumpling, kept the tome from toppling from her grasp. Tired. Depleted. Hopeful.

The world fell into silence. The book's murmurs disappeared. The lake quieted. The sound of her pulse filled her ears, the rasp of her breath in her throat. Nothing else until Tesfira spoke.

"Oh my."

The handler opened her eyes.

Even without sporting a six-foot horn from its forehead, nobody could mistake the creature for a horse. Muscles rippled beneath its purest of white coats. Its long mane and silky tail streamed out behind it as its hooves beat against the grasslands. The closer it got, the more easily she judged its dimensions, and she estimated it at least twice the size of an average steed.

But nobody ever rode this animal.

"The unicorn," Alwin muttered. "It's impossible."

The exquisite beast leaped from the scrubland onto the lake, its steps sending splashes fountaining in its wake. Droplets sparkled in the sunlight like a rain of diamonds and the water creatures fled to the depths.

On the near shore, Shiera waved her arms in triumph. Jubilant, she swung the severed unicorn's horn through the air in a circle above her, its length still tainted with the stain of an ogre's blood.

Now halfway across the lake, the unicorn tilted its head, the wicked tip of its horn directed at the silver-haired woman.

She froze, her elation disappearing as quickly as the lake's water had calmed in the face of the charging beast. She lowered her arms, hesitated, then turned and ran.

The congregation watched her for a second as Shiera struggled up the hill toward the village, the flowing skirt of her shift impeding her. She'd sensed their presence and avoided following the path, instead beating her way up the scrub-covered incline, bare feet slipping in the loose dirt. The unicorn's hooves splashed in the water as it neared the shore, the sound driving her on.

Without prompting, the mismatched group of companions abandoned their position, hurrying the direction they'd come. Llyris carried the tome with her. Alwin retrieved the others and stowed them in the satchel before following. With no words spoken, Hartrek joined them as they passed.

They hurried around the curving palisade, and the dragon, portal, and the crowd of magiks came into view. It appeared as though they'd been frozen since they left, any change in their positions unnoticeable. The Unnamed cowered, the mythical beast simply stood before them, its presence enough to hold anyone at bay. It directed its emerald eyes toward their party as they rounded the corner.

Someone amongst the crowd of magiks shouted and pointed, their exclamation sending a murmur through them. The dragon roared, silencing them.

A second later, Shiera darted past the beast, halting in the space between it and those she'd released from the curse.

"What are you doing?" she screeched. "Don't just stand there. Get out of my way."

The group parted, opening a path to the passageway's entrance. The pounding of hooves in dirt filled the air, and she glanced over her shoulder before hurrying on, bound for the tunnel and the baron's estate at the other end.

Llyris stepped forward, separating herself from her friends. She inhaled through her teeth, drawing energy with the breath as before. This time she tasted it, an acidic tang on her tongue provoking saliva into her mouth. She paused, swallowed, and spoke.

"Stop."

Not loud. She didn't shout or scream. Firm, commanding. The way Rein might have spoken it.

Shiera halted mid-step.

The hoof beats slowed and the great white beast trotted past the dragon, coming into view of those gathered outside the walls of the village where magiks had been banished and lost their lives.

A gasp passed from mouth to mouth of the Unnamed, and a wispy creature with a dark complexion at the front of the group fell to her knees, then the one beside her, and the next. A moment later, every magical being save the dragon—Vyle and Hartrek included—genuflected before the most mystical of magiks.

The air around the unicorn shimmered. Butterflies followed in its wake, fluttering about it when they caught up, alighting on its nose or shoulder before taking flight again. The animal's eyes glimmered with a wisdom and vitality impossible to miss. Blades of grass where its hooves touched went from brown to green; flowers bloomed in its path. It strode forward, paced a circle around the silver-haired woman before stopping before her.

"Shiera Siirist. I believe you have an item which does not belong to you."

The unicorn's mouth didn't move, but they all heard the words. They filled their heads with the clarity and brightness of a pealing bell on a spring morning. Many of the kneeling magiks leaned forward and touched their foreheads to the ground.

The snowy white animal turned its head toward Llyris, nodded.

The handler released a long exhalation before speaking.

"Move."

The tension holding Shiera in place relaxed, and she stumbled, used the severed horn to steady herself, then faced the unicorn. She brandished the length of ivory, the spots of Gartrek's blood dark on its opalescent surface.

The white magik snorted. "You wave my mother's stolen mantle as though you think I should be in fear of it? Do you not suppose it is you who should be fearful for having it?"

The silver-haired woman's lip curled in a snarl. "Return whence you came. This has nothing to do with you."

The animal paced two steps forward. "Nothing to do with me? You threaten me with the horn stolen from my kin and claim I have no involvement?"

"I want to see magiks live in freedom."

"No. You desire for humanity to die."

She shrugged. "If need be. I'll do whatever it takes so my brothers and sisters no longer have to exist under the thumb of man."

The unicorn shook its head, its silken mane flowing and setting three butterflies fluttering into the air. "You broke the Law, Shiera Siirist. The dead pile up in your wake like a cord of firewood to prepare for winter."

"Law?" she scoffed. "You speak to me of the Law? The shackle placed on our kind...on your kind...by our slavers? How dare you?" She shifted away from the animal, faced the group of magiks who'd followed her through the tunnel. "Do you hear this? This creature doesn't deserve our reverence. The unicorn sides with the humans and wants to see you bound again. She seeks to steal the lives I returned to you."

Some of the Unnamed stirred. A grumble passed through their midst. A few raised their heads, glared at the unicorn. The butterflies circling its head settled on its shoulder.

"Hmm," the creature mused. "The foolishness of youth. You all remember the curse and everything after, but you forget how things were before my mother died."

"We don't forget," one of the wispy fae snapped. "We lived free, as we do again."

A chorus of agreement from the gathered Unnamed. The unicorn paid the murmur no attention.

"Yes, to a point. But you have forgotten the Law existed before greedy men stole my mother's life. It always was and always shall be. It is how magiks and humans coexisted for centuries before the mage took matters upon himself."

It tilted its head, gaze directed toward Alwin Pelletoot. The man shrank from its attention, pulled the satchel high enough to hide the bottom half of his face, eyes peering over the top. He stepped behind Cirril Feron.

"He is at fault, not humans. They did nothing to release you from the curse because nobody could until now."

"It has been my life's work," Shiera said, stepping forward, her posture straight, her head tilted and her chest expanded. "I have done everything—"

"I wasn't talking about you, Shiera Siirist. The Law was broken and you are responsible."

Confused expressions passed between those gathered, Unnamed and human alike. The silver-haired woman's attitude sagged. A scowl tugged at the corners of her mouth as a storm crossed her brow. The muscles in her jaw tightened and lightning flashed in her eyes. She raised the horn toward the sky, her lips moving as she whispered an incantation. The air hummed with power, and then she stabbed it downward, burying its tip into the dirt.

Nothing happened.

Her eyelids widened as she shifted her gaze to stare down at the spot where ivory met earth. A rumble of laughter escaped the dragon's mouth, borne on a cloud of sparks.

"Fool," it said. "Do you not understand who stands before you? This is Kaisa, most magical of all. You should bow before her."

"Enough, Aeryz." The unicorn's voice echoed through all their heads. "For a thousand years you were charged with being my keeper and protector. You have done a wonderful job, old friend, but your services are no longer needed." Kaisa faced the group of humans. "Step forward, savior of the Unnamed. Come to me, Llyris Fildarae."

The handler froze, her expression suggesting she'd rather flee than do as the unicorn said. If not for Tesfira's hand on her, ushering her on, she'd have stayed put forever.

The onetime handler separated from her companions, edging toward the horned creature one tentative step at a time, her heels dragging and leaving furrows in the dirt. All eyes lay upon her, the weight of their attention slowing her.

"You've made a mistake," she said, gaze darting from the unicorn and dragon to Shiera and the group of magiks arrayed behind her. The silver-haired woman seethed. "I'm no savior. I'm naught but a handler who lost her Unnamed."

"You are shadow-scarred," Kaisa corrected her. "The bridge between humans and magiks. You are the question and the answer. The truth and the way."

Llyris swallowed hard. "But I—"

Shiera's enraged scream bit off her words and startled them all. She leaped across the space separating her from the handler, the unicorn horn tainted with Gartrek's blood lifted above her head, ready to strike a devastating blow.

It cut an arc through the air, the ragged end whistling. Llyris raised her arms to protect herself, closed her eyes to receive the lethal strike.

The horn struck Hartrek's palm and moved no farther, the repercussion of the sudden and unexpected stoppage jarring Shiera. The ogre twisted his hand, wrenching it from her grip and sending her toppling to the ground.

He stood over her, the ivory weapon gripped in both fists as he used his thumbnail to scrape his brother's dried blood from its otherwise gleaming surface. The woman scrabbled backward, hands and feet scuffling in the dry soil puffing dust into the air. When she got a few yards between them, she struggled to stand, stumbled, righted herself again and lurched across the yard toward her disciples.

"Don't just gawk," she gasped. "Help me, you fools."

Hartrek took a measured step after her, blocking any chance of her going any direction other than the one she'd chosen. The magiks looked at each other. Some glanced at the ogre, the dragon, the unicorn, measuring their chances if they sided with her. None of them did anything.

Shiera's anger roared from her mouth. As she reached the gathering, they stepped aside, clearing a path for her. Leaving her no choice but to enter the portal and escape to the baron's labyrinth. She leered at them as she passed, twisted her neck to peer over her shoulder at the advancing ogre, the horn gripped in his fist.

"You're not the only ones," she barked as she careened toward the tunnel. "I'll return, and then you'll pay. All of you will pay."

She lunged across the threshold, a crackle of energy rippling the air as she departed this place headed for another.

"Halt, Hartrek," Kaisa said. He complied, then the unicorn, who'd watched in silence, faced Llyris. "Close the passage."

She lunged across the threshold, a crackle of energy rippling the air as she departed this place headed for another.

The words reverberated in the handler's ears, rattling around and refusing to allow comprehension. She stared at the swirling entrance, the silver-haired woman already little more than a miniature version of herself. In seconds, she'd be only a dot, and then she'd disappear completely to arrive at the other end minutes later, spilling out on the baron's grounds within spitting distance of his maze.

Llyris hesitated, her head filled with the witch slain by closing a tunnel, the cannibals doomed to whatever lay on the other side. How could she do it again?

What choice do I have?

She blinked, glanced toward the unicorn, hoping for her to rescind her order. Kaisa said nothing. Nobody spoke until Ilkari appeared at her elbow.

"Do it," he said. "She will survive, but in a prison she won't enjoy. Trust me, I know."

Her gaze met the squire's, his eyes watery with emotion, and she recalled the first night after she'd arrived at the baron's, before Misk's searches turned everyone's lives upside down. When everybody else ignored her, or treated her as a lesser, he'd invited her out for a drink, sat with her and talked to her. When did he ever give her reason not to believe him?

And his simple presence attested to the veracity of his words.

Llyris nodded and stepped away from Ilkari, staring at the misty entrance to the passageway. As she'd expected, Shiera had disappeared from sight. The handler extended her arm. She sensed the footsteps of the silver-haired woman, each one pressing into her skin as though a tiny version of her trod upon her hand, and memories flooded her mind. Flayre spinning on her palm, the warmth of the Unnamed spilling through her, the sense of calm and acceptance she got from the tiny magical being. The lone place she'd found them throughout her entire life.

And Shiera Siirist, the granddaughter of Amnayel Prisma, took it from her.

Llyris pressed her lips into a firm line slashing across her face, narrowed her eyes, and snapped her hand closed into a fist.

The passageway disappeared.

The entire gathering stared, their gazes fixed on a rise leading to a stand of bamboo—where the portal had been a second before. Nobody moved or spoke. Birds ceased singing, insects stopped buzzing. The butterflies rested on the unicorn's haunches, their wings pressed together, their antennae motionless.

The world paused.

It stayed so for more than a minute, the sense of awe, and disbelief, and shock permeating everything until Kaisa's voice filled their heads once more.

"There's yet one more malefactor who needs dealt with."

She turned her head and gazed at Alwin Pelletoot.

The satchel shook in his hands. His arms quaked, his knees knocked, his teeth chattered. He lost command of every muscle in his body as the white creature sauntered across the grass toward him.

Alwin's mind raced. He had done nothing, possessed no more control over what the others inside him had done than humans did over the curse laid by their forefathers. He fought to restrain the quakes. If this was his end, at least he could meet it with a modicum of dignity.

He wasn't sure he'd be able to do so without wetting his pants.

His companions, both newly met and more familiar, gathered around him. To his surprise, Sir Jai stepped in front of him, inserting himself between the quivering fellow and the approaching magik. He raised his sword half-heartedly.

"This man has done nothing," he said. "If you are to punish someone, make it me."

"I see your loss, good knight. I sense your pain and grief, but I cannot undo it for you. Only time heals such wounds, and even then the scars will often cause discomfort, as I still lament my mother's loss a thousand years later. It is an unavoidable truth of our world." Kaisa paused, waited until he lowered his sword. "Step aside, brave Sir Jai."

The knight's chin drooped toward his chest and his shoulders shuddered with the intensity of the sigh he drew into his lungs. He did as the unicorn wanted, moving out of her way and stepping into Tesfira's waiting embrace.

"I understand," she said. "We have all lost."

And they cried together.

Alwin's gaze slipped to Kaisa, her eyes unwavering from him. He grasped the satchel tighter against his chest, doubting the ability of the ancient leather and the tomes within to keep the wicked horn from running him through.

"Resistance is futile," the voice told him.

It never offered good advice. If he'd ignored its prompting from the start, perhaps he wouldn't be here. The silver-haired woman wouldn't have gotten the Book of Shadow and he'd be passed out drunk of the floor of the local tavern, no doubt.

The thought caused his heart to sink into his belly. If he hadn't done those things he'd done, none of this would have happened. Rein and the others would yet live, the world functioning as usual, if he hadn't heeded the voice and positioned himself to lose the tome.

"It's my fault," he whispered. "All my fault."

He hung his head and the strength in his arms faltered; the satchel thumped against the ground by his feet. He twisted his hands to face the unicorn, fingers splayed and palms spread flat before raising his eyes again.

"Do as you must."

His companions watched in silence as Kaisa took three more steps forward, stopping with the tip of her horn brushing Alwin Pelletoot's chest. In the short time of his memory, he'd survived myriad ways his life should have ended. Never did he expect it to finish skewered on the horn of a unicorn.

Energy crackled in the air. Alwin's body stiffened, the point pressing against his sternum. He waited for the pain, his face tightening like a fist.

It didn't come.

His torso shuddered, his spine arched. A tearing sound disturbed the silence, and a space cleared inside his chest. His limbs vibrated and a low moan he hadn't expected rose from his throat. He couldn't sense the ground beneath his feet, the touch of his clothes against his skin. Behind his closed eyelids, bright light filled his vision, ragged and purple around the edges and shot through with colorful veins, as though he'd shut his eyes after staring too long at the sun.

After a few seconds, or possibly hours, the sensation passed. His boot soles settled on the earth and gravity expected his knees to support his weight. They refused, and he folded to the ground like a marionette with severed strings.

His face pressed against the dirt, its earthy scents filling his nose, and he wished to stay there forever. If this was death, he'd take more of this, please.

The troll called Vyle had other plans.

He inserted his huge hands under his armpits and plucked him from the ground as easily as if lifting a feather. Alwin's knees continued their refusal to support him, so the beast wrapped a thick arm around his chest to keep him upright, then he whispered in his ear.

"Look."

Against his wishes, his eyelids fluttered open, stealing his kaleidoscopic visions and blinding him with sunlight. It required the space of five heartbeats before his brain made the adjustments for the world to regain focus.

Alwin gasped.

More than two dozen shadowy figures stood around him, most of them old enough to be his grandfather, a few matronly women amongst them. He recognized one man from the box outside the mortuary, with his tangled white beard and his ancient eyes, but the others he didn't know.

The unicorn directed its attention toward the ghostly gathering.

"I'm sorry for what came to pass for all of you." Given he heard its words in his head rather than his ears, Alwin wondered if a phantom could interpret what the creature said. "Your time has come. You can go."

Nothing happened for a few seconds, and he presumed it meant the spirits could not comprehend the magical animal speaking with its mind.

Then a figure—a fellow with a bent spine and a sour expression—turned to mist and floated toward the sky, the vapor dissipating as it rose. Another followed, then a third. A moment later, a fog lay upon the land. When it cleared, two remained.

The one closest to him—the old man he'd heard the others refer to as Viden Misk—faced him. His lips moved soundlessly, but Alwin didn't need to use his ears to understand what he said.

"Thank you."

He faded to mist and followed his brethren skyward, leaving a single figure to face the unicorn alone.

The fellow appeared a cross between a man and a raisin. The loose skin on his naked body folded into sheets. Spots marked his bald pate, centuries had turned his hands into claws.

"Amnayel Prisma," Kaisa said.

The wizened lips around the fellow's toothless mouth moved. He stopped, readjusted, and began again. This time, Alwin heard him, the words wheezed more than spoken.

"What will you do to me?"

"You are old beyond reckoning, mage. You and my mother frolicked in flower-laden fields in your youths. Once, my kind called you friend, one of our own."

The ancient fellow remained silent, all eyes on him as Kaisa approached him. He didn't flinch or try to move. Alwin wasn't sure if he could.

"An age has passed since your transgression, transitioning from the age of dragons to the age of man. Again, you are the catalyst of change. What you did won't be forgotten, but it can be forgiven." The unicorn strode forward the last few steps separating them and touched the tip of its horn against the shadowy figure's chest. "I set you free."

The ghost's wrinkled cheeks smoothed, his posture straightened. For a second, a younger fellow stood before them, a man immortalized in statues and paintings across the land in gardens and dining halls.

And then he faded to mist.

Chapter 22

— · —

T HE FIRE CRACKLED AND snapped, logs hissed as the heat released water from the wood. Flames licked at the underside
of the pyre, though not yet high enough to set alight the oiled
canvas wrapping the baron's champion.

His sword lay upon his chest, the firelight dancing on the silver
steel.

Ilkari stood beside Cirril Feron with Tesfira and Hinter to the
other side of the merchant's man, Alwin Pelletoot to the squire's
left. Jai grieved alone at the head of the pyre. They all stared at the
flames, refusing to meet each other's gaze.

"We're sure?" the squire asked, the question intended for whoever answered.

"It's what she said," the thief replied. "Destroy them."

He tore his eyes away from the fire before it spread to the body
of the man he considered his son. But would it be enough to con-
sume the tome he gripped in his hands? He glanced toward Cirril
and the stave he held, its runes glowing in the night, matching the
fire's intensity. Wood and parchment should succumb to heat, but
this wasn't any normal book and walking stick. Even his gnarled
fingers sensed the power swelling in the volume's blank pages.

He shifted to hold the item in one hand, seating it on his left
palm and forearm as he caressed its cover with his fingertips.
Rough and smooth, hard and soft. Whenever he altered his opinion of what he touched, the tome changed to match. He paused,
his fingers resting on the top corner, the urge to flip it open flowing
from his heart into his arm, heading toward his wrist.

"Ilkari."

Alwin's word startled him. The squire shifted again, pulling the volume against his chest to relieve the temptation. He offered the fellow a sheepish and apologetic smile.

"I wasn't going to," he said. His words didn't sound convincing to himself, but no matter.

The bottom side of the oiled canvas flickered with tiny flames. A minute later, it engulfed the baron's champion.

"Now is the time." Jai's strained voice was barely audible above the conflagration.

Cirril stepped forward, and the squire went with him. The heat from the funeral pyre inched toward unbearable as they approached. The squire's cheeks reddened. He blinked to relieve his drying eyeballs. The insides of his nostrils burned. Any closer and they'd get a whiff of hair melting from their heads.

The merchant's man stopped and Ilkari halted beside him. They didn't look at each other. Neither waited for nor offered a sign. Cirril raised his arms, the stave gripped in both hands, and tossed it into the fire without ceremony. It landed amongst the burning logs, knocking them askew and sending sparks dancing skyward, its runes brightening with the heat.

He paused, turned his face upward toward Rein's body engulfed in flames.

"Goodbye, brother."

He left the squire alone, the tome responsible for starting it all clutched to his chest. It reminded him of how Tesfira always hugged her prayer book, the way she now held it again, her faith restored, her path rekindled. The young woman hadn't said a word since telling them she'd retaken her vows.

Ilkari lowered the volume from his bosom, gazed upon its cover. In the pyre's light, it flickered with the color of blood. Rein's blood. Kove's blood. Aryzath's. The blood of countless others, both now and in the past, its pages drenched in it, the words appearing on them written in it.

He hefted the tome. It felt heavier, as though it resisted his intent, or the blood-soaked parchment added to its weight. His tongue dried up, and he smacked his lips, attempting to create saliva.

A minute passed. Two. The pyre's heat raged against his face and sweat dripped from the end of his nose, sizzling as it splashed on a rock near his feet.

"Ilkari."

The squire looked up, drying eyes wide, his parched mouth fallen open.

Not Pelletoot's voice this time. Rein's.

He raised his head, half-expecting to find his charge's ghost lingering amongst the smoke, watching him, waiting for him to perform his task.

Nothing but smoke.

He wiped his sleeve across his face, relieving it of the tears and sweat collected on his cheeks and not yet dried by the fire. With Rein gone, what life did he have? He'd spent the last two decades training and mentoring. Fathering. What came next?

A log shifted, its charred body falling into pieces, and the crunch of its demise pulled him from his thoughts. His blurred vision cleared to view the tome once more before he threw it into the fire.

Its tinder-dry ancient parchment caught without ceremony, flames swallowing it before he returned to his spot. As he settled in between Cirril Feron and Alwin Pelletoot, he glanced toward Jai Aryn and found the knight returning his gaze.

And the squire realized the purpose of his life.

They all stayed until the posts holding the pyre collapsed, the body of the baron's champion plummeting into the fire in a cascade of embers swirling into the night. Only Jai lingered as the others left in silence, and he remained when Hinter and Tesfira arrived in the morning.

The once and future acolyte tugged her friend's sleeve, pointed toward the knight. He stood in the same position as when they'd retired—the point of his sword on the ground, both hands folded over the pommel, his head tilted forward. She wondered if he'd slept like this.

The young women approached the still-smoking ashes, halting a few paces short and stretching to survey what survived the conflagration. Tesfira hoped not to find a skull, or bones, but it was the stave and tome they wanted to ensure had met their end.

Beyond the ash and a few chunks of blackened wood lining the outside of the pit, Rein's sword remained the lone recognizable item, the leather burned from its grip, the blade tainted black by fire. She expected Jai to claim it, as was his right.

No book. No stave.

She breathed a sigh of relief, the tension in her body expelled on a single breath. But she understood more was to come, and Hinter didn't make her wait.

"Do you really have to go?"

She faced her friend, took both of her hands in hers, and nodded. The thief knew the answer. They'd already discussed it before Tesfira returned to silence, she'd listed all her reasons she needed to follow God's word, seek his forgiveness, and contribute to the healing of the world. But she longed to tell her again how she'd thought long and hard, how all those reasons almost weren't enough because of her. She didn't want to leave. She had to.

God called to her.

She squeezed her friend's hands, watched a tear slip down her cheek as she fought to keep her own from escaping. She realized this was the right course, but it didn't ease the ache in her heart. Only time could offer comfort and relief, and she doubted its ability to erase it completely.

Hinter pulled her forward, wrapped her arms around her. Tesfira melted into her, the tears unstoppable. She cried for Hinter. For Brother Emeryn, and Rein, for Gartrek and Kove and everyone else who'd sacrificed to bring balance to the world. They were with God, celebrating in his kingdom, awaiting the ones they loved. One day, they'd all be together again, but not today. Work must be done first.

God's work.

The acolyte snuffled, separated herself from her friend. If she didn't do it now, she might never leave her embrace. Over the thief's shoulder, she saw Ilkari joining Jai—the last of them gathered as Cirril and Alwin had left at dawn, headed to Carpera's estate to assess the damage.

Tesfira turned her attention to Hinter.

They gazed into each other's eyes, wetness glistening around the edges. She leaned forward and pressed her lips against her friend's, passing warmth and love between them one last time.

Then the acolyte strode away, hugging her prayer book against her as her tears started anew.

Llyris rested against the gate post, arms crossed in front of her chest as the new residents of the village buzzed about tidying, building, improving. She spied Hartrek amongst them, and the troll once called Vyle but who now went by his true name, Kurth. The two had become fast friends.

Despite his size, Aeryz crept up behind her. You'd imagine a dragon should at least cast a noticeable shadow, but he always positioned himself to avoid it.

"Think you can handle it?"

She shrugged. "She didn't give me much choice, did she?"

They both stared across the compound. "More will come. Many more, once the accommodations are built."

A slight figure with wispy hair and pointed ears waved her hand, and a section of thatch rose from the ground to settle in place as the roof of a newly constructed hut.

"It shouldn't take long, judging by the looks of it." Llyris stretched to peer past the ruby behemoth with ash running through its veins. "Where is she?"

"Kaisa has much to attend to."

"Being away for a thousand years will do that. You're letting her go alone?"

The dragon chuckled its throaty laugh. "My time as her protector is done. We have restored peace to the world."

She straightened, faced the beast. "How can you be sure?"

"I have faith in who she has left to oversee it."

A chill ran up the shadow-scarred's spine despite the day's heat. Her mind still reeled with all the recent events, and she couldn't believe the spot she found herself. How much time had passed since her arrival at the baron's castle? She recalled marveling at its opulence, the craftsmanship of the staircase she needed to climb to take audience with him. Then she thought of Rein, and Kove, Emeryn Aryzath. Flayre.

"I'm not so sure. I haven't been successful at anything."

"You halted a genocide."

She shook her head and strode away from the village, heading along the path toward the lake as the dragon trailed her. Dragonflies buzzed and darted about near the shore. The water reflected the sun like a mirror. When she reached its edge, she stopped, her toes sinking into the mud, cool liquid caressing them. Her companion sat behind her, tail wrapped around his body like an enormous cat.

"You have the tomes," he said. "You will find anything you need amongst their pages."

She nodded. The satchel full of tiny volumes and scrolls rested at the end of her bed in the hut once occupied by Shiera Siirist. Would it be safe? What if one of the dark fae or another magik decided they despised this new arrangement? Could she stop them if they revolted?

In the distance, the red and orange bird wheeled, its tail feathers fluttering out behind. It rose high into the air, performed a loop, then spiraled toward the ground before leveling off.

"Show-off," the dragon muttered with a chuckle.

The phoenix disappeared beyond the horizon, leaving the handler staring across the lake.

"Do you think separating us will work?"

Aeryz sighed, the heat of his breath warming her neck. "Both sides need much healing. And humans must relearn how to live without the crutches they called Unnamed. It requires time but, with you as liaison between the worlds of magiks and humankind, I have no doubts about success."

His words made her cringe. How could she be the one responsible? It seemed unreal. Not long ago, she was a handler. Despised, mistrusted...and now this.

She reached up and touched the brooch clasped at her throat.

"But you'll be here?"

"We all will."

Llyris turned upon hearing the voice. Kaisa stood beside the dragon, two other unicorns with her—one larger, one smaller. Her partner and her child. Before this, she'd thought the last unicorn dead.

Now there were three.

She crossed the ground to them, buried her face against Kaisa's neck. When she breathed, she inhaled the scent of her pure white

306

hair—honeysuckle warmed in the sun, the hint of snow in the air. The unicorn tilted her head toward her, rubbed her with her cheek. They stayed that way for a minute before Llyris relaxed her grip and stepped away.

"I won't let you down," she said.

The unicorn's eyes sparkled. "I know you won't...shadow-scarred."

CHAPTER 23

—·—

T HE SCENT OF EARTH and mildew clung to her nostrils as she
sat against the wall beneath the scar in the stone. Above her,
the green moss stretched across the passage's ceiling. No matter
which direction she traveled, or how far she walked, she always
ended up here.

She recognized it, of course. This was where she'd met Rein
Shriken and made the deal with him to get Prisma's stave.

When it happened, she thought she'd won. She'd possessed the
horn since birth, and getting the book seemed an easy enough
task, but she'd assumed she'd have far more difficulty taking the
damned staff from the baron's champion.

Love undoes all.

But things went so wrong. How?

She traced a line on the floor with her fingertip, following its
pattern again and again, always ending in the same spot. Not a
circle—a path without end.

"The shadow-scarred," she said aloud, the words bouncing off
the sides of the passage until they died in the distance. Or perhaps
they didn't. Maybe they'd arrive back here if she waited long
enough.

She levered herself against the wall, pushing to get to her feet.
How many times had she traversed the passageway since her banishment? Ten? A hundred? One trek along the unending corridor
blended into the next, blurring into a smear of gray walls and green
moss.

It didn't matter how often she journeyed its length to finish in
this spot. Thousands, millions. It only mattered how many more
before she discovered an escape.

Because then she'd have her revenge.

THE END

Here ends the adventures of Llyris Fildarae and her companions. I hope you enjoyed reading the Curse of the Unnamed as much as I enjoyed writing it. If you'd like to read more, be sure to check out the Also by section...you may just find something else you'll enjoy!

CAST OF CHARACTERS

In Order of Appearance or Mention

Zero - An Unnamed
Marita - Zero's handler
Llyris Fildarae - handler of Flayre, an Unnamed
Rein Shriken - a knight. Baron Sylleth's champion
Ilkari Vasuk - Rein's squire
Flayre - An Unnamed
Jai Aryn - a knight and friend of Rein
Baron Sylleth - ruler of the fiefdom. Rein's father
Viden Misk - an old man and adviser to Caedric Carpera
Caedric Carpera - a successful merchant
Linian - a handler in the employ of House Carpera
Cirril Feron - Carpera's head guardsman
Cassemir Carpera - Caedric's son
Nsiri Carpera - Caedric' wife, mother of Cassemir
Amnayel Prisma - an ancient mage
Kove Heren - one of Carpera's guardsmen
Mikol Vakkan - one of Carpera's guardsmen
Bettany - a handler
Emeryn Aryzath - a cleric
Tesfira Florithe - Aryzath's student
Hinter Panne - a thief
Priscilla - a woman living in the woods
Prue - lives with Priscilla
Raelle Fildarae - Llyris' mother

Agis - an ancient age
Falkon - an ancient mage
Cystenn - an ancient mage
Mr. Zeir – a powerful merchant
Patriarch Siurin – a high-ranking official in the church
Kayara – Emeryn Aryzath's lost love
Dibue – a guardsman in Baron Sylleth's militia
Ondo – a senior guardsman in Baron Sylleth's militia
Nevan Wynfir – one of Carpera's guardsmen
Neave Wynfir – one of Carpera's guardsmen
Sybel Paray – a handler
Kiall – a guardsman in Baron Sylleth's militia
Shiera Siirist – a mysterious woman
Alwin Pelletoot – a man without a memory
Waul – a street urchin
Vyle – a troll
Breda – Vyle's handler
Behrtio – a Senior of the guild
Hisbid – a were-bear
Zalie – a human child
Yeffez – a store owner
Hartrek – an ogre
Gartrek – an ogre. Brother of Hartrek
Hum – a pisky
Orania – Hum's handler
Quintan – Hinter's former partner in crime
Tialha – daughter of Amnayel Prisma

Curse of the Unnamed epic fantasy:
The Book of Shadow
Shadow Scarred
A Shadow Upon the Land
In the Shadow of the Dragon

Khirro's Journey epic fantasy:

Blood of the King
Spirit of the King
Heart of the King

The Books of the Small Gods epic fantasy:

When Shadows Fall
The Darkness Comes
And Night Descends
When Ravens Call
The Twilight Fades
And Kingdoms End

The **Icarus Fell** urban fantasy series:

On Unfaithful Wings
All Who Wander Are Lost
Secrets of the Hanged Man

Blood of the King (Khirro's Journey Book 1)

A kingdom torn by war. A curse whispered by dying lips. A hero
born against his will.
With a vial of the king's blood in one hand, and a sword of legend
in the other, one soldier sets out on an odyssey that will change
his life... or end it.

Forced into the army, Khirro never wanted to fight. And with the
monarch dead, any hope for the kingdom's survival hangs by a
slender thread. But when the king's shaman charges Khirro with a
curse, he's compelled to undertake a journey to the haunted land
in search of the outlaw necromancer. And if he fails... the very
walls of the fortress itself will fall to the blood-crazed undead.

Can Khirro complete his quest in time to save his realm from a
brutal end?

*"Blood of the King is a masterpiece. It is as close to perfection as
I would consider a book to be."*- Ella Medler, author of *Blood is
Heavier*
"Blake has a knack for bringing you into the story"
*"Mr. Blake's writing is masterful and clear, he draws you into his
story and when it's finished you feel like you're leaving an old
friend."*

When Shadows Fall (The First Book of the Small Gods)

An ancient prophecy threatens the return of the Small Gods to
seek revenge on those who banished them a thousand years before. According to its words, only one person can stop them: the
firstborn child of the rightful king. But King Erral usurped the
throne decades past.

For whom are the words intended?

When the prince and princess discover the long-forgotten scroll,
Teryk is convinced he is the savior of the kingdom and determines
to fulfill his destiny. His sister is not so sure. If he is the chosen
one, why is it only Danya can read the words inscribed on the

313

parchment? And what of the other elements of the prophecy: the Barren Mother, the Living Statue, and the Man from Across the Sea? None of them can possibly exist.

Teryk strikes out on his own to become the hero he is meant to be and prove his worth to his father once and for all. His desperate sister and the kingdom's one-armed champion give chase, but none of them realize the evil they've set in motion.

The prince wants to save the kingdom. The princess wants to save her brother. But in a fight against the gods, who will save them all?

"When Shadows Fall is one of the best fantasy books I have ever read. Its characters are memorable: you adore them, you want to strangle them, you cheer them on."

""It rained fire the day the Small Gods fled" Thus begins When Shadows Fall, the first book in the Small Gods series by Bruce Blake and what a terrific start to one fast-paced and completely engrossing new fantasy it is."

On Unfaithful Wings (Icarus Fell #1)

To some, death is the end; to others, a beginning. To Icarus Fell, it should have been a relief from a life gone seriously awry.
But death had other plans.
Icarus doesn't believe that the man awaiting him when he wakes up in a cheap motel room is really the archangel Michael, or that God's right hand wants him to help souls on their way to Heaven. Icarus doesn't believe there's a Heaven, so why should they want his help?
But the man claiming to be the archangel tempts him with an offer he can't ignore--harvest enough souls and get back the life he wished he'd had.
It seems Icarus has nothing to lose, until he botches a harvest and the soul that went to Hell instead of Heaven comes back to make him pay by threatening to take away the life he hoped to win back.

To save the wife and son he already lost once, Icarus will have to become the man he never was. Somehow, he will have to learn to believe.

"The next book in this series cannot come out soon enough for this reader. Not just my favorite Kindle book of the year, but one of my favorite books ever."
"I loved this book."
"Bruce Blake's On Unfaithful Wings is a great urban fantasy novel. I love good character development in a story's protagonist and Blake nails it with Icarus Fell. I found myself rooting for him from the get-go and laughing out loud at some of his observations."
"On Unfaithful Wings was an impressive first novel. All of the characters were interesting and engaging, but in particular the main character and his struggle to reconcile with his new identity/job. This is one of those stories that stays with me long after I read it and I'll be on the lookout for more from this author."
"This is just, simply, amazing. Icarus is one of the best characters I've ever "met", chock full of virtues and faults and doubts and worries and a simple HUMANNESS that comes through so clearly, I almost expect to run into him around the next corner."
"Icarus Fell is a flawed man but a wonderful character. From the moment I started reading On Unfaithful Wings I was pulled along by this interesting character and wanting to know what would happen next."

Bruce Blake embarked on his writing journey in 2011, immersing readers in the enchanting realms of fantasy. Best known for his **Icarus Fell** urban fantasy series and epic fantasy trilogy **Khirro's Journey**, Bruce crafts narratives that transport audiences to urban landscapes tinged with supernatural mysteries and heroic worlds teetering on the edge of destiny.

Following the success of these series, Bruce launched his six-volume series, **The Books of the Small Gods**, showcasing his ability to weave tales of divine intricacies and impending darkness with the fates of intriguing characters you will laugh and cry with. His most recent project, the **Curse of the Unnamed** quadrilogy, featuring the Florida Authors' Association Gold Medal-winning The Book of Shadow, concluded with the fourth book released February 2024.

Visit Bruce online at **www.bruceblake.net** for FREE SHORT STORIES, signed copies, and to keep up to date with new releases